# GOOD BOYS

## The Visionary

# WORKS BY JEREMY ROBINSON

*The Didymus Contingency*
*Raising The Past*
*Beneath*
*Antarktos Rising*
*Kronos*
*Pulse*
*Instinct*
*Threshold*
*Fracture*
*Torment*
*The Sentinel*
*The Last Hunter – Descent*
*The Last Hunter – Pursuit*
*The Last Hunter – Ascent*
*The Last Hunter – Lament*
*The Last Hunter – Onslaught*
*The Last Hunter – Collected Edition*
*Insomnia*
*SecondWorld*
*Project Nemesis*
*Ragnarok*
*Island 731*
*The Raven*
*Nazi Hunter: Atlantis*
*Prime*
*Omega*
*Project Maigo*
*Refuge*
*Guardian*
*Human After All*
*Savage*
*Flood Rising*
*Project 731*
*Cannibal*
*Endgame*
*MirrorWorld*
*Herculean*
*Project Hyperion*
*Patriot*
*Apocalypse Machine*
*Empire*
*Unity*
*Project Legion*
*The Distance*
*The Last Valkyrie*
*Centurion*
*Infinite*
*Helios*
*Viking Tomorrow*
*Forbidden Island*
*The Divide*
*The Others*
*Space Force*
*Alter*
*Flux*
*Tether*
*Tribe*
*NPC*
*Exo-Hunter*
*Infinite²*
*The Dark*
*Mind Bullet*
*The Order*
*Khaos*
*Singularity*
*Hunger – The Complete Trilogy*
*Nemesis*
*Point Nemo*
*Good Boys – The Lost Tribe*
*Good Boys – Unleashed*
*Kingdom*
*Good Boys – The Visionary*

# GOOD BOYS

## – THE VISIONARY –

JEREMY ROBINSON

BREAKNECK MEDIA

Cover design and title page art by Jeremy Robinson, and Midjourney AI.


Visit Jeremy Robinson on the World Wide Web at: www.bewareofmonsters.com.

*For my current Good Boy,
the actual Grover, without whom
this trilogy would have been
impossible to write.*

# Prologue

"My Lord," he said, bowing lower than he felt comfortable, mostly because it showed deference to the one on the receiving end. In this case: The Visionary. He had been leading the Draun for generations but spent much of his time cowering within his floating metallic sphere. And yet, he was powerful enough to fend off every challenge to his authority thus far.

But Oliver Reinhart had observed every failed attempt on the Visionary's life. Most of them were laughable. Drunk with the power of becoming Draun, a bevy of idiots gave themselves over to the Dunning-Kruger effect (a total lack of knowledge creating a spike in self-confidence). As the attacks descended from the peak of Mt. Stupid, Reinhart watched and learned.

Each attempt on Lumen Sok's life had failed because the attackers did not bide their time. Everyone was in a rush to claim power. But success would only ever occur when subterfuge was thrown into the mix. *Establish trust, gain dependence, wait for the guard to drop.* That's how a good assassin did the job. The only real skills required were time and patience. With the job done right, the only necessary violence was a quick slit of the throat. After a few gagging moments, the Visionary would be dead, and Reinhart would assume control.

There had been a contender—someone Reinhart believed he would have had to kill first—or perhaps wait until she had killed the Visionary herself. Jenna Flood. She'd been powerful and was playing the long game, too. The Visionary knew that, as well as every other Draun. He hadn't seemed to mind or fear an attack from his first acolyte.

Perhaps because he'd known her death was imminent. The task he'd given her proved to be too much to handle—a direct confrontation with the Kynolari. They were the Draun's sworn enemy, who had somehow pushed Reinhart's predecessors to the brink, forcing the Visionary to rekindle his plans on Earth. And yet, the Kynolari had found him already—though their numbers were limited.

Reinhart never had a problem with dogs. He just didn't like the idea of pets. Of anything alive depending on him for food or for taking a piss. He didn't mind supporting a comrade in the heat of battle, but outside of that scenario, living things could fuck off.

It was that lack of dependence on forces outside his control that made him the right person to succeed Lumen Sok. He had the knowledge, skill, and vision to reignite Draun dominance in the galaxy, and then the universe.

Once the Visionary was dead, and Reinhart was in control, challengers would arrive to usurp his newfound power. Such was the life of the Draun. Through competitive combat with each other, they weeded out the weak, and refined the strong. So, he welcomed the challenges. If he couldn't hold on to the throne, he didn't deserve it.

There was no malice behind it, but only the strongest deserved to lead.

And right now, that was still Lumen Sok.

So, Reinhart held his bow until a grating voice said, "Stand."

Reinhart had never had a direct, one-on-one conversation with the Visionary, but recent events had advanced his position. He now found himself a general in an army of telekinetics, many of whom were punch drunk insane with power, out there in the world, wreaking havoc and claiming territory.

Up close, the metal sphere protecting the Visionary shimmered with iridescent colors, as though its surface was both solid and liquid. It made no sound as it hovered a foot above the ground at the center of what was once Japan's Imperial Temple.

Reinhart lowered his eyes, tracing the arrangement of stone and gravel making up the courtyard's floor. For a moment, he got lost in the design's harmony.

"You may look," the Visionary said. His voice sounded different. Less projected.

When Reinhart looked up, he understood why; the sphere had opened without a sound. The Visionary was just feet away, his thin body clad in beige, loose-fitting, Japanese garb. He sat cross-legged atop a plush, red, cushioned interior, like a pampered monk.

*I could do it,* he thought. I *could cross the distance between us in a thought. Crush the life from him. This might be the closest I ever get. Might be my only chance.*

*No.*

Others had attempted the same. Most of them found their heads burst open before finishing their internal debate. The Visionary had survived thousands of attempts on his life. He now had an uncanny ability to sense danger and deception.

Reinhart relaxed his body, showing no signs of aggression. Instead, he looked the Visionary over, taking in every part of the man the world knew as Lumen Sok. He'd seen the man's face before. Everyone in the world recognized the richest man on the planet. He had been eccentric and controversial, and everything he did was for an ulterior purpose: a return to space.

Now, the man's face was hidden behind a metal mask. It was aged with flakes of blue, almost like it was carved from some kind of stone. The mask had several scratches and gouges. Signs of ancient battles. Its sinister eyes held two luminous blue orbs, making it impossible to know where he was looking. On either side of the helmet were two dials over his ears. A strange design. Could serve a function, might just be for protection, or even to look more intimidating than Lumen Sok's pasty white face...if that was even his real face.

"Mmm," Sok said. "Your control is admirable."

"Thank you, sir."

"And you're accustomed to taking orders?" he asked.

Reinhart gave a nod. "Navy SEAL for ten years before being recruited to the CIA, where I performed clandestine wetwork that never happened."

"How many targets did you successfully eliminate?" Sok asked. There was no emotion behind the question. No real curiosity. Whatever number Reinhart gave would pale in comparison to the Visionary's body count. He had wiped out entire civilizations.

Had.

Now he was old, in hiding, and desperate.

"Seventy-two targets," Reinhart said.

"And did you feel any guilt about these kills, before you were with the Draun?"

"Not an ounce. Two of them were kids, if you can believe it. No idea why they were targeted, but I don't ask questions. I just kill who I'm told to kill."

The Visionary nodded. "And since you have become one of the Draun?"

"I haven't been in contact with my...employers since the change," Reinhart said. "Didn't see the point."

"But you *have* killed," Sok said.

Reinhart grinned. "Oh, yes."

"How many?"

"Three hundred twenty-seven," Reinhart said.

"A true member of the Draun. How many of them were your brethren?"

Reinhart suddenly felt like he was on trial, that his bloody confrontations had been reported and he was about to be disciplined. If so, he would welcome the fight. "Fifty-two."

The Visionary nodded. "Your status is well-earned. I am pleased that what I have heard of you was not exaggerated."

"I'm surprised I left someone alive to tell you."

To Reinhart's surprise, the Visionary huffed a laugh. "There is a persistent problem that I need you to take care of for me."

"The Kynolari." Reinhart knew about them. Everyone did. But they hadn't been seen since they disappeared in Mexico three weeks ago.

"Indeed. They have human allies, and together they have defeated all who have preceded you—from the powerful, to the insane, to the inhuman." He glanced to the side where an army of fully formed biologics stood at attention. Giant Helions, hulking Gobi, long-limbed Tyrne, many tentacled Platamots, and others Reinhart had never seen before. The simulations of defeated enemies were intimidating, but no match for the Draun. Apparently the same was true for the Kynolari.

"So now you need a professional?" Reinhart asked.

"Several Straub Hunt Squads were employed to find and kill them. They were able to locate the Kynolari, but unable to defeat them. They are hunters on a level you could never achieve. What I need is someone who is smart, deadly, and willing to wait until the time is right to strike."

Lumen Sok held his gaze for a moment, following it with, "I'm smiling beneath this mask. Your hunger. Your ambition. It radiates from you more than others, and yet, here you sit, willing to take orders. To bide your time. To get the job done right. Admirable qualities."

"Thank you, sir."

"Perhaps you will receive all you believe is attainable," Sok said. "But not today."

"Understood," Reinhart said. "And agreed. Now, who do you need me to kill?"

"Brace yourself," the Visionary said, reaching his hands up to the dials on the sides of his head. Before explaining, he twisted both dials. A high-pitched squeal tore through Reinhart's mind as memories were violently implanted. He saw through the eyes of the dead, watched recordings of the Kynolari in action, saw their capabilities (which were astounding) and their weaknesses. The last thing impressed on his mind was a list of priority targets.

The Kynolari leader, Praxion, who had led the universal charge against the Draun and been integral to their defeat. He was at the top.

The next was a Kynolari Reinhart thought looked like a badass. A German Shepherd sniper. Gruunlokar. The memories of why he was important were blocked though.

*Must be personal,* Reinhart thought.

Third in line was a human. Micah Taylor. Ally to the Kynolari and able to use their technology in ways not seen before. He was also emerging as a leader and needed to be put down.

It was the fourth priority that confused Reinhart.

"A dog?" Reinhart asked, as the memories continued etching into his mind.

The answer came a moment later.

The dog was important to all of them. Like a lynchpin. If it was killed, the others would fall apart. Would weaken, making the rest of his job that much easier.

When the squeal ended, Reinhart rearranged the priority order, putting the dog known as Grover at the top of the list.

# 1

### MICAH

"I count three," Gruunlokar says.

I nod. "Same."

"Go around or clear the path?" he asks.

I look down my binoculars at the three Draun dancing in front of a home that they've recently destroyed. They've created a bonfire from the rubble and are now repeating some kind of self-congratulatory chant, but it's slurred so badly that I can't understand a word of it. The tone is obvious, though. They've got hard-ons about being Draun and want the world to know.

Also means that they're a bunch of Level Ones.

We began categorizing the Draun two weeks ago. Helps us determine whether to engage. We do everything we can to avoid Fours and Fives. Threes are debatable. Twos are doable. Ones...well, these assholes are easy targets and a good chance to practice.

It's not that we can't collectively handle a Five. We could. But it can cause a ruckus, and we are officially incognito. While the others are healing, monitoring Torel's condition, and repairing the *Prowler*, the rest of us—myself, Gruunlokar, Jess, Grover, Jenna, and Poppy—are doing recon. Poppy didn't want to come with us. Said her duty was with Torel, but she's a field medic, and Torel is stable. She just needs to wake up again, and all that's required for that is time. When Praxion ordered Poppy to join us, she agreed. Feisty through and through, but a good soldier, despite her time on Earth pretending to be an average dog.

Our mission is straight forward. Damage and salvageability assessment. Of the human race. How many people are left alive? How many Draun? How vast was the destruction? Is there anyone left to save?

So, we headed diagonally up through Mexico, borrowing vehicles along the way when we could. Took us a few days to reach the coast, and we've been mostly on foot since, headed north across the border. Haven't seen a lot of people along the way. Even in places untouched by the Draun. Doors and windows are shut. Survivors are hiding in the shadows. But there *are* survivors. A lot of them.

Best guess, the Draun have free rein to kill who they want, but they get their kicks from dominating. From ruling. It appears they're claiming territory. Sometimes just a block. Sometimes a whole city. This occasionally leads to conflict between the Draun, usually resolved by a fight to the death. They're shrinking their own numbers, but soon, only the strongest will be left. But there're still a shit-ton of them.

And there are still people transitioning from human to Draun. Not sure when that will stop. Might not until there are no humans left. Makes it hard to trust anyone on the road, so we mostly avoid contact and travel at night. The Draun aren't human anymore, but they still need to sleep...unless they're idiots out partying.

These three must have been pals before shit went down. They haven't turned on each other. Yet. Kind of makes them a unified Level Three, but if we do this right, they'll never know we were here, and will slip into oblivion without feeling any pain.

"You're going to do it again," Poppy whispers, "aren't you?"

"Striking from a distance is more about saving lives than taking them," Gruunlokar says. "It's not the faces of your enemies that stay with you, that keep you up at night. It's the faces of those you couldn't save that haunt you." He turns to face Poppy, a slight grin on his face. "I don't think I could make it a day with your squashed up face haunting me."

She gives him a whack across the snout. She doesn't hold back, but she's also very small. Pretty sure he barely felt it. His uncommon chuckle confirms it. Since we've been on the road, the two of them have become fast friends.

"You have an opinion?" I ask Jess. She's been quiet tonight. Says she's just tired, but I think it's something else. I've put a pin in it, but there's a good chance I'll forget to ask.

"Just get it over with, and let's keep moving. Two hours to sunrise and we need to find a place to hole up for the day—if there's anything left these three haven't burned down."

I take a quick look at what used to be a neighborhood in West Covina, one of many Los Angeles suburbs. All that remains are a bunch of charred foundations and smoldering remains. These three have been busy.

I wonder how many of these homes were occupied when they were reduced to ash, and the thought fortifies my position.

*They need to die.*

But first, my moral compass. "Grover?"

His eyes are on the ground, brows twitching up and down as he ponders the situation. He used to make this face when he was trying to figure out how I hid a tennis ball. Now, he's making life and death decisions.

"They is Draun?" he asks.

"They are."

"They kill Grover friends?"

"If they could."

"Could tell others?"

"Yes."

"No way around?" he asks.

"No easy way," I say. "And no guarantee that they won't find us later. Only way to make sure all of us stay safe is to take them out."

He sighs. Grover abhors the taking of life, even Draun. I loathe asking him to make this call. But he is my moral compass. War can change a person. Make you cold to taking a life. But Grover? He's incorruptible. But he will do anything, including giving his life and taking a life, to protect the people he loves.

"It no hurt?"

"They won't even feel it," I say.

"Okay," he says. "But I no watch."

"Wouldn't ever ask you to, bud."

Jess sits beside Grover and puts her arm around him. "I'll stay with him." She makes eye contact with me. "Make it quick."

"Only way he knows how to do anything," Poppy says, elbowing Jess in the back. "Eh. Eh? Am I right?" She keeps nudging until she gets a smile out of Jess. "There's my girl." Then she rubs her paws together and says, "Alright boys..." She turns to Jenna, who's been sitting silently. "...and moody girl, let's get this done."

We creep to within a hundred feet of our targets, taking cover behind the ruins of a ranch style home that looks like an airplane crash site—minus the airplane. Gruunlokar has been teaching us the ways of stealth, a subject I thought I was proficient in. But he takes it to the next level. He could approach a target through brush and leaf litter without making a sound. I just have to hope the home's charred remains will help muffle our movements.

Jenna has it easy. While Gruunlokar and I need to carefully place each foot and hand, keeping our weight equally distributed and balanced, Jenna just floats along beside us, just inches over the ground, perfectly silent. She sometimes rubs it in by floating past, arms behind her head like she's on vacation.

She's been a solid addition to the team. A real heavy hitter, but also quite confused about her predicament. She has some memory of who she became, that she had served the wrong side of this conflict, but the part of her that had become Draun was cleaved away like it never happened. Her biggest struggle is her new body. The woman who had been Gemma, also a Draun, who was mind-wiped and replaced with Jenna's consciousness. Jenna's not used to her size, her gait, or her reflection. Last she knew, she was a sixteen-year-old blonde cutie from Key West. Now, she's a half-Japanese twenty-something with telekinetic powers, embroiled in a war for humanity with talking dogs as her allies. Every day she doesn't lose her mind impresses me. Takes a strong kind of person to roll with that kind of mind-rattling, Mike Tyson-level barrage.

There's no goofing around tonight, though. She glides beside me as we crawl beneath the frame of a still-standing bay window on what would have been the home's side.

Poppy struts up beside us. She's small enough that stealth takes no effort. Hardest thing she has to do is not talk, but she makes up for it with hand signals. She unleashes them now, telling me to take out the two men on the sides. She wants Gemma and Gruunlokar to work together on the third.

It's massive overkill for these guys, but a good opportunity to practice against the Draun. Risky, though. After the first two drop, they'll wait for the third to throw up his telekinetic shield, and then try to fire a shard wrapped in a telekinetic shell, capable of piercing the shield. If they can perfect the attack, no Draun will be safe from them. Not a Level Five. Not the Visionary.

After all three of us nod our agreement, I lower my arms and charge my Hell Hound gauntlets. We're bathed in orange light, but the Draun are too caught up in their own importance. They aren't paying attention to anything but their loud voices and the bonfire that used to be a home.

"Okay," I whisper to myself, taking aim, which is difficult when there are two targets. There are ways to do this easily, but I want to impress Gruunlokar. Single, brief blasts of laser light, creating clean holes through the heads of both targets.

That's what I want to do.

Gruunlokar takes aim beside me. Aiming isn't a problem for him. He can see through his weapon. Can control his aim to within a micron, with just a thought. Doesn't miss often.

Jenna stands beside him, hands raised toward his gauntlet. I can't begin to understand how such a thing is possible, but when Jenna was in his head, they had no trouble syncing up her abilities with his weapons. Now that she's in her own body, they're struggling to repeat the attack.

"Alright," I say, narrowing my aim. "This baby is crowning and ready to pop. Let's do this."

Poppy slow-turns to me, dead pan, despite her constant lighthearted nature. "What in the name of Scooby-Doo's castrated gonads is wrong with you?"

The soldier in me is locked on target, and with a thought, both gauntlets unleash narrow beams of deadly orange laser light. It just happens to also be the same moment my motor cortex, amygdala, and hippocampus react to Poppy's statement—and I laugh.

# 2

**CHIRK**

"C'mon man, you got this!"

Sean's enthusiasm irks me like a Scarlokian corkscrew worm working its way out of my anus. Because I *don't* got this. My bones might be healed, but the muscles that were torn at the same time are refusing to cooperate. They're technically healed, too, but they've lost mass. The strands of muscle that remain aren't working as a team.

When I try to curl this simple, two pound weight, my whole god-damned arm quivers and eventually flops down. Sean suggested starting at a lower weight, which makes sense, but two American pounds is the lightest weight on board the *Prowler*. Because Kynolari are strong.

A lot stronger than humans. Even me. The fibers that make up our muscles are densely packed, yet flexible when needed. Though not strong enough to stop Xolotl from telekinetically twisting my arms a hundred and eighty degrees in the wrong direction, breaking bones and shredding muscle.

I'm not pals with every Kynolari I meet. There are some real pieces of work out there. But I have never considered one of them my enemy. Until now...I wish Xolotl had one more life in him so I could take it again. Hell, I could resurrect him a dozen times, kill him a dozen times, and still feel rage over what he's done to me.

Because I can't pilot like this. Not manually. And I can't lift my mini-railguns, which weigh—you guessed it—two pounds. So, I'm basically useless right now, unless you're interested in my undercarriage... Can't lift that two pounder, either.

I grin at my thoughts and my arms give in, dropping down. The small weights fall from my hands, bouncing on the training room floor.

"So close, bro," Sean says, sitting cross-legged on the floor. "You'll get it next time."

"Meh," I say and then snap my fingers at him. "Give me that."

He plucks the joint from between his lips and holds it out to me. "Don't let it dangle, dude. We are running low on the mojo."

I take a long drag, filling my lungs with the foul tasting smoke. My body relaxes. The chronic pain in my arms fades. I hold my breath and tap out the roach, preserving what little remains.

After a thirty second hold, I release the smoke from my mouth and nose. When it clears, Sean is staring at me like I just flicked a Draun to death.

"Whoa," he says. "That was the longest hold I've ever seen. Gonna hit you like a motherfucker, little man."

He ain't wrong about that. My lungs are saturated with THC, which is now rushing through my bloodstream, relaxing my mind and body.

I plop down on the floor, sitting beside him. "You know...who cares about being a useless little lump of fur, right? My value is so much bigger than being able to kill things with these two small arms."

I lift my arms and lie on my back, watching my hands as I wave them back and forth.

"How many living things have I killed with these two arms? Maybe this is... What do you call it? Llama?"

"Ahuh, ahuh, ahuh." Sean's belly shakes when he laughs, which gives me the giggles.

"What? It's not Llama?"

Sean snorts and starts doing an impression of some kind of annoying creature. He turns to me, eyes wide, smiling like an idiot. "I'm a llama! But don't freak out, man, cause I'm a no drama llama."

"Pfff! I still don't even know what a llama is!"

"Pajama," Sean says, regaling me with his knowledge of words that rhyme. "Bahama. Diorama. Alabama." He chuckles and says it again. "Alabama."

"Dalai Lama," I say, which gets a big laugh.

"Panorama," he says, and then lets out a sigh that quickly fades into a familiar abyss of despair. "You think she liked me at all, dude?"

I let myself calm for a moment, trying hard not to laugh at the 'ama' rhymes I've got chambered and ready to fire. "What's not to like?"

"I mean, was she even capable of liking a normal person? C'mon man, real talk. Was it all fake?"

I've been hoping this time wouldn't come. That he'd just find a way to move on without asking questions. They were never really in a relationship. Gemma just led him on enough for him to become enamored. Didn't take much, but she strung him along—returning his smiles, laughing at his jokes, saying supportive things, and, on occasion, she took hold of his hand or leaned in toward him. He was smitten. And now he's heartbroken.

"Seriously, dude. Just pull off the Band-Aid."

"No," I say. "She never had feelings for you. Because you are a bad ass motherfucker and a Kynolari. One of us. And we are the god-damned coolest doggos in the motherfucking universe. She was a moth chasing the sun, too stupid to know that it was a million miles away. She was incapable of love, and you shouldn't, not for a minute, have second thoughts about what happened to her."

"Yeah...but...Gemma—sorry, *Jenna*—she's still there, right? Not the same person, but, I don't know. She seems nice, too."

"Whoa, whoa, whoa," I say with a chuckle. "You dog—and I mean that in a very Earth way—you're just after that bod! You don't even care who's inhabiting it. Boy, you nasty."

"It's not like that," he says. "Okay, it's a little like that. It's tricky, you know, I was in love with her, man. And some of that was her body, yeah. She's kind of perfect. Her brown eyes, her slightly chubby curves, the sweet voice. They're all still there, man. It's just..."

"She's inhabited by a woman who used to be in her thirties, but who had her memories erased back to when she was sixteen, now living in a twenty-something body you've already fantasized about doing—"

"So many things..."

"Don't need to know," I say, still chuckling. "I get it. That's fucked up."

"What should I do about it?" he asks.

"For now, not a damn thing. I mean, first of all, she's out there doing recon. Probably having a ball while we're stuck in the *Prowler* trying to lift weights. But there's some serious shit for both of you to work through, *after* we save the world, and dude, bro, she might not be interested."

"Right," he says, "because I look like this." He motions at his unkempt self. His mop of hair and fuzzy face. His dark skin. His total lack of style.

I place my hand on his. "Hey, Lord Sean Huempfner, if I were an Earth chick, I'd fuck you sideways."

He sighs. "I know you would."

We lie there in silence for a moment. Then he says, "I miss *Peregrine*."

"She was the coolest car I've ever been in," I say.

"So cool. So fast."

"Gave her life for the cause."

"Excuse me," Harth says from the room's far side, curling two hundred pounds without breaking a sweat. "Did I hear you correctly? You had a vehicle, worthy of a name, that was destroyed in service to the Kynolari?"

"Saved our asses," I say. "More than once." Then I understand what the big man is getting at. "Oh...oh ho! I can't believe I didn't think of that."

"What?" Sean asks.

"If a personal vehicle is destroyed in service to the Kyno Corps, we are obliged to replace it."

"Replace it?" Sean asks, eyes widening. "Is that even possible?"

I motion to Harth, "You're looking at the man who built this whole ship. The *Prowler* isn't just one of a million factory-built ships, you know. She's a one-of-a-kind custom modification, just like *Peregrine*. And have I not shown you what he built for me?"

"I've heard about it," Sean says.

"It is glorious," Harth says.

"Wanna see it?" I ask.

Sean nods his head a dozen times in a second.

I extend my finger. "To the Workshop! Strap me on, you saucy sonuvabitch." I roll to my feet, take two steps, and then twist around before falling atop Sean's chest. He pulls the BabyBjörn baby carrier up and over my body, strapping me in place.

Then he tries to stand.

Doesn't quite make it. He rolls back to the floor, laughing.

"You!" I say, snapping my fingers at Harth. "Giant! Pull us up!"

Harth does a final curl, lays the dumbbell down, and stands above us. He frowns. "You two indulge too much. If the Draun find us—"

"What am I going to do?" I ask. "Fly us out of here? Kick them in the shins? Berate them to death?"

Harth motions to Sean. "He can fire the weapon systems."

I grimace. "Right." I elbow Sean in the ribs. "No more pot for you!"

Harth groans, leans down, takes hold of the baby carrier and lifts the two of us just as easily as he did the weight. "Do I need to carry you both?"

"Naw, man," Sean says, feet dangling above the floor. "I got this. I'm good."

Harth puts us down and Sean tries to walk to the door, all cool like. Doesn't seem to notice that he's angled to the left like a tree about to fall. Harth catches him, rights him gently, and follows us toward the workshop.

He might not admit it, but the big man is just as bored as we are. Weeks of hiding beneath the ground, not knowing what's happening in the outside world, while our friends might be in the shit, is beyond frustrating. Good news for Sean, when Harth is bored he tends to concoct his most amazing—and dangerous—inventions. He's already got the *Prowler* up to full strength. Still low on ammunition, but she's ready to hitch a ride on the gravity web.

First we need to escape the atmosphere, though. On a world overrun by the Draun, that will probably be impossible without a very big distraction. Also, we can't just leave the others. That's why we all volunteered Baarfolir for the job. He, along with MIMIR's help, will have to run the gauntlet, reach space, and head for home. If all goes well, he can reach Kyno, call in the fleet, and return in a few Earth days.

If we're lucky, we'll have solved the Draun problem by then, though that will be a lot more difficult without a ship to whisk us around the planet, an escape plan, supplies, or heavy hitting weapons.

Sigh.

If we can't take care of the Draun on our own, the fleet will do what they do best…and that doesn't bode well for humanity.

# 3

## PRAXION

Stagnation is my enemy.

And yet, I cannot bring myself to act. The ship is repaired. The team is restless. *I* am restless. This world is being conquered, and I feel frozen with concern for an individual.

For Torel.

She lies as still as she has since Anubis struck her down in Egypt, except for a brief spell where Poppy says she woke, but then quickly slipped to unconsciousness again. It is an unusual predicament for a Kynolari with regulators. Brain damage occurs, but it is quickly repaired. This feels different. Like a part of her is missing.

I flinch at the thought.

Humans believe that they have souls, that some immaterial continuance of their consciousness is separated from their bodies at the moment of death. Kynolari believed the same long ago, but we have…evolved past the need to believe in the eternal.

But I now wish it to be true.

Wish it enough to consider the possibility.

We *are* on another world. While Earth is mundane compared to other planets, it is not unusual to encounter phenomena that defies logic, known physics, and long held beliefs on every world. We Kynolari are advanced, but only a fool believes they have all the answers.

I toggle the ship's internal comms, think twice about what I'm considering, and then look up at Torel, lying still, eyes closed.

I miss her presence. Miss her voice. Her soothing encouragement.

As Micah would say, 'fuck it.' "Sean, Praxion. Copy?"

"Uh, yeah?" he responds after a moment. "This is Sean." Then he whispers, "Since when are comms working?"

In the background, Chirk replies. "Internal comms don't go down unless the ship blows up, dummy."

"Oooh."

"Sean," I say, talking over the open channel.

"Yes. Yes, sir."

"I need to speak with you."

"Oh shit, bro," he whispers. "I think I'm in trouble—"

"Sean," I say. "I can hear you."

"Ah."

"You haven't done anything wrong," I tell him. "I need...your input."

"Oh, wow. Yeah, of course. What's the sitch?"

"I would prefer to speak in person," I say.

"Sorry, boss man," Chirk says over comms. "Captain Beefcake is getting fitted."

My eyebrows rise. "Fitted...for what?"

"Not sure yet," Chirk says. "Harth is working on it. Idle hands and all that."

"The Devil's Workshop," I say. "Strange how humans manage to weave religious ideas into all aspects of life, whether or not they believe."

"You got it," Chirk says.

"On my way." I deactivate comms and lean my elbows on my knees. After a long sigh, I stand beside Torel and take her hand in mine. "If you knew what I am about to do, you'd laugh me out of the room."

I chuckle at the thought and lean my forehead against hers. "But I hope you'd be wrong."

After double-checking to make sure our gauntlets are still synced and her vital signs are still strong, I leave the infirmary behind and head for the workshop. It's a short walk through winding, organic-looking halls, that I have traversed thousands of times.

And yet, the ship feels empty. And not just because Torel is unconscious. I grew accustomed to living with Micah, Jess, and Grover. I was fond of the camaraderie formed between the humans and my crew. I would have never thought it possible, but the human Kynolari now among us—even Sean—have transformed the deadliest Kyno Corps squad into a family. The foundation was already there, but we were missing the kind of closeness at which humans excel.

Speaking of which...

The sound of Sean's laughter is muffled by the closed workshop entryway, but loud enough to hear even from a distance.

"Are you sure this is necessary?" he asks.

The workshop entry peels open before me, the sinews stretching and separating as I enter. Then it seals behind me.

Sean is upside down in a G-force simulator, spinning around in every direction. "Whoawhoawhoa!"

Chirk is on his back, laughing. Harth is operating the machine, looking at the readouts with a raised eyebrow. He sees me enter and waves me over, despite my confusion.

"Look at this," he says, motioning to Sean's readouts.

Not sure what I was expecting, but it wasn't positive numbers. We've all gone through G-force simulations, testing and pushing our limits. I know what good numbers look like, and Sean's are staggering.

"What?" Chirk asks, looking up from the floor.

"He's doing better than you," Harth says.

"What? Bullshit." Chirk gets to his feet. "No one does better than me."

"Whooohooo!" Sean says, settling into the spin. "The G-forces!"

Chirk snaps his fingers up at Harth and is lifted up to see the screen. "I'll be damned." He smiles. "My boy's a natural!"

If the person being tested were anyone else, Chirk's competitive nature would be triggered, and he'd push himself until he beat Sean's numbers. But he's reacting more like a proud parent with Sean.

"Feels like I'm back in *Peregrine*!" Sean shouts.

"Peregrine?" I ask.

"His vehicle," Harth says. "Sacrificed in service to the Kyno Corps."

Now I understand.

They want to build a replacement for Sean.

"It was fast," Chirk says. "Felt faster than it was because it was on wheels."

Harth huffs. "Wheels."

"May I speak with him now?" I ask.

Harth ends the test and Sean slows down from a blur. When he stops, his mop of hair billows around him, flowing like a field of Gavorian Thinsel Wheat. Sean unbuckles, stumbles a few steps, and catches himself on a workbench. "That was...wow." He catches his breath and laughs. "Can I ride it again later? Does it take quarters?"

"Sure this is the guy you want to talk to?" Chirk asks, grinning.

"Hey, I'm good." Sean stands up straight and gives me an American salute. "Okay, I might be a little high—on life...and pot—but that's kind of standard, so I guess you knew what you were getting into."

I hold up a hand, silencing him.

He purses his lips and steadies himself.

"What do you know about the soul?" I ask.

"It is a fiction," Harth says.

I silence him with a look that lets him know my line of questioning is serious.

"Well, it's complicated, I guess," Sean says. "Or is it? I'm not sure. I mean, most humans believe the soul exists. It's like...like we can feel it. There're a ton of different religions on Earth, but the soul is basically a part of all of them, whether it faces judgment after death, or gets transmogrified into a Hercules beetle, which

I think would be pretty sick, actually. Souls...are immaterial, I guess, unless it's a ghost, because they can touch things sometimes. But maybe that's just Patrick Swayze. Give that man some clay and he'll have you batting for the other team, if you know what I'm saying."

"We have no idea," Harth says.

"Anywho, yeah, the soul is a thing. Couldn't tell you if they exist or not, but the United States government definitely thinks they do."

"Explain," I say.

"Well, okay. Keep an open mind. Actually, you know what, this really shouldn't be that far outside of your wheelhouse. The Draun are telekinetic, yeah? Well, we classify that as a psychic ability, or power. Like precognition, telepathy, clairvoyance. Things like that." He attempts to flatten his hair but fails. "There are a few very similar phenomena that fall under the umbrella of parapsychology, which is kind of on the fringe of religion, or spiritual beliefs, I guess. The weird without the dogma. Making sense?"

"Continue," I say.

"Okay, let's talk OBE. That's an Out-of-Body-Experience. Imagine your consciousness kind of slipping out of your body. But it's not just your consciousness, because you can still hear, and see. It's like no-clipping in a video game. You can just float around, invisible to everyone else, and separate from your physical body. Some people can do it at will. Others just spontaneously slip out of themselves. But I think mostly it's triggered by psychedelics...which is what old school secret programs like MKUltra, Stargate Project, Grill Flame, and Sun Streak used. There're a few more, but—"

"You've mentioned these secret programs in the past," Harth says.

"Yeah, well, they're kind of freaky and weird, like me, and I never miss my *Why Files*. Because: 'Lizid People!'"

"I loathe lizard people," Harth says. "They smell like ammonia."

"So, one kind of OBE is called 'astral projection.' That's when you project your consciousness—or soul—because it's definitely not just your brain energy or whatever. Some people call it your 'astral body,' but how is that different from a soul? It's not. Same thing, different word. Government was interested in this so they could spy on enemies without fear of detection."

"It would be a useful ability," I admit.

"The last one, and I think this might be more closely related to why you're asking, is an NDE. Near Death Experience. Sometimes, when people die in the hospital—like really die, for minutes, sometimes longer—they're resuscitated and tell a story about how they were outside their body, floating around the operating room, listening to the doctors. Some drift into other rooms. And they perfectly describe what they're seeing, even though their body is dead. When they're zapped back to the living, they snap back inside their bodies. Crazy, right?"

"And this happens on Earth?"

"It's pretty well documented, yeah. Lots of books. And people have been taking spiritual journeys for a long time. That's like astral projection, but sometimes you speak to your ancestors, or meet your spirit animal. All kinds of stuff."

"And do you...know how to do these things?"

"I wouldn't call myself an expert," he says, and then smiles, "but I have been saving some shrooms for a boring day."

"Shrooms?" I ask.

"Hallucinogenic mushrooms," Chirk says. "A psychedelic."

"I am not fond of mind-altering substances," Harth says.

"Hey," Sean says. "If the big man wants to take a trip outside himself to find Torel and bring her back, I say we give him a chance. Because all your fancy advanced science ain't working. Maybe you just need some old school Earth spirituality? But, you know what they say. 'Any sufficiently advanced technology is indistinguishable from magic.'"

Chirk hitches a thumb at Sean. "I swear, there's a seed of genius buried in the fruit that is his head."

"Agreed," Harth says. "Perhaps it is worth exploring."

"Sweet," Sean says, holding up a clear bag full of gnarled mushrooms. "Let's get the Prax-meister blazed!"

# 4

## MICAH

In war there is often an upside and a downside to every attack—even if you think of an immediate downside. In this case, both are evident right from the get go.

The two men I targeted are dead. Raise a banner on a warship. Throw a party. Mission accomplished. Upside.

Downside? When I unleashed my narrow beam of condensed energy, Poppy snuck past my focus and got a laugh out of me. My hands shook as a result. The two men didn't fall to the ground with neat holes in their heads—they burst apart, carved into a dozen cauterized chunks, toppling to the ground like they were made from blocks.

A high-pitched, "What the fuck?!" follows their instant, steamy destruction.

And it's horrible, I know, I *know*, but the sound of the remaining Draun's voice is so hysterical that every single one of us hiding in the dark bursts out laughing. Gruunlokar holds his fire. Can't aim straight. Neither can I.

To say we have been tense is an understatement. We keep things light, but the weight of the world is literally on our shoulders. If we don't find a way to turn things around, humanity is kaput. The unexpected dismemberment was all it took to break our collective tension.

And now, the real downside.

"You fucking assholes! Do you know who we—who I am?! *Huh?!* Well, you're about to god damn find out!"

"Shield's up," Jenna says, suddenly serious.

Gruunlokar clears his throat and focuses on his aim once again. "Sighted."

"Better make it snappy," Poppy says. "He's reaching for something."

"On three," Jenna says, lifting her arms toward the railgun muzzle extending from the top of Gruunlokar's 1H1K Void Sniper gauntlet. "One, two, three!"

The tungsten shard launches from the railgun with a sound comparable to a whispered *pff.* A moment later, the Draun's invisible telekinetic shield shimmers from the impact.

The Draun inside flinches and spins around, looking at the impact site with wide eyes. But there is no blood. No death. It didn't work. Again.

"Gah!" the Draun man shouts, lifting some kind of gun toward the sky. He pulls the trigger. A red streak of light cuts up into the heavens.

"Shit," Gruunlokar says.

"What is it?" I ask.

"Reinforcement beacon," Poppy says, uncommonly urgent. "We need to relocate right the fuck now."

"I don't think that little beam of light is going to attract too much—" Jess is interrupted by a burst of red that flows out around the flare like the northern lights. "Okay. I stand corrected. But where are we going to go? It's not like there are any basements left to hide inside."

"First things first," Poppy says, turning to Jenna. "Do your thing."

Jenna's response is disgust. Helping Gruunlokar doesn't bother her, but actively taking the life of someone—even a Draun—offends her sensibilities. And honestly, that's a good thing. Helps me trust her. Taking a life, even that of an enemy, should be hard. Sure, you might find the humor in it on occasion, but unlike me, she's not going to accidentally Ginsu the man.

And she knows there's no choice. The man could direct whatever reinforcements arrive in our direction. Only way to leave them clueless is to kill him. And the only one of us that can do that very quickly, without a fight, is Jenna.

"Snap it up, princess," Poppy says.

Jenna shoots an angry glance in Poppy's direction but stands up and does her job. She reaches her hand out toward the Draun man, fingers outstretched.

Her target reacts immediately, spinning toward her, floating over the ground, writhing with manic power. "You! The traitor! I will writhe with delight in your spilled entrails."

"Dude," Jenna says, wincing. "Gross."

Then she closes her fist. In a battle between telekinetics, the more powerful one generally wins, and Jenna has access to all the power her former self had practiced for a decade and honed under the Visionary's direct guidance. The Draun doesn't even get a chance to squeal. One moment he's full of bravado, the next he's compressed into a sphere of flesh—bones crushed, organs reformed, wrapped in skin, and the man's clothing. When it starts dripping fluids, Jenna lets it fall to the ground and roll away.

She steps back. "Ugh." Looks ready to puke.

Poppy pats her leg. "Did good, kid. It ain't fun, but it's better than the alternative."

"What's that?" Jenna groans.

"Being dead," Jess says. "Can we go now?"

"There was a stand of trees a mile back," Gruunlokar says. "We could—"

"That's going to be seen for hundreds of miles," I say, pointing up at the swirling red sky. "A couple of trees isn't going to—"

"Shh," Jess says, snapping her fingers at me.

"What?" I whisper.

"Listen," she says. "I heard a voice."

We all fall silent for just a moment before both Gruunlokar and Poppy spin around toward the ruins of a nearby home.

"What is it?" I ask.

"A voice," Gruunlokar says.

"Sounds young," Poppy adds. "Kid maybe."

"What's it saying?" I ask.

Gruunlokar's brow furrows. "'Who's a good boy? You're a good boy. Yes, you are.'"

"That's how someone talks to a—" My eyes widen and my stomach twists. I search for Grover, but he's missing. "They're talking to Grover."

"Grover!" I call. "With me!"

A moment later, his goofy happy face pops up from a hole in the rubble. "Friend this way. Hide here. Lots of friends."

Before I can decide whether Grover has fallen into a trap, Jess fires the grappling hook from her Stinger gauntlet. It punches into the roof of the ruined home and yanks her into the air. Half the distance to Grover, she retracts the grapple and sails the rest of the distance, landing just feet away from him, the shock absorbed by the boots Harth supplied her with. Lets her bounce around without having to worry about shattering bones or developing shin splints.

She leans down beside Grover, shining a light from her gauntlet inside the hole. Grover is excited by her closeness, sniffing her ear and giving her playful nudges. "Love Jess. You see? Friends."

Jess leans back up as the rest of us arrive. "I think we're good."

"What makes you think that?" Gruunlokar asks.

"Come on out," Jess says into the hole.

A moment later, a dirty little girl pops out of the hole. "Hello," she says, sounding nervous. She can't be older than ten, black hair tied back, dressed like a kid, but covered in dirt and what looks like dried blood. "You're not like the others, are y—" She gasps upon seeing Poppy. "Sooo cute." She looks up and sees Gruunlokar. Her mouth drops in amazement.

"Kids," Poppy says. "You know how many of these little humans have just walked right up to me and touched my—"

"Good girl." The kid strokes Poppy's head.

"You see!?" Poppy points to the girl but doesn't stop her from petting. "At least get behind my ears." She leans into the scratch.

"Is it really you?" the girl asks. "You're them?"

"Them, who?" I ask.

"The ones the bad people are looking for. The Kynolari."

"How do you know that name?" Gruunlokar asks.

"On the first day," she says, "when they all came out from Japan. There was a broadcast about you, with pictures. Called you Kynolari along with some bad words. Said that anyone who told on you would be spared. But we won't tell, and you can hide with us."

"Us…who?" I ask.

"*La Résistance*," Grover says, getting a smile out of me. He must have just learned those words from the girl. Got the pronunciation right, too.

"Good enough for me," I say, looking up at the sky. High above, a Draun soars past, silhouetted by the bright flare. "We have company."

Jess ducks into the hole with the girl and Grover. Poppy dives in next, followed by Jenna. I motion to the hole, and when Gruunlokar moves toward it, I say, "Ladies first."

He pauses. Grimaces. "Axiom or not, I can still put a round through your pecker from more than a mile away."

"Super awesome badass snipers first," I say and motion to the hole again.

"Better." He ducks inside and I follow, pulling a slab of plywood over the hole. Even if the Draun knew there was a hiding spot in one of the ruined homes, they'd have trouble finding it.

I slide through a bumpy passageway of cleared out debris. It's a tight fit, but I manage to worm my way through, into a partially cleared-out basement. There's enough room for all of us, but Gruunlokar and I are the only ones here.

"Where...?"

"Here," Gruunlokar says, lifting another piece of plywood away from the wall. Behind it is a tunnel. A lit tunnel.

"The hell?"

I enter the tunnel and Gruunlokar allows the spring-loaded wooden hatch to close behind us. On guard, we work our way through the winding tunnel that's been dug out and braced by two by fours.

We exit into a large storm drain, also wired and lit by bulbs. Definitely not part of its original design. Voices echo from ahead, where the rest of our crew keeps up with the swift pace set by the girl.

"Be ready for anything," Gruunlokar says under his breath.

"Already at full charge," I say.

When the two of us approach the end of the storm drain, the echoing of voices falls silent. Jess leans into the tunnel, eyes wide, a subtle smile on her face. "You guys… Weapons down. You need to see this."

Jess wouldn't tell us to lower our guard without good reason, so we both follow her guidance and step out of the storm drain, into a massive concrete terminal where several concrete tunnels converge. What we find shocks me silent. I don't know what to say.

But Gruunlokar has me covered. "Well, pull my hair and call me a bescumbering Chortilian dung funnel."

# 5

## PRAXION

"Am I doing it right?" I ask.

"Right now, you're just sitting, boss," Chirk says. "Just try to relax."

He's got a permanent subtle smile, wholly amused that we're trying something so...aberrant. But he has held back teasing me about my desperate gambit to wake Torel. After all, they are comrades as well. We would all like to see her wake.

I'm back in the med-bay with Chirk and Sean. Harth is toiling in the workshop, creating something for Sean that he seems to think will help us in the *Prowler's* absence.

Sean sits down across from me. He claps his hands and rubs them together. "Okay. This is exciting." He takes a deep breath and lets it out slowly.

"Are you feeling well?" I ask him.

"He feels like this is his first real chance to contribute," Chirk says.

"Well, yeah, dude," Sean says. "I mean, I carry you around, and that's cool, but I don't have a gauntlet. Don't know how to fight, or any of the other badass stuff you guys do. I'm not an expert in much, but I am an expert in getting blitzed."

"You see?" Chirk says, motioning to Sean. "Raring to go."

"Okay," Sean says. "First things first..."

"Ain't that the order most things go?" Chirk asks.

Sean ignores him and focusses on me. "You need to set your intentions. What is the purpose of your journey? What do you hope to achieve when you leave your body?"

I nod, thinking the answer.

"No, no, no," he says. "You need to say it. Verbalize it, dude. Really root yourself in it."

Feels awkward to say the words aloud, but I know Sean will not judge me for it. "I intend to locate Torel's soul, or consciousness, and return it to her body."

"Okay, now we need to create a sacred space, but seeing as how we're in the stark white med-bay of a spaceship, not a candle in sight, we'll just have to make do."

"She is here," I say. "This is the right place."

"Rad," Sean says. "Next step. When you begin to feel the effect, you need to visualize the journey, leaving your body, traveling the Earth, being drawn to Torel's location. Just as important, you need to focus on keeping yourself tethered to your body, right? To find your way back and bring Torel with you. While all that's going on in your head, I want you to keep your breathing deep and steady. And well, you guys don't believe in a higher power, so we can just skip that bit and move on to music."

"Music?" Chirk asks.

"Well, yeah," Sean says. "Obviously. It helps keep everything in sync. Flowing. Sets the tone. I don't have any hippy trippy shit on my phone, though, so we're going to have to make do with what I have."

He plays a song from his phone. A series of repeating tones play, creating a rhythmic, inspiring, and slightly ominous feeling. Like an approaching storm. I close my eyes and picture Torel. The music fills me with confidence.

"This is a good choice," I say.

"Can't go wrong with Daft Punk. Believe it or not, this is a movie soundtrack. I play it in my head when things get nuts. I think it fits our story pretty well."

I nod. "Agreed. What's our next step?"

"Right. Uhh, do you have anything symbolic of Torel? Something you could hold onto or wear? Something to remind you of what you're doing? In case you get lost?"

"Well," I say, opening my eyes and turning toward Torel. She's lying on a hover bed, just ten feet away. "She is right there."

Sean's eyes widen. "Right. I got you."

He glides Torel's bed beside me and sits back down.

I nod my thanks and take her hand.

"Check," he says. "So, yeah, that's about it. Probably should spend some time meditating, or practicing your visualization, but I get the feeling that waiting is *no bueno*."

"*Mucho*," I say.

"Well, all that's left is the fun part." Sean pulls his baggie of mushrooms out of his pocket and gives it a shake. "Now, I don't know how this is going to affect you, so we might want to take it slow."

"Give me what you would give an adult human," I say. "We have spent too much time underground as it is."

"Okay, express elevator to la la land." Sean opens the baggie and plucks out a chunk. Weighs it in his hand. "Two grams will get you to a happy euphoria, but it's not enough." He takes out a larger chunk and combines it with the first. "Five grams. That's what we want. Say goodbye to the real world."

"It's not too much?" Chirk asks.

Sean shakes his head.

"It's a high dose for sure, but overdosing on shrooms is hard to do, and even then, it's super uncommon to die from it."

"In people," Chirk says.

"Well, yeah, but if you want to complain about it, tell him." Sean hitches a thumb toward me.

My response?

"If overdosing isn't a concern, give me six grams. I want to make sure this works."

"Bro," Sean says. "First, balls out, I respect it. Second, you sure?"

"I'm always sure," I say with a grin.

Chirk throws his head back and rolls his eyes. "Oh, here we go. The great and mighty Praxion, liberator of the universe, defender of freedom, who never makes a mistake and always gets the credit."

"You're just jealous," I say.

"Yeah, well, if I were a six-foot-tall golden boy like you, it would be me getting the praise."

"Hey," Sean says, giving Chirk a pet on his head. "You're *my* hero."

"Right." Chirk slides out of his chair and drops to the floor. "You two can take it from here. I'm going to go work out my useless arms. Or shoot myself. One of the two. Wait, never mind. Can't even lift my damn mini-railguns to do the job. Work out, get buff, then shoot myself. Later."

Chirk exits, leaving me alone with Sean for what I think might be the first time since we met.

Sean grows quickly nervous.

"How is Chirk?" I ask.

"He's...he's, uhh, having trouble dealing with the arm stuff. I mean, he's a little guy. Everything you guys do is twice as hard for him. Maybe more. He's proud, you know? Of being one of you. He's probably starting to doubt all that, now that he can't really pull his very light weight."

I nod. "You're a good friend, Sean. I'm glad he has you."

He sits up straighter. "Thanks."

"Now," I say, holding out my hand. "Hit me."

Sean chuckles. "'Hit me.' Nice."

He places the shrooms in my hand.

"I just eat them?"

He gives a thumbs up and says, "They taste like shit, but you need to chew them up good. If you don't, the effect will be slow. But since we want it to hit you with a bang, it's time to visit mastication station, which is a very different place from masturbation station. You don't want to go there. It's nasty."

I don't want to know if such a place exists on this world, so I don't ask. Instead, I toss the mushrooms into my mouth and chew. "They're not bad," I say, still chewing. "Honestly, they're pretty good."

"Head back," Sean says. "Eyes closed. Focus on Torel's hand in yours and visualize the journey. Feel your connection to her. Let it pull you. Direct you. Guuuuiiiddddeee yooooouuuu."

I feel like I'm floating. Like I'm leaving myself behind. But it's too quick. I reach my free hand up and look at it. My fingers warble like they're dancing on the event horizon of a black hole, about to be sucked inside.

"I think it's working," and my voice sounds like one of Sean's squeaky cartoon animals.

"Yeeaaah, duuuude," Sean says. His face is distorted. Stretched out. His smile is two feet wide, and not metaphorically. "Youuu'rree trrriiipping baaaallls."

Flashes of color burst around the white med-bay. I can see the music Sean is playing, pulsing out around me, a steady wave. I take root in it, my legs stretching out and burrowing deep.

*My legs aren't roots*, I think, and chuckle.

I gasp as I suddenly can feel every atom flowing around and through me. Can feel the click of every skin cell being shed, and the pop of new ones being created.

"Foooccusss on yoouur intennnsions," Sean's disembodied voice says, flowing around me. "Visualizzzze the jooouurney. Reememmber why yoouu're therrre."

*Torel.*

I am liberated from reality.

The med-bay fades away. All that remains is color, movement, and sound. Yet, I still reside in my body. Can sense its corporeal form.

*Torel.*

A burst of energy sweeps me away into an ethereal realm. A cosmic sea of stars and swirling nebula.

*Torel.*

I feel a connection to a universal fabric binding all things together and it feels...familiar.

*The gravity web.*

Realization clarifies my view of a hundred million strands of energy connecting all things, everywhere, in an infinitely complex mesh.

That I know how to navigate.

*Torel.*

A pulse of color calls to me.

The music evolving around me crescendos.

I visualize traversing the web, sliding through its faster than light network, and emerging at my goal.

*Torel.*

# 6

## CHIRK

I'm not usually one to throw pity parties for myself. I've been injured before. We all have. Sitting out the fight is never easy, but our med-tech gets us back in the fight fast enough.

I should be good to go. My bones and muscles have knitted back together. And yet I still can't perform the simplest tasks, including having a wank in my quarters. Arm just gets all shaky like a Delorvian street trollop with tentaclitus. Causes violent tremors. Looks like a fun time until she gets a hold of you. Then it's like being bound in a copulatory tie with a St. Bernard bounding down the side of a mountain. Just dragged and whacked around until you're flung free forty-five minutes later.

Yeah, so, pity party for me.

Healed, but not healthy.

*The fuck is that all about?*

I sigh, looking at my weights. They're embarrassingly small. And I can't lift them without looking like I'm being electrocuted. It's humiliating. Almost enough to put a scratch in my massive ego.

*You just need time,* I tell myself.

Or am I getting old?

I shake my head. I'm in my damn prime. Top of my game.

"Hi-ho!"

I flinch at Baarfolir's loud voice. His head leans into the training room, all smiles. "Trouble you for a flying lesson? Maybe something with evasive maneuvers, since, you know, every Draun weapon in the atmosphere—and above it—will be trying to shoot me down."

"Here's my best advice," I say. "Let MIMIR do the work. You're on board so that the high council knows our request is legit. If you try flying the *Prowler* through an obstacle course of enemy fire, you won't make it to the clouds."

"Right," he says, sounding nervous. "So, I just—"

"Pucker your butt and hold onto your nuts. When you reach Kyno, transfer and confirm the message. Easy peasy, yo mama's sleazy."

"My mother passed away ten years ago," he says.

"Oh," I say. "Oh, damn. Sorry. Wasn't talking about *your* mother."

Baarfolir's brow furrows. "Are you feeling all right?"

"Fine. Why?"

He raises one of those furrowed brows. "That is the first time you've apologized to me for something rude or insensitive that you've said."

"Really? Huh. Should probably make it the last time."

"It was not an unwelcome change."

I resist making a joke, mostly because I lack the gumption to engage in a fiery dialogue with a guy who uses historical references as insults, resulting in a long historical discourse that makes me feel young and stupid.

But the alternative might not be much better.

"So," he says. "What is bothering you? I know I'm not a gruff operator with nerves of tungsten, but I'm here, I'm still alive, and I've got more life experience than the lot of you."

"Not sure how that's possible," I say, "with all the shit we've—"

"War is not life," he says. "You'd do well to not confuse the two."

I just stare at him for a moment, unsure whether I should be impressed by the insight or make some kind of snarky comment.

He doesn't give me time to decide. "Okay, let's cut right to the marrow of it. You're upset about your arms."

"Well, I—"

He holds up a finger, silencing me. "Not done." He clears his throat. "I'll put this in words that you'll understand. You are embarrassed that your arms are about as useful as two flaccid Mishaquin tube snakes, and by 'tube snakes' I mean cocks."

"I got that, but thanks."

"It's okay to feel useless. It's okay to *be* useless. Around you lot, I feel like that all the time."

"As you should," I say, and smirk.

"What you need to do," he says, "is take some time to figure out how you're *feeling*. You suffered a trauma, as I'm sure you have before, but this time your defense system can't bury it. Why do you think that might be, hmm?"

"We in therapy now?" I ask.

"If you want to be," he says. "It was my profession before I began my history studies."

"Great," I say, hopping down from the bench. "So, your solution is to make this even more humiliating."

"Whatever is said, stays between us."

"Hrm." I feel dirty just thinking about it. In the Corps, after a battle or injury, a therapy session is mandatory. But it's really just about keeping the masses happy. If they knew the kind of shit we went through with the Draun... They might have decided to play defense instead of taking the fight to them. So, we attend therapy, shoot the shit with someone who may or may not be a therapist, get a stamp of approval, and head back into the field. That hour is just about appearances. The real work is done alone, at night, compressing all the nasty things into a box and forgetting it's there.

But now... Kind of feels like the box is full. Or that this is different.

"Come," he says, sensing my waning defense. "Let's go someplace more comfortable."

My legs follow him despite my trepidation, and I find myself sitting in one of his library chairs, surrounded by old timey paper books that give the room an organic feel. But it's a complicated scent, muddied by many thousands of years of fingers that have touched these volumes.

He plops himself down in the chair beside mine. "There now. This is better. Just talk to me like I'm one of your friends, okay?"

I huff a laugh.

"What's funny?" he asks.

"You've been through the shit, right along with the rest of us, man. Hate to break it to you, but that means you're part of the team. Means we're more than friends. You get me?"

"I—I don't know what to say."

"Don't need to say anything. Just know it."

"Then, I suppose talking to me should be easy," he says. "Seeing as I'm in the shit."

I huff a laugh. "Not *in* the shit. Been *through* it."

"On the precipice of the shit," he says.

"Absofuckinlutely." I take a deep breath and let it out. "Okay, here's the thing. I've been shot, stabbed, electrocuted, choked out, shot down, scorched, broken bones, and wrangled a pair of Glorkian twins."

He gasps.

"You damn right," I say. "Don't recommend it. Now, there are two things all those injuries have in common. First, they were graciously bestowed upon me by the Draun. Second, I stood a fighting chance and gave as much as I got."

"Xolotl was different."

"Hell, yes," I say. "He was one of us. A legend. And he turned out to be as horrible and ruthless as the Draun."

"Then this is also the first time you have considered the fallibility of our people?"

"I wouldn't take it that far. I know some guys—and ladies—that would make you question our place at the top of the universal order. But Xolotl was different.

Mad. Power hungry. Even before he gained telekinetic abilities, he was just like them. And that means: it could happen to any of us. Just like it is to the humans."

"Let's leave the big picture out of this and focus on you," he says.

"Not going to let me sneak my way out of this, huh?"

He just grins at me.

"Okay, so problem one. I guess we can call it shame. Problem two. I don't know. Maybe you'll get it. We're small breeds. To keep up with Praxion, with Harth, all of them, I have to put in a supreme effort, all the time. It's why you don't see much of us in combat. And why I'm a pilot instead of on the front lines. Do I care? Not in the slightest. Pit me against any of the Kyno Corps and I'll hold my own, not because we're equals, but because I'm better than the lot of them, operating with an ironically big handicap."

I wait for a sarcastic, 'your brain?' but Baarfolir doesn't partake in conversational jabs. He's genuine and doesn't hold back.

"And with Xolotl…you felt?"

"You know damn well how I felt. How I feel."

"Helpless."

"Like any other quivering terrified chihuahua on this planet. He just held me there. Nothing I could do. He just severed my muscles and bones like they were hotdogs and twisted them around. But you know what else he did? Left my nervous system intact. Wound like that? Arms go numb. But not this time. I could feel the severed bones grinding against each other. I can deal with pain, but helplessness? Humiliation? Those are not things I'm accustomed to."

"Have you told Sean any of this?"

I wave my hand at him. "Don't need anyone here thinking I'm anything but a hardcore badass."

"Is that how you perceive the others?" he asks. "Is Praxion not attempting a desperate gambit for the sake of love? Has he not shed tears about Torel's condition? I know you have seen the kinship and mutual affection between Micah, Jess, and Grover."

"Big squishy mess of slobbering love," I say.

"And yet, Micah is the Axiom, is he not? He was profoundly tortured when Grover died, and yet he is the most 'badass' human we know. My point is that your greatest weakness—and when I say 'your' I mean all of you Kyno Corps operators—is that you bear your pain alone. You should hold the weight of it together. Support each other. Share strength in times of weakness, which *you all have*. Admit it or not.

"And I know you're worried about becoming like Xolotl yourself, corrupted by what's been done to this world's atmosphere. Xolotl was already corrupt. He fled here, a cult figure leading our ancestors astray. That wasn't caused by Earth. From what I've seen, the only thing we need to worry about is lowered guard, increased emotions—positive and negative, and a penchant for humping every bitch we come across."

I laugh. "Yeah, well, that's mostly a me problem. Well, Harth, too, I— You know what, I'm keeping that to myself."

"Intriguing," he says.

"Don't ask," I say. "Not me, and definitely not Harth."

He chortles. "I wouldn't dream of it."

"Yeah, you'd have nightmares if you did." A shiver shakes my body. "If you learn how to erase memories, let me know."

"So," he says. "Feeling better?"

"Yeah," I say. "You know, I think—"

"Catch!" he shouts, tossing something in my direction. There's no time to see what it is, let alone catch it.

The heavy object collides with my head and thumps to the floor.

"What the heck was that?"

"Drat," he says with a snap of his fingers. "I was hoping reflex would activate your arms and you'd catch it."

"Well, you activated a headache." I hop down from my chair and find the projectile beneath. My eyes widen. "You threw a mini-railgun? It could have gone off. Could have broken!"

I bend down and pick it up. Give it a quick inspection. Look down the sight. Seems to be okay. "Listen Baar, next time you throw something at someone—"

He's staring at me. Grinning.

"What?" I ask.

His eyes flick to the weapon.

"Yeah, I know. You threw one of my—"

"Ah-ah!" he says and flicks his eyes again, closer to my body, to my outstretched arms.

"Seriously," I say, losing my patience. "What are you—ohhhh. Oh, shit! You sneaky little mongrel."

I laugh as I lift the weapon with no trouble. Wasn't my body keeping me weak. It was my mind, and this little wizard worked mental magic on my psyche in just a few minutes. "Thanks, Baar."

"It's what we do," he says. "For each other."

I nod. "Understood. Now, how about I give you a few pointers on how to not get your ass shot out of the sky?"

# 7

## MICAH

"That was funny," I say to Gruunlokar. "Since when are you funny?"

"I have always been funny," he says. "I just reserve it for special occasions. The contrast to my normal glowering self makes me seem funnier."

"Ahh," I say, "strategic humor."

"Everything I do is strategic," he says, back to being deadpan.

"Guys!" Jess says, waving us down into the central chamber, which is dry and empty, save for all the gathered people...and dogs. They look up at us with a kind of reverence.

I catch hints of whispers but can't make them out.

"What are they saying?" I ask Gruunlokar.

He leans back close to me. "They know who we are. They are happy we are here. They think...they think we will save them."

"No pressure," I say as I reach the bottom, where Jess, Poppy, and Jenna are speaking to a couple who tell the little girl to go play with the other kids. A pair of happy Pit Bulls sit on either side of them, content, but also on guard. Grover isn't far. He's having the time of his life, bounding around with a springy Boxer, a large black Newfoundland, and a French Bulldog spinning in fast, happy circles. A group of children laugh at their antics while Grover says, "Happy! Am happy! New friends! Happy!"

"Hi," I say to the parents. "Hello. I'm Micah."

I shake the man's hand. He's just an average dude. Receding hair. Bit of a belly. Maybe mid-thirties.

"I'm Ben," he says. "Ben Jackson. Man, we are glad to see you."

His eyes widen when he turns to Gruunlokar. "Wow. I just... She's amazing—" He motions to Poppy. "—but you. I mean look at you." He's lost in admiration until his wife swats his shoulder.

"Ben, you're making a fool of yourself."

The man collects himself and holds his hand out to Gruunlokar. "Ben. Or Benjamin. Whatever you prefer."

"Gruunlokar." He shakes the man's hand, and then nods to the woman. "Pleased to meet you both."

"I—I'm Kim. Kim Jackson. Obviously, I guess."

"Okay, okay, we get it," Poppy says. "The gruff German Shepherd looking guy is impressive." She leaps up, bounds off my hip, does a flip, and lands on Gruunlokar's shoulder, taking a fist full of his hair to keep herself in place. "But he ain't the brains of this outfit, and I have some questions."

To his credit, Gruunlokar just raises an eyebrow and glances to the side at her. I know I wouldn't be jumping on Gruunlokar if I were small enough to pull it off. But I'm also not a loveable Pug, either.

"Who are you? Why are you here? And...anything else?"

"Why are you helping us?" Jenna asks.

"Sure," Poppy says. "That."

Ben looks baffled. "You...you don't know?"

"We've been on the run for a few weeks now," Jenna says. "Whole world is looking for us."

"Yes, of course. We are the Resistance. *La Résistance*, if you ask the kids. Most of us were dog owners during the change, and it wasn't hard to figure out what made us different. So, we started organizing. Preparing. We saw what everyone else did—about you, about the Kynolari, but we knew—felt it in our guts, you know? We're Kynolari, too."

"Dog people," Jess says with a grin.

"Hell, yes," Ben says.

"Alright, Ben, give me a sitrep," I nod.

"Sit...rep?" he says. "I was a structural engineer until a month ago."

"Right. Sorry. Situation Report. Military for 'How are things going?'"

"We're hanging in there for now," Kim says. "But supplies are running low. Some stations are already out. We've got a week left. Two if we really ration. Then we'll have to start scavenging...which is obviously dangerous."

My heart breaks for these people. They're regular folks with a family just living their lives, and now they're hiding out in sewers and rationing food, while the world is torn apart above their heads. I try not to get distracted by their personal plight and focus on the details buried in the answer.

"You said 'stations.' *Plural*."

"Right," Ben says. "We call them 'stations.' Guess you'd call them bases. Basically, each is a collection of people like us. Some are dozens of people. Some are hundreds. There are even some in Japan, if you can believe it. We're connected through a ham radio network set up before the Draun launched their attack from Japan. When they did, we all went underground, literally. We've got underground networks up and down both American coasts, though there are some breaks that need to be covered at night. There're a few ways to cross the country, but I wouldn't recommend it. Some states are entirely dark."

I stand there for a moment, mouth open. Then, I say, "You're shitting me."

Ben smiles, proud. "Not remotely. We've just been waiting for you to emerge."

"Waiting for us, for what?" Jess asks.

"To do what you tell us. We're your army."

Ben is definitely not military material, but defending armies are usually made up of anyone that can fight. Farmers, bankers, chefs. Anyone that can hold a weapon. "Are you armed?"

"Oh, yeah," he says, "not that conventional weapons work against the Draun, unless you catch them off guard, like you guys did up there."

"You didn't see that, did you?"

He struggles to hide his disgust.

"That was not on purpose," I say, and motion to Poppy. "This chick made me laugh."

"And the last man?" Ben asks. "We saw how he died, but I don't understand it. It was like..."

"Like he was killed by one of their own," Jenna says. "Please don't freak. It's a long story. I'm not one of them, but I can do what they do."

Ben and Kim go rigid. It's the first time they've looked anything but friendly. Ben's hand moves down and toward his back.

I put myself between Ben and Jenna. "Stand down, soldier."

He flinches.

"Right now." It's an order, not a request. "We are Kynolari, I am the Axiom, and she—" I point to Jenna. "—is one of us."

Ben relaxes. "Sorry. We've had to be careful."

"Understood," I say, "but from now on, if I trust someone, you trust someone."

"Yes... Yes, sir. But, if you don't mind, can we double check?"

"Double check...if someone is Draun?"

"How?" Gruunlokar asks.

"Tomax," he says. "Xamot."

The two Pits stand ready, broad mouths open, tongues hanging out.

"First," I say. "The names. Hell, yes. Second, no biting."

Ben nods and Kim says, "If she's one of them, they'll walk away. Disinterested."

I look to Jenna. It's her call.

She shrugs. "Never can have too many dog friends, right?"

I can tell she's nervous. Is she still technically Draun because of what she can do? Or is the essential element of our enemy a twisted mind and soul? Guess we'll find out. She crouches down as the two dogs approach her. At first, they sniff the ground around her and slowly work their way up and around her legs, coming to her hands. Putting a lot of trust in the pair, she leans down and lets them sniff her hair.

A moment later, tails begin to wag. The sniffing becomes snuffing, and then licking. The pair bounce and jump up, pawing at her until she gives in and pets them. Then they're on their backs, spread eagle and twitching as she scratches their bellies.

Hard not to smile at them. "We good here?" I ask.

"Yes," Ben says. "Sorry for the doubt."

"You are only keeping your people safe," Gruunlokar says. "Your precautions are wise."

Ben is beyond pleased. "Thanks. Thank you. Means a lot coming from you."

"Yeah, yeah, yeah," Poppy says. "Quit sucking his dick and let's get back to the nitty gritty. You have bases, a network of tunnels, weapons. All of that is good, but how many of you are there?"

Ben smiles. "About a billion."

"Bill...did you say *billion?*" Jess asks.

"Globally," Kim says. "Closer to a hundred seventy million in the U.S., though we can't be sure how many of them are still alive. These are estimates based on the number of dogs owned in the country, and the average number of people in a U.S. household. It's possible half of them are dead and were never able to join the Resistance."

"They won't all be dead," Gruunlokar says. "The Draun have established their dominance over this world. Survivors who fight will be killed. The rest will be enslaved."

Before that happy tidbit can fully sink in, the concrete ceiling above us bows down with a thunderous boom. Did something big crash? Or is it—

A lone man punches through the center of the ceiling, dressed as a Goth priest, and shouts, "Woe to the dog-snakes who crawl through the earth, gnashing their teeth in terror! For I am Scourge, the prophesied one, exalted above all who gaze upon my glorious form! Bow that I might spill thy blood and satiate my unending lust for carnage!"

# 8

## PRAXION

I'm stretched around the world, part of my body locked at the start of my journey, the rest of me elongating as I'm whisked through a kaleidoscopic rainbow. I can see the Earth below me. Its continents. A swirling storm system in the middle of the Atlantic. Africa. The Mediterranean Sea. Egypt.

I've been to a lot of worlds, but Earth is the first one I've stayed at long enough to learn the names of countries—partially because centralized worlds don't have countries, but also because we've had to make this place our home for the time being.

A wave of green energy sweeps through me, and I plummet from orbit.

I'm falling but can't feel it. I have no stomach to lurch. No hair to whip in the wind. No body to burn up from the friction of punching through the atmosphere.

I relax into the descent. Feels like I'm in bed the day after a victory. I begin to drift until, from the recesses of my mind...

*Torel.*

"Gah!" I snap awake, terrified that I've lost my way.

Desert sands stretch out in every direction beneath me. Vast swirling pits open up, gaping maws intent on swallowing me whole. Panic rises, but then I spot a colorful beacon pulsing to the north.

My brain tells me to angle my body. To direct my descent. But that's not how things work now—not in this world. Longing guides me toward the beacon. It grows larger. Brighter.

I pass through the light!

No!

I've missed it.

Missed her.

*Torel.*

*I'll have to find my way back up,* I think, and then face forward again, just in time to scream before impacting the Great Pyramid's angled side. I feel the jolt like I've been slapped by the dessert Sean calls, 'Jell-O.' It's more humorous than painful, and I can't help but laugh as I plow a path through the limestone blocks, through the King's Chamber, and then down into the secret crypt beneath, where we discovered Anbu's power cell, and where I lost Torel.

I strike the floor, which is somehow more solid than the pyramid. My body spasms, but there is no pain.

Head swirling as colors dance through the air, I roll over onto my back and gaze upward at the intricate carvings on the ceiling. Each segment depicts a part of Anbu's life in Egypt, posing as the dog-god Anubis. The last time I saw the images, they were static. This time, they're alive.

The dead march toward judgement at Anbu's feet. One by one, he cuts them down, dropping them into a dark pit, delighting in their demise.

Then he stops. Turns to me, eyes glowing red. "You have been judged, Praxion of the Kynolari, and have been found wanting. You have fallen short of your duties, failed this world, deserted the one you love."

"No," I say, but I fear he's telling the truth. Everything has gone wrong since we arrived on Earth. As the leader of my team, I am ultimately responsible for every failure, no matter how vast the odds stacked against me.

But I am here now.

I can redeem my mistakes.

"There is no forgiveness in this place," Anbu hisses. Strands of color burst away from his body, twisting and coiling as his head enlarges and his mouth opens to swallow me whole.

"No!" I shout, voice feeble and cracking. "I can make it right!"

In my desperation, I shout the only name I can think of from the world beyond. "Torel!"

The jaws close. Encase me in darkness.

The mummified faces of our friends—both Kynolari and human—swirl around me, shrieking in agony.

I scream and flinch back, guarding my face and diverting my eyes.

"No! No! Please! Stop!"

Anbu's growling throat suddenly tears open at the back, letting out a streak of light. The swirling faces howl and fade. A second slash of light is followed by a third. Sparkling light pushes back the darkness, filling me with hope and relief.

Then the darkness fades completely, and I find myself swaddled in light, comforted and safe.

Brilliant sparkles force my eyes to squint until a silhouette emerges, smiling and reaching out a hand.

"Torel?"

"I have you," she says, taking my hand.

I collapse into her arms, weeping openly. She holds me, absorbing my unusual emotion. I feel no judgement. Sense no disappointment. She just holds me, letting her love ease me back to myself.

"You seem lost," she says. "Not yourself."

"I am…'tripping balls'…I believe it's called."

She leans back, looking me in the eyes. "You let *Sean* help you?"

"I needed to free myself from the mortal plane. I needed to find you. You've been lost to us."

"Well, took you long enough. And I'm exactly where I need to be." She places a hand on my cheek. "I can feel my body, even now, calling for me to return. But I am not done here."

"Done here?" I ask, my mind swirling, trying to understand, while the world around me distorts and distracts. My experience of this plane is twisted and confusing, but I get a sense that Torel's mind is unhindered and clear. "What do you mean…*this* is where you need to be? The world…is lost."

She nods, somehow aware of events outside of this place. Sean did say that people experiencing out of body events could see the real world around them, but I can't imagine what would hold her back if she knew the Draun had launched their invasion.

"Come with me," she says, floating away, her outstretched hand bidding me to join her. "I've been waiting for you. I need you to see. To understand."

This isn't what I came here for.

I need to take her. Need to bring her home, to herself. To me.

But I also trust her. If she says there's a good reason, I believe her. And the angelic light emanating from all around her is impossible to resist. I glide closer and take her hand. The moment our grip firms, I feel a tug and am whisked into another realm.

Light envelops us.

I sense a presence beyond us.

Not just one, but hundreds. Thousands.

"What's happening?" I ask, my voice and body stretching out behind and in front of me.

"Humans call it limbo," she says. "A place between frequencies of reality."

"Like Gruunlokar's mental liminal space?"

Her forehead scrunches. "What?"

I forgot she hadn't been around for that. Hard to remember anything. "Long story," I say. "He's okay. Xolotl—Anbu—is dead. For good."

She smiles and color blooms from all around her, caressing me in relief. "The others will be pleased to hear it."

"The others?" I ask.

Our journey ends inside a tunnel of light, the end of which is lost in luminous white. Shadows emerge from the walls. At first, I think they're human souls.

Then one of them steps close enough for me to see her face. She's a Golden, like me.

She nods and smiles. "It pleases me to see a new face after all this time." She glances at Torel. "He is handsome."

"You're biased," Torel says.

Before the woman can reply, other figures emerge. Kynolari, every one of them. All breeds, large and small, dressed in the garb of ancient Egyptians with flairs of ancient Kynolari.

"Is this part of my hallucination?" I ask.

Torel shakes her head. "You are beyond your body and the effects the drug has on your mind. All that you see here is reality beyond our normal perception...without help."

"Humans know of this place," I say, "but have yet to prove its existence, or even that of an afterlife."

She nods. "And Kynolari have always scoffed at the very concept, to the point that no one ever thought to look."

"Who are they?" I ask, but then I turn to the woman. "Who *are* you?"

"Siloquin Dima, Prefect of the Kynolari Guard," she says.

I'm astounded. "The *Guard?* But they... You... *How?*"

"Anbu," Torel says. "Everyone you see here was a member of the Lost Tribe who did not agree with the actions taken by Anbu and his followers. The rebellion, the deception of mankind, the genetic alterations. After Anbu discovered this reality between life and death, he judged and condemned them all to an eternity, lost in this place, unable to move on to what comes next."

"How can I help?" I ask. The Earth is in trouble, but I cannot abandon the Lost Tribe I came all this way to find.

"There is a device contained in the core of the Great Pyramid," Siloquin says. "To free us, it must be destroyed."

"Which means..."

Torel nods. "We need to destroy the Pyramid."

"There is a chance the humans will not even notice," I say. "This world is overrun by the Draun."

"The corruptors of mankind's DNA," Siloquin says. "We know of them."

"That corrupt DNA became active," I tell her. "There are now millions upon millions of them, killing humanity, killing each other, and if they're not stopped here, the universe—including Kyno—will be next."

Siloquin steps forward, her practiced gaze serious and intimidating, as I'd expect from a Prefect of the Kynolari Guard. "Perhaps there is a way we can help each other?"

# 9

## MICAH

"Whoa, whoa, whoa," I say, holding my hands up. "You were prophesied about? Me, too! That's crazy."

The goth-priest's eyes snap to me. "Prophesied to spill thy blo—"

"Yeah, I got that," I say, paying attention to my periphery, where I can see the humans and dogs surrounding us slowly retreating through a variety of tunnels. With no real way to fight the Draun, retreat is their only option. And I'm glad for it, because once the space is free of potential collateral damage, I can let loose. "But I'm curious about who prophesied about you and when? Because, weirdest thing, mine was apparently one of the dog-people from millennia ago. I mean, that's ludicrous, right? You were a priest? Before the change?"

He squints at me, floating closer and higher to maintain a position of dominance. "Before I disintegrate your skin cells and leave you in agony—"

"Not nice," I say.

"—what...is your point?"

"I mean, Biblically speaking, when a prophecy is received there must always be someone there to translate the meaning, right? Because that shit's not always easy to understand. I mean, I only went to church a few times, with an old friend, but I was there for the day on prophecy, so..."

His eyes narrow.

I've called bullshit, and he knows it.

"You believe yourself intelligent?" he says. "And yet, here you stand while others have wisely fled. I will sniff them out. The hunt is thrilling, but you...you I will delight in killing."

"Because you're a sham," I say. "A Draun with a fragile ego, and I'm going to guess you were a sucky priest, too."

He lifts his arms, fingers hooked, ready to tear me apart.

"Here's the thing," I say. "Only one of us was lying about their prophecy."

He hesitates, and I use it. A thick beam of orange light slams into the man's already present telekinetic shield. It saves his life but isn't enough to stop him from being flung back against the concrete wall. He survives the impact, but all his concentration is on resisting my sustained laser blast. In this duel of wills, I'm not sure which of us will tire first, but it doesn't matter.

I've got back up.

"How you want to do this?" Jenna asks, standing beside me.

"I mean, I feel like we'd regret not pin-balling the guy. Look at all the angles in here."

She scrunches her nose and shakes her head.

I realize how cavalier I'm being about taking a man's life. Then again, he's not really a man anymore and is intent on slaughtering a group of men, women, children, and dogs.

"Right," I say to her expression of disapproval. "Quick and easy. Like outside."

Without a word of confirmation, she squeezes her fist, crushing the Draun's brain inside his skull. His shield drops before I'm ready and he takes a full-on laser blast. It's just for a moment, but it's enough to separate his body and limbs, sending them ricocheting away, bouncing off all the concrete angles until finally dropping to the dusty floor as a series of meaty thumps.

I raise my hands. "That...was *not* on purpose."

"But it was awesome," Poppy says, looking down at the Draun's remains. "He had it coming."

"Did anyone see where our hosts fled?" Gruunlokar asks.

A dog bark summons us. Grover peeks out from a side tunnel. Jess appears beside him. "Over here," she says, and then sees the mess, looking at me. "Seriously, what's wrong with you?"

"Why did you assume it was me?" I ask.

She raises an eyebrow.

"Well, yeah, it *was* me, but it wasn't intentional."

"Uh-huh," she says, knowing it will irk me.

"Hey, I'm not psycho," I say, following her into the low tunnel.

Our journey through the tight network of circular tunnels that smell of years-old feces is soundtracked by my defensive speech that makes me sound crazy rather than innocent. By the time we're done, I don't think anyone believes the goth-priest's dismemberment was accidental.

When we reach the end of our ten-minute crawl, led by Grover, Poppy pats me on the leg, looks up at me with her big Pug eyes, and says, "Don't sweat it, kid, we're all *malditamente loco*. Kind of need to be, to fight the Draun."

"*Sí*," I say, smiling down at her. "*Muy loco*."

We find just Ben and Kim, along with Tomax and Xamot, waiting for us in a cramped chamber.

"Where's everyone else?" I ask.

"They know how to get away. We'll catch up with them later. Anyone trying to follow them will just get lost. And there are secret doors, hatchways, and submerged tunnels, some of which lead to safety and others that head in the wrong direction. It's a maze down here," Kim says.

"Okay," Ben says, rubbing his hands together like he's jazzed to be part of the fight. "Where do you guys need to be?"

"Unknown," I say. "We're recon. Collecting intel. Waiting for the others."

"How many others?" Kim asks, eyes wide.

"Six," Gruunlokar says. "One of them human."

"Can't wait to meet them," Ben says, grasping Kim's hand. They give each other an excited squeeze, but then Ben looks uncomfortable. "No offense, and we've seen what you all can do, but that puts your total number at—"

"Twelve," Jess says. "One billion and twelve."

Ben chuckles. "This is true, and while many of us—not me—are military, we already know that conventional weaponry doesn't make a difference."

"Untrue," Gruunlokar says. "Draun are not gods. They need to eat, same as you. Need to shit. Need to sleep, which is when they're most vulnerable. But they also get tired. Telekinesis is a force of will, and its strength varies from person to person. And it takes effort, meaning Draun *can* be worn down. Can get exhausted. With large enough numbers and sustained gunfire, their shield will wane."

"Okay," Ben says. "Wow. Good to know." He turns to Kim. "Let the others know. Spread the word. Sustained fire and—" He glances at Gruunlokar.

"Nighttime assassinations," Gruunlokar says. "While they're asleep. Even better than that, a bomb, explosives, poison gas. However you kill them, it needs to be quick and ruthless. Something that cannot be recovered from."

"We could poison their food," Kim says.

"Difficult," Gruunlokar says.

"Shouldn't be too hard," she says. "They mostly take it from us."

Gruunlokar grins. "Then it is a spectacular idea."

Kim is beaming. "Great." She takes Ben's second hand in hers. "Be careful. Wherever you end up."

He gives a nod. "Always." They embrace and kiss. Passionately.

Tongue.

Fondling.

The whole shebang, right here in this cramped, dank space, surrounded by people who can't really turn around.

I glance over at Jess, who looks just as amused as me. She gives me a wink and then raises her eyebrows twice. When I nearly laugh, she bites her lower lip.

"Are you serious?" Poppy says, looking up at Jess in disgust.

I can't contain my laugh but manage to reduce its volume to a hiss. Jess breaks, too, holding her hand over her mouth to contain her laughter.

"Humans, man," Poppy says. "Always horny. Wake up in the morning? Horny. On an airplane? Horny. Facing imminent doom from an invading alien species? Fucking horny."

"Meh," I say with a shrug of my shoulders. "Guilty as charged."

Poppy rolls her eyes and sighs, stepping out to the front of our group. "Okay, okay, enough with the Plecostomus action. And before any of you small-minded primitives ask, you probably call it a suckerfish."

"Micah," a whisper calls from below.

I crouch down to Grover. "Yeah, buddy?"

"I miss snuggles," he says. "We always run."

Affection between people always makes Grover want some of his own.

"You're right," I tell him, petting his neck. "I'm sorry. Next time we stop, it's snug time, okay?"

"Okay," he says, forlorn. "But…what if…no stop?"

He's breaking my heart. Golden Retrievers are basically the perfect pet. Friendly, loyal, empathic, but they require a constant flow of affection, or they get anxious. It's not a problem for me usually, because I'm basically a Golden in human form. I'm also feeling the lack of snug time with Grover, and with Jess. But, not dying is the priority.

"We will stop," I say. "Eventually. I promise."

I don't take promise-making, to a Golden Retriever that can understand and speak English, lightly. He will be devastated if I don't follow through.

"Love Micah," he says, licking my face.

Jess crouches beside us, smiling. "You two are irresistible. Let me in on that action."

Grover's tail goes wild, smacking Gruunlokar, who is still talking to Kim and Ben, but I have no idea what about. I'm in Grover town.

Jess laughs as Grover slathers her with kisses. "Love Jess. Love Micah. All love."

We're both petting him, reconnecting as a family.

I'm a lucky man.

"Also," Grover says. "Love Poppy."

"Leave me out of it," Poppy says, out of sight.

"Love Gruunlo—" Grover's ears perk up. His head snaps toward the tunnel we took to get here.

Gruunlokar looks down at Grover, curious about why his name was cut short. When he sees Grover's tense stance, he turns toward the tunnel, his tall ears turning forward.

"What do you hear?" I ask.

"Tic-taks," Grover says, and I'm not sure what he means.

"*Tic-taks.* The sound of their talons on concrete. Shit." Gruunlokar looks back at me. "Gron Skitterlings"

"Biologics used to clear out tunnels," Poppy adds. "They're nasty little things. We should move."

"I can handle them," Jenna says, speaking for the first time since we entered the chamber. She's a badass, but I sometimes forget her psyche is just sixteen. She often just sits back and absorbs what everyone is saying, trying to make sense of this new world she's been transported into from ten years in the past.

"No," Gruunlokar says, "You can't. Their numbers will be too great. You would be overwhelmed...eventually." He turns to Kim. "Tell your people to get as far away as possible. At least a ten-mile radius."

She nods, shares one last kiss with Ben and then disappears into a tunnel. "With me," she says, already out of sight, and both Tomax and Xamot chase after her.

"Where do you want to go?" Ben asks.

"Los Angeles," I say.

"LA is a little...crazy," he says.

"Crazy is the new normal," I say.

He gives a nod and enters a square passageway that requires him to crawl.

"I'm last," Poppy says, and before anyone can even think about arguing, she adds, "You bitches are going to be slow-ass motherfuckers in there, and I can run, do somersaults, and shoot. Plus, my Lancer is the best weapon for Skitterling biologics."

Gruunlokar turns to Jenna and motions to the tunnel we exited. "Can you seal this?"

Jenna raises her hands toward the tunnel. "Will it stop them?"

"Slow them down," he says.

She closes her hands and the tunnel crumbles and falls in on itself. "Done. Did the next twenty feet, too."

Gruunlokar nods. "Should give us an extra ten minutes."

Jenna is disappointed. "Ten *minutes?*"

"They are voracious and unrelenting," Gruunlokar says. "Now, we better leave before we're eaten alive."

"Makes sense," I say as Jess, Grover, and Jenna follow Ben. "Eaten alive, huh?"

"They're about my size," Poppy says. "But they'll eat you until you're gone."

Hard to imagine how that's possible. "Big stomachs?"

"Ha!" Poppy says. "If only. More like you get to see yourself digested and shit out, as their mandibles slice, dice, and gnaw your flesh and bones. And they always start to eat at the feet. One of the worst ways to go in the universe."

"Right. I'll go next." I duck down into the tunnel and crawl like a motherfucker.

# 10

## CHIRK

"Now," I say, "if you feel like you're going to pass out, just clench your asshole like you're trying to keep a Glingan Entrail Eel from burrowing its way in."

"I've never had to do that before," Baarfolir says, sounding nervous.

"Some freaks would say you're missing out, but they're not Kynolari, and have very short lifespans, so it's basically YOLO every day, all day."

"YO...LO?"

"Sorry. A Seanism. 'You only live once.'"

"Ahh. *Carpe diem.*"

"Huh?"

"'Seize the day,'" he says, "'because tomorrow may never arrive.' That's a paraphrase of the original saying, '*carpe diem, quam minimum credula postero.*' In the original Latin, of course. It translates to, 'pluck the day, trusting as little as possible in the next one.'"

"Right," I say. "YOLO."

He smiles. "It certainly is a more efficient way of saying it. Either way, it is a foolish way to live."

"How so?" I ask.

"It encourages risky behavior," he says. "The kind that is likely to hasten tomorrow never coming. It's a self-fulfilling prophecy. Better to prepare for the worst and overcome it, rather than give up hope and become part of the chaos."

"Never thought of it like that," I say.

"Strange," he says. "It's what you do. The Kyno Corps. You defeat madness with discipline, order, strength, and preparation. That's the whole reason we've been hiding in this cave, recuperating, repairing, gaining strength. YOLO would have us charge into the fray, and likely die as a result."

"Preparation," I say. "Yes. Now we're coming full circle, right back to ass puckering."

"Right," he says. "Understood. To keep myself from passing out."

"Which shouldn't happen because the *Prowler*'s anti-G-force systems should keep you from feeling anything remotely that strong. But, you will likely be under heavy fire and take some hits. No way to know what systems will get knocked out."

"And the gravity web?" Baarfolir asks.

"Harth relocated the gravity drive," I tell him. "They'll definitely target it, but it won't be where they think it is. Only way to destroy it, is to destroy the ship, and if that happens, only thing you'll be able to do is—"

"Pucker my asshole," he says, getting a laugh out of me.

"Now, you're getting it." I tighten his safety straps and then climb back out of the simulator. "MIMIR."

"Yes, sir?" the ship's A.I. asks.

"Simulate Earth exfil under heavy fire and Draun telekinetic attack."

"Simulation commencing in ten seconds."

I give Baarfolir's arm a pat. "If you feel like you're going to puke, don't. Keep everything inside, focus on staying conscious and keeping your mind sharp."

"Doesn't sound like I'll be helping much," he says.

"MIMIR's systems can take damage like any other. If she bites the dust, you might need to take over maneuvers, or weapons. She has several backup protocols, but one of them is you. Understood?"

He gives a nod. "I under—aahhh!"

The simulation kicks off without warning. Baarfolir, connected to the simulator via his regulators, is now fully immersed in a lifelike sim that will run on repeat, exposing him to a series of worst-case scenarios until he gets a handle on how to respond. Or until he fails them all with no improvement.

I warned him about all of this. That it would be grueling, mentally taxing, and possibly disturbing. He insisted. Which I respect. He's taking his role in all this seriously. At first, he felt horrible about it, as if jetting off back to Kyno was weakness.

Truth is, in this next phase of the fight for Earth, he might be the first casualty, if the *Prowler* can't make it out of the atmosphere. And if it does, and Baar completes his mission, he might be the sole reason Earth is saved.

Or destroyed.

It's kind of a coin flip.

We'll have a lot of work to do while he's gone.

But first he has to get gone. The ship is ready. Thanks to Baarfolir's psychological readjustment, *I* am ready. Harth is always ready. Once the bossman gets back from la-la land, he'll be ready, with or without Torel.

Baar twitches in his seat. Must be going through some intense shit in there. When he's done, he'll feel like hell, but he should have new knowledge about how to handle the ship and the weapons systems. The simulation doesn't just let you try out your skills, it guides you, nudges your psyche in the right direction, and helps hone reaction times and system knowledge. And it does it at the speed of thought. It can't turn a petrified turd into a diamond, but it can shave off some of the crust.

In the meantime...

I guess I'm going to twiddle my thumbs.

Think about that sassy Pug, Poppy.

She's not really giving me the time of day, but I think she's into me.

Why wouldn't she be?

I'm a living legend among our people. A decorated hero. The only one of my breed to receive a Doom Medallion. Of course, she doesn't know any of that. Hasn't been around for the last decade, and won't give me a chance to tell her how awesome I am.

Ahh well, can't win them all. Maybe when all is said and done, I'll find Bacon, relocate to Earth some place tropical, and settle down with a brood. Until Bacon kicks the bucket forty years before me. But hey, maybe that's a bonus? What if she's annoying? What if she's dumb as a Doinkfly? She's definitely close. But there's nothing wrong with a simple lady, right? It's all about love in the end.

But wow, the haunches on Poppy. To die for.

"Hey!"

I nearly fall out of my chair at the sound of Sean's voice booming through the ship's interior comms. "Yo! Chirk!"

"Whoa, whoa, whoa, untwist your panties, man, I can hear you." My little heart is pounding, but I don't know if it's from being startled, or being lost in sensual reverie.

"This is my third try to get you, dude. You taking a shit or something?"

"Or something," I say.

"Ahh," he says. "Deep thoughts."

I smile. "Very deep."

He laughs. "Ahuh, ahuh, ahuh. I'm catching what you're throwing, my man."

"I sure hope not."

We're both laughing now. This is how it goes with us.

"Okay, okay," he says, trying to calm himself down. "Yo. First, *you nasty.* Second, Praxion is awake. And he's looking at me funny. I think because of what we just said, but dude, Torel is awake, too, and they're both jazzed or something. Like ready to go. Maybe they—" He whispers like it will help him not be heard over the open, ship-wide comms. "—did the deed in the mystical hinterlands or whatever they were in? Point is, I think you need to get—wait, no. Praxion says to meet them in ops. They're already en route. Is it en route? In route? Root? Whatever. Just get over there, pronto."

"I'm on it," I say.

"I won't be much longer in here," Harth says over comms. "I will join you all shortly."

I hustle from the training center and weave my way through the ship's winding, white halls. Over the years, I've had plenty of friends injured in the Great War, many of them comatose like Torel, but I find myself more concerned for her than I was for any of them. Maybe because we've been together for a long time. Maybe because of Earth's air. But this team...they mean a lot to me, and I'm relieved she's back.

The doorway peels apart, allowing me into ops. Praxion and Sean are already seated. Torel, looking a bit dazed, stands at the far side of the table in the room's center. Without really thinking, I say, "Torel!" and leap up onto the table, crossing it in three hops and then jumping up to hug her neck.

She stumbles back and laughs.

Nearly falls over.

Just as I start to feel embarrassed about what I've done, she returns my hug, squeezing me tightly. "Missed you too, little man."

She places me back on the table and I head for my seat, giving Praxion a nod as I pass, "Better watch out, bossman. I think you might have competition."

He laughs in a way that says it's ridiculous, and he's not wrong. A Kynolari like Torel would literally break me, and I like my bitches small.

"Nice work," I say to Sean, giving him a high-five as I pass. Then I fall back into a chair, which is higher than the rest, so my head isn't below the table.

"Before we start," Praxion says, and turns to Sean. "I owe you a debt I'm not sure I can repay. You have not only allowed me to transcend the physical boundaries of life itself, but you allowed me to bring Torel back..." He turns his gaze to me. "...and find the rest of the Lost Tribe."

"Excuse me?" I say. "What now?"

"The souls of the Lost Tribe," Torel says. "Those who stood against Anbu. They're imprisoned in what humans call limbo, held there by a machine inside the Great Pyramid of Giza."

"No shit?" Sean says. "Limbo?"

"The hell is limbo?" I ask.

"No place and nowhere, but there and everywhere."

"Can I get an answer from someone who has more than a few stoned braincells?" I ask.

Sean takes no offense.

"It's a frequency of reality...between realities, accessible upon death, or if someone helps you leave your body behind for a bit." Torel smiles and nods at Sean, who's beyond pleased with himself.

"So, you're saying that...souls are real...and they move through this limbo state and into...what? What comes next?"

"No idea," Torel says, "but it can't be worse than the place our people have spent the past thirty-seven thousand years. That's why we need to set them free."

"How?" I ask.

"We're going to destroy Earth's oldest and most prized structure," Praxion says. "We're going to destroy the Great Pyramid of Giza."

Harth chokes in surprise, standing in the doorway. He raises a finger and asks, "What did I miss?"

# 11

## PRAXION

"What do we think?" I ask after laying out a plan that is, at best, risky. At worst, suicidal.

"Impossible," Chirk says, "unless I'm behind the wheel. But I'm not keen on being an errand boy while all of you are eyeball deep in the shit."

"The oceans will conceal much of the journey," Harth says, "but the moment we expose ourselves, I believe we'll have just seconds."

"Unless we don't expose ourselves," Torel says, and turns to Chirk. "Sorry, I know how much you like doing that."

"Why you picking on me?" Chirk says.

"Because," Harth says, "despite your stature, you are an easy target."

I raise my hands before we tumble down a staircase of tangents.

"Listen," Torel says. "There's no hiding from the Draun when we leave Xolotl's cave, but there's no reason for us to take a direct route to Egypt. We're much closer to the west coast of Mexico, increasing the likelihood that we're submerged before an attack can be launched."

"Nothing to stop any nearby Draun from following us," Chirk says.

Torel nods. "For a time, but not even the Visionary can withstand the pressure of the ocean depths. Not like the *Prowler*. Now, instead of taking the fastest route across the Atlantic, we cross the Pacific and wind our way through Southeast Asia. From there, the Arabian Sea, the Gulf of Aden, the Red Sea, and all the way up to the Suez Gulf, which places us just seventy miles from the Giza Pyramids. Assuming we still have long range weaponry, we turtle-head out of the water, take out the Pyramid from a distance, and dip back into the waves."

Sean chuckles and all eyes turn to him.

"You got something to contribute there, bud?" Chirk says.

"Oh, no. It's just that...turtle heads."

"Do I not understand how a turtle head works?" Torel asks.

"You do, you do, it's just also a slang term..." Sean makes a noble effort to let it go at that, but he can't stop himself from explaining. "Okay, look, if you're not actually looking at a turtle, and you say something about a 'turtle head,' people in the States are probably going to think you have to take a shit."

"What?" Chirk says, sounding doubtful.

"I swear," Sean says. "It's like, bro, I need a bathroom. I got a turtle head poking out."

We sit in silence until the visual resolves itself in my mind and I let out the briefest of laughs.

"Oooh," Chirk says. "I get it. Clever. But gross."

Torel leans her head into her hands. "So gross."

"I do not understand," Harth says. "What does an Earth amphibian's head have to do with defecation?"

The question gets another laugh. I wave my hands at that group, determined that we're only going to stumble down this single step. "Unimportant," I say. "Sean can explain it to you later. Right now, we need to evaluate Torel's plan."

"It is feasible," Harth says, quickly moving on, "but it will double the time it takes us to complete that phase of the mission, and I am not yet convinced it will be beneficial. It will also double our time back to our rendezvous with the others." He ponders for a moment. "But it should also confuse the enemy, popping up on opposite sides of the planet, first to destroy a monument that seemingly has no meaning or strategic value, and again in a desperate bid to escape the atmosphere—and destroy the system blocking our external comms."

"Any luck on that?" I ask.

"I am close to isolating the frequency being used to scramble our signals."

"Then we destroy the satellite network being used," I say.

He shakes his head. "That would alert them to the fact that we had recovered and were once again using comms. Lumen Sok has a vast network of satellites surrounding this planet. It is likely he could block our comms within seconds. There is no way we can keep up with his ability to adapt *and* allow the *Prowler* to escape. What we need to do is change our own frequency, and encryption. I've already completed new encryption protocols, but until we isolate the frequencies being used by Lumen Sok's network, we won't know which will work."

Sean raises his hand and before anyone acknowledges it, says, "Idea."

He once again captures our collective attention.

"Look, I know I'm not the most *sciencey* person on the planet, but I've had a few good ideas along the way..."

He's not wrong. Without him, Torel would not be back with us. I give him a nod and fold my hands in anticipation for something between greatness and absurdity.

"Awesome," he says. "So, you guys know who the Borg are, right? 'Resistance is futile.' 'You will be assimilated.' 'The line must be drawn, heeya!'"

He waits, earnest eyes waiting for us to confirm that we have any clue what he's talking about.

"Seriously? You've been on Earth for what? A few months, and you haven't watched *any* Star Trek besides *Khan*? Not even Next Gen? This is like pop culture 101, like 'Get to da choppah!'"

"What is a choppah?" Gruunlokar asks.

"You know what? Not important. I'll just have to edjumicate you." Sean cracks his knuckles. "The Borg are a collective of species that have been cybernetically enhanced and controlled, becoming part of a hive mind that's directed by the Borg queen. They're really nasty fuckers. Kind of like pale fleshy cyborgs that wear a lot of latex. They have all kinds of wacky tech, including these crazy shields. When they take a hit, like from a phaser—it's like a laser—the collective evaluates the frequency and modulation of its energy. The next time the weapon is used, it has zero effect because the shields adapted. Basically, you get one shot and you're done—*unless*, you're the crew of the motherfucking *USS Enterprise*. D. Or E. They overcame the Borg shield adaptations by rapidly modulating their energy weapons, preventing the adaptation. So, let's say the satellite network up there, blocking your usual communications frequencies, are the Borg, and you want to get a signal past them—"

"We modulate our communications frequencies," Harth says, leaning a thoughtful hand on his chin. "We would need to use uncommon frequencies. The energy boost will be detectable but will sound like solar noise. Comms would be… unstable. Occasionally garbled." He looks up at me, eyes wide with a little bit of shock. "It *could* work."

Sean leaps from his seat and pumps his fist. "Lord Sean Huempfner for the win!"

"Get started," I say to Harth.

"Won't take long," he says, standing from the table, giving Sean's shoulder a pat, and then heading for the door.

I let myself feel a measure of relief. Getting comms back up will allow us to coordinate with the recon team and, "Now all we need to do is make sure Baar… Where is Baarfolir?"

Sean shrugs and makes a sound that resembles the words, 'I don't know.'

"Last time I saw him…" Chirk says, thinking on it.

His eyes bulge.

"Oh, shit. Ohh, shit." He leaps down from his seat and scrambles for the door saying, "Shit, shit, shit."

I glance to Sean.

"Clueless," he says. "I didn't leave your side."

"You better go with him," Torel says, placing her hand on my arm. "I'm fine. Just a little weak. I don't need a caretaker."

"Stay with her," I tell Sean, and before she can protest, I move in Chirk's footsteps, following his fresh scent, now tinged with the smell of worry.

"You got it, boss!" Sean shouts after as the door seals behind me.

Halfway to my destination, I figure out where Chirk is heading. Running, actually. I can hear his feet on the floor. And his hands. He's running like an Earth dog, putting everything he has into it. Wherever he left Baarfolir, it's not good. Feeling concerned myself, I double my pace and charge through the halls until I reach the training center, stumbling to a stop just inside the open door—just in time to see Chirk disengage Baarfolir from the training sim.

"How long was he in there?" I ask.

Chirk flinches at my voice. "Eh, well, since you contacted me."

"That was an hour ago," I say, moving to Baarfolir's side as he opens his eyes. He looks stunned, like he has just woken from a deep sleep. He blinks a few times, glancing back and forth between Chirk and me.

"What sim was running?" I ask.

"Oh, you know," Chirk says, feigning a casual demeanor. "A few. Atmospheric ascent...under fire. Evasive maneuvers, space explosions, and survival. Uhh, combat scenarios—" Chirk gives Baarfolir's shoulder a squeeze. "I'm sorry, Baar. I shouldn't have—"

"Sorry?" Baarfolir asks, blinking a few times. "Sorry for what?" He sits up like he's spring loaded. "That...was amazing!" He hops down to the floor. "Let's do this!" He gives Chirk a shove. Then me. "Hell, yeah! I was all—*pew, pew, pew,* and 'hold on!' and '*Pekersh!* It was—wow. I just..." He leans forward, hands on knees. "I never knew. Never understood the exhilaration."

"It hits a little different when you can actually die," I say.

"Must feel even better," he says, "assuming you don't die."

"It *is* a rush," Chirk says. "But...you were in there for a long time. How are you feeling?"

"Honestly," he says, looking up at me. "I feel great. I feel ready."

Chirk twists his nose. "How many times did you die?"

"At first, a lot. Like a lot." A smile spreads. "But not once in the last thirty minutes. I got the hang of it. Got in the flow. It was like turning pages. I just knew what to do. I think there was a latent part of me, a warrior I never knew existed. I could also feel the sim guiding me. But it wasn't until I accessed my encyclopedic knowledge of historical wars, battles, tactics, and our most successful leaders—includeing you, Praxion, that I was able to calmly overcome whatever the simulation threw my way."

"He found clarity," Chirk says to me. "Faster than most of us, too."

"What is 'clarity?'" Baarfolir asks.

"A state of mind soldiers fall into, where they can see everything clearly, through all the chaos. It allows us to act and react, sometimes to things that haven't happened yet," I tell him.

"That's how it felt," he says. "It was like a dance to which I knew all the moves without needing to be taught."

"Ready to do it again?" I ask him.

"Looking forward to it," he says, and then to Chirk, he adds, "Thank you for allowing me to spend so long in the sim."

Chirk forces a laugh. "Yep. That's what I did, all right. Knew you could do it with enough time."

"Talon-Actual, Talon-One, how copy?" It's Harth in my ear. His voice sounds a little jumbled. For a moment, I think the ship's comms are bugged. Then I realize that he's speaking to me through external comms.

"Talon-One, Talon-Actual, copy loud and almost clear. Well done."

"Sean gets the credit for this one," Harth says. "I just rewrote some code and flipped a few switches."

"That's my boy!" Chirk says, clenching his fist, proud of his friend.

"Fuck, yeah!" Baarfolir shouts, thrusting both fists in the air as he struts out of the training center. "I'm gonna growl, prowl, and I'm ready to howl! Let's do this shit! Whoo!"

# 12

## MICAH

I've had to endure a lot of uncomfortable situations since the Kynolari dropped down into my parent's property, but few compare to the feeling of speed-crawling in a cramped concrete tunnel for several miles.

Can't see much, other than the floor beneath my hands.

Can't hear anything, aside from the heavy breathing of the humans and the Kynolari in front of and behind me. It's approaching what could genuinely be considered torture.

We're all thinking it, but no one wants to speak the words, because that would make it worse. The acknowledgement of discomfort has a way of giving it power. And stopping, or even slowing, will end up being worse, as one by one, we're eaten from the feet up by a horde of who-knows-what biologics.

"Almost there," Ben says from ahead, and a collective sigh of relief rolls through the tunnel.

"Contact ETA," Poppy says from the rear. "Two minutes, tops. They've got our scent. Closing in."

"Hey, Ben," I say. "Where is 'there?'"

"Junction..." His voice is muffled and hard to hear over the shuffle of hands and knees, but his hesitation comes through loud and clear. "Twenty-one. Or is it twenty-two? No, it's twenty-one. I wanted to give each junction a name, like parks, or street names. Make them easy to remember. But Kim thought number codes would be easier, and we usually go with what Kim says. Makes life easier, you know."

I keep my mouth shut, unwilling to jump on Ben's quasi-sexist bandwagon.

"And where does this junction go?"

"Three tunnels," he says. "But we're taking Twenty-One B. Toward Los Angeles, as requested."

"Right," I say, "Any chance there's an open space nearby where we can handle these Skitterlings? You know, before they eat through us?"

"No," he says. "Not really. Unless..."

"Unless what?" Gruunlokar asks from behind.

"Unless you want to surface," he says.

"Thoughts?" I ask Gruunlokar.

"We don't have any other choice," he says. "Facing them in these tunnels, which are similar to their species' natural habitat, would put us at a severe disadvantage."

Light flares behind us, crackling with energy. It's followed by three quick snaps and the sound of biologics shattering.

"Whatever you're doing," Poppy says, "better do it now!"

"Take us up," I shout ahead.

"Okay, almost there!"

I take a breath, trying to focus on crawling and ignoring the pain, when I get a nose full of stank. I cough and say, "Oh, god."

"Sorry," Grover says from ahead. "Me nervous toot."

"Silent but deadly," I say. "Dude."

"Soorry."

"Silent but deadly," Gruunlokar says, "like Saligordian Assassin Worms, but far more repugnant."

Can't help but laugh. I want to hold my breath. I'm desperate to tuck my nose into my shirt but can't do either. Just need to plow through the noxious cloud and find some humor as the others pass through.

"Oh, gawd," Poppy says, gagging. "What did you eat, Grover?"

"From big room floor," Grover says. "Squishy. Taste like cheese."

The details somehow make the stench worse. My stomach clenches, but it's a short-lived reaction. A moment later, I reach the tunnel's end and find myself knee deep in stagnant, oil covered water. There are three branching tunnels, which are actually labeled, and a ladder leading up to an open manhole. Jess is halfway up, and Grover is waiting. I haul him up onto my shoulder and he clings to me, digging in his claws. I ignore the fresh pain and climb.

Below, Gruunlokar spills out of the tunnel. Behind him, flashes of blue light and sound-suppressed *thumps* of thunder as Poppy lays down a constant barrage.

"Clear the exit!" Gruunlokar shouts.

"On it!" My legs burn as I double time up the ladder while carrying Grover's extra eighty pounds. I envy the Kynolari's natural strength. Even Poppy could probably carry Grover up the ladder, and here I am struggling.

That is, until an invisible force lifts my dog off my shoulder and pulls him through the manhole. I emerge like a whack-a-mole a moment later. And am helped to my feet by Jess.

We're in a mall parking lot. Looks a little bit like...

*Holy shit, I think it is.*

"Jess," I say, reaching out for her arm. "Look," I say, pointing to the far side of the parking lot.

She shakes her head. "It's a parking lot, and I don't think— Holy shit, I see it."

"Right?" I say, lost in a memory.

"1.21 gigawatts..."

"The Twin Pines Mall," I say, "or Lone Pine, depending on what time you're in."

Poppy bounds out of the manhole, flipping at the crest and landing on her feet, snapping me out of my nostalgia. I catch sight of her gauntlet's power gauge. She's already half empty. Will take a little while to recharge.

Gruunlokar springs out of the hole behind her, landing with equal grace and a whole lot less flourish. "Everyone back. They're coming."

"I can slow them down," Jenna says, reaching her hands out to the manhole.

"Wait," Gruunlokar says. "Don't."

Jenna cringes. "Why?"

"We've got them bottlenecked," he says. "If we seal it, there's no telling where they'll emerge."

"Oh," she says, wincing. "Sorry."

The manhole tunnel and sewer beneath fold inward and collapses.

Gruunlokar rolls with the punch and says nothing to make Jenna feel bad about the error. "Form a circle, facing out. Ben, Grover, in the middle."

We fall into position quickly, forming a defensive ring around the unarmed. I have Jess to my left and Gruunlokar to my right.

"Now what?" I ask.

"We wait," he says.

"How long?"

A rumble answers my question. Twenty feet away, the pavement bulges upward. Then again to my right, thirty feet out...and a dozen more times all around us. They're burrowing up from underneath. "This is some real *Tremors* bullshit right here."

*If only Valentine and Earl had futuristic laser Hell Hounds,* I think and charge both gauntlets to full. *Maybe Chang would have survived.*

Watching the growing mounds, I ask, "Jenna, can you put a shield around us that will let things out, but not in?"

"What?" she says. "Is that even a thing?"

"Well, I just made it up, but it would be awesome."

"Strategically beneficial," Gruunlokar says.

"Okay, but no. There's nothing rattling around my head that's anything like that. I can do all sorts of gross things to...other things...though."

"Good enough," I say and fire my first, precise laser blast. It drills a clean hole in... What is that? A face? Hard to say, but it's definitely dead, and instead of being pushed out by the next in line, it's yanked down, body shaking as the biologic is devoured from below.

Motion in my periphery tempts me to look away, but I can hear the others unleashing hell. I watch as the dead Skitterling is dragged down and reduced to sludge, giving way to a second, which hops out of the hole, landing on its single-talon-tipped, exo-skeletal limbs. Four of them. It resembles an insect, but it's built for speed and…eating.

The creature spots me and snaps open at least twenty mandibles, behind which is a double set of thick, constantly chewing, pointed teeth. One set masticates vertically. The other horizontally. Everything about it exudes power and manic hunger—

Until I fire a second laser, slicing it clean in half.

For a moment, I think this might be easy. Just slice and dice as they come up, one at a time and—

The ground shakes.

Geysers of Skitterlings erupt from the pavement, shooting twenty feet up and spilling down in every direction.

"Can these things fly?" Jess asks, whipping her super-heated grappling line back and forth like an exercise battle rope, incinerating everything it touches. Arcs of electricity bounce through the horde, fired from Poppy's Lancer. Gruunlokar fires a steady rhythm of shards, taking down lines of the enemy with each shot.

But they've all got limitations. They can't keep this up forever.

"They can't fly," Gruunlokar says, "but they are agile, fast, and strong despite their size." He flinches back, as one of the Skitterlings proves him right as it nearly tags his face with a talon. He fires a single round into the underside of its head and ducks as the creature sails past, rolling to a stop in front of one of its brethren, which begins devouring the dead one until Jess drops a line of sizzling hot death atop it.

"Yeah!" she says. "Eat it, little assholes."

"You sizeist?" Poppy says, having no trouble arcing her lightning strikes between three to five Skitterlings at a time.

"I grew up watching *Critters*. Freaked my ass out."

"Ha!" Poppy says. "Love that movie."

I unleash a broad, continuous laser strike, evaporating a dozen of the biologics on the ground, but twice that number are still leaping toward me.

"There're too many," I say to Gruunlokar.

"That's why they're so effective," he says.

I glance at Poppy. She's on ten percent.

Jess won't be far behind. No idea how long Gruunlokar can hold out, but his ammo won't be infinite.

All at once, half of the Skitterlings redirect straight toward me, leaping en masse. Maybe because I have the most charge. Maybe because they know who the Axiom is. Who knows. Point is, I can't hit them all in time.

But I don't have to hit them all.

The first wave compresses into little carapace balls, their insides violently spraying out from between the seams before falling to the ground and rolling to a stop at my feet. I'd thank Jenna for the assist, but there's no time.

Taking a lesson from my confrontation with a Draun while crossing the country, I focus on shaping the light that emerges from my two gauntlets. The orange beams broaden, coalesce, and form a shield that expands to fend off the attack.

One by one, the Skitterlings throw themselves into the laser shield and are flung back with a crackle of energy. They're surviving the impact, protected by their shells, but prolonged contact will destroy them.

"Jenna!" I shout. "I'm going to throw up a wall of energy. When I do, create a telekinetic wall around the Skitterlings!"

"Then what?" she shouts.

"Trash compactor!" I focus my laser light out and around us. It spreads left, right, and up, obeying my will until we're encased in a sphere of destructive energy.

"What..." Gruunlokar says, stunned, reaching his finger toward the wall.

"Wouldn't do that unless you don't mind having one less digit."

He withdraws his hand and turns to me. "How?"

"Haven't been the Axiom long enough to understand how it works," I say. "Only that it does." I turn back to Jenna. "Your turn!"

"On it," she says, eyes closed, hands lifted to either side.

There's no way to know if she's succeeding. Telekinetic forces are invisible. But, like the wind, you know it's there, not because you can see it, but because you can see its effect on the world.

While many of the Skitterlings continue their attack, bouncing off my energy shield with singed talons, those on the outer periphery fight against a second force, pulling them closer.

"Keep going!" I shout.

"I...am!" She grits her teeth, pulling the massive sphere of telekinetic energy in toward us. She might not remember all the tricks of the trade her older self had, but her strength of will is the same.

While my gauntlets aren't running low on energy, I can feel my mind and body weakening. Like Jenna, I still have human limits to what I can do. Need to end this before one of us gets too tired.

"On three," I say. "Give it everything you have!"

I catch her nod out of the side of my eye.

"One," I say. "Two..."

I close my eyes, focusing on what I want to do. "Three!"

The orange sphere surrounding us bursts out like the first moments of a nuclear strike. At the same time, a telekinetic wall smashes into them from behind. A brilliant light explodes as the two forces collide and everything between them is atomized.

Jenna's shield fails first and the last of my laser light bursts out and away from us. Jenna collapses to her knees, breathing heavily. A moment later, I fall beside her, lying on my back, looking up at the stars. "Well...that...worked."

Jenna laughs, and then moans. "Did we get them all?"

"We're clear," Gruunlokar says. "But we should not remain. All that light is sure to draw attention."

"Okay," I say. "Okay. Just give me a second to—"

A burst of static in the ears of everyone with regulators cuts me short. Then the sound repeats and gives way to a familiar voice. "Talon-Two, Talon-Actual, how copy?"

# 13

**GRUUNLOKAR**

I would never admit the level of relief I feel upon hearing Praxion's voice over comms. Not just because it means the others are still alive, but because comms have been restored. Without the ability to communicate, we wouldn't stand a chance. "Talon-Actual, Talon-Two, hard copy."

"Good to hear your voice," Praxion says, and I note that he has quickly disregarded comms protocols. "Have you encountered the enemy?"

"A few times," I say, looking at the Skitterlings lying in the empty parking lot around me. "Nothing we couldn't handle."

"How far have you journeyed?" he asks.

"I'm not sure I should say that over—"

"Our comms are encrypted and scrambled," Praxion says. "Even better, the Visionary won't know they've been restored."

"How did you manage that?" I ask.

"Believe it or not," he says. "Sean."

"Aww, yeah!" Sean says, suddenly joining the comms. "Ricardo Montalban is in the hiz-ouse!"

I turn toward Micah for an explanation. He just shakes his head and says, "Too hard to explain quickly."

"Bro," Sean says, "Montalban was an actor who played an evil space dude named Khan who had a superior intellect. Wham, bam, thank you, ma'am. That's how it's done, Micah, my man."

Micah huffs a laugh.

"Is there a safe location at which we can rendezvous in twenty-four hours?" Praxion asks.

I turn to Micah.

"I've never been here," he says.

"Did you not recognize this location?" I ask, while he and Jess try to shush me with their fingers. "You named it yourself. Twin Pines?"

A high-pitched gasp from a very excited Sean comes over the comms. "You... are at the Twin Pines Mall? Legit?"

"Right in the parking lot," Micah says, "but we need to stay focused."

"Got it," he says, "I'm focused, Marty!"

When Micah sighs and shakes his head, I understand that this is what he and Jess were trying to avoid. This location has some kind of historical or maybe even religious attachment to it.

"Catalina Island," Jess says, raising her voice to overpower whatever quip might be coming next. "It's off the coast of Los Angeles and there isn't much there. No good reason for a Draun to claim it. We just need to get through LA, reach the coast, and find a boat…in twenty-four hours."

Micah turns to Ben. "Doable?"

"We'll have to take some risks," he says, "but I think so."

"We'll be there," Micah says. "But, what's the plan after that?"

"Still working out the details," Praxion says, "but I aim to have us on the ground in Japan, shortly after meeting up with you all, twenty-four hours from now."

I punch the timeline into my gauntlet. "Copy that. Twenty-four hours. Catalina Island."

"We will mostly be underwater and off comms until then," Praxion says.

"And we will be underground," I say.

"For a long time," Ben adds.

"Who was that speaking?" Praxion asks.

"Oh, that's Ben," Micah says. "We've made a few friends out here. About a billion of them."

"Oh, snap," Sean says.

"I'm sorry," Chirk chimes in. "Did I hear that right? A *billion*?"

"Dog people," Jess says. "And if we're counting dogs, one point five billion. Roughly. They're networking. Arming. Living underground and ready to rise, if need be."

"They would be slaughtered," Praxion says. "Let's hope it doesn't come to that."

"Agreed," I say. The humans we've encountered are kind-hearted and brave, no doubt capable of fighting Draun with enough time and the right training. But neither of those things are possible.

"Do you know what they're talking about?" Ben whispers to Jenna.

"Best guess," she says. "You. But I don't have those things on the sides of their heads. Regulators. I can't hear them either, but I get the impression they don't want your people fighting."

"That's bullshit," Ben says, then turns to me. "That's bullshit." He storms over and gets right in my face, something I would not allow in most other scenarios. "Do you know who we are? Where we come from? Our history? When the most powerful empire on Earth tried to crush our people beneath its boot, we rose up and fought against incredible odds. Farmers. Normal people. We adapted. We bled, died, and killed for this country. And that's not just the United States's story. Happens all the time. Humanity is often strongest when our backs are against the wall. You better damn well believe that we're going to do the same for our planet."

I remain silent but raise my eyebrows.

He pats my chest. "Sorry." Backs off a step.

"You heard?" I ask.

"Every word," Praxion says. "And he is right. If the humans wish to fight for their world, we cannot stop them. But we will not ask for their aid unless there is no other option."

"Copy that," I say, and then to Ben, I add, "Nice speech."

"Th—thank you? Does that mean..."

I nod. "We will call upon humanity if necessary."

"That's all fine and dandy," Jess says, "but not one of you have asked the right question yet."

After a moment, Praxion says, "Torel is awake."

Those of us who are close to Torel sag in relief, and Grover joins in. "Torel okay? Love Torel. I talk to Torel? Please, oh, please."

Praxion's muffled voice comes over the comm, followed by a click as someone new joins. "Grovey Grove," Torel says. "I miss you, buddy."

"Torel! Love Torel. Miss Torel. When I see?"

"Tomorrow, Grover. We'll see each other tomorrow."

I can almost hear her smile. Earth dogs are not the most intelligent animals, but they have a way of emanating, maybe even transmitting, love and affection. I have not witnessed this capability in any other creatures I've encountered out in the universe, or in other species on this planet.

"Tomorrow!" Grover cheers.

"Okay, buddy," Micah says, crouching and petting Grover, easing his growing excitement and volume. He looks up at me. "We shouldn't hang around much longer."

"Oh!" Ben says. "Right. We should go!"

He scurries toward a different manhole at the edge of the lot. I motion for the others to join him. Jenna, Jess, and Grover follow him. Micah remains behind with me. I toggle us over to private comms.

"We're private on our end," I say. "Just me and Micah now."

"How are things out there?" Praxion asks.

"It's a hellscape," Micah says. "Cities are in ruins. Fires. Bodies. Patrolling Draun. Honestly, it's hard to imagine a path back to civilization."

"Humanity is resilient," Praxion says, "and your survivors will be united. Perhaps a centralized world government will emerge from the ashes."

"Mm," Micah says, not entirely impressed by the idea of a centralized government. For reasons I cannot fathom, humanity revolts at the idea of global unification. That said, nearly being wiped out by the Draun tends to realign a people's priorities.

"For now," Praxion says, "focus on the mission ahead. Chirk is showing me a map of the area. It is a congested population center. The Draun presence will be significant."

"Yeah, well, unless Draun enjoy the stench of death, shit, and urine, I don't think we'll have any problems." Micah winces at the thought of what lies ahead. "Then again, maybe we'll take our chances with the Draun."

"And your journey across the ocean?" Torel asks. "How will that be accomplished?"

It's a good question. A boat, even a small one, will stand out in the open ocean, and if our vessel is damaged or sinks...

"Yeah," Micah says, and I can tell he's running through the same scenarios I am. "There are a lot of Great Whites out there." He notes my confusion. "Sharks. Big ones. Man eaters."

"Lovely," I say.

His eyes widen. "Is the *Prowler* ready to leave the atmosphere?"

"Confirmed," Harth says, speaking for the first time.

"And I am ready to rock," Baarfolir says, sounding uncommonly confident.

"But," Praxion says, "to ensure the success of Baarfolir's mission, we must part ways when we rendezvous."

"Meaning we need a way to Japan...from Catalina Island," Micah says. "Even if we find a badass yacht, that's going to take a good month, in the open. I don't know if Draun will be flying back and forth from Japan still, but I have a hard time believing we won't be— Hold on a fucking second." His eyes widen. "New plan. Meet us at LAX."

"Umm," Chirk says. "What does L-A-X mean?"

"Sorry. Los Angeles International Airport...where there's a big ass statue of a horse in front of a P.F. Chang's."

"Another horse statue," Torel says. "Fantastic. I'm still having nightmares about the last horse's engorged testes."

"I have yet to experience engorged horse testes," I say. "Sounds like a treat." I motion for Micah to descend into the sewer. "We'll see you there. Out."

# 14

## CHIRK

"Everyone feeling up to this?" I ask, glancing back, letting my gaze linger on Torel. The rest of us are downright eager. But we weren't in a month-long coma, lost in limbo with a bunch of long-dead Kynolari. I mean, you'd think something like that would fuck a person up, but Torel, she's a badass of epic proportions. Aside from some exhaustion from not using her physical body for several weeks, she seems like her old self.

"Don't look at me," she says. "I just have to sit here."

She's not wrong about that. Harth and Sean are manning the weapon systems. Praxion is doing his man-in-charge thing, sitting beside her with his stoic gaze, ready for things to go wrong. And Baarfolir...he's not hiding out in his study. He's right beside me, watching and learning from the best.

"Let's blow this joint!" Sean says.

Harth leans back to look at him. "I thought one was meant to suck on, or inhale, a joint."

"Well, not that kind of joint." Sean holds out his hand. "Okay, okay..." He resets himself. "Let's blow this popsicle stand."

"What is a popsicle stand?" Baarfolir asks.

"I've had a popsicle," Harth says. "Tasty."

Sean sighs, and with much less enthusiasm says, "Let's...leave this cave."

"Why not just say that?" Harth says.

"Cause it's lame sauce."

Harth grunts in frustration. "What is 'lame sauce?'"

"It's just..." Sean's patience is also being tested. "It's a made-up word. Can we go now?"

I have a laugh at Sean's expense, and say, "Don't worry, bro, I gotcha. Let's blow this Tarkin Fornication Bake."

"Ahh," Harth says. "I think I understand the humor now."

I cut any possibility of a continuing conversation short by launching us out of our hiding place inside the mountain lair that hid Xolotl for so long. We burst through the raging and redirected waterfall, curving up into the air just above the tree line.

"Which way is west?" I ask Baarfolir, testing him.

He points, and I adjust course.

"Can't MIMIR keep us on course?" he asks.

"Obviously," I say, "but if the A.I. is damaged, or you find yourself, you know, on your feet, it's always good to know where you're going, even if you don't know where you are."

"That might be the smartest thing I've ever heard you say."

I glance over at Baar. He's grinning. Trying to not laugh.

"Oh, you think you can be the short, plucky pilot now? She's all yours." I disengage my controls and transfer them to him. MIMIR will keep us from crashing, but he's driving.

"Are you sure that is a good idea?" Praxion asks. "Baarfolir's training was—"

The *Prowler*'s speed jumps forward. Mexico passes beneath us in a blur. Then we zig and zag, do a few spins, and slide into a maneuver that points our nose to the sky and redirects us in an instant ninety-degree turn that I actually feel in my seat.

Before we get too high, he reverses course, swings us down, and levels out just feet from the ground. Then we're off again, streaking through the air, well below any watching radar systems.

"You haven't seen anything yet," Baarfolir says, looking mischievous. "Next, up—"

The *Prowler*'s nose tips straight down, facing the ground as we continue forward. As the terrain flows past, it rises and sinks beneath us. It's a dangerous move that few can pull off, and aside from impressing bitches, it's basically useless.

"The hell are you doing?" I shout.

"It's not me!" he says, lifting his hands away from the controls. The moment he does, MIMIR is in full control. The ship's position relative to the ground doesn't change.

Because we're being affected by an outside force.

"MIMIR," I ask. "How close are we to the Pacific?"

"Ten miles," she says.

"Gonna be close. Alright boys and bitch, we've got company. We've lost partial control, which means an outside force is influencing the *Prowler*, and that means—"

"Draun," Praxion says. "Harth, Sean, find us a target. Chirk, do everything you can to get us into the ocean."

"What I'm doing," I say, a smidge annoyed that I was in the middle of saying everything he just did. Which is out of character, for me, not him. Praxion is the boss. He gives the orders. Talking over us is his right, and it's never bothered me before. Ahh, the emotional joys of breathing Earth air.

Can't move, no matter how much power I give the ship. We're just frozen in midair, fifteen feet above the ground, and ten miles from relative safety. Whoever has us, they're powerful. We might only have one chance of escape.

"MIMIR," I say, "Find me a gravity thread large enough for a snap."

"Yes, sir," MIMIR says, scanning the space around us. There are an infinite number of strands in the universal gravity web, but we're looking for something special.

"What's a snap?" Baarfolir asks.

"Something you won't enjoy."

"Contact," Harth says. "Directly overhead."

"How far?" I ask.

"One mile."

"Impressive range," I say. "He's powerful."

"*She's* powerful, my dude," Sean chimes in. "Kinda hot, too. Black latex. Black cape. Black hair. Looks like a superhero. Or supervillain, I guess. I mean, she *is* scowling."

"Is she alone?" I ask.

"Adjusting sensors," Harth says. That the sensors weren't already attuned to human biology—in the sky—is a massive oversight, and all of us know it. Doesn't need to be said, and we all know the reason why. The planet is making us soft. Protocols have been replaced by instinct. Planning has been reduced to a quick meeting around a table. In the past, operations were carried out with meticulous plotting. Now, we're stuck in a pattern of reacting.

The Visionary hasn't had the stones to reveal himself since hiding in orbit during our fight with Jenna Flood 1.0. He knows we're a threat. To protect himself, he made this entire planet hostile territory, keeping us from forming an airtight plan. Sure, we've got some ideas. Some random strands of ancient bullshit that might work if we figure X and destroy Z, and hey, I know, why don't we invite some long dead Kynolari to the party? Not that it will do anything. They're dead. And if they still somehow exist, they're intangible here.

And now, every time we show our faces, some asshole with a massive ego and an eccentric outfit comes to dominate us like an Earth dog with a hard-on.

"I'm not detecting any life signs for several miles in every direction," Harth says.

"How long until we're ready to snap?" Praxion asks.

"MIMIR just needs to find a strong enough strand," I say.

We're surrounded by strands. We move through them all the time, like atoms. They're both separate from us, and a part of our beings. But we need something bigger, like the kind created by a planet, and Earth has millions of them, coalescing from every person, grain of sand, and atom that makes up this world and everything on it. They stretch out into the cosmos, connected to every other world, star, black hole, and grain of sand in existence.

The sound of rail-shards and lasers blasting up into the sky is subtle until you look at the target. The laser blasts refract off the invisible telekinetic shield, splitting into a burst of smaller beams. Some of the shards shatter on impact. Others pancake the way bullets do. It's a mess. If there was anyone around, it could be deadly. I hone in on her, locking our nose on target. The Draun has us locked in position, but we can still wiggle.

"Structural integrity?" Praxion asks.

"We're feeling the squeeze," Torel says, "but it's nowhere near stress limits."

Ships like the *Prowler* look funky. Inside and out, she's constructed from what look like random organic white structures. Almost fungal. But that lattice helps the ship resist powerful pressure.

"Powerful," I say. "But not enough."

"Think she just figured that out, too, dude," Sean says.

I focus on the target again. She's fired a bright red flare into the air. It billows out, filling the sky with light that will be seen for hundreds of miles around.

"That can't be good," Sean says.

"Oh, dear," Baarfolir adds.

"Hurry, MIMIR." Praxion uses his indoor voice, but I can feel the weight of his words just as surely as I can the weight of my ponderous schlong.

"Gravity strand acquired," MIMIR says. "Lock in ten seconds."

"Hold your fire!" I shout. "And keep your mouths shut. I swear to this world's gods, I will fillet anyone who pukes. I'm looking at you, Seany-boy!"

"Five... Four..."

"Hey, it's been a while since I barfed on anything," Sean says.

"Two..."

"And besides, I had oatmeal and sausage for breakfast, so it won't—"

"One."

"—be that ba-lllaaarrrfff!"

# 15

## PRAXION

Riding a snap is more kinetic than a shard being fired from a railgun. There is no experience of acceleration, of easing into the speed of gravity—which far exceeds the speed of light—despite what human physicists believe. One moment, you're stationary, the next you're winking through time and space. It is a violent act, only survivable thanks to the minds of Kynolari far more intelligent than me. I can't even begin to guess how the ship is able to keep us from being vaporized against the bridge's back wall. But the system isn't perfect. We experience an intense slap of G-forces. Some vomit. Some pass out.

Some…much worse.

A snap is an act of desperation, used only when a ship has been caught in a Draun's grasp. It is our only means of escape, but the bravest among us managed to turn flight into fight.

When the *Prowler* snaps into a gravity strand inside an atmosphere, moving from stationary to speed beyond comprehension, it generates a momentary pressure wave that dissipates upon entering the vacuum of space. In the moment that pressure wave exists, it becomes one of the most powerful forces in the universe, eradicating everything it comes into contact with, including the Draun. Their telekinesis is no match.

Toward the end of the great war, we attempted to use several ships as projectiles, aimed at killing the Visionary. But he always seemed to know when they were coming. He avoided our attacks thanks to his Visionary Sphere, which also has access to the gravity web. It's a one-man spacecraft, and he's never been seen without it.

Only Gruunlokar, master of stealth, came close to killing him. So close that we all believed the Visionary was dead, until we came to Earth.

A wave of nausea comes and goes in an instant. Anyone watching us would think we just teleported two miles straight up. The only real evidence that we didn't is a gentle pink mist drifting away on the breeze.

"Confirm contact?" I ask.

"Confirmed," Harth says. "Draun is KIA."

"Resume course," I say, and Chirk swings us west and accelerates faster than anything humanity has, but relative to a snap, it feels slow.

When we're up to speed and cruising low over the terrain once more, Chirk leans over and turns to Sean. "So. Sean. My man."

"It's okay!" Sean says. "Caught it in my shirt! No muss, no fuss."

"Is your shirt dripping?" Chirk asks.

"Uhh…" Sean glances down and then up to me. "Permission to change my shirt?"

"Make it quick," I tell him, knowing that all of us will be distracted by the smell, and not just because it is repulsive. Ever since arriving on this world, we have found ourselves intrigued by rancid odors, and at worst, ravenous for whatever horror is generating the stench. Sometimes that includes vomit. It's especially difficult for Chirk, whose small body makes him more susceptible to the instincts being awoken in us by Earth's atmosphere.

Sean shuffles away, as Chirk shakes his head.

"If anyone ever catches me scarfing puke," Chirk says, "feel free to put a shard in my head."

"Likewise," Harth says.

Chirk swats Baarfolir's shoulder. "Hey. How you holding up?"

Baarfolir's head lolls to the side. I'm concerned until I see his grin. "That… was amazing. Why can't I just exit the atmosphere like that?"

"Odds of survival are less than an extraction under fire," Chirk says, "but higher than letting a Draun have its way with you."

Baarfolir's smile fades. "What's the survival rate?"

"Thirty-five percent," Harth says.

The historian's eyes widen. "And how many times have you survived the maneuver?"

"Four," Torel says, "including that one."

Baarfolir's jaw drops. "Statistically—"

"We shoulda been paste," Chirk says. "But statistics and odds don't take into account that I'm the best god damn pilot in the fuckin' Kyno Corps. And despite your enthusiasm, you're not. Ipso facto: you're not snapping into space or even into one of Sean's Slim Jims."

"Contact," Harth says. "Two behind, approaching from north and south. Not fast enough to catch us. But there is a third target to the west on an intercept course."

"Draun?" I ask.

"Affirmative."

"Attempt long range engagement," I say.

"I'm back," Sean says, bumbling back into the cockpit, pulling on a fresh T-shirt. "I'm back. What did I miss?"

"Incoming, twelve o'clock," Chirk says. "Knock it out of the sky."

Sean takes his gunner's station and sets about trying to hit a fast-moving target heading straight for us. Accounting for our speed, the Draun's speed, and multiple other factors affecting the trajectory of the shards Sean fires, is a difficult task for anyone. But Sean doesn't account for anyone. 'Spray and Pray' is what he calls his technique, and he claims it works well in something called *Call of Duty*, which he most often refers to as '*Call of Booty*.' I do not know what is meant by these phrases, nor have I asked.

Harth, on the other hand, controls our laser cannons. Traveling at the speed of light and completely unaffected by the atmosphere, his odds of striking are considerably higher, especially with MIMIR's assistance. Sean could do the same, but he has expressed revulsion at the idea of 'auto-aim.'

"Damnit," Harth says. "Approaching target is shielded. Coming in hot, but not stupid."

"He's gonna plow right through us," Chirk says. "Same as we did his buddy."

"First," Sean says, spinning around. "You really need to stop assuming the gender of every Draun is a dude. It's sexist, man. There are more chicks on the planet than men, so—"

"*Second?*" Chirk says, impatience brewing.

"Okay, hear me out," he says.

"As long as we hear you quick!" Chirk says. "Running out of time."

"Right. Fast. Okay, so, the Draun shields, they like block everything, right?"

"They do," Torel says, somehow the calmest of us all.

Sean raises a victorious finger. "But they don't!" He pauses, waiting for someone to react.

"Oooh," Chirk says. "Ahhh. Please dazzle me."

"Well, if the telekinetic shield blocked everything...they wouldn't be able to see. But because they can see, we know that—"

"Visible light!" I say. "MIMIR, adjust laser cannons to emit only the visible spectrum, maximum strength."

"Aww man," Sean says. "I was going to talk about spectrums and wavelengths and shit. Would have sounded dope."

"You did dope enough, pal," Chirk says. "That one brain cell you've got left is pretty good at thinking outside the box."

"Aww, thanks, man. That means—"

"Spectrum adjusted," MIMIR says. "System at full power."

"Hold," I say, as we close the distance.

"Target holding steady," Harth says. "Two miles and closing."

The group falls silent, waiting.

And then...

"Is this what they talk about?" Sean whispers. "The silence before the storm?"

Chirk glances at him. "I have no god damn idea what you're talking about."

"You know," Sean whispers. "Like when a thunderstorm is rolling in and all the birds and bugs are like, 'Bro, this shit's about to get real. Let's hunker the fuck down and hold our breath.' And *then*—"

Torel snorts beside me. Then bursts out laughing.

The dam breaks, and the rest of us join in.

Sean is instantly amused, though he's also confused about why we're laughing.

"It's okay, buddy," Chirk says. "We're laughing *with* you."

"One mile," Harth says, containing the volume of his laugh, but I can see his shoulders bouncing out of the corner of my eye.

We settle down again.

"Three quarters," Harth says.

"Show it to me," I say.

The viewscreen in front of us shifts from an open view of the sky ahead to a zoomed-in view focused on the lone Draun rocketing toward us.

"Huh," I say. "That...is unexpected."

"People come in all shapes and sizes, Dude," Sean says, "just like you guys."

He's right, of course. I've just never seen a person so small. "Is there a word for...this size of human being?"

He shrugs. "Yeah, but who knows what's kosher to say these days, you know? Uhh, Dwarf... I think that's okay. Little people. Definitely okay. Hobbits? I don't know. They definitely used to be a thing, and not just in Middle Earth, but on some island somewhere. Not sure if people use the term, though."

"Works for me," I say, and then "Harth?"

"Quarter mile. Impact in ten, nine, eight—"

"Fire on the Hobbit."

It is the least climactic encounter of my military career. The Hobbit flares bright, its body reflecting the glow of unfiltered, raw illumination. There isn't a set of eyes in the universe that could gaze into that light and not be blinded.

The Hobbit slaps his hands to his eyes, twists around and plummets toward the Earth.

"Well done, Sean," I say. "Again."

He beams, and I can't deny getting some pleasure from his excitement.

"Good boy," Chirk says, giving Sean a head nod.

The viewscreen tracks the small Draun's progress toward the ground. He's flying again, but still can't see. Has no idea he's accelerating straight down.

"Well," Harth says. "He's going to hit hard."

"Little crater, though," Chirk says.

Sean gives him a single eyebrow raise. "Dude."

"Look at me," Chirk says, motioning to his small body. "I'm allowed."

Sean considers and nods.

"True dat, my man. I guess shorties can roast shorties."

"Damn right," Chirk says and then puts the *Prowler* into a dive down toward the Atlantic Ocean, plunging us beneath the waves and out of sight from the Visionary's omnipresent satellite network.

# 16

## MICAH

Navigating a combination sewer/drainage system across Los Angeles is a new kind of nasty. The Resistance has done what they can to clean things, and there are Little Trees air fresheners hanging in the opening of every tunnel. They help, but not much. Not sure I like the scent of lemon slice shit any more than I do actual shit. It just confuses me.

On the plus side, there aren't many toilets being flushed anymore. There are dozens of 'flush zones' though, avoided at all costs. Because a regularly flushing toilet means a permanent resident, and right now, that means Draun. Basically, if the shit you smell is fresh, go the other way.

And since the Resistance doesn't go anywhere without their four-legged shit-detectors, new flush-zones are easy to avoid.

I will say this, though. Despite our gnarly surroundings and an uncomfortable journey, we are joyfully welcomed every step of the way by survivors and their pooches. I've never met so many dogs in a day before, and I'm honestly loving it. Each one of them doles out the love without asking for anything in return, except maybe a scratch. Despite our circumstances, both short term and long, I find myself buoyed and positive.

And Grover… The little man is having the time of his life. He loves meeting dogs. Loves meeting people. Doesn't mind the smell of shit. And he's easily the most popular of our group, not because he's a dog, but because he can translate what dogs are saying for their owners. He's been passing messages back and forth all day, giving the momentary gift of direct communication between human and animal that leaves most owners in tears, squeezing their loving dogs, and reaffirming that we are all in this together, and that we are *all* Kynolari.

It's pretty damn close to magical.

The response to the actual Kynolari among us is a combination of respect and intimidation (for Gruunlokar), and adoration (for Poppy). I thought it would annoy her, but she's soaking it up and ribbing Gruun for being so scary looking.

Right now, we're in an underground section of the LA river, which is less of an actual river and more of a concrete aqueduct meant to redirect rain runoff into the ocean. Only reason most people knows it exists is because of movies like *Terminator 2: Judgment Day*.

But there is room to stretch here, so I'm not complaining. The smell isn't so bad, and right now, there is no river to speak of. If it rains, our whole underground route will become a wet, disgusting slog that could leave us saturated in bacteria, diseases, and people's old drugs. But this is LA. What are the odds? Whatever they are, I don't want to know them, or dwell on the subject. Gonna jinx this whole thing.

We parted ways with Ben about an hour ago. We've been passed along to different cells, each an expert in their section of tunnels, all of them armed with ARs and shotguns.

Right now, we're being led by five adults and their seven dogs. They're an interesting collection of people from all walks of life. Pretty sure one of them was a movie star, whose name I should know. One of those guys from *Good Will Hunting,* maybe. And then there is our guide, who used to clean all the trash, industrial waste, and literal shit from these tunnels, keeping the water flowing out into the Pacific, something he's currently explaining to Jess.

She smiles and nods at the old man in grimy blue coveralls and a matching cap. The name tag on his coveralls says 'Jim,' so I'm assuming that's his name. He's carrying a very groomed looking Pomeranian that's adorable, but also looks a little bit like it sustained a good whack to the head at some point. Not quite all there. And unable to put its long tongue away.

"You see," he says, "if no one cleans out the tunnels, all that water—it collects on the roads. And let me tell you, the only people who know how to drive in the rain in Southern California are the people not *from* California. A little rain. A whiff of fog. Three hundred car pile-up. Without fail. I basically help reduce that number."

"He's still doing it," the famous guy I'm going to refer to as 'Will' says. "Probably shouldn't. Eventually they're going to wonder why the roads aren't flooding."

The old man waves him off. "Would have to rain for them to wonder anything at all. And that's going to happen, what? Once? Twice a year in any amount significant enough to be noticeable? No one gonna notice. Especially not them egotistical assholes flying around up there. They're too busy fighting over who gets to control the rubble."

"Well," Poppy says, "given my nose's proximity to the floor, I appreciate what you do."

"You see?" Jim says to Will. "Even the Kynolari think I'm doing a good job."

Will smiles. Holds up his hands. "Okay, okay. You win." Then he turns to Jess and says, "Jim here might be salty, but some of us can be sweet, if you get to know us." Then he winks.

*Hold on a god damn second.*

"Hey!" I whisper-shout. "Good Will Hunting! She's spoken for."

He raises his hands again. "Sorry! Didn't know, man."

Jim has a laugh, shaking his head. "Thinks because he used to be famous that people are still gonna be impressed. Ain't no movie theaters anymore, hotshot."

"Yeah, yeah," Will says, trudging ahead in dual rejection.

"He'll be fine," Jim says. "He's got self-esteem to share. Right, Chuck Norris?" He pets his little dog, and I nearly guffaw.

He glances back at me. "You can laugh. It's supposed to be ironic. Little guy is a few cents short of a nickel." He nods down at Grover, who has just fallen in line beside me, head under my hand for a scratch. "That guy of yours is something, huh?"

"He's the best," I say.

"Micah is best," Grover replies, nudging my leg with his head.

"Pretty sure Chuck wouldn't have much to say, if he could talk," Jim says.

"Chuck no talk," Grover says. "But I sniff. He love you."

"He's talking about pheromones. Dogs can smell how people and other dogs feel. Can smell the difference between a good guy and a bad guy. Can even smell a person's intentions."

"Well, I'll be damned," Jim says. "And here I just thought they were cute."

"A lot more than that," Jess says, falling back. "The reason you're down here, and not one of the Draun is that their presence in our lives changes our brainwaves. Not just *what* we think, but the way we think. They protect us from the Draun corruption. Keep us human, by making our minds Kynolari."

Jim holds Chuck up in both hands, giving him a playful shake. "You hear that, you little shit? Kept me human." He smiles and kisses the little guy's forehead.

"Sniff love," Grove says, letting Jim know that Chuck shares his affection.

"Thanks for that, Grover," Jim says, and then slows to a stop. He gives a whistle and snaps his fingers. "You all missed the turn again."

He points to a round tunnel so small that we're going to have to Army crawl through.

"Don't worry," he says. "It's short. The tunnel ahead goes in the wrong direction. Just head through this here pipe. It converges with a large runoff tunnel that leads all the way to Marina del Rey. From there, you'll need to hoof it through the Ballona Wetlands Ecological Reserve, which being located in Los Angeles, ain't that wet. But there're no tunnels through there, and it's an empty stretch of land. So, wait until night. After that, there're plenty of subterranean tunnels that will eventually connect you with LAX's service and maintenance corridors."

"You're saying this like you're not coming," I say.

"Because I'm not," he says. "I might know the way, but this is where our stretch of LA's 6500 miles of tunnels end. You'll find Arlo on the other side. He's a loner, and kind of—"

"He's a whack-job," Will says.

"But he's one of us," Jim adds. "Loyal beyond question. And don't let his girls intimidate you. They're sweethearts." He glances up at Gruunlokar. "Imagine they'll like this one, though."

"I have seen horrors across this universe," Gruunlokar says, "far beyond anything this world has evolved, or you could conceive. Whatever the personality of the man on the other end of this pipe is, it will not surprise me."

Jim smiles. "Hope you're right."

Poppy takes the lead, hopping up into the tunnel and zipping away. The rest follow with the very quiet Jenna taking up the rear, leaving just me. I lean down to the tunnel, look back at Will and say, "How you like dem apples?"

He laughs and says, "Fuck off, asshole."

I have a chuckle and dip into the tunnel. It's a hard slog. Really tight. Makes me glad that food has been scarce lately. I barely fit. But Jim is right. Takes me just two minutes to squirm my way through.

I roll onto a dry concrete floor and back to my feet right next to Gruunlokar, who leans over to me and whispers, "I may have been wrong."

"About what?" I ask, and then catch sight of our new guide.

"What the fuck?" I whisper.

Gruunlokar nods. "Mm-hmm."

"*Privet, tovarish,*" the man says to me with a Russian accent, his broad, toothy smile never faltering. "I'm Arlo."

# 17

## CHIRK

Good news: it's been smooth sailing since we entered the ocean. These newbie Draun haven't figured out how to breathe underwater, even though their old school predecessors could pull it off using telekinetic bubbles full of compressed air. All the telekinesis in the world can't save them from a deep dive in the abyss, though. So, we're sitting pretty.

Bad news: I need to piss. And that is most definitely against the rules whilst in the middle of a mission cruising through an alien ocean, evading capture, and prepping an assault.

"You okay, dude?" Sean asks, squinting over at me.

"Dandy," I say. "Never better."

"You're acting funny," Sean says.

"He needs to urinate," Harth states.

"Thank you, Harth, for saying it out loud." Here's the thing about Kynolari. We smell everything. What you've got going on outside your body, and inside. If someone's got to piss, like really got to go, everyone knows it. Sean might have been the first person to notice my discomfort, but everyone else could smell the pressure building inside my bladder. It's normal for us, and only embarrassing if someone calls you out on it.

"If you need to—"

"I'm fine," I say, cutting Praxion short.

"Wait, wait, wait," Sean says, "hold on. You guys are like the most sophisticated alien species in the universe, right?"

"Not remotely," Harth says. "Just the most sophisticated who are willing to fight for those not as powerful. There are several more highly evolved species, but they do not take part in things such as war."

"Okay," Sean says, "but, like, more than humans."

Harth's only answer is to laugh.

"Harsh," Sean says, "but I don't think you're right. Not all the time. Because there are some basic things you guys just don't think of."

"I ain't stopping the *Prowler* to take a piss," Chirk says.

"What if..." Sean says, "you don't have to?"

My eyes flick over to him for a moment. He's being earnest.

"How big is your bladder?" he asks.

"Oh, c'mon, man!" I throw one hand up. "This is getting into some private territory."

"Twelve ounces," Torel says.

"Seriously?"

"I know all of you," she says. "Inside and out."

"Gross," I say. "Can we please stop saying uncomfortable things out loud? I'm starting to feel violated over here."

"I can hold twenty-five ounces," Baarfolir says, eyes on the viewscreen, taking his co-pilot duty very seriously.

"Bullshit," I say.

"It's true," Torel adds, "but he's a little larger everywhere else, too."

I close my eyes, sensing things are about to shift to appendage sizes.

"Sean," I say in my best 'I'm trying not to explode' voice. "Can you get to the god damn point?"

"Right!" he says and pulls out a nearly empty water bottle. "When I was a kid, my uncle would take us out on his boat. We'd spend the day off the coast, exploring islands, catching crabs—the animals, not the STD—and there're no bathrooms out there. So, if you're in transit and don't want to get arrested for pissing in the wind with your dick out—" He unscrews the bottle cap, swigs the last of the water, and holds the bottle out to me. "Piss in this. Twelve ounces of relief, my man."

"You're serious?" I ask.

"Works in a pinch," he says. "And it's not uncommon on Earth. On a boat, while gaming. Hell, if you work at the Zon, I hear it's a thing. Better than pissing your pants."

"Or bursting your bladder," Torel says. "From what I'm smelling, you have about ten minutes before I'm performing surgery. And since I'm still a little shaky from being in a coma..."

"I hate all of you," I say and snap my fingers at Sean.

He caps the bottle and tosses it to me. "Ain't no shame in taking care of business, brah."

I mutter to myself, unscrewing the cap.

"You have control, Baar. Just keep us straight and for the sake of all that is bacon, no sudden movements."

"Of course," he says. "I won't let you down."

"Do you need me to turn around or something?" Torel asks, snickering.

"Woman!" I say. "You've seen me piss before."

I whip it out and angle myself so no one can see how easily my business end fits inside the bottle's opening. Then, I open the valve and unleash the pressure.

To say it's loud is an understatement, and as the bottle fills, the pitch changes. "Fuck's sake..."

"Sounds like a clown taking a leak," Sean says. "Like a slide whistle."

"Well thank god I— Oh, shit." The piss has passed eleven ounces and is still going strong. "Oh, shit!"

"Pinch it off, man!" Sean says.

"I'm trying!"

"Use the power of kegels!"

"Whoa, whoa, whoa," I say, lowering the bottle until...it stops. All at once, my bladder is drained. I quickly cap the bottle and stow it, doing up my body armor at the same time. I shoot a glance back at Torel. "Twelve ounces, my ass."

She shrugs. "Give or take." She gives me a wink. Was fucking with me on purpose. I smile and shake my head. Good to have her back.

"Entering shallow water," Baarfolir says, snapping me out of humiliation and back to work.

I strap myself back in and take the controls. "Approaching the surface now. MIMIR, should we expect any guests?"

"No Draun detected in the immediate vicinity," the ship's A.I. says. "Long range scans show three possible targets several miles away. I suggest staying low to the ground to avoid detection."

"Low to the ground is how I do everything, baby." I pull back and follow the sea floor's natural slope up through turquoise water. We emerge from the Gulf of Suez with nary a splash, cruising just a few feet above the barren sand, between a power plant and some kind of refinery. All the buildings are roughly the same color as the surrounding terrain, glowing yellow in the morning sun. We're going to stand out like a shining white beacon. There's nothing tall to hide us. The sun will gleam off the white hull, and we're moving at a speed that can't be mistaken for human, or even anything the Americans have. We're also leaving a monstrous plume behind us.

Low to the ground or not, we're going to have company.

Glad I pissed now. A full bladder would not be fun for what's going to come next.

"MIMIR, get us to a freeway that leads to the Giza pyramid. Maintain speed and altitude."

"Copy that," MIMIR says, "I'm on it."

I give control to the A.I. and look back at Praxion. "Things are going to get dicey. Last chance to call off destroying one of this world's most precious monuments."

"It *needs* to happen," Torel says, using her 'Don't screw with me' voice.

"Right, right," I say. "The ghosts of the Lost Tribe. But…since when do we believe in ghosts?"

She counters with, "Since when do you piss in a bottle?"

"Don't deflect," I say.

"Look, I know how it sounds. I'm a damn doctor. But I was there, for a month. I know many of them by name."

"And I confirmed they existed," Baarfolir says.

"Wait, what?" I ask.

"You did?" Torel asks.

"Of course. You documented your encounters thoroughly. I compared the names you wrote down to the original Lost Tribe manifest. Every one of them was a match."

Torel points at me. "Ha!"

"Well, all right then. Let's put a hole through forty-five thousand years of history!"

Ahead, the viewscreen shows a freeway, partially covered in sand and abandoned, burned, and torn-apart vehicles. It's an apocalyptic trail of destruction. My initial thought was that someone might discount a glint of light from our hull as an 18-wheeler on the freeway, but there's too much debris to do anything but fly over the road.

"Time until contact?" I ask, taking back control of the ship.

"Thirty seconds," MIMIR says.

"Harth," Praxion says. "Sean."

"Ready," Harth says.

"Ready spaghetti," Sean says. "Where are we aiming?"

"Dead center," Torel says. "The device is ten feet above the King's Chamber, encased on all sides by solid limestone."

"So, we punch through one side," Sean says, "using lasers and shards, but is that going to be enough?"

"There's a power core in there, bud," I say. "It'll be enough."

"Target in range," MIMIR says, as the Great Pyramid of Giza rises up over the horizon, glowing in the sun.

"Locked on," Harth says.

"Ready to rock!" Sean says, sounding more eager than someone should at the idea of destroying a national monument.

"Fire," Praxion says.

Harth's solid beam of energy strikes first, glowing white hot as it disintegrates solid stone, burrowing a hole that is then suddenly widened by a barrage of tungsten shards, each one powerful enough to pulverize a hundred feet of solid stone.

There's a bright red flash at the core of the fusillade, and I say, "Hold on to your taint and try not to faint, this is going to get bumpy!"

That's when the Great Pyramid of Giza volcanoes into the sky, a plume of luminous red energy launching its ancient blocks out and up, many of them headed straight for us.

# 18

## MICAH

I stand in stunned silence, looking at the strangest human being I've ever seen. He's short. Sub-five feet, for sure. But not because of anything that might end with an 'ism.' Looks like he just hit the short branch when he fell out of his family's genetic tree. But his height is hardly what stands out most. Nor is it his authentic Russian accent.

The eye-patch covering one eye stands out, but it's overshadowed by his black mohawk. Then there's his clothing. He's dressed for night ops, in all black, wearing body armor and carrying spare shells for the shotgun in his hands. But the clothing beneath the armor…it's a latex body suit. Form fitting. Leaves nothing up to the imagination, including the man's prodigious third leg. When I notice the thing, I feel like I've been slapped in the face. I find myself flinching back, over and over, as I scan his body.

Slung over his back is a sound-suppressed Barrett M107A1 sniper rifle. Only reason it's not dragging on the ground is because it's hanging at an angle. Along with the shotgun, the ammo, and the machetes hanging on either hip, he might be carrying close to his own body weight in weaponry.

*Must have been an athlete,* I think, and then the truth slaps me in the face and blurts out of my mouth. "You were a jockey."

"Ahh!" Arlo says. "You recognize the *Aerodynamic Arlo*, then?"

"No, sorry," I say. "Just a hunch."

"Because I am short, da?"

I nod. "And strong."

He grins at this. "A keen eye, then." He waves my tension away. "I was a horrible horse jockey." A smile creeps onto his face. "I was a much better spy."

"You were a spy?" Jess asks. "For the Russians?"

The grin becomes a toothy smile. "Who would have thought? The answer: no one! Everyone discounted me because of my size, never guessing that I was absconding with state secrets. Who knew that my affection for canines would make me one of the good guys when there were no countries left?"

"Okay," Poppy says. "I get that, and kudos to you for using size discrimination to your advantage, but if no one else is going to say it, I'm going to: Pick a lane, buddy. What are you supposed to be? A sniper? Spy? Pirate? Punk rocker? A BDSM master?"

"And sadist," he says, turning his attention to Poppy. "But not toward Kynolari—" He turns to me. "Or their friends. I am all of the above and more, and no part of my eccentric garb is a mistake."

He pats the sniper rifle. "I strike from a distance, silent and gone like a ghost when enemy arrives. Twenty-two confirmed kills."

"Kills?" Jenna says, brow furrowed. She's encountered a lot of strange things since waking up in a new body, but she's still relatively new to the madness that has claimed the whole world, and the kind of eccentricities that emerge when there's no one left to judge. "Who?"

Arlo is confused by the question. "What do you mean, 'who?' The enemy, of course."

"You have killed *twenty-two Draun*?" Gruunlokar asks, sounding doubtful.

"Twenty-two confirmed," Arlo says. "Five unknown. Several dismemberments. If they don't know the strike is coming, they don't defend against it. The smarter ones are shielded all the time, but most of them are not smart."

"Agreed," Gruunlokar says, turning his attention to Arlo's sniper rifle.

"Would you like to see it?" Arlo asks, unslinging the rifle and holding it out to Gruunlokar, who accepts the weapon and begins inspecting it, looking down its lines, feeling its weight, peering into the scope. "Barrett M107A1. Aka: Light Fifty, though I call it 'hooy morzhovy.' Is walrus penis, because when it shoots you in the ass, you'll definitely feel it."

"Ugh," Jenna says, turning away. Her discomfort with all of this is becoming more evident. She's pulling away. Growing quiet. Has lost her sense of humor. It's easy to forget she's only sixteen, but in my core, I fear what her discontent could become.

"A well-crafted, yet crude weapon," Gruunlokar says. "It would take a steady hand to—"

Arlo holds up his hand. Perfectly still.

"How many have *you* killed?" Arlo asks. "I see the cold gaze of death in your canine eyes."

Grunnlokar grunts at the man's assessment. "Two thousand five hundred thirty-seven." He lets that sink in for a moment, and then adds, "At range," and leaves whatever that means a mystery.

"Holy shit," Poppy says, looking up at Gruunlokar with a newfound respect.

"It's not that impressive," he says. "Chirk has far more."

Poppy and I lock eyes, both of us surprised.

"Well, that's great," Jenna says. "Can we stop talking about all the people we've killed and—"

"They're *not* people," Gruunlokar says.

"Unless we can bring them back," she says. "Isn't that the point of all that Xolotl shit?"

"Sugar," Poppy says. "It's highly unlikely that a mind occupied by a Draun can be made normal again."

"*I'm* here," she says.

"But you're not you," Poppy says. It's the brutal truth.

I raise my hands, hoping to defuse the growing tension. "Jenna, your other self–"

She raises both eyebrows at me. "My real self, you mean."

I purse my lips and take a moment. "She was…different. Powerful. What she accomplished with you isn't something anyone has done before. Gemma, the woman whose mind you inhabit, was also Draun, and when *her* self was erased by Praxion, she was an empty vessel. I like the thought of bringing them all back, just as much as you, but I don't think it's possible, or something we should pin our hopes on."

"The people whose Draun selves are erased can't inhabit their own bodies again," Poppy adds, "because they *are* Draun. Their old selves aren't tucked away somewhere like a saved video game waiting to be reset. A Draun is a mind evolved and changed, by choice."

Jenna crosses her arms. "So, if we pull this off, if we somehow send Praxion's signal out through the world and kill all those people, what's the point?"

"They are not human," Gruunlokar says. "Not anymore."

"The point," I say, "Is to save everyone else that remains. Before they convert or wipe out countless other civilizations throughout the universe. Like it or not, we need to stop thinking of ourselves as part of an Earth community–not that we ever really did that. We're so tribal we're still considered primitives by species from other worlds. But that needs to stop. We are part of an interstellar community now, and we are on the front lines of a war that could consume worlds and lives beyond our understanding. If we need to kill the people who accepted the call to become Draun–and we know it *was* a choice–then that's the sacrifice we're going to have to live with. It's what you would have wanted. It's why she spared you the choice, and it's why you're here now, to finish this fight in a way she couldn't. Or wouldn't."

"It okay, Jenna," Grover says, stepping beside her and lowering his head against her leg.

She looks down at him, face tense.

Screwed up with emotion.

"Me no love fight," he says. "But we fight…for love."

Jenna's stiff upper lip begins to quiver.

She crouches down and wraps her arms around my boy. She cries into his fur, while he does what he does best. "Love Jenna. It okay. World is scary. You safe."

"Sooka sin..." Arlo whispers, and then looks at me. "He can *talk?*"

"Glad you're not the only one full of surprises," I say.

He chuckles, looking back at Grover while rubbing a hand through his short mohawk.

Desiring to give Jenna a little privacy, I turn to face Arlo's two dogs. They're just about as tall as him. Definitely weigh more. Probably twice as much. "And who are these two?"

He motions to the dog with a red bandana around its neck. "Crip." He slides his hand over to the second. "Blood."

"You're shitting me," Jess says. "Don't you think that's..."

"Dangerous?" he says. "When such things held meaning. It's like he said—" He motions to me. "We are now one people, done with tribal life. A world."

"They are impressive," Gruunlokar says.

"They're huge is what they are," Jess says. "What breed are they?"

"Part German Shepherd, as I'm sure you can see." He smiles with pride. "Their size comes from their father, a Great Dane."

"So, basically, if you and Harth had babies," Poppy says, nudging Gruunlokar's leg.

"A biological impossibility," Gruunlokar says. "But impressive."

"They know you're friends," Arlo says. "In case you were concerned."

"How do you know that?" Jess asks.

"Because you are alive," he says, deadpan. Then he smiles. "And they can sniff out the difference between a human and a Draun. Now! The sun is setting, and we need to cross the wetlands in the dark."

Arlo catches me off guard by shouting, "Let's ride!" and grabbing a mount on the back of Crip. He flings himself up and onto the massive dog's back, highlighting the size difference between the two. The dog hardly even notices.

"I'm not sure—" Gruunlokar says, uncomfortable at the sight of a dog being ridden like a horse.

Poppy cuts him short. "Hell, yes!" She hops up onto Blood's back and loops her hand around the dog's riding harness.

"Been a long time since I had a riding companion," Arlo says.

"Probably been longer since you won a race," Poppy says, eyes full of mischief. Their eyes lock and almost at the exact same moment, Arlo and Poppy both urge their dogs into a sprint, racing away at impressive speed.

"Well," Jess says. "I guess we go that way."

A distant "Whoohoo," echoes back to us.

"If we get lost, we can always follow the sound of Poppy's delight," Gruunlokar says, striking out. Jess goes with him. I linger behind as Grover and Jenna separate. He walks to my side, calmly wagging his tail.

When she joins me, I ask, "You okay?"

She nods, but I can tell she's still holding back.

"Any time you want to talk about it—"

"I miss my father," she says.

"Is he—"

"Dead," she says. "Happened before all of this. Long time ago, I guess. But recent for me."

"I'm...sorry," I say. "I didn't know."

She catches me off guard by leaning her head on my arm.

"If it helps," I tell her. "You're not alone." I put my arm around her. "I've got your back. We all do. And I know Gruunlokar would never let anything happen to you." Up ahead, I see his ear twitch at the mention of his name. I take his continued silence as confirmation. "He cares about you, even if he won't say it. Respects you, even, and that's rare. We're family now. Means we won't let anything happen to you."

"Unless you all die first."

"Well, yeah," I say with a laugh. "Obviously."

I give her a shake, and she laughs, too.

"We got this, though."

"We're in a sewer," she says.

"Runoff tunnel," I say. "What you're smelling is just us."

She laughs again.

"Everyone smell good to me," Grover says, trotting ahead.

"You see?" I ask. "All good. And it should be smooth sailing until we reach the airport."

"And then?" she asks.

I smile. "Well, that depends on whether or not there's secret alien technology hidden inside a horse statue's asshole."

# 19

### PRAXION

"Whooo!" Chirk says, letting out a laugh as he reacts to the debris catapulted towards the *Prowler*. We plow straight through the small chunks of limestone, which pose no threat to the ship, but some of the airborne bits of pyramid weigh tons and could damage the ship if we collided with them at our current speed.

The *Prowler* twists her way through the approaching debris, spinning and weaving. The viewscreen shows the action, but we barely feel it inside, as the ship moves around the cockpit, allowing us to stay upright.

A massive gray block flutters into the air, directly ahead. It's immense. Nearly twenty feet across.

"Chirk," I say.

"I see it," he says. "MIMIR?"

"Flight path erratic," the A.I. says. "Total weight, eighteen tons. Recommend destruction over avoidance."

"Take care of it," Chirk says.

"Of course."

Chirk leans toward Sean. "MIMIR is taking control of the rails."

Sean takes his hands off the controls like he's just been caught with one of his joints by this world's authorities.

A moment later, a hail of shards fire from the *Prowler*. They're impossible to see, but the effect they have on the slab of granite is easy to spot. It starts as four converging lines of grit spraying away. Even as the massive block twists up, MIMIR accounts for the movement, carving perfectly straight lines. When the four lines of shards converge, momentum flings the four segments apart and away—just before we pass through.

"Sick," Sean says, watching the viewscreen, smiling like a kid.

It *is* 'sick,' but as the captain of a warship in the process of destroying a world monument in order to free thousands of trapped Kynolari souls and attract the attention of any Draun in the vicinity, I keep my feelings to myself.

As we cruise above the scene, I say, "Give me a view of the destruction."

A holographic display is projected in front of me and Torel.

Our view of the pyramid below us is a sudden blur. We're there and then we're gone. MIMIR is smart enough to know what I'm asking, though. The flicker of movement replays, slowed down, every frame a crystal-clear, three-dimensional hologram.

Torel points to the hollowed-out core. The thick, solid stone floor is cracked and dented down. The immovable Earth below the pyramid forced most of the explosion's energy up and away. "That's the base of the King's Chamber. Everything above it is gone."

"Pretty sure that explosion confirmed the target was destroyed," Chirk says, avoiding the last chunks of debris, now moving in the same direction as we are, but far slower. "Unless rocks explode on this planet."

"Wait," Torel says. "MIMIR. Go back three frames."

The video skips back. I don't see anything out of the ordinary.

"One frame forward." Torel says, and then points at the new frame. "There! Zoom in."

The image expands revealing a luminous blue wispy cloud.

"Residual energy," Harth says, glancing over from his station. "Left behind from the explosion."

"Or it's them."

"There's no way to know how a thirty-seven-thousand-year-old power cell will react to an explosion. The effect really isn't that surpri—" He leans in a little closer, then abandons his station completely and peers at the hologram from the other side. "Is that a face?"

MIMIR intuits that he wants a closer look and expands the image at the outer edge of the glowing cloud. The revealed shape really does look like a Kylonari face, eyes up, mouth open. Happy.

"Siloquin," I say recognizing her face from our time in purgatory.

"We really did it," he says, stunned. "Set them free. The Lost Tribe?"

Torel nods, and then turns to me. "And I'm afraid you're not going to like what comes next."

"What do you mean?" I ask.

"MIMIR," she says. "Scan the ship on all sides for any visual distortions similar to that we're seeing inside the ruins of the pyramid. Enhance it, and then display."

"Scanning," MIMIR says.

"What are you hoping to find?" Praxion asks.

It's Sean who answers, his railguns swiveled to aim behind us. "They're behind us. And closing."

"*Who* is behind us?" I ask Torel.

"Holy shit!" Sean says. "They're gaining fast."

Torel takes my hand in hers and places a second on the side of my face. In that still moment, love radiates from her along with something else.

Regret.

"I'm sorry," she says, kissing me gently. Then she leans back, releasing my hand.

MIMIR joins in. "Incoming anomaly approaching faster than we can—"

The *Prowler*'s interior blinks and flashes, all our systems, including MIMIR, have been disrupted.

A moment later, I feel something no one ever should while on board a ship like this—gravity.

Before I can start shouting commands, Torel stands from her chair, propelled by a blue beam of energy pulsing through the ship and into her back. Arms wide, spine arched, she turns her head to the ceiling and screams in agony.

I reach for her but am driven back by the blue energy's electric field. All I can do is watch as my love is torn into—by the souls we freed.

They enter her en mass, silently sliding out of purgatory and into a new host. Thousands of them. Torel isn't just saving them, she's housing them. But for what?

She knew this was going to happen.

Apologized for it.

And kept it from me, because she knew I'd never allow it.

All at once, the blue beam ceases, and the ship's functions return.

I leap out of my chair and catch Torel before her unconscious form can crash into the floor.

"All systems back to normal!" Chirk shouts.

"Get us out of here," I say. "Fast as you can."

"Draun targets en route," MIMIR says, her calm voice a drastic contrast to the rest of us.

"Target anything that gets in range," I say, placing Torel back in her seat and strapping her down. She might need medical attention, but that has to wait until I'm sure the rest of us aren't going to die. "Goal is to slow them, not kill them. Harth, use visible light. See if you can't make them think twice about looking directly at us."

Harth nods and returns to his station.

"Sean," I say. "Just give them hell."

"Right," he says. "Cool. But…there is a red square in the bottom right of my head's up display that's blinking."

"MIMIR," I say. "Confirm."

"Confirmed," the A.I. says. "Shard stores are nearly depleted."

"Then give them hell until you can't," I say. Not fond of using up the last of our shards while running away from a fight, but situations don't get much more desperate than this.

"A-firmative," Sean says. "Giving hell."

While my people do their jobs, I turn my attention back to Torel, assessing her condition. She's breathing. Has a pulse. Doesn't appear to be in distress, but she is once again unconscious, and that fills me with a familiar dread I thought was in my past.

A hand rests atop mine. It's Baarfolir. "I can take her to the med-bay. Run a full diagnostic."

The idea of not going with him breaks my heart. The burden of leadership sometimes means putting yourself last.

"Got one!" Sean shouts. "Asshole didn't have a shield up. Dropping like a fly over an open barbeque."

"Two more have been slowed by light," Harth says, "but I see many more approaching now, rising from the cities along the Nile."

"How many?" I ask.

"One hundred seventeen," MIMIR answers.

"Where are we at?" I ask.

"Diverted toward the Mediterranean," Chirk says. "No way we're getting back to the Red Sea. ETA until splashdown, thirty seconds."

"Take her," I say to Baarfolir, and turn my attention to the viewscreen, while he frees her from the chair and with surprising strength, moves her limp form toward the infirmary.

"Contacts approaching from ahead," MIMIR says. "Two Draun."

"I see 'em," Chirk says, performing a maneuver meant to confound the Draun. If either of them is powerful, they might be able to reach out and catch us—if they can see us. Their eyes are still human, and we're moving quickly. If they can't focus on us, they can't exert their will upon us either.

We rocket up into the sky while swerving back and forth. The Draun rise to meet us, and when they do, Chirk does something they can't—changes direction, straight down, without first slowing down. To anyone watching it would look like we bounced off an invisible wall. As expected, the fast-moving Draun are unable to react nearly as quickly, and they need to slow down before chasing us.

And once they're behind us... Not even the most powerful Draun could match the *Prowler*'s top speed.

"I'm out," Sean says, sliding back away from his controls, hands raised. "Hit a bunch. Slowed a few."

"No worries, *compadres*, we are..." Chirk says, as we slip into the Mediterranean Sea and cruise into the depths. "...clear! Next stop, Los Angeles."

"Uh, bros," Sean turns around looking concerned. "We're in the Mediterranean, yeah? And the Draun can obviously talk to each other."

"What's your point?" Chirk asks.

"Only one way out of the Mediterranean. Strait of Gibraltar. Read about it in this book called *Pulse*. Cool history, but the water is like seven miles across. Point is, we might not be out of trouble yet."

"MIMIR?" I ask.

"The human surprises again," MIMIR states, getting a laugh out of both Chirk and Sean. "The Strait of Gibraltar is indeed a narrow crossing. With enough Draun, it could be perilous. If they are organized, it would be the likeliest location for an ambush."

Chirk looks back. "All I'm hearing is that there's going to be more Draun for me to kill."

MIMIR attempts to shoot him down. "That is statistically unlikely—"

"If you had lips," Chirk says, "this is when I'd press my finger against them and say, 'shh, shh, shhhh. Trust me, baby.'"

"If I had a sense of humor," MIMIR counters. "This is when I would laugh."

Chirk gets a fiendish grin on his face. "Watch and behold with magnificent gasping and exclamations, as I dazzle you all with my knowledge of space, speed, time, and pressure to create a counter-assault that will leave all aghast at its horrible splendor."

"Is this one of those times you pretend you know what you're doing, hoping that you'll figure out what to do by the time shit goes down?" Sean asks.

"Shush, human!" Chirk says. "I never do that. But also—"

Harth turns around with a sigh. "He's going to—"

"Ah, ah, ah!" Chirk says. "Don't spoil the surprise. Just let me entertain Captain Beefcake."

"MIMIR," I say. "ETA for the Strait of Gibraltar?"

"Three minutes," she says.

"Do it," I tell Chirk, very aware of what he's going to attempt. We all learned about the strategy long ago but have never had a chance to try it. Then I stand and head for the med-bay, where I fear I'll discover that Torel won't be returning this time.

# 20

## MICAH

"There, you see?" Arlo points across the wetlands, which are, in fact, bone dry and covered in scrub brush. The dry vegetation helps conceal us, but it's also noisy, scratching against our clothing and crunching beneath our feet. Thankfully, this patch of empty earth has no appeal to the Draun and isn't watched over.

He hands me his small binoculars, and I take a look. A trio of Draun—young men—hover over LAX. Every now and then, two of them square off and charge toward each other. Their telekinetic shields collide, and they're bounced away.

"They look like rams fighting for territory," Jess says.

"That's exactly what they're doing," Arlo says. "I think. They come here every night for several hours, smashing into each other. I believe they're trying to claim the airport. I've allowed them to continue because they're more focused on each other than on what's happening around them. I suspect they were friends before the change. Draun aren't normally so civil about territorial disputes, and whenever a fourth arrives to claim the airport, they work together to defeat them."

"Interesting," Gruunlokar says. "It is an unusual arrangement."

"Which I'll be more than happy to help bring to a close," Arlo says, unslinging his sniper rifle. "If we strike all together, between their impacts, we might catch all of them unprotected."

"A solid strategy," Gruunlokar says, getting a smile out of Arlo, and then just as quickly he decimates it, "if the surrounding territories were unpopulated. The sudden disappearance of three Draun would be felt by others in the area, who would likely come to claim the airport as their own. They would know ahead of time that an adversary had killed the others. These three would be dead, but we'd have a very large target on our backs."

"Mm," Arlo says. "Really was hoping to shoot something tonight."

"The night is young, my friend," Gruunlokar says, patting Arlo's shoulder.

"So, we go slow and low like the Beasties, sneak past the Three Stooges, and pull an Ocean's Eleven escape with a horse's anus," Poppy says.

I nod. "Sounds about right."

"I don't know anything about a horse's anus," Arlo says, "but I think it could work."

"I'm in," Jess says.

"What…are you all talking about?" Gruunlokar asks. "Beasts? Oceans? *Stooges?"*

"Pop culture references," Jenna says. "People use them as analogies when they can't think of a smart way to describe something."

"Hey," I say. "It worked for Peter Griffin and Deadpool."

"Yeah," she says. "Because they embraced the stupid. You all think you're being clever."

Jess drops her jaw. "Is she calling us stupid?"

"I believe she is," Gruunlokar says, with a subtle grin.

"Been called worse," Poppy says, hopping away and slipping through the field without a sound. "Move your asses, this cooch ain't gonna fuck itself."

"There," I say. "You see? No pop culture… Just a vulgar reference comparing our mission…to a vagina…that needs… You know what? I'm good. Let's, ahh, let's just go."

Staying low, we follow Poppy through the field. She could take an even more concealed route and leave the rest of us to fend for ourselves, but she moves along ahead of us, clearing a path and making sure we're hidden and silent. She pauses in a small clearing, behind some brush. Waits for us all to arrive and then turns to Arlo. "All right, tunnel rat, where to?"

There's a road just ahead and a neighborhood beyond. A few blocks farther is the airport. Really not a bad location to live in. Walking distance from the beach, which I can smell. But the sound of airplanes coming and going must have been incessant.

"Manhole cover in the middle of the street. Leads to a runoff tunnel that will take us to a sewer line straight to the airport. From there we can transition to a maintenance tunnel."

"Hard to believe it's all connected under there," Jess says.

"They weren't. I might have made a few holes of my own. In the early days. When things were still chaotic, and explosions weren't uncommon." He lifts his binoculars and looks out at the airport. "Looks like they've stopped for the night."

Gruunlokar takes a look using the scope built into his sniper gauntlet and relays what it's seeing to his regulators, allowing him to see what the weapon does. "Confirmed. The Draun are no longer visible. But that does not mean they are no longer present."

"Yes sir, ma'am, sir," Poppy says, and then breaks from cover, heading toward the manhole.

"Was that a pop culture reference?" Gruunlokar asks.

I shake my head. "More of a playful taunt."

"She was calling you a chick," Jenna says. "Pretty sure she was flirting with you." She smiles and follows Arlo and his girls out into the street.

Gruunlokar looks befuddled.

I pat his shoulder. "And that was Jenna screwing with you."

He sighs with relief. "That is good. Poppy is an elegant creature, but my loins would–"

"No," Jess says. "Nnnno. No more loins, or vagina talk."

He grins. "You lived with Kynolari, in close quarters for more than a month. Our hearing is exceptional. We all know how much the two of you discuss loins, female anatomy, and things no one could–"

"No," Grover says. "Nnnno. I see all. I hear all. No relive."

Gruunlokar nearly bellows a laugh. "Perhaps we should all move on."

"Let's do that," I say, and head for the road.

We gather around the manhole, which is still closed. Arlo is crouched beside it. "Bad news," he says at my approach. "Someone is on to us." He leans aside to reveal the manhole cover. It's been welded shut.

I scan the area, looking for danger, but see nothing. Whoever did this isn't here. That, or they're very patient.

"Well, let's not stand here all day gawking at a sealed hole in the road like it's the Statue of Liberty's asshole," Poppy says.

Arlo stands and makes a series of whistles and clicks at Crip and Blood. He finishes by snapping to the right, sending Crip running in that direction, sticking to the shadows cast by the neighborhood homes. With a second snap, Blood bolts in the other direction. "If anyone is waiting for us, they will sniff 'em out." Then he jogs toward the nearest home, hiding in its shadow cast by the moon.

"There are three more entrances to the tunnel system we're looking for." He peeks around the home's corner. "I will check them all and return as soon as I gain entry."

"And if you do not?" Gruunlokar asks.

"Return?" Arlo asks. "Or gain entry?"

"Both," Gruunlokar says.

"Well, we can always duck and weave through the neighborhood, cut through the LAX security fence, cross a few runways, and kick open a door." Arlo shrugs. "Wouldn't recommend it, but that doesn't mean it wouldn't work in a pinch. If you're lucky. Until then..." He motions to the large modern homes on the neighborhood's fringe. There was a time in my life when the minimalist clean lines, large windows, and seaside vibe would have appealed to me. Now, each building looks more like a mausoleum that might actually be full of bodies. "Pick a house. Try to relax."

Then he's off, his little body just a blur in the shadows of buildings and palm trees.

"Well," Poppy says. "This is a shit show."

"What isn't?" Jenna says, stepping up to the nearest home's rear sliding door. She gives it a tug and finds it locked.

"I know how to pick—"

She cuts me short with a twiddle of her fingers. The door unlocks and slides open without her ever touching it. "Thank you, Captain Mansplain. I think I can handle it."

She steps inside, and the rest of us follow. I bring up the rear, closing and locking the door behind us. We're in a wide-open living space that's two stories tall and capped with a ten-foot-wide skylight that allows the moon's light to illuminate the sparsely decorated space.

Each chair is a work of art, along with the actual art hanging on the large walls. One, which looks like it could be an authentic Jackson Pollock, stretches eight feet wide.

"Dibs on this place after we save the world," Jenna says, spinning around as she takes everything in.

"You can have it," Poppy says. "I'm going home."

"Agreed," Gruunlokar says, trying out a seat that looks like a tongue. As soon as he settles his weight, he stands back up, glowering at the chair. "I am uncomfortable here."

"In this house?" Jess asks.

"House smell funny," Grover says, slowly wagging his tail as he sniffs around every nook and cranny of the futuristic multi-million-dollar home. "No people live."

"It's abandoned, buddy," I tell him. "Just like everywhere else."

He looks back at me. "No one live ever."

Gruunlokar takes a long sniff, while Poppy turns her head up and takes several quick sniffs through her nose.

"He's right," Gruunlokar says.

"No one has even taken a shit here," Poppy adds. "Place was never occupied."

"Because it was never sold," Jenna says, pointing out the large front window, where a 'For Sale' sign sits in the miniscule front yard. She pulls the shade closed. "Which is fine by me. No dead bodies or dead body stink? Bonus."

I pick a chair that's more of a sideways bowl and sit down. The whole thing swivels down, sliding smoothly and tipping me backward until my feet are above my head and my ass is in the air. "Umm."

Gruunlokar appears above me, looking down with a grin. Jenna joins him and covers her mouth to hide her laughter.

Jess arrives next, amused and shaking her head at me. "Idiot."

Poppy leaps up onto Gruunlokar's shoulder and looks down at me. "You know, I thought the Axiom would be, I don't know, like, a thousand times more impressive."

"Just...help me up," I say, reaching a hand up.

No one takes it. They're all getting a kick out of my misfortune.

Then Grover leaps up, paws on the bowl, tipping it slightly in the right direction. He's beyond excited, leaping on his back legs up over and over, trying to get in the bowl with me but never succeeding. "Fun! Me have fun, too! Micah! Micah! I get in! I get–"

The three of our group with canine ears suddenly stop, go rigid, and snap their heads to the left.

"What is it?" I whisper past my ass.

Gruunlokar stays focused on what he's listening to and whispers, "Suppressed sniper fire."

# 21

### CHIRK

"Why are we stopped?" Sean asks.

"All part of the master plan," I tell him.

"The one you just pulled out of your ass," he says.

"I'll have you know that it's pulled from an ancient tomb of Kynolari strategy that is admired by civilizations and military minds throughout the cosmos." I smile. "I just keep it in my ass, so I understand why you're confused."

"Dog," he says. "You crazy."

"Just getting started," I say. "How are we looking, Harth?"

"Structural integrity is at 99.999 percent." He gives me a nod. "Well within safety parameters."

"MIMIR?" I ask.

"I concur," the A.I. says. "Risk of total destruction is minimal."

"Total destruction?" Sean says, sounding concerned. "What percentage counts as minimal?"

"Four percent," MIMIR says.

"Shit, man." Sean runs his hands through his mop of hair, making it stand every which way. "Four percent? If you told me I had a one percent chance with Jennifer Love Hewitt, I'd be psyched. With some work, I can make that shit happen. But *four* percent? I mean, that's kind of a done deal in Lord Sean Huempfner's land of Ain't Gonna Happen."

"What is he trying to say?" Harth asks.

I wave a dismissive hand toward Sean. "Ahh, he's just nervous."

"Only because you shut off... What did you shut off?"

"Transmedium field," I say.

"And that does what?" he asks.

"You know how we can fly through different...stuff? Air. Water. Space. That's because of the transmedium field that surrounds the ship. Makes us... What's a good word? Slippery. With that off, water clings to us just like it would anything else. All we're going to do is move through the water, at speed, with no transmedium field."

"And that does what?" Sean asks.

I grin. "You'll see."

I toggle my comms. "Attention all *Prowler* passengers, we're about to pull off the maneuver of the century. Please strap yourselves in, or down, or whatever you need to do. Things could get bumpy."

"Bumpy?" Sean asks.

Harth turns to Sean. "The transmedium field is also the part of the system that absorbs shocks and sensations of movement. The ride will be significantly more..." He turns to me. "What is a good word?"

"Jouncy?" I propose.

"Disconcerting?" he says.

"I don't even know what those words mean!" Sean says.

"Agitating?" Harth offers. "Agitating."

"Let's go with jiggly," I say, and then to Sean, I add, "You like jiggly things, right? All humans like jiggly things."

"While I appreciate things that jiggle," Sean says, "I don't really picture myself riding *inside* them. I mean, motorboating doesn't count. That's more on top and doesn't actually go anywhere."

Praxion's voice comes over our comms. "We're good to go back here. Engage when ready."

"We have discussed this for far too long," Harth says. "The time for action has arrived."

"It'll be just like cruising down the street in *Peregrine*," I tell Sean. "Just a thousand times faster."

"A thousand times—"

"Engaging," I say, and I manage to shove the throttle all the way forward before being crushed back into my seat. Won't be able to reach forward to slow us down until we're at full speed.

The viewscreen becomes a blur of shifting blue light as we rise and fall with the ocean floor, building speed and creating a wall of pressure.

A bow wave forms in front of us, rising higher and higher. We're plunged into darkness as the water above and around us can't get out of the way fast enough, growing into a tsunami the likes of which this planet hasn't seen since before there were human beings.

Behind us, the rapid displacement of water creates a vacuum. Sea water rushes into the void, filling the space and creating a turbulent and cavitating wake where pockets of vapor explode to the surface. It will cause chaos for the coastlines to our north and south, but I doubt there will be anyone sunbathing on the beaches.

From above, our passage through the Mediterranean will look like a giant wave chased by boiling water. Something like a scene from the *Project Nemesis*

TV series Sean had me watch. The beast, roiling with vengeance, rising to the surface in search of evil. What we're doing isn't all that different, except we're using real science here, not the stuff of TV and novels.

"E...T...A?" I manage to force out of my lungs.

"Thirty seconds until we reach the Strait," MIMIR says. "Ten seconds later, we will be through."

"Sssensor contacts?" I ask.

"There are a growing number of Draun in the air above the Strait, stretching from Gibraltar itself, to Point Cires in Morocco."

"How...many?" I ask, teeth grinding as the G-forces continues to push me into my seat.

"Currently," MIMIR says, and pauses like it doesn't want to say, even though it's a damn A.I. and doesn't feel an emotional attachment to whatever horrid news it's about to deliver. "One hundred fifty-three, with more arriving by the moment."

The pressure holding me back eases as we reach the ship's top speed while traveling through water without a transmedium field.

"What are they doing?" I ask.

"Removing the water," she says.

"How much water?" Harth asks.

"I believe they are attempting to drain the entire Strait, but we will arrive before they have succeeded."

"Any good news?" I ask.

"Actually," MIMIR says, "I've run hundreds of simulations, and all came to the same conclusion. The sudden entrance of our fast-moving tsunami will quickly fill the cavity they've created and burst vertically into the air, resulting in an explosive ejection of water a mile tall. Any Draun close to the cavity will have their skin whisked from their bodies. Those higher up will be caught by the water and dragged into the depths where they will be crushed by the pressure."

"Survivors?" Harth asks.

"If there are any, they will, to quote our pilot on many occasions, 'Run away like little bitches.'"

"Ha *ha!*" I shout. "You see, Beefcake?"

When Sean doesn't respond, I glance over. He's passed out. "Huh."

"Humans," Harth says with a chuckle.

"Ahh well, guess he's going to miss the grand finale." I take the controls. "MIMIR, engage transmedium field as we pass through the waterline. I don't want to feel the transition out of—or back into the water."

"A wise decision," MIMIR says.

"I know that," I grumble. "All I make are wise decisions."

"I seem to recall—"

"Silence, computer mind!" I shake my head. "A.I.s and their perfect memories, am I right?"

Harth doesn't reply. Probably because we're about to slip out of the water and into the open air created by hundreds of Draun.

Hundreds.

That much power in one place should be enough to destroy us. I'm counting on their egos to keep them rooted in place, aware of the approaching wave, but not fully understanding the threat it presents.

"Give me an omnidirectional view," I say.

The large viewscreen at the front of the cockpit accesses all the ship's sensors to give me a complete view of everything around us.

In front, a wall of luminosity approaches. "Here we go..."

I zoom in, focused on the viewscreen, gripping the controls. Laser focused.

We slip out of a wall of water and into the open. There's a half mile of open terrain between us and the Atlantic ocean.

We make it halfway across in the blink of an eye.

And then we're stopped in our tracks.

The Draun to our left and right, release the portion of water they were holding back, rushing toward us, chased by the released ocean.

"Dumbasses," I say. "All of them."

Just as the first warning light indicating hull damage flashes to life, I watch three walls of water converge, two from the sides, and one moving at roughly fourteen thousand miles per hour.

The viewscreen shows water, and a sky full of converging Draun humans. Then, all of it is replaced by dark blue. A shockwave follows, rumbling through the ship as water collides with water, snapping upward with incredible force.

Thanks to the transmedium field, all that water slips right on past.

But the Draun... It would be like being struck by a seven-mile-wide, overpowered water jet strong enough to cut through steel. Draun shields take force of will to stay up, and I don't know of any Draun that can take that kind of brute force attack for more than a second. Then it's bye-bye skin. See you later, muscles. *Adios* skeleton and everything inside it. There won't even be chunks left for the fish to eat.

"And that," I say, "is why we're the fucking best."

Harth sits beside me, a satisfied smile on his face. "You're damn right." He holds his large fist up and I bump it with mine. It's one of few human gestures we've adopted.

I launch us forward into the Atlantic depths, "Next stop, after a quick jaunt through the Arctic Sea and the Bering Strait: Los Angel—"

"Uh..." It's Baarfolir, leaning into the cockpit. "Does that mean we won?"

"We decimated the enemy," I say, "and—"

"Great. That's, ahh, great." Our historian turned co-pilot looks shaken. "You both need to see this."

# 22

## MICAH

We scatter throughout the home, peering through windows, hoping to see something. Anything. But all we can see are the other nearby modern seaside mansions.

"I'll check it out," I say, heading for the door.

"A mistake," Gruunlokar says.

"Our man is out there," I grumble, "fighting for his life."

Gruunlokar nods. "Experience has taught me to be wary of unseen comrades in distress. The Draun do not take prisoners, but they would use the dead to draw us out of hiding."

"We don't know he's dead," I say.

"We don't know he's not," Poppy says, full of regret. "Gruunlokar is right. I've seen it happen. We need to wait."

"Wait for what?" I ask.

"For them to reveal themselves," Gruunlokar says. "Draun are not known for their patience."

"And if Arlo is out there fighting for his life?" I ask.

"Then we wish him well, and if he is subdued, a quick death."

I grind my teeth. This goes against my every instinct.

"It makes sense to me," Jess says, nearly knocking me over in surprise.

"What?"

"Try to see it from their perspective." She motions to Poppy and Gruunlokar. "They've been in this situation before. They've run out to help only to find an ambush that got more of their people killed. Maybe once. Maybe ten times before they learned to ignore the sounds of distress."

"Eleven, actually," Gruunlokar says. "The last was my brother. My reaction to his cries of pain resulted in the deaths of twenty more."

That sobers me up.

I can't discount their experience with the Draun. They know—*really* know—the depths to which the Draun will sink, while I'm still learning. "I don't like it."

"No one likes it, asshat," Poppy says. "We just—"

Heavy thumps on the rooftop cut her short. Without speaking, we all slide back into the shadows.

"What was that?" Jenna asks.

Gruunlokar lets out a quiet, "Shhhh."

We wait in silence. I can hear my heart pounding. Reminds me of playing flashlight tag when I was a kid. I took it too seriously, climbing high into trees, in the dark, to avoid being caught because no one would ever think to turn their light straight up. I thought myself a ninja. Lucky is all I actually was. That I didn't fall and break every limb and rib on the way down. That my parents never found out. That it impressed the shit out of Debbie Radloff. Physical feats of dumbass derring-do impressed fourteen-year-old girls for some reason. In the end, she dated Mike Hall, and I risked my life for nothing.

The thumping works its way across the rooftop until it reaches the large skylight overhead. Hard talons tick on the glass. Just two of them, tapping again and again.

*Tap.*

*Tap.*

*Tap.*

*Testing its weight on the glass,* I think.

Then it scurries out onto the window and stops in the center. I can barely see the shape of the thing's body against the backdrop of stars, but I get a sense that it's looking down, searching for occupants. They know Arlo wasn't alone, but not where we are. Luckily, we're invisible in the deep shadows. Despite knowing where everyone is, I can't see any of them. Only reason I know exactly where Jess and Grover are is because Jess is holding my hand and Grove is leaning against me.

I flinch when a broad band of red laser light shines through the glass. The light is narrow at the top and as wide as the room at the bottom. It slowly scans down the room's far wall, headed toward the floor, where both Gruunlokar and Poppy are hidden.

Poppy's feet tap across the hard floor, scurrying away from the light. Can't see her, but it sounds like she's moving deeper into the house, well out of sight. Gruunlokar moves next, his steps slow and careful, his body silhouetted by the beam behind him, sweeping closer.

When the light is about to strike the back of his tail, he leaps forward and rolls without making a sound. Impressive stealth, which I guess is what he's known for. That, and dismembering the enemy from a mile away.

It's Jenna's turn to move now, but unlike Poppy and Gruunlokar, she can't see in the pitch dark. She bumps into an end table, trips over a wire, and stumbles into Gruun's arms. I'm guessing. I can't see shit. But I can hear and imagine. I can also sense Gruunlokar's position, and his emotional state, thanks to the regulators connecting us all.

He's not exactly afraid, but his dander is up for sure. The Skitterling above would be easy to destroy, but that's not what makes them dangerous. They're not solo biologics. They move in herds.

*They* do *move in herds*, I think, unable to stop my mental reference despite not being able to say it aloud.

It's our turn to move. The Skitterling's scan is halfway across the room. We have time, but there are three of us, and two of us can't see.

I focus my attention on the regulators, willing Grover and Jess to feel my intentions without having to speak aloud. A moment later, Jess gives my hand a single squeeze. Grover nudges my elbow with his nose.

Somewhat coordinated, I bend down and scoop Grover up, lifting him so his head is parallel with mine. He gives me a lick on the cheek and then we pull out a trick from the old magic box. There's a strange perspective shift as my vision shifts from my black view to Grover's limited-color view.

But, I can see.

When Jess places her hand on my back, I start walking. Moving while seeing from a view that's just off center is on the fringe of nauseating. Feels like walking after binge drinking. My center of balance is off, so I take my time, planting each step and waiting for Jess to do the same.

We reach the kitchen where the others are already waiting, ducked down behind the counter. The three of us join them and crouch low.

A moment later, the scanning beam sweeps above us, up the fridge across from me, and then goes dark.

The Skitterling lingers and then moves along, its talons tapping across the glass and then thumping on the ceiling.

After waiting a solid minute, Gruunlokar whispers. "Well done, all. That was a Skitterling scout. Had it seen us, we would have been inundated."

"What does that mean?"

"Inundated?" Gruunlokar asks.

"What? No. I mean, like, big picture. Where are the others? The normal Skitterlings."

"They're here," Poppy says. "Probably in every house, dormant, conserving energy, just waiting for the scouts to find someone."

"Like Arlo," Jenna says.

"And Crip and Blood," Gruunlokar says, sounding forlorn.

Poppy nods. "Afraid so."

"But they're not *here* here?" Jess asks.

"Oh yeah, they are," Poppy says. "In the bedrooms. Shit ton of 'em. That's actually what I meant by 'here.'"

"What?" Jenna whispers, a little quieter. "What do we do?"

"Stop talking," Gruunlokar says. "Then you will all follow me without saying a word. You will step where I do, breathe when I do, and not once make a sound, no matter what happens, no matter what you see. Failure means being set upon by the Skitterlings *and* the airport Draun, who have certainly not yet left the area. Am I understood?"

I see the test for what it is and nod without a word. The rest follow my lead, even Grover. We're all on the same page.

Gruunlokar nods and then leads us back to the door through which we entered the building. He pauses in the door frame, nose lifted, breathing deep. Then he steps outside and heads to the left. We follow in single file, me bringing up the rear, feeling that old flashlight tag energy again. But if we get caught, it won't be a flashlight on us, it will be a horde of quick digesting biologics that will eat—and shit—us alive. Jenna and I handled the first bunch, but that was in an open parking lot. We could see them coming. This neighborhood...it's a maze. Could be hiding thousands of the little assholes.

I nearly trip and bump into Jess. She gives me a 'Seriously?' look and I re-focus on not dying rather than thinking about the possibility of us dying in one of the worst ways imaginable.

Our progress through the neighborhood is agonizingly slow, but no one complains. First, they can't. Second, we've seen several more scouts, moving from rooftop to rooftop. They're running a search pattern, one that Gruunlokar has already figured out. He leads us right where we need to be, when we need to be there.

Along the way, we pass countless apartment buildings, tragic scenes of destruction, and more than a few corpses—dressed skeletons, some of them torn apart, either by scavengers after death, or by the Draun while still alive. Every manhole we pass has been welded shut. They don't want anyone entering the airport underground.

Must have found Arlo's tunnel breach into the service entrance.

It's not long until we find ourselves at a high school flanked by a soccer field on one side and a baseball diamond on the other. We skirt along the side of the first building and are headed across the small gap between it and the next when I catch something strange in the moonlit basketball court to our right.

Grover senses my interest in the hard-to-make-out object and glances toward it. The moment his eyes lock on, my vision snaps to his and I'm forced to stop.

It's Arlo.

What's left of him.

His limbless torso has been tossed onto the hoop, his head hanging down through the net.

# 23

## PRAXION

"Torel," I say, reaching out for her luminous body, floating four feet above the med-bay bed. Blue energy swirls around her like wisps of cloud, twisting and churning, holding her aloft.

She doesn't respond. Still unconscious, she is at the whim of whatever force is controlling her.

"Torel, if you're in there, you need to fight this. You came back from Egypt once; you can do it again. The path remains the same. Just move toward my voice."

Her body slowly rotates.

*Is it a response? Just part of what's happening to her? There's no way to know.*

The rotation persists until she is face down over the bed. Then she spins horizontally, forcing me to take a step back. She moves a full 180 degrees and then stops. She rotates one more time, stopping again when she's face up, and then spinning the final 180 degrees until she is right back where she began.

It's like watching a machine calibrate itself.

"What in the name of Gozank?" Chirk asks from the doorway, looking like he's been slapped in the face. He gazes up at Torel, hovering over the bed. "The hell happened?"

"We don't know," Baarfolir says, pushing his way into the room. "She began to glow, and then floated off the bed."

Harth enters last. If he feels surprised, he does a good job hiding it. "Have you searched her body armor? Perhaps she is wearing an anti-gravity—"

"Where would she get that?" Chirk asks. "We don't carry them—" He turns to me. "—and no offense—" Then turns back to Harth. "She ain't you. Whipping up quantum tech isn't her forte. This is something else."

"Something supernatural," I say without thinking. Kynolari aren't known for being spiritual or believing in what Earthlings call *supernatural*—existence beyond science. But just because we don't yet understand a phenomenon doesn't mean it's breaking the laws of the universe. There was a time when faster-than-light travel was believed to be impossible. As long as that belief was held, no one looked for anything different. Until one person, prone to rebellion against the norm, assumed the speed of light could be surpassed. By the end of his life, the gravity web had been discovered, and Kynolari civilization changed forever. That was seventy thousand years ago.

And now, here we are, facing the unknown once more.

In Torel…

Levitating.

Chirk bounds off the floor, onto the bed, and angles himself for a second jump.

"You probably shouldn't," is all I get to say.

"Not a good idea," Baarfolir blurts.

We're both too late. Chirk leaps up onto Torel. He lands on her stomach, perfectly balanced. His lower body is consumed by light, swirling around him, attracted to his body.

If it were anyone outside of her team leaping up onto her at a time like this, I'd shoot them right off. But she's like a sister to the team. Chirk has as much right to react with his heart as I do.

"Hey, yo," he says, stepping onto her chest. "Torel." He turns to me. "Permission to slap her face?"

I nod. "Granted." If he didn't try it, I was going to.

He winds up. Going for a big hit. Sounds horrible, but Torel is not only tough, she's also padded by thick fur on her cheeks, and Chirk is the smallest of us. He packs a punch against a human, but Torel might barely feel it.

Chirk's hand remains locked above his head, ready to strike.

But he holds back.

"What stays your hand?" Harth asks.

"I…can't…move," Chirk says, his jaw locked.

The churning blue light has begun crawling up his waist. It's burrowing into and out of him.

"We need to get him down," Harth says, "before he is consumed. But I fear if we also touch the light—"

"What the—" Sean leans on the side of the open door, holding the white wall. He's groggy and confused, looking up at Chirk. "Hey, I don't know what happened, but—" He squints, looking up at Chirk, frozen in place, teeth gritted, brow furrowed.

He straightens up and blinks fully awake. "The hell?"

"We need to get him out of the blue light," Harth says. "Without touching it."

"Throw me!" Sean says.

Harth picks him up and throws him—into a nearby wall.

"Oof!" Sean hits hard and slumps to the floor.

Above, Chirk manages to laugh through his locked jaw.

Sean shoves himself up off the floor.

"Not...what I meant..."

"Apologies," Harth says. "I believed you desired to be fully alert."

Sean staggers two steps back to Harth. "Naw, dog, just... Just...Tom Brady me at Chirk."

Harth looks down at him. "How does one '*Tom Brady?*'"

"Throw me at Chirk!" Sean says.

"Ah." Harth hauls Sean up again and tosses him across the room. He pinwheels through the air, his shout of surprise coming and going as he rotates. Then he collides with Chirk, grabs hold of his torso, and wrenches him away.

The blue light clings and stretches, holding on, hooked in. But it can't match Sean's force and slips away, allowing Sean to crash to the floor, cradling Chirk in his arms.

"Bro," Sean says, lifting his head to look at Chirk on his chest. "Little man, you okay?"

Chirk manages to lift his head. Gives a small smile. Says, "My hero," and then passes out.

Sean surprises me by immediately checking to see if Chirk is breathing and has a pulse. "Little man is good." He picks himself up off the floor, holding Chirk's limp body in a way that would enrage our smallest team member...if it were anyone else. His bond with Sean is such that affection like this isn't just acceptable, it's expected.

"And what about Torel?" Harth asks.

"Felt cold. The blue light." He faces Torel. "I mean, my knowledge of this shit is basically from *Poltergeist*, *The Sixth Sense*, and a bunch of other movies you don't want to watch alone. But I assume someone—the writers probably—did some research on the subject. The blue energy, the swirling wisps, the cold... Dude... Torel is possessed."

"Possession is a phenomenon that is not unknown to us. Several psychic species—"

"Psychic? What? No. This isn't psychic, bro. She's possessed..." He looks me in the eyes. "By dead people. Or demons. But dead people sounds less horrible."

"And more accurate," I say, nodding as everything suddenly makes sense. "The souls freed from Limbo. The trapped Kynolari. They have entered her body. Are using it to maintain their connection to this plane of existence. She knew this was going to happen. Apologized for it. Arranged it."

"She hopes you will understand," a voice says, feminine, but not Torel. The accent is wrong, but it did come from Torel's body. And she's now looking at me, eyes glowing bright white.

Her body flickers with energy and she rotates until her side is perpendicular to the floor. Then she spins until she's upright. The flickering continues as she lowers to the floor, but it stops when she's no longer floating.

"Torel," I say.

"I am not Torel," she says.

"Called it," Sean whispers to himself.

"Nor am I a stranger," she says.

"Siloquin," I say, placing the voice.

"Who?" Harth asks.

"Harth..." I motion to Torel. "This is Siloquin Dima, Prefect of the Kynolari Guard. Leader of the Lost Tribe, whose...*souls* were trapped by Anbu, and held in a conscious stasis state for thirty-seven thousand years. They are the Kynoloari who resisted, the ones whose descendants we came to rescue."

"Oh," Harth says, stunned. "That's...strange."

"For us all," Torel says, turning to Harth. She holds her hand out, elbow bent at a ninety-degree angle, hand ready to clasp. It is the old greeting used between Guard members. She is bestowing him with a great honor and recognizing us as an extension of them.

Harth looks at her hand but holds back. "It is dangerous to touch you." He motions to Chirk's unconscious body. She glances at Chirk, and then down at her hands, dancing with excited energy. Eyes closed, brow furrowed, she pulls the swirling spirits fully inside Torel's body.

"Our bodies were not made to contain more than one soul." The glow around Torel's body fades and disappears as the wisps are pulled inside her skin. "The number Torel holds within her is...difficult to rein in."

Transformation complete, she offers her hand to Harth once more.

He looks to me for approval. I nod.

He clasps her hand, both of them squeezing, snarling their teeth at each other, neither breaking eye contact.

Then she smiles. "You know our ways."

"They inspired me in my youth," Harth says. "Helped shape who I would become."

Torel gives him a once over that makes both Harth and me uncomfortable. "You were shaped well."

I clear my throat. "Siloquin."

When she turns to me, it's difficult to not think I'm speaking to Torel. "I assume you and Torel had a plan."

She nods. "And now it is complete."

"Excuse me?"

"Torel assured us that you—" She glances from me to Harth, to Sean and Chirk, and finally to Baarfolir, who is just standing silent, jaw agape. "Would figure out what comes next."

"We are about to launch him—" Harth points to Baarfolir, "into space with the hopes of reaching our brethren, while the rest of us wage war against a far more numerous and powerful force."

"Then it is good I am here," Siloquin says through Torel's mouth. "I excel at such things."

"Gah!" Chirk shouts, suddenly sitting up in Sean's arms. He spots Torel up on her feet and looking normal. He thrusts two little fists in the air. "Yes! Success! Bow before the—"

"Chirk," I say, motioning to Torel. "Say hello to Siloquin Dima, Prefect of the Kynolari Guard."

"Prefect of the Kyn—oly shit. Are you serious? Torel is possessed by—You're screwing with me." He hops out of Sean's arms and struts over to Torel, hands on his hips, looking up at her with scrutinizing eyes.

She returns his gaze and says, "Greetings."

Chirk throws his hands up in the air, frustrated. "Well, what in the hell are we supposed to do with this? Please tell me someone has some kind of plan, or strategy, or even a fucking machination?" He looks at me.

"Machination? No?" He turns to Sean. "*You* definitely don't have one." Chirk turns to Harth. "You? Machination? *Anyone?*"

"A plan has already been proposed, little one," Siloquin says, looking down at him. She grins. "*War.*"

# 24

## MICAH

The first squeak of a scream pulls me out of Grover's vision.

I find Gruunlokar with a hand over Jenna's mouth. We all stand there for a moment, looking at the horrific display. Arlo was a strange man, but he was an ally, and an asset. I was wary about getting to know him, but I regret not really having the chance. He must have had stories to tell, and now no one will hear them.

Gruunlokar peels his hand away from Jenna's mouth, holds a finger to his lip, and then motions for us to follow him again.

The silence that follows feels heavy. Arlo's gruesome death is going to take some processing. We've seen horrible things. We've *done* horrible things. But the casual way he was just dumped there speaks of an inhumanity that is hard to imagine. It also means that we are not alone.

The three Draun claiming the airport haven't been seen, but they seemed more...stupid than maniacal. And it wasn't Skitterlings. They consume what they catch. Which means there is someone, or some*thing*, else out here, hunting us.

Probably a Draun.

And the same person who welded the manholes shut.

It was all a trap—for Arlo. We're just a bonus.

All we can do about it is keep moving and stick together. For now, we're the hunted...but that doesn't mean we're prey. Whoever is stalking us is in for a rude awakening when they show themselves.

After clearing the high school, we're forced to cross an open freeway that is blessedly full of ruined taxis and buses that provide at least a little cover. On the far side of the highway is an artificial rise topped by a tall, razor-wired, chain link fence.

The airport.

We crawl on our bellies, up the ten foot hillside toward the fence. I nearly laugh when I find Grover beside me, also crawling, tongue hanging out the side of his mouth, eyes wide. He's a Golden Retriever, so of course he's having fun.

Stopped by the fence, we pause to take in the airport beyond.

There's a shit-ton of open space between us and any kind of cover. Service roads and large patches of empty earth crisscross the land ahead, surrounding two massive runways. A pair of airplanes sit abandoned on the taxiway. For all we know, they might even be ready to fly.

But not nearly fast enough.

We'd be set upon before the engines were warmed up.

And I'm pretty sure none of us is a pilot.

Beyond the runways are a massive number of parked planes, hangars, and fuel depots. It's a maze, and it's the only way we're going to reach the main terminal, where the P.F. Chang's is located. Luckily, Chang's is at the western-most end of the terminal. Won't be hard to find, if we can make it all the way there, and get inside without any more trouble.

Which I find doubtful, given the fact that we are no doubt being watched by Arlo's killer.

"I'll take care of the fence," Jenna says.

"Quietly," Gruunlokar urges.

She nods and holds her hands out toward the fence. Starting at the top, the metal strands unwind with the ease of a breadbag twisty tie. The links slip apart, gently bending out and away. When she's done, there's a hole in the fence that looks like it was blown open by an explosion. The razor wire is untouched, stretching over the opening above our heads.

"Well done," Gruunlokar says, getting a smile out of Jenna.

"Okay," I say. "So, what's the plan? Run like hell to the nearest plane? Then like fuck to the next, and then like a pack of sunzabitches to the airport, where we can lose whoever is following us?

"Someone is following us?" Jess asks.

"Hunting us," Gruunlokar says. "Arlo's killer." He looks across to me. "Caught their scent. Human. Male. Draun. That is all I know."

"He's just guessing," Poppy says with a smirk. "It's like 50/50 because, of course it's a Draun, and a human. Could be a man, could be a butch lesbian. You don't know."

"I have never smelled a 'butch lesbian,'" Gruunlokar says.

"And you don't want to," Poppy says, scurrying to the top of the rise. "Point is, doesn't really matter if it's a man or woman. We need to GTFO, pronto. Everyone good for a sprint?"

We don't really need to confirm readiness. There is no choice. Ready or not, we're about to run like a bunch of streakers at the Super Bowl, hoping security doesn't notice our dicks and tits flopping about. But we each take a moment to look into each other's eyes, determining the readiness of everyone around us.

But when I look to my right, toward Grover, I nearly scream in shock, but manage to reduce it to a whispered, "Fuck me!"

Lying beside Grover, looking right into my eyes, are two of the largest, most intimidating dogs to have ever walked the Earth.

Crip and Blood. With Arlo cut down, they've rejoined the group. Their eyes say they're looking forward to revenge. But, both of them are looking at me.

"Why are they looking at me?" I whisper to Grover.

"Crip and Blood," he says. "Yours now."

"*Mine?*"

"I say it okay." Grover pants for a moment. "Family now. We love."

I put my hand on the back of his head and pull him closer, "You're one of a kind, Gro Gro."

I then turn my attention back to Crip and Blood.

*My* dogs.

I reach a hand out, and Crip ducks her massive head beneath it. I pull her closer and rest my forehead against hers. She exudes power. "You're a good girl."

I repeat the process with Blood. "Good girl."

It's a simple thing but establishes a bond of trust between us. I don't know how I know what to do, or how I'm able to communicate with most dogs using a series of clicks, whistles, gestures, and body language. But I can. And I understand them in the same way. We're all on the same page now. These two would die for me, and I for them. Same as Grover. They'll probably just need fewer cuddles, and a lot more food.

When I turn back to the others, everyone is staring at me like they've just witnessed something otherworldly.

"What?" I ask.

Jess, who's right beside me, wipes a tear from her eye.

"You welcomed them to the pack," Gruunlokar says.

"It was the right thing to do," I say.

"Many would not," he says. "Our breed is often feared."

"Ain't nothing to fear," Poppy says. "You're all a bunch of softies, if you're brave enough to get past the furrowed eyebrows...and big teeth...and haunting eyes."

Gruunlokar levels his ever-serious stare at her.

"You see? Haunting." Poppy reaches up, pinches Gruunlokar's cheek, and gives it a shake. "And a softy."

"Never do that again," he says, trying to hide a smile, and failing.

"You all did the same for me," Jenna says. "This body was a Draun. My older self was, too. You have no reason to trust me...but you welcomed me. I'm sure Crip and Blood are just as grateful as me."

Gruunlokar places his hand on her shoulder and gives her a silent nod.

"Don't mention it," Poppy says. "But I think it's time we end the kumbaya circle jerk and hot-foot it across this doom clearing before we get railed in the ass by a sneaky Draun. My tail is curled enough as it is."

"Fast as you can to the other side," I say. "Go!" I turn to the girls, tilt my head to the side, and give a single click as I stand and start running. The pair launch forward like missiles. Grover chases them, but is more like a chaotic rocket, bounding back and forth, occasionally bouncing on all fours like a deer. He's ridiculous, but he keeps up with the pair. Poppy is quick on her feet, too, but she has to take four steps for my one. She'll tire first at full speed. So, she hangs back, just like Gruunlokar and I are... And Jenna apparently. She looks like she's casually jogging.

"Just...go," Jess says. "Don't slow down on my account."

"Leaving you behind would almost certainly ensure your death," Gruunlokar says.

"Okay," Jess says. "In that case, thanks for slowing down."

"Are you sure you can't run any faster?" he asks.

"You try with great big tits and tell me how that works out for you."

"Mm," he agrees. "Human women do have rather engorged mammaries. Point taken."

"And subject *dropped*," Jess says. It's rare to see her self-conscious, but she is kind of bouncing all over the place. I nearly trip over myself when I notice. And when she notices me notice, she snaps her fingers at me and points forward. "Eyes on the road! Fuck me. We're running for our lives, man."

Properly scolded, I turn my eyes ahead. The girls and Grover have reached the other side and are ducking into the shadows between two hangars. Not thrilled with how far they went, but the girls are used to operating independently, and they'll keep Grover safe if it comes to that.

It's the rest of us I'm most concerned about, moving through the open, not exactly quietly, and only halfway to cover.

"I believe it is time," Gruunlokar says to Jenna.

"I don't know if it will work," she says. "For all of us."

"You need not carry us all," he says, reaching down and plucking Poppy from the ground. She's not thrilled at first, smacking at his hand, but when he places her on his neck, she grabs hold of the hair on his head and says, "Hell, yes. This is more like it. Mush, boy, mush!"

"You can do it," he assures Jenna and then bounds ahead, moving as fast on two legs as the girls did on four.

"Okay," I say to Jenna. "Whatever *it* is, do it now."

She closes her eyes for a moment, which is kind of dangerous when running, but then she floats up off the ground, carrying herself aloft with her telekinesis. We all knew she could do it. Draun fly all the time. The big surprise comes next, when Jenna opens her eyes and Jess lifts off the ground—far less gracefully than Jenna, flapping her arms, spinning head over heels. I'm ready for it when it happens, and do my best to look like a natural, lifting off with calm confidence.

Jess levels out beside me, eyes widening as our speed increases. "We're flying?"

"Technically," Jenna says. "Being carried. But you can pretend if you want."

Takes just a few seconds to cross the rest of the runways. When we set down again, I put a hand on Jenna's back and say, "Nice trick. Don't be afraid to use it again. You're far more powerful than you know. You could probably carry one of those planes."

She surveys the planes with raised eyebrows, considering the possibility, but then we're off again, moving through the shadows between planes and buildings, working our way toward the main terminal.

"Look," I say, pointing to a terminal door labeled "Maintenance."

I lead the way and find the door locked. I give Jenna a nod and step aside. With a blink, the door unlocks for her. Then we're inside, moving through dark hallways in search of a stairwell. The girls lead us, finding the way up, and then out into the terminal.

The lit terminal.

I get my bearings, and then point to a large statue of a horse, one flight up, standing boldly between two moving escalators. The Draun trio have kept the power on...

"Hold," Gruunlokar says, sniffing the air. "Food is cooking. Smells like Jess's Lo Mein."

"No way," I say, looking up at the top of the P.F. Chang's sign. "They didn't..." I point to Jenna. "You're on point. Try to emanate enough raw power that it seems like we're Draun, too." I point to Jess. "You're with us. Everyone else with dog ears stay here. If we need help, you'll know."

I crouch down to Grover, who wags his tail at my approach. I kiss his forehead. "Won't go far." When I'm done, I notice Crip and Blood waiting beside him. When I turn toward the pair, their tails twitch. "You guys..." I give them both kisses on the forehead. "Keep them out of trouble."

Both dogs open their mouths to pant, a sign that they understand and are on the job.

All necessary goodbyes said, Jenna leads Jess and me to the escalator. At the bottom, the smell of cooked Chinese food is easy to detect. When the sound of laughter rolls down from above, all my suspicions are confirmed. The trio has kept the P.F. Chang's up and running, and despite being Draun, are still just a bunch of 'bros' at heart. I'm sure I'm older than they are, but I was in the military.

I can speak the language of bros when I need to, and it won't hurt that I'm flanked by two beautiful women.

At the top of the escalator, I whisper, "Just follow my lead." When my head rises high enough for the three young men seated outside the food court style P.F Chang's to see me, I lift my arms and say, "My dudes!"

# 25

### CHIRK

"I'm serious," I say, sitting in the *Prowler*'s bathroom, in the stall beside Baarfolir. "How are we supposed to trust her?"

"You don't believe there is anything left of Torel in there?" Baarfolir asks.

"No way to know," I say, "but there's also no way to find out. And we were both too flabbergasted to ask anything intelligent. I said 'machination' three times, and you just stood there with your mouth open, looking like one of those little houses humans make for birds."

"Bird houses," he says.

"Yeah. Those. So Torel is possessed by Siloquin, a supposed Prefect of the Kynolari Guard from thirty-seven thousand years ago, whose soul was trapped by Anbu/Xolotl because she—and the several thousand other souls contained inside Torel, which is fucked up by the way—didn't go along with his grand scheme, and we're just going to let her join the team? Fight alongside us? Take Torel's place?"

"I do believe that is Praxion's request," Baarfolir says.

"It's bullshit. And you know I don't say that often, not about Praxion's orders. But this time it's a pile of viscous, nutty, ass-slop."

"Perhaps his motivation for allowing her to join the team is a way of keeping her close."

"I bet he wants to keep her close," I grumble.

"To keep an eye on her," he says.

"I bet he wants to keep—"

"You know what I'm saying, Chirk," Baarfolir says. "You've trusted Praxion for your entire career in the Kyno Corps. Why not now?"

"Praxion used to be a calculating son-of-a-bitch. He'd go into battle with a rock-solid plan and a handful of backups for when things went sideways. Now... he's making decisions with his heart."

"Aren't you doing the same?"

I sigh, unsure what he's getting at.

"With what?"

"Sean," he says. "He is...unpredictable, lacks discipline and training, and at times he can be rather uncivilized. In the eyes of any Kyno Corps leadership, he'd be a liability. No offense."

"None taken, my man," Sean says with a grunt from the third stall. "All true."

"And yet, he is part of our crew now. He operates the ship's *railguns.* And he has provided insights along the way that has saved this crew and turned the tides of battles."

"Also true," Sean says.

"All of that trust in him has nothing to do with his qualifications—" I start.

"True dat."

I bang on the stall wall to my right. "Stop being his hype man and finish taking a shit."

"Aren't you taking a shit?" Sean asks.

"Naw man, I cleansed the colon an hour ago. I'm just here because it's a safe space to think."

"Same," Baarfolir says. "I often meditate in here. Back to my point. Sean is here because he is, 'your dog.' You love him. As your friends, the crew accepted him as well, despite how clearly unqualified he is."

"Okay," I say. "Fair point. But Sean isn't dressed up as my bitch."

"I'd do it, though," Sean says.

"Yeah, you would." I shake my head at how easily he can sidetrack me. "But that doesn't change my point. Siloquin just looks like the person Praxion trusts."

"I think it's about respect, dude," Sean says. "She was a perfect, or whatever. That's a big deal, right? And the Kynolari Guard? They must have been important, right?"

"You know that movie we watched? The one with Leonidas and the Hot Gates?"

"*300,*" Sean says. "Sickest movie ever. Yeah."

"The Kynolari Guard were our equivalent of Spartans. Real badasses."

"Then it's good she's on our side."

"If she *is* on our side," I say.

"I have tested her knowledge of the Kynolari Guard, and her own personal history. She is who she claims to be. And we know Xolotl had the ability to lock souls, or intellects—whatever you want to call them—away for long periods of time."

Baarfolir is sincere and competent. If he says she's the real deal, I should probably believe him. But, "How do we know she's not Xolotl? How do we know that every single one of those souls isn't a copy of Xolotl, just waiting to be implanted? He was the kind of douche bag that would make an army of himself."

"Mm," Baarfolir says. "If he had thought of that possibility, I believe he would have avoided it."

"Why? Safety in numbers. Power in numbers."

"But who would lead? Like the Draun, each iteration of himself would share the same ambition. They would have destroyed each other until only one remained."

"Okay," I say, "so your hypothetical is a little more well thought out than mine, but I still don't have a good reason to trust her."

"Because Praxion trusts her."

The baritone voice of Harth silences the bathroom. I did not know the big man was here, too. He must have been the first arrival.

The silence lingers until a long squeak of a fart fills the air, lingering for a full five seconds. "Oh man, that was a squeaker," Sean says with a chuckle. "Sorry, we can go back to being intense now."

"There is nothing to be intense about," Harth says. "Praxion is trustworthy, and an excellent judge of character, even when his heart is involved. He met Siloquin in Limbo, with Torel. Our current situation was arranged by Torel. If you're questioning Siloquin's intentions, you are actually questioning Torel's. I, for one, believe she is beyond reproach, and keen enough to not be fooled by a madman pretending to be one of the noblest of Kynolari ever to serve our people."

"Okay, see?" I say. "Take notes, Baarfolir. That was a lot more convincing than all your gobbledygook, and you'll need to be a *lot* more convincing when you reach the Council. They're not just going to send the fleet across the universe on the word of a historian."

"That's why I had Praxion record his request, and explain the situation. We made a video addressing the council, along with all pertinent information about this world, the Lost Tribe, Anbu, and the Draun, including their effect on this world and our hope that the people of Earth—with brainwaves matching Kynolari—will ultimately be saved."

"Ah," I say. "Smart. Well, then, Baar, I think it's time to launch your ass into space where you will either catch a ride on the gravity web and snap across space and time—or be blown out of the sky."

He chuckles. "I'm ready. For either scenario."

"You are a brave Kynolari," Harth says. "Worthy of the Kyno Corps. It has been an honor to serve with you."

"Is it just me," I say, "or should we save the complimentary goodbyes for when we're not sitting in the head?"

"Right," Sean says. "Just let me..." He activates his stall's cleansing unit. There's a high-pitched whine, as a jet of water cleans him off, and a repeating puff of air that reminds me of the pneumatic dart guns used by the Plingo people of Darkquin Prime. Sean laughs. Never gets old for him. The procedure is finished up with a puff of drying powder, if needed, and a spritz of scented oil.

"It's like a pedicure for my asshole," Sean says with a satisfied sigh.

"I suggest you all leave now," Harth says. "I was in here before you all arrived, not for a pedicure, but to wage war with yesterday's meal. This room will not be a safe space for much longer."

"That's my cue," I say, hopping down. The stall door melts away. Sean and Baarfolir exit their stalls on either side of me. We swipe our hands under the three sanitizing Gondinese seashells and hustle for the door, which opens and seals behind us, muffling what must have sounded like a mini-nuclear explosion.

"Close one," Sean says.

We head for the cockpit and enter together. Praxion and Torel—Siloquin—are there already, watching us as we enter together.

"Is this what it feels like to be a girl in high school?" Sean wonders to himself, and I have zero idea what he's getting at, so I don't bother asking. "Coming back from the bathroom in a gaggle... Did you do that, Torel? Sorry, Siloquin."

"You may call me Torel if it is easier for you," she says.

"Naw, it's cool. What I was wondering... Back when you were younger, and in school, did you and ahh...other females..."

"Bitches," she says.

"Right. Those. Did you go to the bathroom together? Like socially?"

"Social defecation?" Her brow furrows. "Is this a common practice on Earth? It sounds...revolting."

"Right," he says. "Totes. Would never do it myself."

He gives me a cringing look, which I return, while we both sit at our stations. Baarfolir buckles himself in and looks back at Praxion. "I'm ready, sir. Commence Operation: 'Hold On To Your Nuts...'" He leans over to me. "Do I really need to call it that?"

"That is what I named it," I say.

He sighs. "I am ready when you are, sir."

"Very good," Praxion says. "Where is Harth?"

"Finishing some last-minute business," I say. "Shouldn't be—ahh, here he is."

Harth hustles onto the bridge, walking a little funny. Must have been a monster. "I'm here." He takes his seat, trying to not act conspicuous about what he was doing, which somehow makes it obvious.

Praxion cracks a smile, but Siloquin either doesn't notice, or doesn't care.

"Flight path?" Praxion asks.

"Programmed and keyed up," I say. "We'll reach LAX in ten minutes."

Which is when we'll jump ship and Baarfolir will begin a ride rougher than a Scantilorian's armored prepuce.

# 26

## MICAH

The trio react as expected, flinching at the sound of my voice. One spits out his drink. Another tries to scarf down the lo-mein noodles hanging from his mouth, chokes, and then disgorges it all like a startled snake.

"Who the fuck are you guys?" asks the only one of the trio not expelling food or drink. Looks Chinese. Sounds American. Feels racist to even think, but I'm guessing he's the one of these three who worked at this P.F. Chang's before the world went to shit.

I hold up both hands, which is exactly the moment I realize I'm just wearing a black T-shirt. The gauntlets on my arms are totally exposed. "We come in peace. Smelled the food. Came to see if the current Mr. Chang would be willing to share."

The second kid—can't be much older than twenty, all three of them—squints at me with the ferocity of a hawk. Which strikes me as funny, because he's clearly the biggest eater among the three. He's not quite obese, but he looks like he's got elastic bands squeezing his joints. Kind of like a chubby baby. "Bullshit. You're here for the airport, just like the rest, but I got news for you, buddy. LAX and all that you survey inside and around it belongs to *me*."

"Dude," the third guy, says. He's scrawny and tall. And completes the picture of who we're dealing with here. I thought they were bros, but they're not. They're *nerds*. Probably play Pokemon or D&D when they're not knocking heads over LAX. Guessing there's a stack of comic books around here somewhere, too. "LAX doesn't belong to anyone yet."

"True, true," the big guy says. "Verily."

*Okay*, I think, *D&D confirmed.*

"Look, bud," I say. "I don't care who owns the airport. Don't want it. Don't need it. We're just looking to take a plane."

"First, my name is Stephen," elastic band wrist says. "Second, why in the name of the Seven Kingdoms would you need a plane? Can't you fly?"

Jenna smartly hovers off the ground and glides over to the buffet, which is half full of steaming food.

It makes my next lie a little more believable. "You mean, you guys haven't tried flying a plane, yet?"

"Why would we—"

"Because you're not supposed to," Jess says, turning a chair from their table around and sitting on it backwards. She's taken her long-sleeve shirt off and tied it around her waist. Her tight black tank top always looks like it's struggling to hold her ample chest back, and she uses it to her advantage now, leaning forward against the chair back, pushing her cleavage up until she looks like a medieval bar maid.

I nearly burst out laughing when all three of the musketeers ogle her without an ounce of shame or self-awareness.

"Don't break them," I say, sitting down.

Jess leans back, and the spell is broken. Stephen is flushed. Looks confused. The other two look at each other, slight grins on their faces. It's like they've just seen an eclipse for the first time. Probably been a while since they saw an attractive woman in person.

"You guys are breaking rules, right?" Jess asks. "The old rules?"

"We've killed people," the scrawny guy says, trying to impress.

"We've *all* killed people," Jenna says, sitting down with three plates, piled with food. "That's like Draun 101. But it's not *creative*. Crashing a plane into a building full of hiding humans..." She chuckles. "Now *that* is something."

The three of them huff laughs, nervously looking at Jenna-in-Gemma's body, which doesn't need to flash cleavage to enamor them. Her Japanese good looks and smile are wooing the nerds just fine.

Jenna slides two of the plates to Jess and me. Smells amazing. I pick up the plastic fork she's provided, twist up some noodles, and shove them in my mouth. "Oh. My god. Kudos to the chef." I snap my fingers twice and point at the Chinese guy. "Name?"

"James," he says. "And thanks. Worked here for two years before...you know."

"Oh, wow," Jess says, slurping up some noodles. "So good."

I point at scrawny guy. "Name?"

"Sebastian."

"We call him 'Bastion,'" James says, "because it's cooler."

"So cool," Jenna says, giving her eyebrows a double tap and then sucking in a mouthful of noodles in a way that makes me uncomfortable. But the guys...they can't look away.

They are at our mercy.

Well, Jess's and Jenna's mercy.

Stephen clears his throat and attempts to focus. "So, you guys *aren't* collecting territory?" Stephen tries to keep his eyes on me, but they keep flicking back and forth between Jenna's mouth and Jess's chest, and I'm honestly starting to get a little creeped out by the amount of pent-up hormones trapped in these three Draun.

No way this doesn't end in a fight.

They're Draun, nerds or not, and they've fought and killed over this airport. I doubt they've ever looked at the airport the way they are at Jess and Jenna.

"Don't need to," I say. "What's going on out there… What you guys have been doing? It's a waste of time."

"You don't feel the drive?" James asks.

"Feel it," I say. "And overcame it. You keep what you claim, right? Claim and hold. But if you're focusing on taking bits and pieces of this planet, you're thinking *small.* You got to think bigger than that. Like a Mormon."

"Like a Mormon?" Stephen says, and then his eyes widen. "*Planets.*"

I nod. "Entire planets. Millions of them. Populated, Earth-like, and just waiting to be ruled."

"A realm of my own," Stephen says. "Getting excited about the idea."

"Now you're talking," I say. "You just need to get ready, and that means learning how to not just devastate the enemy, but also *rule* over them. That's what the strongest of us are doing. Turning our eyes to the sky. Won't be long before the Visionary finds a way to return our people to the stars."

All three of them do their damnedest to turn away from the ladies and look up at the ceiling.

"JABS," Stephen says. "I propose we refocus our efforts on planetary domination."

"Seconded," James says, still looking up like they can see any stars past the ceiling. Would have been a time when it was impossible to see stars through LA's smog, but that's not a problem anymore. Whole world has stunning views of the stars now.

"Agreed," Bastion says, picking up his paper cup. "I propose we find a planet with three co-equal land masses and rule the planet as a tribune."

The other two don't seem immediately convinced.

"Think about it," Bastion says. "We can have wars. It would be like Warcraft, but real!"

Stephen starts chuckling. It slowly becomes a maniacal laugh. "Yyyes!"

James cheers. "JABS!"

"JABS!" the other two shout, and they clunk their paper cups together before sipping through straws.

I'm about to ask what the hell 'JABS' is, but then I figure it out. "What happened to 'A'?"

"Huh?" Jess says.

"James, A, Bastion, Stephen," I say. "JABS. 'A' is missing."

"Andrew," Stephen says, sounding sad for a moment. "He loved his dogs."

"Until we tied them all up and burned them alive," James says, giggling.

"Yeah, we did!" Bastion adds.

I clench my fists beneath the table. I was beginning to think I might let these guys just walk away. I sold them on the idea of ruling a planet like an old-fashioned snake oil salesman. They probably would have left the airport when their food was done.

"Before we part ways," Stephen says, turning to me. "I noticed your armbands, but I did not recognize them."

I lift my arms up, showing off the gauntlets like I've got nothing to hide.

"Fascinating," he says. "But what are they from? The craftsmanship is magnificent."

"We broke into a props department at the Warner Brother's studio. These were labelled as unused for *Pacific Rim*, but I thought they were awesome. And check this out." I tap the gauntlets' touch screens, bring them to life, randomly tapping on them like they require touch to function. I turn both to the side, showing them the orange light spreading from my wrist to my forearm. When the bars are full, I say, "Fully charged!"

"The LED work is exquisite," Stephen says, all but salivating over the gauntlets. Then he stands to his feet. "Before we take our leave, I'm afraid you'll have to give them to me, along with one of your women. I will be a gentleman and let you choose who may stay and who must come."

The other two stand behind him in solidarity.

I give a nod. "A fair deal." I turn to Jess, give her a wink, and say, "Sorry babe, but you're going with them."

Her jaw drops, but she knows I'm screwing around...and preparing to be deadly. Agreeing to their demands keeps them at ease and, I'm hoping, their shields down. Jenna would know, and when I glance to her, she just seems slightly amused by the whole situation.

"Okay," I say, holding out my forearms toward the trio. "Last thing you need to know about these babies..."

"Hold on a second," Stephen says. "If those were *unused* props from *Pacific Rim*, why would they be stored at the Warner Brothers lot? The props for that film were developed by Industrial Light & Magic. Thus, any unused props would be stored in one of their facilities, not on the WB lot." He glares at me. "Where did you really find them?"

I shrug. "A dog gave them to me."

All three blink in surprise. It's the last thing their minds process as orange light blasts from both gauntlets, quickly severing their heads, while simultaneously forming a scoop shape that whisks them away to the Chang's kitchen and deposits them out of sight.

"That's disturbing," Jess says.

"Sorry," I say. "Wasn't sure how else to—"

"Not that," she says, tapping her ear. "That."

I turn my head and listen. Can hear the three men's bodies still sizzling from their brief contact with my laser light. "Yeah, that's not great." I pick up my plate of food and hustle out of the Chang's. Jess and Jenna do the same, joining me in the large second-floor food court, where the heart-covered asshole of a massive horse statue stares back at us.

I tap my comms, connecting to Gruunlokar. "Clear."

# 27

## PRAXION

I glance to my right, at Siloquin in Torel's body. Sitting beside me, focused on the viewscreen, it's almost possible to think she's Torel. When she doesn't notice my glance and smile back at me, I'm reminded who is in control.

I am intensely uncomfortable with this arrangement. Torel has been taken from me twice now. The evolution of our relationship—intense at first—has been put on hold by a coma and supernatural interlopers. It is difficult to not feel anger toward Siloquin, but I know this was not forced upon Torel.

She agreed to it.

Apologized for it.

And I will forgive all of them…if Torel is returned.

If not… I don't know. For the first time in my life, I think I might feel lost.

Damn this planet and its emotional air. I shake my head. My superiors would have a good laugh at me, knowing that while on the brink of a suicide mission against the Draun, my thoughts were of a single woman.

But here we are. My heart has been conquered and occupied.

"If it would help you focus," Siloquin whispers to me, "you may mount me."

I flinch, glancing around to see who else heard the proposition.

She smiles at me. "It has been a very long time, and you remind me of—"

"No," I say.

"This is your bitch's form," she says. "You would betray no one."

"No," I repeat.

She smiles at me. Swats my arm. "Then I suggest that you either go lick yourself off like an Earth dog or snap out of whatever romantic thoughts have you glancing my way every few seconds. It is irritating."

"Agreed," I say, doubling my efforts to not think about Torel's fate.

"ETA to continental shelf?" she asks, raising her voice.

"Five minutes," Baarfolir says, now in Chirk's pilot station. While MIMIR is currently plotting our course through the ocean depths, he is now in full control of the *Prowler*. Until he reaches Kyno and returns, the ship is his.

Torel—Siloquin—stands and heads for the door. "I am going to relieve myself. If any of you need to do the same, I suggest you do so now."

"Already took a social shit," Chirk says. "Remember?"

"Ahh, yes," Siloquin says. "Like schoolgirls." The doorway separates for her, and then reseals behind her as she exits.

Silence fills the bridge.

Chirk's head slowly swivels toward me. I catch a glint in his eye. A smile on his face.

They heard *everything*.

I breathe the subtlest of laughs.

All at once, Chirk, Baarfolir, Sean, and even Harth burst out laughing. Sean's "Ahuh, ahuh, ahuh," is the loudest.

"Lick yourself like an Earth dog!" Chirk says. "This lady kills me."

"Do you think she was serious?" Harth asks. "About mounting her?"

"Dude," Sean says. "So serious. Who wouldn't want to be mounted by this golden champion stud?"

"The moral implications of offering a body for coupling when it does not belong to you—"

"She wasn't being serious," Baarfolir says. "Siloquin's records mention her penchant for grating humor. It was a frequent sore spot for her superiors in the Guard."

"Good to know," I say, wondering how much more of it will be directed at me.

"Well, it *was* funny," Sean says.

I take a deep breath and let out my tension. "I suppose. Micah would have enjoyed it."

"Speaking of," Chirk says. "About time to get in touch with them. See if LAX is clear."

I give a nod and toggle my comms. "Talon-Two, Talon-Actual, how copy?"

"Talon-Actual, Talon-Two," Gruunlokar responds, sounding calm. "I hear you."

"Sitrep," I say, using Micah's slang for 'Situation Report.'

"Airport is clear," he says. "Thanks to Micah. But our guide was killed during the journey, and his killer is close, and hunting us."

"A Dragnar?" I ask.

"Possibly," he says.

Dragnars are Draun that fully embrace the madness and in doing so lose their minds. They have no real ambition beyond killing. Human, or Draun, it doesn't matter. Dragnars are exceptionally rare and unpredictable, making them dangerous foes. That said, their telekinetic abilities aren't refined. They can't fly. And they don't consider defense. But if they strike, it is always with the intent to kill.

It's what they do to the dead that leaves the real impression. Dismemberment is common. Disembowelment, too. They arrange bodies in places others are sure to see them. So, they know, without a doubt, who committed the atrocity and that *they* will be next.

If Gruunlokar believes the Draun tracking them is a Dragnar, they must have discovered their ally displayed in this manner. I don't bother asking.

We're nearly there, and when Dragnars are concerned, safety is always in numbers.

"We will be on site in three minutes," I tell him. "Keep your comms live and we will land close."

"Copy that," he says. "We are inside the structure. I suggest landing on the roof just south of my current position to ensure you do not break through the glass ceiling and crush the...horse."

"Understood," I say, and then hear barking in the background. It's a joyful sound. Like pups wrestling.

"What is that?" I ask.

"New friends," he says. "Earth dogs that belonged to Arlo—the man who was killed. They've bonded with Micah and are playing with Grover, who is half their size."

"*Half* their size?"

"Think Harth, but on all fours...with my face."

"Horrifying."

"Funny," he says, not giving me even a hint of a laugh. I'm sure he's smiling, though, so I count it as a win.

When Chirk gets up from his station and snaps his fingers at me twice, I know it's time to go. He jumps on the comms, "All right, wrap it up, ladies. We'll be on the ground in less time than it takes Harth to shit."

"You time me when I defecate?" Harth asks, amused.

"Hell, no," Chirk says. "No one has that long."

"My movements are substantial."

"Dude," Sean says, joining the conversation as they move toward the doorway. "This one time, I was at summer camp. And you know what it's like, barely any time to drop a deuce, so I ended up holding it for a whole week."

"That sounds unwise," Harth says, as they exit the bridge and the door seals behind them, leaving just me...

And Baarfolir, head hung low.

"Are you unwell?" I ask.

"They didn't say goodbye," he says.

"It is a custom of the Kyno Corps," I say. "When a solitary member of the team runs a solo mission, we never say goodbye, because there is no doubt we will see you again. Saying goodbye...curses the mission."

"Please tell me no one really believes that superstition," he says. "It sounds far too illogical for any Kynolari to—"

He notes my smile and stops in his tracks. "I have never said goodbye to a teammate in your situation…and have always seen them again. To me, that's evidence."

He smiles and shakes his head. "In all my years, I'd never have imagined the great Praxion, hero of the Great War, would partake in such…nonsense."

"Maybe so," I say, backing away toward the door. "Baarfolir, the bridge is yours."

"Thank you," he starts and then has an epiphany. "You said, 'part of the team.' About me. About *us!* Does that mean—"

The door slides apart behind me.

"A discussion for when you return," I say, and then turn away before either of us says goodbye inadvertently. Door sealed behind me, I head for the workshop's airlock. I tap my comms and connect with Harth.

"Launch status?" I ask.

"Orange."

"Everyone present?"

"Just waiting on you," Harth says. "Siloquin was here when we arrived. I get the feeling she is annoyed that you are late."

"By seconds," I say.

"Perhaps it is Chirk's and Sean's banter," he adds. "Yes, now that I'm listening, it's most definitely their banter."

I enter the workshop and wave to Harth, standing by the airlock hatch. The contraption carrying us to Earth's surface rests inside. This is my first time seeing it, and I have no idea what I'm looking at.

"What *am* I looking at?" I ask.

"A surprise," he says, and smiles. "For when we need it most. Most of what you're seeing here is a containment unit designed to bring us down to the ground, and then look unassuming until the time is right."

"Thank you…for being vague. Exactly what I was hoping for when launching a two pronged mission."

He laughs and pats my shoulder. "Your sarcasm is noted and ignored. Now, take a seat and strap yourself down."

Siloquin gives me a nod as I pass by and take the seat to her right. Harth's containment unit is a broad cylinder, like a can of Earth soup. Five crude seats have been welded to the exterior, each with safety belts that I suspect are there to keep us from falling off rather than making us safe in the event of a crash.

After tightening my belt, I activate comms so everyone on the *Prowler* can hear me. "Kyno Corps, mission status?"

"Orange," Chirk says.

"Orange," Harth says.

"Tropicana," Sean says, followed by a quickly whispered conversation with Chirk, and then, "Sorry. Orange."

"If 'Orange' means I am prepared to engage the enemy," Siloquin says, "Orange. *Always* orange."

"Orange," Baarfolir says.

"MIMIR," I say, "Initiate sequence: Chirk 0734."

"Understood," MIMIR says. "Beginning sequence…now."

# 28

## GRUUNLOKAR

"Jenna," I say. "With me."

She stands up from the table where she and others are finishing the food prepared by the Draun that Micah dispatched. I did not see what happened, but the scent of scorched human flesh lingers in the air. His control over the laser light emanating from his gauntlets is like nothing I've seen before. And it gives me hope.

But I do not depend on hope. I prepare for it to fail.

"Yeah?" Jenna says.

"Come," I say, breaking open a stairwell door that leads down to the first floor, and up to the roof.

"Everything okay?" she asks.

"The others are arriving shortly. I thought this might be a good time to... connect. Just the two of us."

"To find our mojo," she says.

I glance back at her as I climb the steps. "I do not know what *mojo* is."

"It's like, a lot of different things," she says. "Depending on the context. For us, it's like our flow...our ability to sync. To be *in sync*, but not like the boy band. Not that you know about boy bands. Sorry. Rambling."

"Mm," I grunt. "But you are also correct. If I am given the chance to slay the Visionary from a distance, I cannot fail this time."

"And that depends on me," she says.

"It would seem so."

"I'm sorry," she says. "That I haven't gotten the hang of it yet. I'm not the me that you knew before."

"That is a good thing," he says. "She did...horrific things. But at her core, she was still the person I'm speaking to now. It's the only reason she was able to connect with me then. I hope the same is true now."

"What's different?" she asks, "I mean, aside from her being a psycho and power hungry?"

"When I first met your older self, she had been Draun for ten years. She was powerful and confident. Believed in herself and her ability to take the throne from the Visionary. But she was also wise enough to create a backup plan."

"Me," Jenna says.

"And she entrusted *me*, with you." I break the second door's lock and push it open to reveal the airport's rooftop. It's a flat surface littered with metal boxes containing machinery and windows, with various levels and a gravel surface that crunches under foot. Before stepping out into the night, I scan the area with my eyes, ears, and nose. Detecting no nearby threats, I exit the airport and glance up at the stars.

I've seen a lot of night skies since our arrival on Earth, but this view of the heavens still feels strange and unfamiliar.

"Do you miss it?" she asks, standing beside me, looking up. "Your home?"

"I do not think about what I might or might not miss."

"Well, that's—"

"Depressing," I say. "I know."

"Then why do you—"

"Depression in the midst of battle all but guarantees your demise, or that of your teammates. It is unacceptable."

"And those doohickies—" She motions at my regulators. "—don't help with emotions?"

"They do," I admit, "but they cannot subvert one's will."

"You think depressed people *want* to feel depressed?" she asks.

"Sometimes, when everything is bleak, and war has numbed the spirit, even depression can feel like an escape."

"Huh," she says. "If you're telling me to not think about my father—"

"I would never." I look down at her. "But I am wondering if you will allow me to stand in his place. For a time."

She gives a nervous laugh.

"You want to…adopt me?"

"The trust between us needs to be an unshakable bond. I can think of no stronger bond than that of father and daughter, even if they are not formally assigned roles."

"Huh," she says, eyes still on the stars. "That's…" She turns her head away, but I can smell her tears. And her intentions.

"Thank you," I say.

"For what?" She sniffs. Wipes her nose. "I haven't said anythi—hold on, did you smell me?"

"Not intentionally," I say.

"You know how unfair that is?" she asks. "Sniffing what people are feeling?"

"Does it change your answer?" I ask.

She turns to me, tears still brewing. "I accept."

I'm caught off guard by my smile. This is a place I have never pictured myself being, nor a role I ever considered filling. I…am a killer. All that I have to offer leads to death. But that is what Jenna—and this world—needs more than anything else, and I am happy to provide it.

I'm surprised for a second time when she hugs me. "Thank *you*."

We linger there for a moment, letting the bond between us weave together more tightly.

"My father would have liked you," she says. "He was kind of a no-nonsense guy, too."

"He was a good man," I say.

"How do you know that?" she asks.

"The proof stands before me: strong, noble, willing to risk her life."

She smiles. "I also became a monster."

"That Jenna didn't have me," I say. "Now, let's move on before someone hears us speaking and my reputation is irrevocably tarnished."

She laughs. "Move on to what, old man?"

"West," I say motioning to the clear view we have from the airport roof, stretching out to the moonlit ocean and the infinite stars above.

"Okay, pretty view, but—"

"One minute," I say. "Be patien—"

A low growl spins me around. Crip and Blood have joined us without me seeing or hearing them until they were on top of us. They even managed to stay down wind. And their attention is not on us.

Hackles raised, they lower themselves to the roof, disappearing in the shadows, ears and eyes locked on to something to the east.

"Talon-Actual, Talon-Two, ETA?"

"Thirty seconds," Praxion responds.

"LZ might be compromised."

"Can you uncompromise it?"

"TBD," Jenna says and looks up at me. "But we're going to try."

She places her hand on my back, the way she does when we're trying to encase a shard in a telekinetic shield. "Find him."

I raise my sniper gauntlet and shift my view of the world to its scope. I sweep back and forth, in and out, switching between spectrums. I find a target through the thermal view. "Two hundred feet out, behind the air conditioning unit."

"Can you hit him?" she asks.

I look at the small strip of yellow visible underneath the unit. His feet. Shifting about. "He's moving a lot. 50/50 hit or miss."

"Take the shot," she says, closing her eyes. "I'll try to help."

I take aim at the machine's core. I have no concern about the shard's ability to punch through the primitive metals, but I will likely need to take several shots before striking our target. And there might not be time to finish the job before the others arrive, seconds from now.

"Ready," she says.

"On one," I say. "Three, two..."

As I mentally pull the trigger, I feel a surge of energy flow up my spine, down my arm, and out through the gauntlet. It's intense, but quicker than a thought.

And the result is immediate.

The air conditioning unit implodes as though struck by a boulder moving at the speed of a shard. Splintered metal bursts away, matching my projectile's speed and shredding the target hidden behind the machine. He doesn't have time to scream in surprise, pain, or fear. One moment, he exists, the next, he is erased.

My vision snaps back to normal as both dogs launch across the rooftop, chasing down their fallen enemy. I glance at Jenna. "What did you do?"

She looks disgusted by the result. "Gave it a telekinetic shield. Like we were trying."

"That is *not* what we were trying," I say.

She winces away from the scene, looking disturbed by the sight of what we've done. I feel bad for her, but we can debate the morality of killing later.

Motion draws my eyes back out to the ocean in time to see the *Prowler* emerge from the depths without creating a ripple. It's coming straight for us, gliding silently as it banks upward. The ship spins to the side when it reaches a forty-five degree angle. Gravity pulls a large metal tube from the workshop's airlock, dumping it just five hundred feet above our heads. As the tube falls, the *Prowler* angles up and then becomes a blur, launching toward space. The ship becomes a streak and then fades from sight.

I step back as gravity discs, attached to the bottom of the tube, slow its descent. The landing isn't what I'd call graceful, but Praxion is smiling when they touch down. Probably just happy to be alive, strapped to the outside of a tube.

"Whoo! Yes!"

Sounds like Sean made it down, too.

"All good?" Praxion asks, unbuckling.

"Dragnar neutralized," I say. "I think. Still need to confir—"

A thump turns my eyes down. I find Crip standing over an arm he has dropped at my feet. Blood carries a footless leg.

"Confirmation received," I say.

"That was fast for a Dragnar," Praxion says, sounding impressed.

"Had help." I motion to Jenna.

"Excellent." He nods and taps his comms. "Baarfolir," he says, ignoring all communications protocols. I tap into the conversation.

"I'm here!" Baarfolir responds. "Under heavy laser fire!"

The connection crackles.

"Taking damage!" he shouts. "I don't—if you can—*"

More crackling. And then silence.

"Baarfolir?" Praxion asks. "*Baarfolir?*"

All eyes turn to the sky, but none of them can zoom in like me. Following the ship's last trajectory, I zoom farther and farther out until I spot a bright burst of infrared energy.

The kind made by an explosion in space.

Praxion doesn't need to ask.

He sees the look on my face.

Then clenches his fists. "Fuck."

# 29

## MICAH

Dogs don't cry. Doesn't mean they're not sad, they just don't express it like people. Where people might wail and shout and make a scene that's more about us than the dead, dogs internalize their despair and grow quiet. Best thing you can do for them is hold them close and go through the pain with them.

I sit in a stairwell side-by-side with Grover, arm wrapped around his back, absentmindedly rubbing his scruffy neck. We sit like that for several minutes before he feels comfortable talking.

And this is where our master-dog relationship goes into uncharted territory. "We know what happen?"

I don't know how much to hold back. Not sure what he can and cannot handle. We've been through the shit together. He deserves the truth, but I need him to push through it. Past it. Everyone on the team does. Gruunlokar, Praxion, and Harth are dealing with the *Prowler*'s destruction the same way that I am—later. They're professionals. Torel, who is apparently possessed by the soul of a long-dead Kynolari named Siloquin—some kind of badass warrior, with no ties to Baarfolir—is just waiting, arms crossed, ready to throw down with our enemies.

Poppy didn't know Baarfolir well, but she's been on Earth the longest and is quite small. She doesn't want us to see, but this turn of events is a blow. I was happy to see Chirk attempting to comfort her, despite also being hit hard by Baarfolir's demise. They'd grown close, and I wonder if Chirk is comforting Poppy, or if it's the other way around.

"It was the Draun, buddy," I say. "They got him."

Kind of vague, but I'm trying to be.

"*Prowler*...explode?"

I nod. "It did."

"But Baarfolir not dead, right?"

He's gutting me. "Grove...if the *Prowler* exploded in space..."

"He not dead!"

I hold him closer. Tighter. He starts whimpering, puffing his jowls with each breath. Breaks my heart to see him suffering.

I lean my head against his. "I'm sorry, Grove. Baarfolir is gone." It's probably not fair to word it in a way that leaves a nugget of doubt, but speaking the words with certainty might sneak past my defenses and get me all emotional, too. I'm not inhuman, but we need to keep our shit together or Baarfolir won't be the last of us to fall.

"Why?" he asks, and I'm pretty sure it's rhetorical. "Why Baarfolir die? He small. He old. He nice! *Always* nice! No hurt anyone. I don't—" He snarls, growls, and then lets out a string of angry barks laced with pain. He's furious. Never seen him so angry.

He settles back down to a whimper and then looks up at me. "Maybe not explode? Maybe leave ship?"

"No reason to think so," I say. I want to give him hope, but that would just extend the pain. "Gruunlokar said—"

"Gruunlokar doesn't know *everything*," he says. "Baarfolir smart. Maybe he…maybe…" Grover lets out a long sigh, deflating under my arm and leaning his heavy body against me. "I sad."

I just continue petting, letting him express.

"My chest hurts."

"Mine, too," I admit.

"You know why?" he asks.

I shake my head. Better to keep him talking and expressing. Usually the only way to get through these things.

"We do this before," he says. "But not here. Not on these steps. Home steps."

He transports me to another time. Another place. The memory is sharp. Potent. We sat at the top of the staircase at home, same as we are now. It was after the funeral for Mom and Dad. We were both sad and lost. But we had each other, and that was the moment I promised him I'd never leave him.

"Remember what you said?" he asks, looking up at me.

A lump forms in my throat.

I clear it and say, "Ain't nothing we can't overcome together."

Tears fill my eyes, and I find myself reeling, leaning over into his scruff, weeping for Baarfolir, for my parents, and for the rest of the god damned human race who are either dead, remade as monsters, or hiding underground hoping that a pack of people and dogs will save them.

When I calm and lean up, I find Grover's big brown eyes looking up at me, his brow furrowed in concern. After I wipe my tears, he puts a paw on my knee. "Micah. We still together."

I nod, placing my hand on his. "We are."

"We still love."

"All the time."

"Then we can do this, too," he says.

"Hold on a second," I say, letting out a laugh. "I was comforting you. How did we get all spun around?"

"No spin," he says, confused by the concept. "We together, but two pieces. Connected. Feel same."

Could that be true? Grover and I are connected in ways that even the Kynolari don't fully understand. My ability to experience the world through his senses is beyond their science. Could our emotions be entangled now, as well?

"I think so," Grover says, answering the question in my thoughts.

The idea of it buoys me. And in turn, him. Doesn't take long before our mutually rising emotional boats bring us up out of our Slough of Despond and back to the surface, where things look a little less impossible.

"Okay," I tell him. "That was the fastest rollercoaster ride through the five stages of grief I've ever experienced."

"I try rollercoaster?" he asks.

"A metaphorical rollercoaster."

He squints at me.

"Never mind." I scruff his head. "We should find the others. Won't be long before troub—"

Jess opens the stairwell door, bursting in.

"You see?" I say. "I say 'trouble' and she just—"

"Shut up," she says. "We have incoming."

I'm on my feet, leaving my jokes behind. "How many?"

"Don't know."

"Where from?"

"No clue," she says. "I was just sent to get you." She holds the door open, and we exit back onto the airport's second floor. Praxion and Gruunlokar are wrangling the rest of the team, gathering them by the P.F. Chang's horse.

I look down to Grover and motion to Jess. "Stick with her. Keep her safe."

He cracks a tongue waggling smile and shifts from my side to hers. I head for Praxion. "What's going on?"

"Incoming," Gruunlokar answers. "From north, south, and east. Far too many to resist. To fight is to die."

"Tracking the *Prowler*'s launch back to this location would have been a simple task," Harth says, standing at the horse's ample backside. "We should have already departed."

I stand beside the big Kynolari, watching as he pries up the heart covering the horse's asshole. But where there should have been a puckered sphincter, there is a hand scanner.

Shit.

"Don't suppose anyone hung onto Stuchbury's hand?" I ask.

"A hand?" Jenna asks. "Who is Stuchbury, and why do you need his hand?"

"Security measure," Harth says. "Stuchbury was human, but an ally of the Draun."

"So, then we need a Draun hand?" Jenna asks. "Maybe the guy on the roof? I could—"

"No," Harth says. "We…need *your* hand."

"But I'm not—"

"You can do what they do," Harth says, "and your body belonged to a woman—"

"Yeah, yeah, I get it," Jenna says. She's definitely not happy about it. Must be hard knowing that every part of your past self and current body had given themselves over to evil. But it's also a blessing. Without her, we might not have a way to use the Leap Node hidden beneath this horse.

Jenna heads for the back of the horse.

"All hands," Sean says. "Pick a spot and think happy thoughts."

"Anything else?" she asks.

"Japan," I tell her.

"Anywhere specific?"

Praxion shakes his head. "The only two node locations we know of are compromised. It would be dangerous to return."

"Might be dangerous to choose at random," I point out. "Also, Japan is a pretty big place. If the Visionary is in the Imperial Palace…"

"So, Tokyo," Jenna says. "Big place. Lots of places to hide. Probably a few node things, yeah?"

"No idea," I say.

She looks to Gruunlokar. He shrugs.

"Cool," she says. "So cool. Nothing like a total lack of intel to start a world-saving mission."

"No plan survives contact with the enemy. So why bother?" I give her a smile, and she shakes her head. Places her hand on the horse-ass hand scanner.

She glances around the group, ensuring that each and every one of us, including the dogs, have a hand on the horse. "Always wanted to see Japan." She closes her eyes, focusing, and we slip from one part of the world—to another.

# 30

## CHIRK

"Okay," Jenna says from within a sudden darkness. "Did the lights just go out?"

"Smells different," I say, but can't see a thing, even with my Kynolari eyes. "Wherever we are, there isn't any light seeping in."

"A lot of synthetic plastics and rubber," Harth says, pin-pointing the odor.

"A factory?" Praxion guesses.

"How does this thing work, anyway?" Jenna asks.

"No one told you?" I ask.

"When a leap node is tethered to another, there is no choice but to move between them," Harth explains. "But in this case, there is an interconnected network of nodes allowing the user, or users, to choose the destination simply by thinking about it."

"So, like, if I was thinking about Antarctica, that's where we'd be?" she asks.

Jess laughs. "Please tell me you weren't—"

"Nope," Jenna says. "Tokyo. But nowhere specific."

"Weapons hot," Praxion says. "If we come under attack, try to keep it quiet. If we are in Japan, we are deep in enemy territory. No need to stir up a Dungt nest."

"Copy that," I say.

"I do not know what a 'dungt' is," Siloquin says through Torel.

"Like an Earth bee, but the size of a coconut." I draw my twin mini-railguns and watch as the others' gauntlets charge to full power.

"Illuminate," Praxion says, and the team switches on an array of head, shoulder, and gauntlet lights. Our surroundings are lit up so brightly that I need to squint and shield my eyes for a moment. Then I see it—a warehouse, full of wooden crates and strangely shaped objects covered in tarps. That includes the large statue we all had our hands on when we arrived.

"Ooh," Sean says, eyes wide. "'We have top men working on it right now.'" He turns like he's playing another person, and I realize that's exactly what he's doing. "'Who?'" He turns again. "'Top. Men.'"

"I have a feeling this isn't that kind of warehouse," Micah says, starting to lift the tarp covering the local jump node statue.

Gruunlokar whistles and clicks his mouth at Blood and Crip, the way Micah did, and apparently their previous owner before him. They seem to understand

and bolt away down two different aisles. Gruunlokar steps back and fades into the shadows. Nothing strange there. He's just being his cautious self.

"How could you know that?" Sean asks Micah.

"Well, for starters," he says, "this statue is pink, and I'm pretty sure—" Micah pulls the tarp away revealing a statue of a giant pink erect penis.

"What the fuck is this bullshit?" I ask, thrusting my hands while giving Jenna the stink eye.

"What fuck is this bullshit?" Grover says, attempting to repeat the phrase while imitating my indignation.

"You," I say to him. "That was pretty good." He wags his tail. I turn to Jenna. "And seriously, the hell were you thinking about?"

"Umm," Poppy says, raising a hand. "Yeah, this one might be on me."

Mouth agape, I turn toward her. "This is a human dick."

"Well, I wasn't exactly thinking about the Jolly Pink Giant's pecker," she says. "Just…it's been a while, okay?"

It occurs to me in that singular delicious moment that, thanks to our similar sizes, Poppy was standing next to me, our hands just inches from each other on the horse leg that became a dick, while she was thinking about… *Could it be?*

I open my mouth to ask, and she gives me a whack under my chin. "Don't you say it. Don't you even think it."

"Okay, okay," I say, lifting my mini-railguns up in supplication. "Geez, lady. The fuck was that chin whack, anyway?"

"Seen humans do that to dogs," she says. "Dogs hate it. Wanted to see if it worked on Kynolari, too." She gives me a grin. "Question answered."

"I hate to say this," Jess says, looking up at the megalithic penis. "Like *really* hate to say this, but…I know where we are." She looks at Micah. "Please don't judge me."

"We're way past that, babe," he says.

When they smile at each other, I roll my eyes and smack Micah's leg, "Ugh, you two need to hurry up and have pups so she gains a lot of weight and doesn't keep you distracted all the time."

"If I gain weight in the same places my mother did," Jess says, "then it's just going to get worse. Also, we're in Kawasaki, just south of Tokyo. And this…" She motions to the giant pink junk. "This is part of the Kanamara Matsuri."

"Which is?" I ask.

"The Festival of the Steel Phallus," she says.

"The patriarchy is strong in Japan," Jenna says, rolling her eyes.

"It's a fertility festival," Jess says. "Which became important in Japan after World War II, and more recently because 'Why have kids when you can crank one out to your anime pillow?' But all the money went to HIV research—"

"Which doesn't matter at all," I say. "So, can we get out of this sausage festival now?"

"Gruunlokar?" Praxion asks into his comms.

"Clear," comes the reply. "Warehouse is secure. Doors locked. No signs of occupation."

"Nor here," Torel's voice says over the comms.

I spin around looking for her, but she's a ghost. Didn't even hear her sneak away. I close my eyes and focus, sensing her on the north end of the building. Gruunlokar is to the south.

When I open my eyes, I catch Praxion doing the same. Then he says, "Rendezvous on the north end."

"Copy that," Gruunlokar says.

"Going to be hard to keep an eye on Torel if her current operator can disappear without us noticing," I say to Praxion as the team moves toward the north end.

Harth lingers behind with us, nodding in agreement. "It will be hard to stay attuned to her whereabouts while evading or engaging with the Draun. Ensuring Torel's continued safety might require endangering all of us."

Praxion nods. Grim.

"I'll speak to Siloquin," he says. "She is a good soldier. Perhaps she'll follow orders."

"Or start giving them," I say. "I mean, she's been around a *lot* longer than you. She might outrank you."

"Glad to see you've decided to be helpful." He delivers the sentence with a stoic expression, but I know him well enough to hear the subtle tinge of sarcasm.

"Doing my best to be my best," I say.

I hustle along, catching up to the others. "Yo, Sean. Strap-on time!" I leap into the air, spin around, and expect to be caught by Sean's hands and then fastened to the baby carrier. Instead, I roll across his back and topple to the floor. He's doubled over laughing.

"Slick," Poppy says, shaking her head.

"Sorry, my dude," Sean says. "It was just…your choice of words…ahhh. 'Strap-on time.'"

"What?" I say, feeling pretty annoyed that I don't understand.

Sean glances to the side, where a wooden case has broken open and spilled its contents—plastic wrapped dongs that may or may not also be lollipops. "Context, bro."

"Real mature," I say, holding back a laugh. "Ha. Ha. So funny. Now, pick me up."

I lift my hands over my head. Sean hoists me up, spins me around, and secures me to the carrier like a pro.

More like it.

Gruunlokar arrives last, and silently, making me jump when he says, "Hey," from the shadows above us. I jump again when Crip and Blood arrive just as silently. Granted, I don't make a hell of a lot of noise when I walk, but all three of them are like thirty of me. You'd think they'd be a little less stealthy.

We've gathered by a set of double doors at the north end. Micah's opening one of the two, keeping it slow and quiet. He leans his head out of the door for a moment, then leans back inside and closes it. "Clear. Some destruction. Purple glow looks like the sun just set, so we've got some time to operate in the dark. No contacts in sight, but that doesn't mean they're not out there."

"How far are we from the Imperial Palace?" Praxion asks Jess.

"Right," she says, "let me just access Google Maps on my gauntlet." She pretends to push button. "Beep, boop, beep. Yep, I have no frikken idea. I'm not Japanese, you know."

"You seemed to know a lot about Japanese penises," Praxion says. "I assumed you'd also have knowledge of more useful information."

Jess gives him squinty eyes. Then says, "It's a few cities north. Maybe four. But who knows how much distance that actually is. Japanese cities could be smaller or larger than ours. But I think it's close enough that we can sneak our way there by daylight."

Praxion looks to Micah, conferring with their eyes. When Micah gives a nod, Praxion returns it. "We move out as a group. In line and tight. Don't make a sound, stay in the dark, and we might survive the journey. Micah, you're on point. I'll bring up the rear. If we encounter the enemy, you all know what you're good at." He grins. "If this isn't our finest hour, it will be our worst."

When he finishes speaking, we all just stare at him.

"Not your peppiest pep talk, boss," I say.

"It was meant to sober you," he says. "We might face the Visionary himself before the night is through. I do not expect all of us to survive, if any of us do."

"Right," I say. "Well then, mission accomplished. Sobered up and dick shriveled. Now, let's go—"

A distant rumble cuts me off. Everyone with mobile ears turns them toward the door.

"It sounds like a human vehicle," Harth says. "Something large."

"The Draun don't need trucks," Sean says.

Micah opens the door and looks for just a moment. Then he opens it the rest of the way, revealing a road that leads straight toward the warehouse. In the background, a nightmare horde of biologics. All shapes and sizes. They're chasing down a single human vehicle, its bright lights nearly blinding.

When a glowing orb of plasma shoots past the vehicle, detonating inside the first floor of an apartment building, we get a clear view of what's coming.

"Is that..." Jenna says. "Is that a panda?"

# 31

## MICAH

I stick in place, unable to look away from the spectacle racing toward me. It's like a fever dream combining *Willy Wonka and the Chocolate Factory* and *Mad Max*. The familiar Panda Bus races toward us, but it's been modified, weaponized, and armored.

Behind it is a writhing mob of biologics.

Skitterlings race beside the vehicle, throwing themselves into it, only to be chewed up by the spiked wheels. Two Helions are at the back, side-by-side, their dual tardigrade bodies too wide for the road, plowing through the buildings on either side, spraying blue-lit debris in every direction.

Between those behemoths and the small Skitterlings is a collection of hulking Gobi, long-limbed Tyrne, and the writhing tentacles of three Platamots. Unlike the unfinished versions of these monsters we fought last time we visited Tokyo, these are fully formed and hard to look at.

By human standards, alien life is mostly nasty looking. Except for the Kynolari. They're still adorable, even if they're also badasses.

Not that any of these things are actually alive.

Which means I don't need to hold back...except, we are deep in Draun territory. How long until one of them hears the commotion? And if they get a flare off here, we're toast.

We've already lost any semblance of stealth, but if there's one thing we're good at, it's rolling with the punches as they come.

I look back to Sean and Chirk. "What do we do?"

"Hell, if I know," Chirk says, almost amused by the tidal wave of destruction coming our way. "But I'm guessing it rhymes with...I don't know. What rhymes with 'retreat?'"

"Well, I'm taking a pic, cause that's totally epic." Sean pulls out his phone. Starts snapping photos. Zooms in. "Yo! Haruto!" He waves. "Guys, it's actually Haruto!"

Praxion pushes past the team filling the double doors, watching the madness rushing toward us, still a few blocks off. "There are too many to engage without drawing more attention."

Like me, he's more worried about the Draun than biologics.

"Just mow them down," Sean says. "We got the firepower. We got the skills."

Praxion shakes his head. "The moment we use Kynolari weaponry, the Visionary will know we are here. The longer our presence remains unknown, the longer we will survive."

"So, we run," Sean says. "I'm even better at that."

"We cannot leave an ally to perish. We owe Haruto our lives. It is a debt that will be repaid." He looks back into the warehouse. "Quickly, search the area. Find something to—"

"Got it," Jess says, standing over a pried-open crate. While we've been talking about how to handle the situation, she's been looking for a solution. She tilts the wooden box in our direction, revealing two heavy blocks of fireworks.

I rush to her side, picking up one of the two blocks. "Just like the battleship fireworks in Ashland, yeah?"

She nods. "Exactly what I was thinking."

The others part for us, allowing us to carry the blocks just outside the open doors and position them to fire straight down the street. They'll be here in seconds, so there's no time to waste. I heat the claws on my right hand Hell Hound gauntlet and touch them to every single wick extending out of both cases. They're designed to fire in sequence, but that's not exactly what I have in mind.

The first firework launches a moment later, whistling down the street, striking the Panda Bus head on and bursting up and around it with a boom. I swear I can hear Haruto shouting at me, but there's no time to switch strategies. After a quick adjustment the rest of the wicks burn down to nothing, and a glorious pink and gold display is launched down the street. Hundreds of fireworks, the force of them pushing Jess and I back until Sean and Harth help support us.

"I fail to see how this will not attract the Draun," Harth says over the racket.

"Oh, it will," I say, "but they won't know it's us, right?"

He grunts and adjusts Jess's aim, sweeping the fireworks across the street, just over the Panda Bus.

And then, all at once, the fireworks burst. It's a magnificent display, twenty feet off the ground, unleashing hot white spheres of light that *thump* through the air and my chest when they explode. White hot sprays of twirling, whistling fireworks twist up into the air. Pretty sure they're meant to resemble sperm. But the *coup de grâce* are the bright pink explosions. Down low and congested by smoke and the enemy horde, they're hard to make out. But a few of them deflect into the air, bursting to form massive majestic pink penises.

The blatant fireworks display will look more like a Draun dicking around than an elite enemy force infiltrating the conquered island nation.

The effect on the enemy is hard to make out. There's as much smoke as there are colorful displays. I lose sight of the biologics—and the Panda Bus. Good news is, they can't see us. Bad news, the bus might plow into a building or a telephone pole.

Emerging from the luminous, exploding clouds like a water-birthed child, the Panda Bus launches from the street trailing pink and white lines of smoke. Loud laughter emerges from the bus, followed by a string of Japanese curses directed at the horde.

The bus heads straight toward us, and just as I think it's about to careen through us, it skids to a stop, the vehicle's back end swinging around so its side is facing us. The door opens to reveal Haruto, smiling wide. His uniform is gone, replaced by black fatigues. There are three scars on his cheek. Really thin, like he was cut by a scalpel. Tortured. But free now.

"Micah-San!" he shouts, and then smiles wide when he sees all the Kynolari and dogs behind me. "My friends! Come with me if you want to live!"

Before I can consider the request, a charging Helion emerges from the smoke, flanked by dozens of Skitterlings, their sharp talons tapping over the pavement. No way we're all getting on the bus and speeding away in time. Haruto sees my eyes dart to his side and has a look for himself.

He slaps an ominous looking red button on the dash. Don't remember it being there before... Then he turns back to us, waving us away. "Run away if you want to live! Run!" He passes between us in a blur. And he's moving so fast that he pulls the rest of us, without question, into his wake.

Haruto is faster than I'd have guessed, sprinting through the warehouse, fully understanding how much danger we're in.

As he runs past the giant pink dildo, he leaps up and gives the left nut a slap. "Onegai shimasu!"

No one else bothers. We just run. Because each and every one of us knows what a Helion can do, especially if it's experienced. They learn from every battle they, or one of their brethren have survived. They'll know how to counter everything we've done to defeat them up to this point. And whatever that might be, it won't be enough to stop all the others—especially if we're holding back on our gauntlet usage.

Jenna might be the only one of us who can fight back, and I doubt she could handle the army on her own. As powerful as she might be, she is still human. Telekinesis is like sprinting. Uses a lot of energy and it takes a toll. Too much and she'll get mental cramps...or something like that. I've never asked what it feels like. But I've seen her run out of steam. Same way I do with extended gauntlet use. The force of will it takes to sustain a gauntlet charge can leave me feeling numb and off balance if I'm not careful.

Haruto slides to a stop at the far end.

He lifts a radio from his body armor—the kind cops use—and speaks into it. “Denji! Atarashii nigemichi ga hitsuyō da, toho de!”

The sentence starts in Japanese, but translation services kick in, and I hear his words in English. “Denji! I need a new escape route, on foot!”

“Nearest entry point is south. Across the Keikyu Daishi Line and 409 to the 7-Eleven. Between the store’s backside and Daishi Nishimachi Jido Park is a manhole. It’s a mostly unused route, but you’ll be out of sight. Once you’re inside, head west. Poke when you reach Route 15, and I’ll guide you from there.”

“Hai!” Haruto says with a nod, then waves us on faster. “Come, come, come! Mou! I thought dogs and dog-people would be fast, but no, here you are taking sweet time when bus is about to explode!”

“What?” I ask, surprised by the revelation. “You never said anything about—”

“When!” he shouts, as I slam into the rear door, shoving it open for the others. “When I tell you? When running for life? When calling for escape? I just stop and say, ‘Oh, haroh, Micah-San, I tell you whole plan that won’t work now because I took time to explain plan.’”

As the last of the team—Jess, Sean, and Chirk, race past us, Haruto and I release the door and sprint after the others.

“Go, go, go!” Haruto shouts. “Straight across train tracks and freeway! To 7-Eleve—”

A shockwave reduces the warehouse behind us to splinters and launches Haruto and me into the air as a fireball chases us. I see the others, knocked to the ground below us, all alive and moving. But Haruto and I are about to pull a Greatest American Hero landing on the train tracks.

And just then, when the reality that one or both of us might be about to bite the dust hits me, a giant pink dildo passes between us. Instead of shouting in fear, Haruto and I embrace whatever comes next by laughing hysterically.

# 32

### PRAXION

When I lift my head off the pavement, the last thing I expect to hear is laughter. I recognize Micah's belly laugh before I see him sail past overhead. A moment later, Haruto is laughing as well. And they're both pointing to the large pink fertility phallus spiraling between them.

They're likely going to die on impact, but I can't help chuckling as well.

And not just because it's a funny sight, but because their laughter in the face of certain doom is contagious.

And brave.

They arc toward the train tracks, where they will certainly crack open their skulls, snap their spines, or be rendered otherwise immobile and easy targets for the biologics that will storm through the warehouse's flaming wreckage.

I want to stand and fight. To defend my friends until the end. But there is a bigger picture to consider. The fate of humanity and all the people living in tunnels beneath Earth's cities. As well as the future fate of Kyno, should the Draun escape this world.

I cringe as they topple downward. Micah is upside down. Going to land on his head.

Averting my eyes wouldn't honor their deaths, so I watch.

The phallus strikes first, clanging against a railroad track and shattering into three large pieces, which bound and roll onto the freeway beyond.

But Micah and Haruto...

They've stopped. Both of them. Just inches from contact.

Haruto reaches down to the train track with which he was about to collide. "Yatta!" He turns to Micah as they both begin rotating. "Micah-San! We are floating."

"Not exactly floating," Micah says, and motions to Jenna.

I turn to find her a few feet away, still on her stomach. Blood trickles down her head from where it struck the ground. She's been dazed, but she still had the clarity of mind to telekinetically catch the two men.

"Ahh!" Haruto shouts, now flailing around and trying to escape.

"It's okay," Micah tells him. "She's one of us."

"She is Draun!" Haruto says, thrusting his hands out at her. "She will tear our limbs off and drink our blood!"

"First," Jenna says, pushing herself up onto her feet. "Gross." She walks closer to Haruto, who remains hovering while Micah is placed on his feet and released. "Second, if I were one of them, why would I have saved you? Why would I be running around with a bunch of dogs being chased by biologics? Huh? I can do what they can, that's it. I'm still a normal person. Understood?"

Haruto looks to me as I join Jenna. I give him a confident smile and nod. "She's with us."

"Oh," he says. "Why no one tell me, eh? Hey Haruto, glad to see you again. Oh, BT-Dubs, one of us is like Draun, but not Draun. Circle of trust, dog-people! Circle of trust!" He waves for us to follow and then continues his charge across the freeway.

As the others start moving, I join Jess and Grover as they connect with Micah. Grover slides between his legs, back and forth, wagging his tail, while Jess inspects the singed material on the back of Micah's body armor.

"Time to go," I say, moving them along. No one questions me. The rumbling ground beneath our feet does that for me. The enemy is close.

Jess and Grover head out first, followed by Micah and me. His gauntlets remain at full charge, despite my orders not to use them. I don't think he intends to defy the order, but I think he will if a life hangs in the balance. And I cannot fault him for it, so I don't mention it.

"Are you injured?" I ask.

"Was like landing on a soft pillow," he says. "She's getting better."

I nod. "Gruunlokar seems confident in her abilities."

"They're close," he says. "Like father and daughter."

"Hrm." I'm surprised and pleased. I have always believed Gruunlokar's life experience and calm demeanor was well suited to raising pups. I never expected he would find that connection with a human. But the ties between humanity and Kynolari are undeniable. An almost innate bond that allows Earth people to become more Kynolari...and Kynolari...well, more Earth-like.

I would have feared and fought the change before arriving on this planet, but I cannot deny the gifts granted to me by this world.

Torel is at the front of our group with Gruunlokar, Crip, and Blood. Though she is currently not the woman I love, I intend to do everything I can to get her back—even if it means another trip to limbo.

Gruunlokar reaches the building marked with a large green, white, and red '7-Eleven' sign. The front windows are broken, the gas pumps bent and twisted. The buildings surrounding it are in an equal amount of disrepair. Crumbled walls. Tilted at precarious angles.

Scorched by flames and pocked by gunfire.

Tokyo and its surrounding provinces are this planet's largest and most densely populated metropolitan cities. In the first days of the change, it must have been hell on Earth for those who did not accept the Draun's offer, or worse, for the dog people. They wouldn't have just been killed for fun. They would have been tortured as enemies of the Draun. Their dogs would have suffered the same fate.

Gruunlokar leaps through the broken window without making a sound. Torel—Soliquin—is right behind him, followed by Crip and Blood. They're a stealthy and confident advance team, clearing the way for the rest of us. But they can't do anything about the enemy behind us.

The telltale shriek of Helion rockets draws my attention back. A dozen of them curl out of the smoking warehouse wreckage. They twist past us, striking buildings and tipping one of them further to the side.

"They're firing blindly," Micah says. "Are they trying to get lucky?"

"Biologics don't believe in luck," I say. "There is a purpose behind everything they do—which is one of their weaknesses. We just need to—"

Micah grasps my arm as we near the freeway's far side. "Check your periphery."

I glance left and right without moving my head. Out of the corner of my eyes, I see them. Tyrne. Their long limbs carry them across the roadway in three quick strides, far outpacing us. But they're not attacking directly.

"They're surrounding us," Micah says. "The Tyrne will get in front." He motions to the rooftops of buildings beyond the 7-Eleven. Skitterlings, attempting to stay out of sight, wriggle with frenetic energy that gives them away.

And behind us...

I glance back in time to see the armored, six-legged Helions, the muscley Gobi, and the tentacled Platamots emerge from the smoke behind us, a massive force designed to intimidate and nudge the enemy forward.

"Feels a lot like a trap," Micah says.

"But you trust Haruto," I say.

He nods. "I do. *If* it's Haruto."

We reach the 7-Eleven together as another poorly aimed salvo of rockets slams into the buildings around us. A crumbling sound fills the air as one of the stricken structures gives way and topples onto the freeway, scattering the Skitterlings on its roof.

We move through the ruined storefront, find the back door, and enter a short street that ends in a playground that's surrounded by buildings. If the biologics can congest the streets in all directions, there will be nowhere to run...if Haruto has betrayed us.

When we round the corner, it would appear our worries are unfounded. Haruto holds a manhole cover open while the others climb inside. Gruunlokar was first in. Siloquin is lowering Blood down. Crip must already be inside. Once both dogs are down, Siloquin leaps down with Poppy right behind her. We arrive as Sean starts down the ladder with Chirk on his chest.

"Oh, god," Chirk says, wincing at the smell. "I thought the sewers in LA smelled bad!"

"Too much sushi, Japan!" Sean says, almost at the bottom. "Too much sushi!"

Jess motions for Micah to help her with Grover. They pick him up together and lower him down to Sean who knew to wait without being asked. Once he's down, Micah gives Jess a nod and she follows Grover.

Micah motions to Haruto and says, "Sniff test."

Then he faces back the way he came, gauntlets charged. If he uses them, at night, he'll be visible for miles around. Just like that explosion. We don't have long before someone shows up to inspect.

So, I perform my 'sniff test,' breathing deep as I move my nose from Haruto's knee, up to his head. When I'm done, we're eye to eye—his being open wide.

"Micah-San," he says. "Why is dog leader Praxion smelling me?"

"Making sure you're human," Micah says, backing toward us.

Micah looks to me and I nod confirmation.

"What else would I be?" Haruto shouts, his voice high pitched. "I no Draun. I no biologic. I Haruto! Rescuer of Kynolari. Savior of Japan!"

"Savior of—" Micah shakes his head and sighs. "Just get in the damn hole!"

"Mou, Mou! *Geez.*" Haruto climbs down the ladder, muttering to himself. "I drive like crazy. I sacrifice Panda Bus. Risk my life. And now they *smell* me?! This is some bullshit."

Once he's down, Micah follows without a word. When he reaches the bottom, he looks up at me and says, "Move it!"

"Do not come back," I tell him, voice grim. "No comms until I reach out."

He's about to question me, or argue, but he doesn't get a chance. I close the manhole cover over his head, just as the building behind me gives way to a charging Helion, spraying debris into the playground. The beast slides to a stop, spots me, and lets out a shrill electric scream, alerting the horde to my solitary presence.

# 33

## CHIRK

The slurping sound of feet through sewage justifies the baby carrier. I'd be nose deep in shit right now if I were on my feet. Even Poppy isn't risking walking. She's perched on Harth's shoulder, holding on to his ear to keep from falling off.

Poor Grover is the least lucky. He's too big to carry in the cramped tunnel, the rancid muck coming up to his chest. He doesn't seem to mind much, and Jess has to keep dragging him away from things that catch his nose.

Jenna is also strangely unfazed by the tunnel of Earthly tortures we're being led through. When she steps forward, lifting her left foot out of the muck, I understand why. The sludge clinging to everyone else, slides easily away from her—because it's not actually touching her leg. Smart kid. She's put up a thin telekinetic shield around her body, allowing her to stay clean and dry. Too bad she lacks the control to do that same thing for all of us.

We move through the tunnels at a Haruto pace—fast and chaotic. Our lights dance with every step, creating a strobe effect that once again makes me glad I don't need to walk.

Sean is handling it fine. He's got one hand on the wall, sliding through layers of filth. We'll need to disinfect his fingers, but he doesn't seem bothered by the lights. Probably been to enough drug-addled parties that he's just reliving happy memories. That said, he is breathing through his mouth, which isn't much better than through the nose.

The air is so thick with digested seafood that you can taste it.

The only one of us talking is Haruto, communicating with this 'Denji' guy, guiding us through the underground maze.

"Approaching intersection," Haruto says.

"Right," Denji says from the radio.

Haruto doesn't question the instruction. He just takes the right and the rest of us follow. Crip and Blood are on his heels, Gruunlokar and Torel right behind them. They're all focused. Eyes forward or looking down.

I'm the only one with real freedom to look around. As we round the corner, I glance back. Catch a glimpse of Micah. His path is illuminated by the orange glow of his charged gauntlets.

Praxion is nowhere to be seen.

I'm about to question Micah about where he is but I'm interrupted by the sound of a muffled *whump*. An explosion. A big one. But was it in the tunnels, or above them?

I run through the possibilities. Praxion is slow? Not remotely. Praxion is lingering behind to set a trap? Unlikely. Praxion is being a noble dickhead so the rest of us can escape?

"Shit," I mutter.

A shockwave rolls through the tunnel, spraying a cloud of aerosolized fecal sludge at us.

"Go!" Jenna shouts, rushing toward the back of the group, motioning us past.

"Stay with her!" I tell Sean.

He 180s, steps to the side, allowing Jess and Grover past, and then stays on Jenna's six. I know it's still weird for him—being head over heels for Gemma, having been betrayed by her, and then having her body reanimated by a chick named Jenna. Seriously, what are the odds? And now he has to deal with the fact that the body and voice he fell for belongs to someone who is too young for him and is more interested in spending time with Gruunlokar than anyone else. That's saying a lot, because Gruun ain't exactly the kind of guy that puts people at ease. It's enough to fuck with anyone. But Sean doesn't question me or complain. He just sticks close to her.

Micah rounds the corner at a sprint, nearly falling onto his face. He stays upright by digging his Hell Hound claws into the concrete wall and swinging around the corner. Jenna thrusts her hands out toward the junction just as the pressure wave reaches us. A tsunami of shit launches past, following the tunnel straight ahead and to the left. But nothing gets through Jenna's telekinetic wall.

Micah pauses, catching his breath—also through his mouth, but wincing with each mouthful of air. "Thanks..."

Before Jenna can reply, I point a finger at Micah. "Where is he?"

Micah looks me in the eyes and raises a brow. "You need to ask?"

"He's going to get himself killed," I growl.

"I think he knew that," Micah says. "But that explosion? It wasn't for us. Only reason we're escaping down here is because he's up there, leading them away."

"Or, you know, dead."

Micah shakes his head. "Listen."

When the roar of sewage bursting past settles, the sounds of battle reach through the tunnels and tickle my ears. Micah is right. The battle above still rages, but it's a one-sided fight. I recognize the weapons being fired, and not one of them is a Sonizer or a railgun.

He's still holding off on using his weapons.

Drawing their attention without increasing the alarm. If enough Draun showed up, they could peel the skin off the streets above and reveal us like ants.

Sean nods above me. "Yo, even I can hear that shit. We can't just leave him though, right?"

He looks down at me when I don't respond. "Little dude. C'mon, man. It's Praxion."

"That's why we can't go back," Micah says. "It was his call. He's the boss. Staying behind so we can escape is no different than ordering us to continue. Nothing any of us could have done about it. Nothing to do about it now. If he can find us, he will."

Micah's not wrong. My concern for Praxion is both justified and reasonable, but the level of anxiety I feel about his situation is uncharacteristic. Not because I didn't care about him before, but because it was easier to remember how much of a badass he can be when he needs to be. It's the Earth heightening my emotions. Praxion has survived worse.

He can do it again.

"Means you're the boss now," I tell Micah, and he takes the mantle of leadership with a nod. Technically, either Gruunlokar or I should take charge, but Micah and Praxion have been working as a leadership duo. Micah's become just as much our leader as Praxion. And this is his world.

"Catch up to the others," Micah says. "Jenna and I will follow and make sure nothing else catches us by surprise."

"You got it, boss," I say and backhand Sean's chest. "Captain Beefcake! Mush!"

"For the record," Micah says. "He closed the manhole above me. I never got a chance to tell him he was an idiot."

I have a laugh. "Sounds like Praxion. Don't sweat it. That's just his style."

Sean hustles to catch up with the others, their lights beckoning to us like a spectral haunting.

"Looks like *Poltergeist*," Sean whispers, and then spits the taste out of his mouth.

"Was just thinking the same thing," I admit. "And thanks again for making me watch that movie. While high."

"It's a classic, bro. Don't Kynolari do scary things for fun? You know, like adrenaline rush material?"

"You serious?" I ask him. "Spent most of my life fighting a war."

"Right," he says. "Right. So why does *Poltergeist* frighten you?"

"Because based on what Torel and Praxion saw, not to mention that Tor is currently possessed by a thirty-seven-thousand-year-old spirit, all that shit is real. Which means life after death, might be a thing, and I haven't ever had to consider what that might be like or how to prepare for it."

"Just, I don't know. Chill about it. Make peace with it. A lot of people don't believe in life after death. Other people have pretty strong opinions about it, but disagree about what it looks like, what we'll find there, or if everyone will be welcome. You can think all you want, but unless you're willing to have faith in something without tons of proof, you're probably not going to find any answers. It's like the origins of the universe. The Big Bang. They say everything came from a single point in space. It exploded...for some reason, and everything just raced away from that point. But really? Galaxies are floating away from a single point in space, they're *accelerating*, dude. Something is pushing them apart, faster and faster, but no one knows what that is. We can only make sense of five percent of a universe that is bigger than we can see. That's like standing in a tide pool and declaring you understand the ocean. Brah, who would say that...without faith? A few observations of a tide pool, accurate or not, can't explain the universe."

I rotate around in the baby carrier so I'm facing him. I place my hands on his cheeks. "First, I'm proud of you. Really. That all sounded very smart."

"I watch a lot of—"

"I know," I say. "I know. But...please... Tell me you—and by 'you' I mean the human race... You guys know about the *Architect*, right?"

"The who-what now?"

I burst out laughing. Can't help myself. I throw my head back and release my tension into the sewers. "Oh, aww, that's rich. Big bang! Pffft. You guys. Oh. Wow. Listen, when all of this is over, we'll have a chat. You can tell me about the afterlife, or whatever the hell you know about it, and I'll teach you about the origins of the universes."

"*Universes*?" he asks.

"Dimensions of reality," he says. "All connected, but better if kept separate."

"Small dog-man!" Haruto shouts from ahead. "You shut mouth now!"

"Later," Sean whispers.

I nod and spin back around. We're just a few feet behind Jess and Grover now. Micah and Jenna are about twenty feet back. Sounds like he's giving her a pep-talk, which is ironic since he called her former self a 'dick-whore' before killing her. At Sean's request, but still. We should leave that out of any future recounting, because we need her on our side. She's already saved our asses on more than one occasion, and given the power displayed by her predecessor, she might actually help us get the job done this time around—or at least help us die less quickly. We've only been in Japan for about twenty minutes, and she's already saved Micah and Haruto, not to mention kept us from being flushed through Tokyo's sewer system.

I squint at the light ahead and don't wince when I take my next breath.

Cool night air flows past me and it feels like I've just taken a drink of water after trekking through the desert.

"Shh, shh, shh." Haruto shushes everyone, even though no one's talking. "This most dangerous part of journey."

"Pretty sure the biologics were—"

He shushes me. "Little man-dog. Do not make me lose patience!'

I raise my hands in casual defeat.

"Outside this grate—" He steps to the side, revealing a large open tunnel ending in a circular mesh of metal bars. Past the grate, darkness. "Beyond is Tama River. Large river. Flow out to sea. We need to swim across while fighting the current. Large bridge overhead will keep us hidden, but only if we stay beneath it. Understand?"

"Affirmative," Poppy says, "but some of us won't be able to fight the current no matter how fast we paddle."

"I got you," Harth says to her.

"Was hoping you'd say that," she says, straddling his neck and taking hold of both ears.

I've never wanted to be the back of Harth's neck until this moment. But there it is. I'm officially smitten. What a big, lucky bastard.

"I got you, broski," Sean says. "Took swim lessons at the YMCA for like five years when I was but a wee lad."

"YMCA?" I ask. "You Make Cannabis Available?"

"Ahuh!" Sean slaps a hand over his mouth, keeping himself from laughing loudly again.

Haruto pinches his nose in exasperation. "Mou..." He looks past us as Micah and Jess catch up. "You hear plan?"

Micah gives a thumbs up.

"Everyone here?" Haruto asks, looking past Micah. Looking for Praxion.

"All here," I say.

Haruto turns away from me and focuses on Micah. He knows Praxion is missing and wants confirmation that we know.

Micah nods. "All here. Move. Now."

Haruto gives a nod and pushes the grate on one side. It swivels open without a sound. Then he leads us out into the night, down a slope, and into the water of a frigid river that's moving much faster than I expected...and is littered on either side by the dead.

# 34

### PRAXION

My proximity to the Helion is what saves me. While these biologic Helions have been outfitted with rockets, they're still melee fighters by nature. It dives toward me, curling its body into a sphere and rolling over the spot where I'd been standing a moment before.

I lunge to the side, tumble back to my feet, and spin around.

A divot of compressed road is left behind the Helion, including a crushed and distorted manhole cover. No one will be returning, and I will not be following.

Not that I was planning on it.

What I have in mind is far more—*How would Chirk put it?*—dumbass stupid.

But it is the only path forward that I believe will allow us to avenge all those lost to the Draun and end this war before it can leave the planet.

The Helion's body snaps open. It digs its six thick feet into the pavement, gouging troughs as the creature slides to a stop. The back end punches a hole in one of the buildings surrounding the playground—buildings that are now raining Skitterlings. Some take the smart route, running down the walls. Others are so lost in their bloodlust that they leap from the rooftops.

They might survive the fall, but not all their limbs will. And a Skitterling that can't move quickly isn't much of a threat.

Which reminds me of the flanking Tyrne. They'll arrive soon, and when they do, I won't last long out in the open. The Gobi are only a threat if I'm trapped. They're too slow to catch me, unless—

Rumbling turns me around as a second Helion arrives.

*Unless that,* I think, when I see three Gobi clinging to the Helion's back like Galorvian Spilk younglings clutching to their hunting father, learning the ways of the Florf hunt. It would be humorous if they weren't charging straight for me.

I turn tail and sprint straight toward the first Helion, which is distant enough that it won't resort to melee. Not yet. Instead, its rocket pods snap open, one over each shoulder. Only half the creature's rockets remain, but it's enough for what I'm hoping.

Twelve rockets fire at once, six from either side.

They twist and scream through the air, each one following a chaotic path meant to confuse the enemy. They're impossible to hide from because you don't know where the unguided projectiles are going to strike. But I don't need to know where they're going to hit, because I charge straight toward them. Unless a rocket scores a direct hit, I won't be anywhere near their detonations. I'll be safe from shockwaves and shrapnel alike.

The Helion behind me… It's shit out of luck.

Rockets shriek past me on either side. Some nearly get me, but I'm not in any real danger until the last of the rockets makes a sudden course adjustment straight toward my head.

I slide beneath it, turning around as I go, to see my plan come to fruition. Unlike me, the Helion carrying the three clinging Gobi, is a large target. All but three of the rockets strike the quartet head on. The other three strike the pavement on either side, and launch asphalt chunks that pelt the Gobi, a moment before the Helion's ruined front end dips down, catches the road, and flips the beast forward.

Without spinning again, I leap at the end of my slide, shoving off the ground as hard as I can. It's been a while since I had to move like this, but instead of hurting, it feels good. Before I was a team leader, I was a solo operator. A forward operating recon specialist—and an assassin when need be. The tactics used as a lone operator are very different from that of a squad, or an army. You need to think fast and move faster, staying several steps ahead of the enemy. And every move is a risk, because the only asset you have is yourself.

And if the mission fails, no one knows what happened. You just don't return to base, or home, or wherever you might normally rest your head at night.

My leap carries me up and over the first Helion. I flip over its back. When I'm upside down above it, I reach out with my gauntlet and slide my hand over its metal carapace. When I land inside the second floor of the building pulverized by the Helion's backside, I've got the beast's resonant frequency.

And I put it to use, unleashing a sonic wave that will be heard for miles around as a shrill scream, announcing my presence to the Draun.

But it also achieves my primary goal. The Helion comes apart, breaking into its component parts and toppling into a pile of rubber. While Helions are capable of adapting to nearly any combat tactic, they cannot change the resonant frequency of their metal parts. Unfortunately, the biologics accompanying the Helions aren't made of the same materials.

Before I can smile over my small victory, my eyes are drawn back to the second Helion. As it completes a topple forward, it crushes two of the Gobi beneath its back. The third, closest to its backside, is catapulted straight toward me, fists cocked back, ready to pulverize.

It's an intimidating attack.

If it made contact, the Gobi could kill me with one blow. But I am not defenseless.

I draw my sidearm, a railgun loaded with thirty spiral shards. They rotate as quickly as they cut through the air and shatter upon impact, sending dozens of spinning shards in every direction, like razor sharp fan blades. The effect is devastating.

A single round slips soundlessly from my weapon. Quicker than a thought later, the Gobi topples away from a mist that was its head a moment before. I step to the side, allowing the inanimate body to fall into the apartment behind me, crash through the far wall, and plumet to the roadway on the building's far side.

I look out the fresh hole to find the ruined Gobi lying atop a struggling Tyrne, not strong enough to free itself from the limp body pinning it down. I notice the ten other Tyrne at the same moment they spot me.

Every single one of the biologic doppelgangers of actual creatures, even the one pinned, lets out a quavering shriek. They don't sound anything like the real thing, but they're not really meant to. The scream is meant to keep the horde on target.

As I dash out of the room and into the next, the sound of pursuing Tyrne is easy to hear, mostly because they're climbing the building's outside. They are too tall to effectively pursue me through the building.

But the Skitterlings… They enter the building from all sides, crashing through windows like special operators assaulting a stronghold.

I burst through the apartment door and into a stairwell.

The window beside me shatters.

I catch the Skitterling by its mandibles.

A brief battle ensues as it attempts to sever my fingers, and I pull in the other direction. Both mandibles give way, and I tear them from the creature's face. Green fluid spurts from the open wounds. When the Skitterling falls to the floor, I drop with it, driving both mandibles back into its insectoid head. By the time I release the creature, I've also got its resonant frequency.

I get to my feet as the sound of sharp little legs *tap, tap, tap,* across every floor in the building. Taking the stairs three at a time, I make it two flights up before the creatures break through the stairwell doors.

The first to emerge never see me. They just leap out and fall to pieces, caught in a sonic wave that vibrates at the exact frequency needed to disassemble their biologic bodies.

I leap past the dead before more of the creatures can exit the apartment. On the fifth floor, one of the little bastards nearly gets me. Ducking low so I can't see it until my head clears the top step, it lunges at my face, limbs and mandibles open and ready to snap closed like a toothed trap.

If it connected, my head would be punctured in several spots. And while they might not get deep enough to kill me right away, I would be vulnerable to the horde, and quickly torn apart.

Instead, I manage to turn my Sonizer straight up, hitting it with a burst that peels the creature's body apart as it passes through. Happily, my own resonant frequency is different than a biologic's. If it wasn't, my head would have detonated.

I'm struck with a wave of fleshy debris and fluid that nearly knocks me back. I stagger a step, firing a blind shot into the next apartment just in case. Then I'm on the sixth floor, rounding the next landing toward the roof. Beneath me, the stairs rumble from the sound of a thousand Skitterling talons.

When I reach the last flight of stairs, I'm moving at full speed and the horde is gaining. I don't slow down to open the door, I just put my shoulder into the wood and crash through.

The impact knocks me down—and saves my life.

As I roll forward, the sharp inner limb of a Tyrne whooshes just above.

They beat me to the top. And a second one is waiting.

Gets a spiral shard in its slender mid-section. The biologic comes apart and topples in different directions, clearing a path toward three more waiting for me on the roof's far side. Behind me, the lone Tyrne and the Skitterlings chase me down.

A quick glance left, right, and up completes the picture. The only path to survival lies straight ahead, but threats are coming toward me from behind, in front... and above.

The glowing body of a coiled Helion descends toward the rooftop. Its body shines with brilliant light, meaning the creature is priming to explode. It will crush this building and everything on it. When the Helion reaches the ground, it will detonate, erasing everything.

The Tyrne ahead don't charge.

The mob behind me slows.

They're waiting. Coordinated. Working together. These biologics have been upgraded. I wouldn't call them smart, but they're more strategic.

Too bad for them, I've been all those things and then some.

I aim my Sonizer toward the sky, shift my resonant frequency back to that of a Helion, and unleash a full power blast straight up. It drains the weapon system's power but has the intended effect.

The plummeting Helion comes apart. Its explosive ability is negated, and its body reduced to a very large cloud of heavy, deadly projectiles.

I use the momentary distraction to my advantage, charging forward, raising my railgun and firing three rounds, each one of them connecting with my targets.

The shots aren't what I'd call accurate, but with spiral rounds, they don't need to be.

The two Tyrne on the left and right lose their one long forelimb each and topple to the side. The one directly ahead takes a round to the chest, leaving a hole large and clean enough for me to leap up and dive through.

As I clear the creatures, the Helion's debris crashes down like a rapid-fire artillery barrage, smashing through biologics and the roof.

I fall into an alley between buildings. Twisting myself around, I strike the brick wall with my hands and feet. I slide a few feet and then leap back to the apartment building's outer wall, controlling my descent.

Above me, the apartments explode outward as the Helion's body destroys the entire building. I'm now stuck in a race to the ground where I need to find an equilibrium between being caught by the building falling above me and the ground rushing up.

# 35

## MICAH

"No one needs to swim," Jenna says, grimacing at the river lined with the dead, strands of decomposing insides warbling in the current. "I can get us across. I think."

"Think?" I ask.

"She can do it," Gruunlokar says. "So long as she doesn't doubt her abilities."

"My bad," I say, raising my hands. "You got this, girl."

Jess backhands my shoulder. "Don't be a dick."

"What? I was being serious."

She raises a moonlit eyebrow at me. "'You got this, girl?'"

"Serious *and* funny," I say. "You know how I get, around corpse-lined rivers. Jenna, you know I was just—"

When I turn to address Jenna, I find her looking surprised.

Haruto is behind her, a knife against her throat.

"No one is going anywhere," Haruto says, "with Draun-girl, until I know she is *not* Draun-girl."

"Haruto," I say, feeling personally wounded by the betrayal. "The hell?"

"I know her," he says. "Hard to forget the face of your torturer."

*Shit,* I think.

*Sounds like Gemma told the truth about that.*

"Jenna. Gemma. Not even a convincing name change! So stupid!" He eyes each of us, looking for a threat against him. No one moves, probably because his actions, given the circumstances, are understandable.

"I can explain," I say, taking a step closer.

He faces me and tightens his grip. "Look in my eyes, Micah-San. Do you see doubt? Any sense of hesitation? Come no closer. All of you."

"Okay, okay." I relax my stance and take a step back.

Blood and Crip on the other hand fade back in the shadows. I don't know what they're thinking, but if they return, I suspect it will be quick, quiet, and without warning. I let them go, curious to see what they're up to. Haruto never sees them leave.

"Listen, Haruto, I can explain. I swear to you."

"Make it snappy," he says, glancing up at the edge of the bridge giving us cover from above, but leaving us exposed on either side.

"Gemma...was real. She was Draun. She tortured you. We know that. She *told* us that, after she betrayed us. She found us in New Hampshire. Used your name to convince us she was a friend. Said she was your niece, and that she needed our help to rescue you."

A look of profound guilt sweeps over Haruto's face.

He gave us up.

"She lived with us. Fought with us. Became one of us. And then—"

"She stabbed us in the fuckin' back, man," Sean says, eyes on the ground. "Nearly killed us."

"Then how is she here now!?" Haruto whisper-shouts, trying to control his conflicting emotions. "How did you forgive her?"

"Didn't," Harth says. "Praxion erased her mind."

"And we replaced it with Jenna," Poppy says, "who, by the way, also was a Draun. The first human on Earth to become Draun, I've been told. But these bozos killed her, too, if you can believe that."

"Jenna was a conflicted soul," Gruunlokar says. "A part of her always fought against being Draun. She dreamed of overthrowing the Visionary. But she also longed for his power. Before her death, she left a copy of her essence, her memories, her soul, I suppose, hidden inside a liminal space in my mind."

"That's some science fiction bullshit," Haruto says.

"I'm a talking dog from space," Gruunlokar says.

"We teleported here from Los Angeles by putting our hands on a horse statue's asshole," Chirk says, "and appearing with our hands on a giant dick. There's nothing normal about any of this, my man."

Haruto nods, accepting the point.

"The consciousness left in my mind—" Gruun motions to Jenna. "—was transplanted to this body thanks to Kynolari technology developed by Anbu, aka Xolotl, but best known to humanity as Anubis."

Haruto waves his free hand back and forth. "Wait, wait, wait. Are you serious? Egyptian dog-god was Kynolari? Not jerking chain?"

"Wouldn't dream of it," I tell him. "She is *not* Gemma. She is *Jenna*. A J and two Ns. She has the powers of a Draun, but the heart of a human. Of one of us."

"And if you'll give me a chance," Jenna says. "Gruunlokar and I are going to kill the Visionary."

Haruto twists his lips. He leans around Jenna and looks at her face. "You are not Draun, but you do not seem concerned. You are calm like one of them."

"Only because I'm starting to get the hang of this telekinesis stuff," she says.

"I have a knife to your throat," he says.

"Well, yeah, but you can't move it," she says, grinning.

"Eh?" Haruto tries to pull the knife away, but it's frozen in place. He lets go of it completely and it floats in place. Jenna turns to face Haruto and the knife floats between them. The blade turns to face her, the handle toward Haruto. Then it floats over to him. He reaches up and plucks it from the air. "Thank you."

Jenna's confused. "For what?"

"For not killing me," he says. "You could have. It would have been understandable. I am in your debt." Haruto gives her a deep bow.

"Not necessary," I say, pulling him back up. Then I look past him and say, "We are *all* Kynolari."

Haruto follows my gaze around to find a very serious looking Siloquin, armed with an extended laser-tipped spear, which I didn't know she was carrying. "Does this mean I do not get to slay him?"

"You do not," I tell her.

She retracts the spear, extinguishing its laser blade, and snaps the weapon to a magnetic sheath on her thigh.

Haruto nods and says, "Woof."

When we don't respond, he says. "The underground here. We say 'woof' to identify ourselves as Kynolari."

Gruunlokar crosses his arms. "I am not saying 'woof.'"

"Nor I," Harth says.

Haruto throws both hands in the air, shaking his head. "You have dog faces! Dog ears. You do not need to identify yourselves."

"Mm," Harth says. "Praxion, what do you—"

He stops upon turning around and discovering Praxion missing.

"Where is Praxion?" he asks.

"Okay," Chirk says, beating me to the punch and taking the heat for me. He raises his hand, gesturing for everyone to stay calm. Then he smacks Sean and whispers, "Pace seriously."

When Sean is moving, hands behind his back like a general, Chirk says, "Okay, listen up, and no complaining. Praxion stayed behind and ordered us to not say anything until we were too far away to do anything."

Gruunlokar and Harth are both incensed. While Harth is about to let loose on Chirk, Gruun moves to activate his comms.

"No comms," I say. "Until he reaches out. Was the last thing he said to me."

Siloquin has a different perspective and stands in front of the pair. "Praxion made a noble decision. His sacrifice should be honored, not whined about."

The jaw muscles on the side of Harth's face are twitching. Then he says, "I like Torel better."

Gruunlokar turns to Chirk.

"He would not leave without assigning his replacement. Who is in charge?"

Chirk redirects all attention to me when he hitches his little thumb in my directions. "Human Badass-Actual over here."

Harth grunts and nods. Gruunlokar steps in front of me. Eye to eye he's as intimidating as a swarm of wasps. The big ones. That cut off bees' heads. "You knew he left?"

I nod.

Grover steps between Gruunlokar and me, looking up at us, his eyes uncommonly serious. "He gave no choice."

"Would have stopped him if I could," I say.

Gruunlokar nods and claps my shoulder. Gives my arm a squeeze. "He honors you."

"I know."

"Then don't fuck this up." His gaze lingers for a moment, then he gives me a subtle grin. "Your orders?"

"Jenna," I say. "Get us across this river. Everyone else, fall in line and stay quiet until we reach our destination. No complaints. No dicking around. Understood?"

Before I can continue, a high-pitched shriek echoes through the city above and behind us.

"Praxion," Harth whispers.

"He's fighting for all of us. So we can finish this war," I say. "Once and for fucking all."

Gruunlokar looks up and grunts.

Looks like he might say something but keeps it to himself.

"Jenna," I say.

She takes my cue and raises her hands toward the group. A moment later, my feet come off the ground. Then we're all floating. It's not like low gravity. I can't move. She's got all of us in a vice grip. For a moment, I'm concerned, but then she rises up next to us and we start floating across the river."

"Find the second star to the right, and fly straight on 'til morning," Sean says, a ridiculous smile on his face, jazzed about floating through the air. He might be the most dog-like human I've ever encountered.

Speaking of dogs, Crip and Blood have yet to return. They can handle themselves, but we are deep in enemy territory. They'll have no trouble tracking us, but I hope they don't wait too long.

When we touch down on the river's far side, Haruto opens a second drainage grate and turns to Sean. "This not the way to Neverland. Down this path is only hell, formerly known as Tokyo."

# 36

## PRAXION

I hit the ground and dive through the window of the neighboring building. Tons of debris crashes down behind me, cracking the walls and spewing bricks that pelt my back. I pick myself up off the floor and turn toward the window.

Death nearly caught up with me then. It's been trying to catch me for years, but I'm still at least a step ahead. I make for the rear door of what I think is a sushi shop, moving through a small kitchen. It's clean, but the scent of rotting fish seeps from the refrigeration unit.

The back door opens without a sound. I lean out into the night, breathe fresh air, and look for enemies.

Given the one-track mind of biologics on the hunt, any near enough to track me down in the fallen building would have been there. Certainly not all of them, but enough.

The rest of them will be confused now. They'll have seen the building's destruction. They'll know I was there when it fell. But until they start digging, they'll have no way to confirm my demise. Some will burrow. Others will patrol. But I've got a head start.

The neighborhoods beyond the playground are packed tight. Winding streets, small homes, and large apartment buildings comingle to make a maze. Finding anyone in the mass of buildings would be a challenge. Finding me will be nearly impossible—until I want to be found.

I dash from the building's rear door, cross a small driveway, and enter a small, but modern home. I repeat the process three more times, moving between darkened doorways and windows, until I'm on the far side of the block.

Here, I take a moment to catch my breath.

The home's interior looks like a battle scene. Furniture is in ruins. Blood on the walls. Someone became a Draun here, and when it happened, they were not alone.

Curiosity draws me to a mantle where a lone framed photo still stands. It's a girl. Straight black hair. Bangs. A cute smile. Couldn't be more than four. Her face is spattered by blood.

I look down at the floor, where several more frames lie. I pick them up and shuffle through them, finding images of the same people. A man, a woman, and the girl. They look happy. Silly, even.

After returning the photos to the mantle, it looks a little bit like a shrine to the memory of these people that maybe no one living remembers at all. I failed them all. It should have never gone this far.

"All I can do is avenge you," I tell the little girl, unsure which parent turned on their family. Children lack the ambition and greed to become Draun. Many will be slain by their parents. Others will be underground with the resistance. Those that remain will either by hunted down and slain or enslaved, while a few will remain hidden, perhaps long enough to be rescued...or long enough to starve. There is no version of conquest by the Draun that does not involve these horrors.

And I can't stand to look at them any longer.

I move through the neighborhood, soundless and invisible. Behind me, the noise of struggling biologics from within the rubble, merged with the crunching of Skitterlings chewing their way through brick, stone, and wood, searching for a corpse.

My corpse.

But I'm not interested in them.

I'm hunting bigger game.

At the end of the street, I get a good view from a second-floor window of a home that looks like it was abandoned long before the change. Uphill to my left is a fourteen-story tall, beige apartment building. The tallest around.

That's where I'll find my prey.

High above.

Looking down.

I work my way through the maze of homes, some of which are pristine, while others look like nightmares. Some smell new, others like death, corpses of the dead littering the floors—some intact, some in pieces. While we were hiding behind a waterfall in Mexico, the rest of the world was enduring unimaginable horror.

*We should have done more,* I think, but it's a silly idea.

At the time, all we could have done was die along with everyone else.

Now...now there is a slim chance we can do more.

I pause by a shade-drawn window. Footsteps outside. Between the home I'm hiding in and the fourteen-story building. The gap between the shade and the window frame gives me just a sliver to look through, but it's enough.

A Gobi.

Nearly tall enough to look me in the eye, here on the second story. Its slick dark skin glimmers in the moonlight. The creature's massive arms ripple with muscles.

Out in the open, Gobi aren't much of a problem. They're easy targets. But in close quarters combat, they are extremely dangerous if they get their hands on you.

But it's not searching for me.

If anything, the creature seems bored.

*It's guarding the building*, I realize, the servant of whatever Draun has decided to come see what all the noise is about. In a battle, the Gobi are your frontline…not your guards. They bore easily and get distracted. This one has its eyes locked on the distance, watching its brethren dig through rubble in search of my corpse.

If a Gobi can be avoided in combat, that's what you do. I head to the rooftop and peer over the edge. The Gobi is ten feet below, still watching the distant action. The lowest balcony of the apartment building is just fifteen feet away. I back up, get a running start, and leap the distance.

The only evidence of my passage is a slight *whoosh* and a muffled *thud* as I land and roll back to my feet. One of the benefits of being covered with fur is that we're equipped with sound-dulling padding, even while wearing clothing or battle armor.

I crouch at the back of the balcony for thirty seconds, waiting to hear any sign that the Gobi has detected me. They're not quiet about such things, so I'm confident I haven't been found out when I slip from the shadows, climb over the railing, and clasp on to one of two rectangular columns that stretch from the first floor, all the way to the roof.

The column is smooth but is more decorative than a weight bearing part of the structure. It's metal beneath the white paint, and my claws have no trouble puncturing it. Moving slowly, I scale the tower without making a sound.

But I am at my most vulnerable. Anyone looking in this direction might wonder about the small object moving up the building's side. Even a missed projectile fired at me might make me flinch and fall away.

I focus on the ascent. Reach. Puncture. Cling. Climb. The cycle repeats over and over, each minute passing as though time has slowed.

When I'm five feet from the rooftop, I stop.

Head raised, I sniff the air.

Two humans, both tainted by the blood of many more.

I perk my ears and listen. They're silent for a moment, and then one of them says, "Do you think they'll find it?"

*It.* The biologics got a good look at me then. Probably seen by whoever is watching their video feed on the other end.

"If we'd been here to see it, I might know."

The second voice is female. Older than the first.

"How was I supposed to know the fucking Kynolari would come here at the exact moment I got hungry?"

"You're lucky you're my brother," the elder sister says. "I'd have killed you by now. Still might."

The boy laughs, but he's nervous. We both know it wasn't a joke. Familial bonds have little meaning to the Draun. If he gets in her way, she'll kill him.

I'm not going to give either of them a chance to live long enough to see if she'll do it.

I climb higher, reaching the top without making a sound. I lift my head over the precipice without worry of being spotted. Their voices are directed away from me, toward the ruined buildings.

They're both wearing hooded cloaks—the boy in green, the girl in black adorned with a red symbol I do not recognize. It resembles a diamond, with lines extending outward in four cardinal directions. If I were explaining it to Sean, I'd say it was two 'X's, one stacked atop the other. When they turn their heads, I see that they're wearing masks. The boy's is unrecognizable, but the girl's is a low polygon styled Earth fox. Strange.

"Easy for you to say," the boy says, "being one of the 'Protected.' If I killed you, Lumen Sok would kill me."

"Damned if you do," the sister says. "Damned if you—"

She tilts her head at an angle, listening.

She's heard me creeping up behind them. But she's too late.

The boy falls to the rooftop, his head removed by a spiral rail shard. At the same moment, I draw my blade across the sister's throat. When she falls forward, I take hold of her mask and cloak and yank them away from her head and the spray of blood that follows. The pair lie motionless on the roof, their faces hidden—or removed—which is a mercy. I don't know how old they were.

Neither were children, but it is difficult to see a young life twisted by the Draun, especially after you've just ended it.

The mask is firm plastic. Sturdy, but easy to break. Despite its low detail, it's an accurate representation of a fox, albeit much larger. The only oddity is that it has two round, white circles for eyebrows. And kanji scrawled on each white cheek in red ink.

# 悪い犬

"Warui inu," I say, reading the kanji, and then I repeat it in English out of habit. "Bad dog... Cute."

I turn the mask around and place it against my face. Perfect fit. Even room for my nose. After fastening it tight, I whip the cloak around me, secure it around my neck, and pull the hood up over my head. To any outside observer, I'll look like one of what the boy called 'the Protected,' some faction of the Draun under the direct protection of the Visionary. To test the theory, I slide back down the building's exterior, climb back to the balcony, and leap down, landing directly in front of the Gobi.

# 37

## CHIRK

"Fifteen minutes," I say to Sean.

"Huh?"

"That's about how long I can stand being in this stench before the urge to murder someone overtakes me."

"How long have we been down here?" he asks.

"Sixteen minutes," I grumble. "Only thing stopping me is being strapped to your chest."

"Huh," he says. "You know you can undo—"

"Silence!" I say. "I'm trying to express my bedraggled emotions through the use of a vivid metaphor."

"Ah," he says. "Then mission accomplished, *mi amigo poco*."

"It would be easier to bear if you would stop reminding us about the stench," Harth says, looking back, one hand over his mouth.

"Stop whining," Haruto says from the front, waving a hand at me. "Fishy poop smell better than dead."

"That's up for debate," I say.

"I don't smell anything," Jenna says, wrapped in her telekinetic bubble of fresh air.

She flashes a smile back at me.

"Yeah, yeah," I say. "We'll see who's laughing when you run out of air and pass out."

She rolls her eyes and faces forward again.

"We almost there," Haruto says. "Just...lick butthole or something for few minutes."

"Did he...?" I look up at Sean. "Did he just tell me to lick my butthole?"

"No offense, my man, but it's something the pooches do. If they can. Mostly little guys like yourself. Big dogs? Not so much."

"I no reach butthole," Grover says. "But I do reach—"

"Uh-huh. Stop there," Jess says. "This is about to devolve into a masculine masturbation joke-fest and I cannot handle that right now."

"What mast—ur—bation?" Grover asks.

"I'll tell you later, bud," Micah says, petting Grover.

Grover wags his tail at the physical contact, looks up at Micah and says, "Okay. Love Micah."

"Love you, too, Grove," Micah says.

"Always a love fest with you two," I say.

"Better than a bitch-fest," Gruunlokar says, leaving me aghast and everyone else laughing.

Haruto is the loudest. "Ha! Aha! Ha! Bitch-fest. Who knew scary dog-person is also funniest dog-person!"

I cross my arms, determined to not respond and give them more ammunition to fire my way. Because I'm actually close to losing my shit. Not because of any of them, but because I'm disturbed about the smell. I've smelled worse. Slogged through it. But that was before Earth. Before this damn atmosphere started affecting me. I've always been kind of a loose cannon. I know that. But now, it's difficult to control my emotions. I feel a low-level anger unless I'm blazed or just chilling with Sean. I feel impatient. Like I want to snap at people who look at me the wrong way. And god-damnit, the smell in these tunnels is the worst of all. Not because it's making me nauseous like it is everyone else, but because it smells so...damn...*good*.

The fouler, the more I'm drawn to it. I find myself leaning toward the same rank scents that Grover is held back from. The worse it is, the more enticing.

What I hate the most is that I'm pretending to be disgusted by these tunnels. I could spend all day here, inspecting all the wondrous scents. Just me and Grover, running from heap of something, to smear of something worse.

"Just ahead," Haruto says, granting mercy.

Less than a minute later we leave the sewer behind and enter a water runoff system that smells more of algae than shit. There's a cool breeze, bringing fresh night air from somewhere far away. It rolls past us, heading downward...downwind, hiding the scent of the people hidden beneath the surface.

"All quiet now," Haruto whispers. "Large tunnels echo to surface." He then follows the path I suspected, leading us downward, back toward the coast. Downwind. Our scent will be swept along ahead of us. If a Skitterling were to pass through, it would never catch our scent, which is mostly fish shit now anyway. It might not recognize us as living things at this point. Maybe that was the point of our shitty journey?

Twenty minutes later, I'm nearly asleep in the baby carrier. The air is cool and clean now. The darkness calms me. And Sean is humming a pleasant tune.

When Haruto claps his hands and says, "Okay, we talk now!" I flinch and snort.

"You sleeping, little dude?" Sean asks me.

"Don't think so," I say.

"You were snoring."

"Okay, maybe a little asleep," I admit. "What was that song you were humming?"

"'Bouncing Around the Room' by Phish, with a PH." he says.

"Knocked me right out."

He laughs. "You're such a hippie pothead."

"Come, come. This way!" Haruto leads us down a concrete staircase. At the bottom is a metal door.

We're all a little bit nervous. I can smell it. What lies on the other side of that door might very well help turn the tide of this war. If it's anything like the organization seen in Los Angles, we'll be off to a good start.

The door swings open and Haruto motions Siloquin inside. The team enters one by one with Sean and me at the rear. When we enter, it's to a wall of backs, spread to the right and left, all looking at something.

Sean shuffles to the side, until we step around Harth's broad back and see it for ourselves.

There is a man in a wheelchair seated at a tray table, upon which is a glowing laptop. The scene is lit by a single hanging bulb.

The man in the chair gawks at us, pushing up his glasses and doing nothing about his agape jaw.

I nearly laugh when Poppy catches my eye. Her face is all screwed up like she smells something rank, and she's hitching her thumb toward the man in the chair. Everything about her exudes, 'Can you believe this shit?'

Before I can respond, Haruto pushes his way through, leaps beneath the light, and extends his arms out to the lone man. "You see! The resistance of Tokyo. Me and Denji. To the last!"

They perform an elaborate rehearsed handshake that ends in explosions. Then they turn to us, waiting for something... Applause maybe?

What they get is me saying, "Please tell me that this is Japanese humor. You..." I point to Haruto and then Denji. "...and him, are the Tokyo resistance?"

"Resistance of Tokyo," he says, correcting me. "Hai. I am like ninja assassin. Stealthy. Know all secrets of Tokyo. In my head. From tour bus. I also escaped from Draun Imperial Palace. I know the layout. Where they keep prisoners. Where they sleep. Where they poo. They think I sooo stupid, but they are stupid ones. I sneak out into tunnels. And that's when I find Denji, hiding here from the beginning with laptop and hoarded food."

He motions to a wall stacked with cans of Japanese labeled goods. The images on the labels do *not* look appetizing.

"I'm not fast or a ninja," Denji says, "but the Internet is still up, the power is on, and I'm kind of a genius. I've got access to the Tokyo's CCTV cameras and the Japanese Defense Force's satellite network. We've identified more than ten thousand Draun operating in all of Japan, tracked them to their domiciles, outlined their territory, and identified the greatest threats—most of them being here, in and around Tokyo. They're either protected by the Visionary or hoping for a chance to replace him."

"The Visionary does not protect those who seek to usurp him," Gruunlokar says.

"He does when he intends on replenishing the Draun population with his own spawn," Denji says. "Look." He turns the laptop so we can see it, and in a few clicks an image is displayed. It's a Draun, photographed in flight from above. Their body is hidden by a black cloak with a red symbol on the back.

"Looks like two Xs on top of each other," Sean says.

"He's right," Micah says. "About the breeding. That's a Viking rune of fertility."

Harth huffs. "And the Draun wearing this are..."

"Protected," Haruto says. "By the Visionary himself. They are, or will be, his child bearers."

"Unusual," Siloquin says. It's the first word she's spoken in a long time.

"Makes sense to me," Poppy says. "He's the OG Draun. Been in power forever. No one has come close to his power level. He survived a bullet to the head courtesy of Gruunlokar..."

He grumbles.

She continues. "If you want to create a master race of Draun powerhouses to wreak havoc, what would be better than a million sons and daughters of the Visionary? And now that the *Prowler* is... Well, they have the time."

"I mean, I've seen photos of Lumen Sok," Sean says. "He's no spring chicken. If he can pump out a full load per day, I'd be impressed."

"He's not human," Jess says. "No way to know how—"

"Draun hatchlings are laid in egged broods," Gruunlokar says. "That your females' biology doesn't match has no bearing. All they need is a womb in which to gestate for two weeks. Then they will emerge as soft-shelled eggs, in which they will grow at an accelerated rate until they hatch—and consume each other until only the strongest half remains. The process will repeat every few months and millions more Draun will walk this world, more powerful than those already present. If that happens...there will be nothing we can do."

As the weight of Gruunlokar's revelations settles upon us, Haruto lets out a half-hearted laugh and a feeble and fading, "Yeah... Resistance of Tokyo..."

# 38

## MICAH

"Okay, we've got a few different plays," I tell the others, seated around the small concrete room, sitting on pads that Haruto has gathered. "Gruunlokar and Jenna can assassinate Lumen Sok. But that doesn't do much about the Draun populating the planet."

"It would throw the enemy forces into chaos," Gruunlokar says, "until a new Visionary is established."

"How long does that take?" I ask.

"Depends on how powerful the next in line is," Chirk says. "If there are a bunch of them, they could level the city before only one of them is left. If one of them is stronger than the rest, they might all just fall in line and bide their time. There're always a few contenders, though. Not that any of us have seen it. Lumen Sok has had control for a very long time."

"How confident are you two?" I ask Jenna and Gruunlokar.

"Ninety percent," he says at the same time Jenna says, "Fifty percent."

"Let's call that seventy-five percent confidence that you can put a shard through his head," I say.

"*If* we get a clean shot," Gruunlokar says.

"Could be a challenge if he doesn't have a reason to stand in the open," Chirk says.

"What about the satellites?" Jess asks.

"What satellites?" Denji asks.

"SkyLink," I say. "Lumen Sok's..." I stop talking when Denji's eyes go wide with abject shock.

"SkyLink!" He slaps his forehead. "Kami-sama! I'm so stupid!"

"Eh?" Haruto says. "What is SkyLink?"

"Now you so stupid," Denji says, working his keyboard. "SkyLink is a satellite network put in orbit by Lumen Sok. Thousands of them. They surround the planet."

"But they're not just for looking at porn," Poppy says.

"They can shoot lasers," Jess says, ticking off fingers. "They can spy on us. And, they can send and receive signals."

"What kind of signals?" Denji asks.

"All kinds," Harth says, "which is why we require access. Though I'm not sure how much good that will be without Praxion's Sonizer. He was the only one with the Draun frequency."

Denji looks back. Doesn't need to ask.

"The simple version is that a Sonizer has the ability to detect the resonant frequency of, well, anything. It can then use that frequency to disrupt an object's stability."

"Like fat lady singing shattering glass," Haruto says. Pretty sure he's referencing a cartoon, but...

"That's right. Except in this case, Praxion used the Sonizer to detect the resonant frequency of the Draun. He can erase them. All of them."

"If we use Lumen Sok's satellite network against him," Denji says, face lit up like it's Christmas in 1990 and he's just opened a Super Nintendo. Then his face falls flat. "One problem. SkyLink's wireless network is separate from its control network. The control network is an intranet, meaning we need to be onsite to access it."

"And where can we do that?" Harth asks.

"There are only four access sites in the world," Denji says, "but one of them is right here in Tokyo, at..." He looks at his computer screen, scrolling through information faster than I can read. "At the top of Azabudai Hills Mori JP Tower." He taps a few keys, accessing information about the tower. "Sixty four stories. Recent construction. Tallest tower in Tokyo."

"Sounds like Lumen Sok," Jess says.

"He didn't have anything to do with the complex's development," Denji says, "but he's on the lease for the top two floors. The top floor is listed as a business suite. The floor beneath is...residential."

"Does he live there?" Chirk asks. "Because the guy has to take a shit just like the rest of us. Maybe we catch him with his pants down."

"He rarely leaves the Imperial Palace," Denji says. "But when he does..." Denji runs some kind of tracking software. Brightly colored dots move around a map of Japan.

"These are all Draun?" Harth asks, leaning in for a closer look.

"Only when they're airborne, and higher than the surrounding buildings," Denji says. "The application is my own, but we're using Japanese Defense Force satellites and data to track all objects moving around Japan. I'm not sure how useful it is, but I figured I would gather all data and maybe some of it could be beneficial."

"Which one of these is Lumen?" Harth asks.

Denji zooms in several times, until there are just a few dozen spots coming and going. "Lumen Sok is the only one colored purple. Look, here." He points to a purple spot, moving out from the Palace, connecting with several other dots, and then going back to the Palace. We watch it happen two more times, and then on the fourth trip out, he stops at the center of a building and a moment later, disappears from view.

"What happened?" Sean asks. "The dude just poofed. And how'd he get inside the building? There a hole in the wall?"

Denji shakes his head. "He landed on the roof, and either stayed there or—"

"—entered the building," Jenna says.

"Hai," Denji says, overlaying street and building names. The label over the building Lumen Sok stopped at… Azabudai Hills Mori JP Tower.

"Holy shit," I say. "How long was he there?"

"Fifteen minutes," Denji says.

"Yeah, that's enough time," Chirk says.

"Time for what?" Grover asks, tail wagging, clueless about how long certain male tasks take to perform.

"Copulation," Siloquin says from the back of the room, where she's still standing, arms crossed. "I prefer a partner that can last several hours. Endurance is an attractive quality in a mate."

"Oookay," Chirk says. "Well, it looks like Lumen is more of a two-pump chump."

"How often does he visit?" I ask.

"Looks like once a day," Denji says. "And there is only one other daily visitor… but…strange. One other person visits the building every day, but it's always someone different—and they never leave."

"The lower of the two floors isn't a domicile," Gruunlokar says. "It's a brood den."

I tilt my head toward him. "And that means…"

"The Protected would be the daily visitors, carrying the spawn of Lumen Sok. Depending on how long the practice has been going on, there could already be Draun younglings."

"Baby…Draun?" Jess shakes her head. "That sounds…horrific."

"The Draun young accelerate their growth when consuming the remains of their fallen brethren," Gruunlokar says. "While there could very well be newborns, it's more likely that you'll encounter younglings. What you would call 'teenagers.' They're not as powerful as their elders, but they are erratic, mentally unstable, and unpredictable. It would be wise to avoid them."

"Right," I say. "We skip Floor Sixty Three. Go right to the top. Nice and quiet. In and out. Chirk, Sean, Harth, Jess, and Grover, can you handle it?"

"Like you have to ask," Chirk says.

"I can guide them from here," Denji says.

Harth nods. "This is acceptable."

I turn to Jess and Grover. "You guys can stay here, but I didn't think you'd stay behind, as much as I wish you would."

"And here I thought you believed we'd be useful." She slugs my shoulder. "Jerk."

"Didn't say you wouldn't be. I just don't want you guys…you know."

"We'll be good," Jess says. "Grover will keep us all safe."

"On duty," Grover says, nuzzling Jess's leg. "But miss Micah."

I crouch down and give him a hug. "You're a big man now. And Jess needs you."

"Grover needs Micah."

I shake my head. "Grover might be the strongest of us all."

He wags his tail. "Micah might be big liar."

I shake his scruff and laugh. "Let's get this done and go home."

He nods, and it's really weird to see your dog nod. "Love Micah."

"Love Grover." I stand to find everyone watching us.

Chirk pretends to wipe a tear. "Oh! Gets me every time. Now that we're done with the love-fest, what the hell are the rest of you going to do?"

I point at Haruto. "Can you escort us to the Imperial Palace?"

"Hai. There are tunnels. But they will be guarded that close to the Palace."

"Biologics?" I ask.

He nods.

"Won't be a problem," I say.

"We need someplace tall," Gruunlokar says. "With a clear view of the Palace's inner courtyard."

Haruto nods. "Hai. I know of a place."

"Great," I say. "Gruunlokar, Jenna, let's see if we can't cap this asshole and cause some chaos. Siloquin, you and I will back them up."

"Hold right on a damn second," Chirk says. "I see what you did. You think you've got all the heavy hitters, don't you? Send the rest of us on an errand mission, while you guys with the big guns take on the Visionary."

"Nonsense," I say, even though he's right. Then I remember that I've missed someone. She's almost out of sight, sitting quietly. "Poppy is with us."

Poppy flinches and looks around. "Huh? What? Someone say my name?"

"Nice of you to join us," Chirk says. "You doing some self-reflection or—"

Poppy shoots him a look that silences him. Then she points at her ear, and then the closed metal door.

She hears something. Just outside.

Then we all hear it.

Screaming.

# 39

## PRAXION

I land in a crouch, ten feet in front of the Gobi standing guard for a Draun it doesn't know is dead. Its proximity is intimidating, the massive body standing fifteen feet tall, its immense arms stretching nearly the entire distance to the ground.

It's not until this very moment that I realize that the Gobi and Tyrne have similar builds—short back limbs, long arms. But where the Tyrne are narrow and lithe, built for speed, the Gobi are all bulky twitching muscle. Raw power. And this one is close enough to pick me up and crush me to pulp.

But it doesn't.

The creature's only acknowledgement of me is to casually turn its eyes toward my mask-covered face.

Waiting...

"Bow," I say, testing its response to my natural voice.

The Gobi drops to a single knee and lowers its head. No hesitation.

I nearly express my shock as a spoken curse. An Earth habit that humans frequently partake in, and which Chirk has fully adopted. I manage to keep the words contained because whoever I'm pretending to be right now would certainly not be surprised by the Gobi's obedience.

"Extend your hand," I order.

When the creature lowers its open palm to the ground, head still bowed, I step upon it. I'm now the only Kynolari to touch the open palm of a Gobi's hand and not be crushed to paste. "Lift me to your shoulder."

It does as commanded, and I claim my perch beside its head.

"Stand tall," I say, and the Gobi obeys.

It's not exactly a stable place to stand, but I have no trouble adjusting to its every movement. And that's important if I'm going to ride the thing. My disguise's primary weakness is that I cannot fly. The Draun don't just walk around. It would be a sign of weakness—unless, I hope, you're being carried. Tyrants on all worlds prefer to be carried by their subjects. It's the ultimate sign of superiority.

In fact... I lean my back against the Gobi's head, trying hard to not imagine how easy it would be for the creature to crush my skull inside its jaws. I sit on its shoulder, lazing back like I'm enjoying the luxury of being transported by the Gobi. While the recreated creature is a biologic, built to serve the Draun, rather than a true slave of the original species, it might still fool those who don't know better.

At least for a time.

Once I'm settled and doing my best to appear casual, I give another order. "Take me..." There are several options. Home. The Imperial Palace. I settle on, "to the Visionary."

Without even a grunt of acknowledgement, the Gobi leans forward onto its hands and swings its legs forward, moving like an Earth gorilla—with smooth skin, that up close looks like a synthetic fabric covered in faint yellow lines, forming a pattern of hexagons. I have no idea if the design was original to their species, or if it's just part of being a biologic. Probably will never know, since the Draun wiped them out and scoured their home world clean of life, right down to the microscopic.

Since I don't know my way around Tokyo, there is no way to know if I'm being carried into a trap, or toward my intended destination. Even if I had memorized the city's layout, I'm not sure I'd know where we were. Pockets of the city are intact, but just as much of it has been leveled.

The first Draun to change would have started testing their powers on inanimate objects. Some might find their limit at crushing a car. Others, a skyscraper. With their hatred for humanity, for all non-Draun life, they would have turned on the millions of people living in the city, destroying everything in their quest to spill blood.

In those first days, most of the human population would have been slain. Those who survived those days of carnage would have been captured and made into slaves. For those poor souls, the ones who died were the lucky ones.

As I'm carried through the broken and charred city, I start noticing the bodies. At first, the rubble is just a mash of materials, colors, and smoke. But then I see an arm. A crushed face. A limp baby.

It's a scene I've witnessed before. Genocide perpetrated by the Draun, but now coupled with humans, whose history of slaughter is long and reaches the present day. Humanity's potential for good is matched only by its capacity for evil. They are the perfect species for the Visionary's corruption.

My ears perk up at the sound of something distant and high pitched. A scream, not of pain, but of anguish. The kind of wail made by living things who have lost all hope.

"Stop," I say, and the Gobi obeys.

I listen.

There's more than one voice.

There are hundreds.

Immobile. Crying out unintelligibly. They are tormented.

Slaves.

I pinpoint the sound's origin and give a new command. "Northeast. Go."

The beast continues our tour of the ravaged city. The mask does little to block out the smell of grit, chemicals, and dried blood covering the pavement like a carpet.

The Gobi doesn't mind the carnage. It just tramples everything in our way. Walls. Vehicles. The dead. I'm glad for the mask. It hides my disgust. I close my eyes for a moment. Not seeing the scene of a massacre will help me maintain the ruse, and feigning sleep amidst all this gore, will convince anyone that might be watching that I don't give a shit.

Because no Draun would.

At best they'd be bored by it, at worst—enamored by it, and I don't think I could convince anyone of that.

The giant continues its slow lumber. I find it easy to close my eyes and relax, probably because I'm exhausted.

My thoughts wander to the others. I know they got away. I felt them fade into the distance as I ran the maze of apartments. Like the paths through Los Angeles, I'm sure it's a labyrinth. And if there is anyone who knows how to circumnavigate Tokyo's underground, it's the guy who has every street, and its history, memorized.

But I can't feel them here. Wherever here is.

I want to reach out.

To let them know I'm okay.

But that would instantly alert the Gobi, and so far, I haven't made enough progress to justify rejoining them. I just need to get close to Lumen Sok... Close enough for my Sonizer's area of effect to include him.

To undo him.

With him out of the picture, chaos will consume the Draun, and the rest of our mission—transmitting that signal around the world—will be completed without interference.

In theory.

That's how it worked out in the second it took me to think it and decide on my current course of action while standing at the top of that open manhole. Micah would say I had followed my gut. I would argue that every decision I make follows the same logical course, whether it's made in months, or seconds.

But I'd be lying. The term 'gut decision' doesn't translate into Kynolari. That's not how we operate on the battlefield. Emotions get people killed when lasers are flying, and the enemy attacks are impossible to see coming. But where is the logic in leaving my team to ensure their safety by luring a small army on a wild chase through a city I've never been to? In retrospect, it wasn't a logical choice. It was a desire to protect my family, more than it was about completing the mission.

I'll still try to do that, but this might not have been the best decision of my career. It was purely emotional.

I can hear Sean's voice in my mind, 'That's a shocker.'

I smile beneath the mask, close my eyes, and very nearly fall asleep.

That's when the Gobi stops, and I flinch fully awake for two reasons. The first is the screaming. It's loud in my ears, building so slowly through our journey that I didn't notice how close we'd gotten. But the second reason is, someone is speaking to me.

"Huh?" I say, sitting up.

I look down to find a mustached Japanese man in his twenties, hands on his hips, sword on his back, blood staining him head to toe, showing no fear of the Gobi. He shakes his head at me. "You sleep too much."

He's expecting a response...from someone he knows.

All I know about the woman whose identity I've stolen is that she was young... but not a child. I decide to attempt acting young, sliding around and then down the Gobi's arm to the ground.

"Look at you," he says, "having fun. Not a care in the world. How's it feel to be one of his 'Protected?' You haven't had to bone him yet, have you? I mean, the guy was old when we thought he was human, and now...he's Draun and his life is measured in hundreds of years. Hope he blows the dust off his—"

I grunt, trying to elevate the pitch of my voice. At the same time, I lower my head and pinch the space between my eyes. It's a very human thing to do and usually means the same thing.

"Headache?" he asks.

I nod and hold a finger to the end of my fox mask snout.

"Right," he says, whispering. "I'll keep it down, but I don't make any promises about the Yokocho of Despair back there."

I look beyond the man and see an alleyway full of glowing paper signs advertising dozens of small restaurants, each with a colorful door, and glass walls all around.

There's movement inside each.

I point to my head, and then to the alley or 'Yokocho.'

"Wait, wait, wait," he says, keeping his voice lowered. "You have a headache, and instead of taking Ibuprofen, you're going to what—take your pain out on them?"

I casually point both fingers at him.

He starts laughing and shaking his head. "You know we're not supposed to mess with these guys too much. But hell, we're also supposed to listen to the Protected—lucky bastards. Well, sort of. Once you get knocked up, you'll be stuck in that tower for nine months at a time, right? And how many babies do they want you to have in a single lifetime?"

He pauses for an answer, and I don't give him one.

"Like fifty or something. Which got me thinking. Fifty babies take a long time, and if you're still up and about when you're like seventy, does that mean we're going to live hundreds of years, too? Or will you just be pumping them out until you croak?"

I cross my arms.

"Okay, okay. Fine. Live and learn, I guess." He waves for me to follow him into the alley. What I find snaps me to a stop. The restaurants are crammed full of people. Naked people. They're cold, bloodied, beaten, and helpless. They wail and scream, begging for mercy that will not be coming.

The moment they see me, a hush falls over them.

They know me.

Recognize me.

*Fear me.*

And in that moment, any guilt I had about killing the young man and the woman who granted me this disguise evaporates.

"Look at these nasty fuckers." The man pounds his fist against a window. The people inside fall away, clinging to each other in horror. "Don't blame you for wanting to mess with a few. It's good fun. But hey, what do you think? About living for a long time. That would be so awesome. Living a thousand years. Getting to see the empire expand, the defeat of the Kynolari. Hell, maybe I'll make it two thousand years?"

"Unlikely," I say in my own voice.

# 40

**CHIRK**

Despite the veritable super team tucked away inside this dank-ass fortress of post-apocalyptic desperation, not one of us moves for the door. The sound coming from the other side is...inhuman.

Two people are screaming.

Human.

Hopefully, Draun.

The screams are just the beginning. Bones crunch and break. Blood sprays against the metal, sounding like rain. Loud thumps echo through the confined space as bodies are thrashed about.

My mind fills in the blanks. It's either a powerful Draun murdering two of his competitors, or there is some kind of mythical creature with a bunch of heads... I tap Sean's leg. When he crouches down, I speak close to his ear. "What's the dragon-thing...with the heads...you cut off one and a bunch grows back?"

"Hydra," he whispers, then his eyes widen. "It does kind of sound like—"

"Shh." It's Gruunlokar. Serious. Ready for a fight.

One scream is cut off with a gurgle. The second continues for a moment longer as the body is dragged back and forth, thumping past the door until it too falls silent.

Then...nothing.

It's like whatever attacked them just faded away.

"So..." Micah says. "Thoughts?"

"Draun," Harth says. "A rivalry. The attack came from far away."

"They sounded horrified," Jenna says.

Jess nods. "Like whatever was killing them was horrific. Up close."

"I no like those sounds," Grover says, eyes on the floor. Micah crouches and pets the dog.

"*Nobody* like those sounds," Poppy says, "but you're all overlooking the obvious. Whoever attacked the people outside this door...they might have saved us. At least some of us."

"Your point?" I ask.

"Let's not go out guns-a-blazing," she says. "Don't want to kill a friendly."

"Maybe it's Prax?" Sean asks, sounding hopeful.

"Wasn't him," I say, remembering the audible gore. "Too messy. Not his style." I clap my hands together. "All right, heavy hitters. Time to show why you get to do the fun stuff. Jenna, shield up and take this guy with you." I point to Micah. "And you, oh Axiom, you can do the dirty work. The rest of us will kick back and wait in here to see if you're vaporized."

Jenna shakes her head while rolling her eyes—it's a real talent—but she heads for the door without complaint.

Micah gives me a much more serious nod, which I appreciate, and stands behind Jenna at the door. Puts his hand on her shoulder. "I'm with you. Whenever you're ready."

Jenna's snark melts away, replaced by a serious demeanor that's intimidating. Note to self: If Jenna looks at me like that, run the other way.

There's no sign that a telekinetic shield has been erected around them, but I figure it must already be there when Jenna takes hold of the metal handle and shoves it down. The door opens without a sound. Haruto must have oiled the thing because it looks like it should all but scream when it opens.

The smell of blood washes over me like a viscous tide. Every Kynolari in the room, and Grover, flinches when the door is just a crack open. Because it's not just blood in the air—it's everything you might find inside a human body, but now on the outside.

"Careful..." Harth warns.

I move in close to Micah. Despite my orders, I have no intention of sitting back while Micah handles the fight and hogs the glory. Just need to make sure I don't dive out the door and bounce off Jenna's invisible shield. The team would never let me forget it.

Jenna shoves the door open without touching it, telekinetically expanding her presence. I can see the blood outside between their legs. Bits of gristle, too. The moment she clears the door and has a look around, she puts a hand to her mouth and mumbles, "Oh my god."

I want to chalk her revulsion up to her age, but Micah looks like he might regurgitate some of that P.F. Chang's. Despite his revolted expression, he stays professional, aiming his charged gauntlets up and down the tunnel outside the door. Seeing no immediate danger, he forms a ball of swirling laser energy at the end of one gauntlet. It illuminates the tunnel beyond in bright orange.

"Clear," he says.

"Neat trick," I say, stepping out behind them.

"Hold on to this for me?" he asks Jenna.

She lifts a hand toward the glowing sphere. "Got it."

Micah releases the energy and steps back.

A moment later, it rises to the tunnel's ceiling and sticks to it like a bubble. I could see fine without the extra light, but the orange glow leaves nothing to the imagination.

And when I see the carnage, I kind of wish it did.

There are enough whole pieces left to identify the remains as human. Given their clothing, they were definitely Draun. Now, they're sludge.

Gruunlokar steps into the tunnel, looks over the scene and grunts, unfazed by the collection of entrails, organs, and shredded muscles. He holds a hand up to Sean, who's about to step out. "Stay there. All of you."

"I can handle it," Sean says, even though he's definitely wrong.

Before I can correct him, Gruunlokar comes up with a reason to stay back that will help the others save face. "You'll disturb the scene."

"Right," Sean says, stepping back. "The scene. Cop shit, yeah? Sick."

Gruunlokar crouches by the largest conglomeration of body parts. Then he closes his eyes and breathes through his nose, putting his exceptional sense of smell to work.

"They were Draun," he says, no trace of doubt in his voice.

"How do you know?" Jenna asks.

"I can smell him on them."

"Him who?" she asks.

He opens his eyes and turns to Jenna. "Lumen Sok." He turns to me. "We're close."

He stands up, still serious, but unconcerned about our current situation.

"No reason to worry?" Micah asks, sounding doubtful.

Gruunlokar shakes his head. "We're fine."

I motion to the dead. "*'Fine'* didn't do this."

He smiles. "No. That was the girls. They're watching over us."

"The girls—" Micah looks like he's just been slapped. "*Crip and Blood?*"

Gruunlokar nods.

"Holy shit," Micah says, meeting my eyes. "Glad they're on our side."

I've seen some Kynolari rip through the enemy something fierce, leaving a wake of blood and body parts in their wake—including Harth—but it was nothing like this.

"No kidding." I take a deep stanky breath and then let it out as a sigh. "Okay, Team AwesomeSauce, let's get the show on the road. Just, ahh, form a single file line, put your hand on the person in front of you, close your eyes, and I'll lead you through."

To my surprise, they fall in line.

Jess says, "This is embarrassing," but it's half-hearted.

"It'll spare you some nightmares," Micah says, scooping Grover up in his arms. "Close your eyes, buddy."

Sean, Jess, and Harth get in line, but Harth says, "I will follow the line out of solidarity, but will not close my eyes. The sight of my enemy's sanguineous viscera will only embol—oh god." He's seen the mess. "Wow. That is…impressive."

"That's a word for it," I say. "Take them up there." I motion further up the tunnel.

Micah leads the way with Grover. I reenter the hideaway. "Okay, Haruto. Denji. Who wants comms?" Both hands shoot up. "Thought so." I remove two comm dots from my belt. "Put these in your mouth. Let the shell dissolve. Do not swallow them."

"What happens if we swallow?" Haruto asks, taking the dot, which is about the same size and color as an Ibuprofen pill.

"Will our stomachs explode?" Denji asks. Can't tell if he's excited about the prospect or horrified. Both, I think.

I huff a laugh. "What? No. You'll have to take a laxative, shit it out, and then put it *back* in your mouth."

"Oh," Denji says, taking the dot and popping it in his mouth. "Not so bad."

Haruto places his dot on his tongue and then grins. "Is sweet!"

Denji makes a funny face. "Ish shtuck to roof of my mouf."

"Leave it," I say. "Just let it do its thing. Short of getting regulators, this is the best way to stay in contact. Undetectable to the Draun. Now, at least. Just say the name of who you want to speak to, and it will connect. If you want to connect to all of us, just use the name of our teams. AwesomeSauce for my people. DickRodeo for the rest of them."

"How…how did you program those names into the comm system?" Denji asks. "You just made them up now, right?"

"Moment I spoke them, they were programed into the system." I wiggle my fingers in a rainbow shape. "Advanced alien technology. Ooooh."

Both men begin to twitch, scrunching up their faces.

"What is…" Haruto grunts. "In my head?"

"Nanowires," I say, "connecting to your audio receptors in your brain. You'll be able to hear us, but it will have nothing to do with your ears. Comes in handy if you lose your hearing."

When they both look as normal as they can again, I say, "Block your ears."

They both comply and I say, "Haruto, comm check."

His mouth drops open. Gives two passionate thumbs up.

"Denji, comms check."

"Holy shit," he says. "I hear you."

"*Muy bueno,*" I say, and point two fingers toward Siloquin. "Catch you on the flip side, crazy lady." I shift the fingers to Poppy. "Time and place, baby. I'll be there." I give her a wink and head for the door, hoping to leave before she dashes my hopes.

"We pull this off and you might just get your wish," she says.

I don't let her see my smile and double time it away, so she doesn't catch sight of my swelling bulge. After a distant and sideways goodbye with Gruunlokar and Jenna, I rejoin my team, where Micah is kissing Jess goodbye.

"Is it just me or do humans kiss too much?" I ask.

"Entirely too much," Harth says.

"I kiss, too!" Grover says, leaping up onto the pair. They bend down and receive his licks.

*So* much saliva swapping on this world.

"Take care of him," Micah says to Jess.

"You know I will," she says.

"All of you," he says, adding what could be perceived as a threatening tone to his voice.

"I will put his life before my own," Harth says.

Micah stands and shakes Harth's hand. "Thank you."

"Okay, okay," I say. "Let's get the show on the road. We got a planet to save."

Micah extends his fist down to me and I bump it, hitting just two of his fingers with my fist. Micah and Sean bump fists next. "All right, Captain Beefcake, strap me up, and let's go unfuck this Florph."

Everyone freezes.

"What's...a Florph?" Jess asks.

"Like an Earth goat," I say.

"And how does one *unfuck* an alien goat?"

I sigh. "Man, you guys killed what would have been a great line to transition to the next stage of our mission. Would have looked great in my mission logs. It's an expression. Means, 'Let's get this done.'"

"Huh," Jess says. "All right then, let's go unfuck this goat."

She starts down the tunnel and everyone follows.

"What the... She stole my line. Ugh." I lift my arms and Sean picks me up. Straps me in. Leans his head next to mine.

"Don't worry, if you really need someone to do it, I'll fuck your goat."

I close my eyes, center myself, and say, "That's great, Sean. Thanks for that. I'm thrilled."

"Awesome," he says, pleased with himself and double-timing it to catch up with the others. "So, what's your goat's name?"

# 41

## PRAXION

Before the man can turn around, raise a shield, or yelp, my raised Sonizer hits him with an inaudible pulse that effectively snatches the soul from his body. He collapses to the ground, still alive, but lacking a Draun consciousness. I had hoped the effect would revert people back to their old selves, but the Draun we're encountering welcomed the change. They are evil, through and through, and the resonant frequency that deactivates the Draun segment of the human genome—acquired from Gemma in Mexico—removes everything conjoined with it, leaving behind empty living shells. I don't know if it's more humane than killing them outright, but it's quiet, clean, and the result could be confused for any number of physical human ailments.

I haven't used it since Mexico because I didn't want Lumen Sok to know the technology existed. He'd have taken steps to protect himself, possibly relocated. Instead, he's remained in his chosen city, denning in an ancient citadel. I've learned a little about Japan's history during my time on this world, and the Samurai Bushido code suits Lumen Sok. It's the kind of creed that, while rooted in honorable values—justice, courage, and compassion—is easily twisted into a dogma of violence.

I crouch and check the man's pulse. Alive...but without a soul, how long will it take him to die? Days. It will be a slow, torturous death, but this body is an empty vessel now. There is no one left to endure the pain. And I would prefer my presence here remain a mystery, so I drag the body between the small restaurants-turned-cells and tuck it behind some potted plants.

Back in the alley, I survey the scene. Twelve restaurants have been converted into cells. Each one of the small spaces holds upwards of thirty people, most Japanese. They're naked, shaking, and terrified.

Of me, I realize.

To them, I'm just another Draun who has swept in, magically killed my predecessor, and taken his place as their jailer. It is the Draun way. Survival of the fittest—often the most deceitful, insane, and violent.

I approach the nearest cell and the reaction from the people within reminds me of two magnets oppositely polarized, pushing each other away, never able to close the distance. Except these people are stopped by the back wall. And me by the glass.

I attempt a friendly wave and am glad for translation services when I say, "It's okay. I'm not going to hurt you."

Not a one of them believes me.

Because of the mask, I realize. Everything about me tells them I'm nothing but a Draun.

I scan the alley, back and forth. Then I scan the sky overhead. We're alone. For now.

After peeling the hood back from my head, I lift the mask over my snout and away, revealing my face. I put on a smile and say, "Kynolari."

A lone young woman separates from the huddled mass. Her eyes are sunken, but now wide and hopeful. She's nearly in tears as she approaches the glass and places her hand against it. I raise my hand out from under the cloak and place it on the glass, opposite hers. She looks at my furry fingers tipped with claws. I wouldn't call them friendly looking, but they still carry a message of hope.

"Kynolari," she whispers.

"Yes," I say.

I turn toward the locked door and then back to her. She nods and heads for the exit. I meet her there, take hold of the door, and yank it open, shattering the lock.

These people are in shock. They've suffered innumerable traumas. I have no intention of adding to that, so I remain outside the cell, allowing the young woman to approach me. She's beyond feeling shame and makes no effort to cover herself. Instead, she reaches a hand up to my face.

She pets my cheek gently. With each stroke, more feeling seeps into her face. She's about to collapse with emotion, but she has no concept of how much danger we're all in now. I've freed these slaves because my heart broke for them, but it was not a sound strategy.

I place my hands on her arms, getting her full attention. "What is your name?"

"Makima," she whispers.

"I am Praxion, leader of the Kynolari on this world."

"Yes," she says with a nod. "I...saw you...in my thoughts. When..."

"I know," I say, hoping to keep her from reliving the change, when Lumen Sok sent out the signal that awoke the Draun DNA hidden in humanity's genetic code. "Do you trust me, Makima?"

She nods without hesitation. "All of us." She motions to all the cells. "We are all Kynolari in our hearts." She places her hand over her chest. "They killed our dogs, but that does not change who we are."

"Indeed," I say, bowing down and placing my forehead against hers, allowing a connection to be forged. When I stand again, I look her in the eyes and say, "I need your help, Makima."

"Anything, but—"

Before her fears about what I might ask of them fully manifests, I say, "I need you all to hide."

Sighing in relief, she nods.

"We need an entrance to the underground," I say. "Sewers. Drainage system. Anything to get you all out of sight."

She nods and limp runs toward one end of the alley. While she's looking, I move from one cell to another, tearing away the lock and setting the people free. When I'm done, hundreds of people crowd the alley.

Makima finds me in the crowd. Tugs on my cloak. "This way. Come!"

She leads me through masses, who part for me, whispering as I pass. I can hear their hope and desperation. It's heartbreaking, and it blinds my strategic mind. I just need to save these people. Then I can—

I slide to a stop at the end of the alley.

Twenty feet ahead, in a cobblestone courtyard, is a manhole cover. It just needs to be opened. Then all these people can file into the city's depths.

But my eyes don't linger on the escape route. Instead, I focus on the man standing thirty feet behind the manhole. He's dressed as a ninja, wearing black head to toe. There are two swords sheathed on his back. He's leaning casually on a staff, like he's bored.

"That was a fun trick," he says, speaking English. "What did you do to him?"

I say nothing, assessing how to handle the Draun. But I am at a severe disadvantage. His relaxed demeanor tells me he knows the same thing. There are more than three hundred desperate, naked humans behind me, depending on me to save them. If they're smart, they'll start running out the alley's far side and try to get lost in the vast, empty city, but I don't hear any feet slapping into the distance. They're all watching, waiting for their savior to dispatch the enemy as quickly as I did the first.

I could, if they weren't here, if I could move, use the buildings, and confuse the man until his guard drops. With them at my back, I'm forced to defend.

"Yeah, I get it," the man says. "State secrets and all that, but..." He breathes through his teeth. "I really want to know how you did it."

"Lumen Sok would sense your deceit before you got close enough," I say.

He peels down the mask covering his lower face, revealing a broad smile and a thin beard. The man is built like Harth and stands six inches taller. He also has the calm confidence of a man who has fought and killed before.

"Maybe we got off on the wrong foot," he says. "I know who you are, Praxion. But you're in the dark about me, so let me fill you in. Name is Reinhart, former military turned private security turned badass motherfucker who does whatever the hell he wants. You know, I think I might have destroyed half of Tokyo. Unlucky for them I was on vacation here when we changed." He laughs. "And I was just getting used to sushi. Long story short, we both want the same thing. Teach me how to use that fancy wrist band, and I'll let these sad bastards walk."

It's almost tempting, but, "The technology isn't compatible with Draun biology. Let me leave in peace with these people, and I will finish my mission. You'll still get what you want."

He considers my offer a moment, and then squints, smiles, and waggles a finger at me. "You... So clever. You're not here to just kill Lumen Sok."

"We both know that," I say, my ear twitching when I finally hear people at the back of the alley realize they can make a run for it.

They don't make it far.

The buildings at the alley's far end collapse inward, sealing off their escape. Means he either has help, or he's incredibly powerful, and I am at a severe disadvantage.

"What you need to consider," I say, doing my best to sound confident, "is when I turn my sights on the rest of you, who will be strong enough to stand against me. You, or Lumen Sok?"

I've put him in a hard place for a Draun. He'll never admit Lumen Sok should be their leader, but if he does anything other than let me go, it signals the same weakness.

"Unless," he says. "I just kill you now, bring you to Lumen Sok, and slit his throat while he gloats over your corpse. That is what I'm meant to do. Hunt you all down. Bring you to him. I've been following you since your friends dipped into the sewers. You're impressive. Ruthless. Posing as one of the Protected? Chef's kiss. But you're outclassed, outsmarted, and—"

I remove the gauntlet from my arm for the first time in many years. I place it on the cobblestone beside me. I draw my sidearm and drop it beside the gauntlet. The cloak goes next, falling behind me. "Let's find out," I say, "how outclassed I am."

Fists clenched, I start toward him. He laughs, but it fades when he realizes, "Wait, you're serious?"

This would never work in the heat of battle, but Reinhart is so confident and headstrong that he might go for it. To not fight me would show fear, and that is something Draun can't stomach. Because they are superior. They're sure of it. The possibility of their own defeat rarely crosses their mind. Hubris is one of their few weaknesses.

He starts toward me, twirling his staff. He hasn't agreed to not use his abilities, but we both know to do so would show the same weakness. He won't resort to telekinesis until things get desperate. By then, I hope all these people will be gone.

"Makima," I say. "Run."

She doesn't hesitate, sprinting away and unleashing the floodgates. The freed slaves break out of the alley, running in every direction except toward Reinhart. Some follow the original plan, lifting the manhole cover and dropping down into the sewer.

"Oh, I don't think so," Reinhart says. Dozens of cobblestones shake and lift up from the courtyard. They then launch with the force of shards, plowing through several people. It would take only a few of them, thrown down the alley, to kill nearly everyone.

I'm forced to charge, lunging for his throat, hoping I'll get lucky and tear his jugular open. I never make it. I'm struck from the air and knocked to his feet, not by a telekinetic blast, but by his spinning staff. He twirls it around, plants one end on the ground, and leans his weight on it again. "C'mon, old dog. You're not going to make this easy, are you?"

I growl and get back to my feet, squaring off with a Draun that could crush me to a pulp, explode my brain, or turn me inside out. Then I charge again.

# 42

## GRUUNLOKAR

"How are you feeling?" I ask.

"I'm fine," Jenna says, rubbing her elbow.

"Uhuh," I say, and wait. Jenna often leads with what she wants the truth to be and then one of two things occur. The truth appears to her like a burst of light, or her guilty conscience catches up with her. Either way, it never takes long for her to acknowledge and admit the truth.

"If feeling like you're going to throw up is fine," she says.

"It's normal," I say.

"Because we're going to kill a person?"

"Lumen Sok is *not* a person, even if he looks like one."

"But isn't that the same kind of bullshit people use all the time to justify, I don't know, like war crimes and genocide? Dehumanizing a person is the first step to killing them without guilt."

"I never promised you wouldn't feel guilt for helping kill Lumen Sok," I tell her, "but you shouldn't."

"I guess," she says, and sits on the hotel room's bed. We're currently in the top floor penthouse of the Hotel Grand Arc Hanzomon, positioned on the building's curved east side, hidden behind mirrored windows. Aside from this room, which appears to have been used by a young girl, the penthouse is a warzone. Dead bodies, some torn apart, some full of bullet holes, litter the main living area. Blood everywhere. Haruto said the penthouse belonged to a gang he called Yakuza. Given the state of things, I'd say some of the well-armed gang became Draun, and some didn't. The result was a bloody battle too messy to clean up. Which is why the space hasn't been claimed by a Draun.

Our view through the window is of the Imperial Palace's east side. Reaching the Palace was a simple walk through the sewers. Uneventful other than the smell. Jenna and I are in position while the others are attempting to enter the Palace under the cover of darkness. Their first obstacle...a moat.

*A moat.*

I shake my head. It's embarrassing. Stopped by an artificial body of water.

With only one bridge on the compound's east side, they'll be totally exposed to anyone standing watch...which is why I am looking for whoever that might be.

While speaking with Jenna, my vision is focused on the view through my 1H1K Void Sniper gauntlet. I can see the entire compound and most of the buildings inside, including the Imperial Residence, the Fukiage Omiya Palace and the reception hall with an open courtyard at its core. Using other visual spectrums, I can peer through the windows of every building. I haven't seen any movement yet, but I can only see through the windows, not the walls beyond. Every structure could be full of Draun, like cream filling in one of Sean's Twinkies, and I'd never know.

"Think it out," I tell her. "Don't be emotional about it, or precious about life in general. Think of the big picture. Lumen Sok has committed genocide on a galactic scale. Many planets have fallen victim. Trillions of lives lost, including your own people.

"Now imagine that the remnants of humanity, however many million are left, huddling in the world's most repulsive living conditions, will all perish with the push of a button—a button held by Lumen Sok. You have ten seconds to pull the trigger before he pushes that button. His death will free your people and prevent scores of other worlds from suffering the same fate, not to mention prevent my people from having to spend several more decades hunting him down. What would you—"

"Pull the trigger," she says. "But you can still feel bad about having to take that one life, right?"

I glance out of my sniper scope and look her in the eyes. "No."

Her answer unsettles me. Could she really be that compassionate? And if so, how did she become the Jenna Flood that removed the bones from a man's body and then animated his malleable form with her mind? How could *this* person become that monster?

"How?" I ask.

"How, what?"

"I'm struggling to comprehend how someone, as hopelessly naive and idealistic as you, could become the Jenna Flood we first met."

"Been wondering that, too," she says. "I guess that's my concern. What if we do it? What if we kill Lumen Sok, take his head right off... What if I enjoy it?"

"Then I won't be celebrating alone," I say.

"But I mean like *really* enjoy it," she says. "Like I want to do it again. To anyone. Just for that thrill. What if killing Lumen Sok turns me into him... Into *her?* Before my father died, I felt rooted. But now, I'm alone. No family. No roots. I'm not even in my body anymore, because it's dead." She rubs her head. "Fuck. What am I supposed to do with that? I'm basically no one. Probably don't have a soul. Does it really matter if—"

I take her hand, hoping to cut off her downward spiral that's going to lead to a panic attack. "Hey."

She blinks out of her thoughts. Looks me in the eyes.

"The person you became before is not the person you are now."

"But how? Why?"

"She didn't have me, kid. Ten years from now, you won't be a genocidal maniac, you'll be a hero known throughout the universe. Along with me, of course."

She smiles. Nods. "A hero, huh?"

"The kind that people write books about," I say.

She rolls her eyes. "Laying it on kind of thick, don't you think?"

I shrug. "There is a whole series of books based on our time during the war. Non-fiction, but the writers embellished a bit...and reduced the most graphic details and events. We're not supposed to be fond of them, but I like the way I'm portrayed."

She barks a laugh and then covers her mouth with a stuffed animal of a stylized white cat.

Resisting the urge to take the stuffed toy in my mouth and shake it around, I turn my gaze back through the sniper gauntlet's scope. "Now, how are you feeling about replacing the Visionary's head with a telekinetically shielded shard?"

"Not great," she says. "But better."

"You want to practice?"

"On what?"

I point out the window. "The bridge. Far side guard house. Single target."

"Don't have a zoom lens in my eyes and can only see colors that are reflected by light...of which there is none outside. You're basically just a silhouette against the night sky, and you're like three feet away."

"You don't need to see the target," I say. "Just focus on wrapping the shard when I fire it."

"Right," she says, standing beside me now. "What's going on?"

I zoom out and spot motion on the bridge.

"Poppy. She's...she's naked."

"Got news for you buddy," she says, "but that's not a weird thing for dogs on Earth."

"I believe that's the point," I say. "She's contorted herself to look like an Earth dog. Fucking hell. She's crossing the bridge in the open."

I adjust my aim back to the guard house. There is a single heat signature moving around, but I don't know what I'm looking at. If we don't get a kill shot with our first attempt, the alarm could be sounded.

And Poppy knows that, so why is she—

The guard exits the small building. Stands on the far side of the bridge, watching Poppy trot happily toward him. He crouches down. Holds out his hands. Claps his knees. He's calling her over.

She turns her head back and looks right up at me. This was her plan. To expose the guard.

I whisper, "Firing in three, two, one!"

The shard slides out of my gauntlet moving so quickly that it punches a clean hole through the glass without shattering it. I don't know if Jenna took her chance to practice on another living target until the shard streaks across the road below, the moat beyond, and the bridge with nearly enough force to sever the atoms it passes on the way.

Then the man drops, his head still intact, but his brain scrambled by the pressure wave created by the shard that buried itself deep in the Earth beyond. The man crumples down on himself, just a drizzle of blood leaking from the two clean holes in his cranium.

Poppy stands and waves the others over. Micah, Haruto, and Siloquin emerge from the bottom of the hotel and race across the bridge. They pick the body up and drag it back into the guard house.

"Sorry," Jenna whispers. She never put her hand on my shoulder. Didn't even try to enhance the shard.

"If he'd had a shield up," I say, "Poppy would be dead."

She sits on the bed. "Oh, god... I didn't..."

"Like it or not, Jenna, we're in a war. I know it's a lot of pressure, but there is a chance that its outcome will depend on you and me."

"Sorry," she says. "I just keep thinking about that guy on the roof. What we did to his body. It...it was everywhere. What kind of person does something like that?"

I raise my hand. "This kind. And apologies only matter if you take action to correct the mistake."

"Ugh," she says. "You even sound like my father. Stupid one-liner life lessons."

"Was he ever wrong?"

"Not usually," she admits.

"Would he want you to help me finish this war?" I ask.

She nods without hesitation. "He'd do it himself if he could."

"Good," I say, "because our people have incoming, and he's definitely shielded."

"How can you tell?" she asks.

"Because he's also flying," I say. "Get ready."

I take aim at the man swooping down toward the guard house.

He definitely saw something but doesn't know what. They must have guards stationed in some of the other buildings surrounding the Palace. Good to know.

Gauging his velocity, angle of approach, and distance, I hold my fire until, "Three, two, one!"

This time I feel her hand grasp my shoulder. My spine tingles. Energy flows through me, into the gauntlet, and out with the shard.

The round punches a fresh hole in the glass—this time the size of a tennis ball. A moment later, the Draun's head bursts into mist and the body topples into the moat. There's a splash, but then he sinks out of sight, water rushing down his exposed esophagus and filling his lungs. He'll surface in a few days, when his body fills with gas.

"What happened?" Jenna asked.

"Target neutralized." I lean back and come out of the sniper gauntlet's view scope for a moment. "Nice work."

"Just glad I couldn't see it."

"Mm," I say. "Will make your future therapy sessions easier."

She slugs my shoulder. "Asshole."

I toggle my comms. "Micah."

"Copy," he says. "Thanks for the cover."

"Two down," I say. "Second is in the moat. You're clear."

"Second?" he says. "Never knew he was there."

"Airborne," I say. "He was en route."

"The hole in this guy's head was neat, did Jenna—"

"Not the first target, but the second." I turn to Jenna. "She did well. When the time comes, she'll be ready."

# 43

## PRAXION

I pick myself up off the cobblestone courtyard for the second time in less than a minute. Reinhart has struck me down again. Unlike most Draun, who rely on their newfound abilities to do everything, this man's long history of capability trumps his need to do things the easy way.

Including killing.

As I get back to my feet, I wonder how many people he cut down with those swords. I can smell the mix of bloods clinging to the blades.

But he's cocky. And doesn't know his enemy. While I understand the limitations of the human body, he doesn't know how strong or fast a Kynolari can be. Doesn't know how much of a beating I can take, thanks to my light body armor and the fur beneath it.

He also doesn't know that I'm holding back, allowing him to strike, feigning injury, studying his technique.

"You know," he says, spinning his staff around his body before snapping to a stop. "I was hoping to nab that mutt. Grover. First, who names their dog Grover? Fucking floppy-armed Muppet."

"Super Grover," I say.

His face scrunches up. "What?"

I stand up tall again, which is nearly a foot shorter than Reinhart. Then I repeat the phrase Sean said to me when I didn't recognize the name Super Grover. "Somebody never watched Sesame Street as a kid."

"Sesame—what the fuck are you… Why do you know what Sesame Street—You know what? Doesn't matter. Point is, you're the one the bossman wants. I can find the dog when I deal with your sewer rat pals. If they're not dead already. You guys know that there're still thousands of us here, right? The weakest of us were given the planet, the strongest are here to rebuild the empire."

He presses the attack, spinning his staff as he approaches, making it nearly impossible to predict where he will strike. Nearly.

When the staff comes down toward my neck, I reach up and catch it in my hand. Before he fully comprehends what's happened, I yank on the staff. Reinhart topples toward me and gets my forearm across his chest. He flips backward and lands on his stomach.

I casually walk a few feet away and turn around to face him. "You show off too much. It gives me time to calculate your next strike."

He pushes himself up. "Calculate, huh?"

"Every fight comes down to simple math," I say, speaking to him as though he were my student. "If you're smart enough, you can predict everything your opponent will do."

He spins the staff but stops faster than usual. "Didn't predict my first two strikes."

"Meh," I say with a shrug. "Just needed to understand what level of math you were using. I'm not an expert on human education, but I think you'd fall into the kindergarten range. Strange word, kindergarten. Did you know it's German? I only do because I've had every language on Earth programed into my regulators. Means, 'child garden,' which is just as strange a concept as a Super Grover, I think."

My casual demeanor irks him. His next strike has no flourish. He's abandoned his showmanship. He's also completely forgotten about the people fleeing the alley.

I am his world now and will be until one of us is defeated.

He unleashes a series of staff strikes, putting me on the defense. My hands slap the staff as I back away, keeping my expression laid back. The man's hubris is his weakness. I take advantage of that by stoking his anger, forcing him to focus harder.

The staff clatters to the ground, bumping away over the uneven terrain.

"Fight me," he says, losing his patience.

"Don't need to," I tell him. "I'm outsmarting you."

He tears his mask away and throws it to the ground, signifying that he's done having fun. His face is Caucasian, covered in scruff leading up to a shaved head. Given his name, I'm not surprised that he's not Japanese. Even Micah had a copy of American Ninja in his old VHS collection. I watched it twice with Harth, who believed it was meant to be an ironic comedy.

"My people have been at war with the Draun since my birth. I've been steeped in battle beyond your comprehension, in places your people would consider hell. I have faced monsters—Draun, biologics, and beasts that would have you pissing in your adorable costume. And you think I'm worried about *you?* A human being, with swords?"

His jaw muscles pulse, betraying his effort to conceal his irritation.

"Whenever you're ready," I say, keeping my stance casual.

He charges, both swords raised.

The blades whoosh through the air together, passing each other as they arc in opposite directions.

I step back, just out of range.

He swings again and again, the swords glinting and singing through the air. The weapons were likely stolen, taken from a master Japanese swordsmith. I can hear their quality. He does not deserve them.

On his next swing, I take them.

As each blade streaks past my chest, I slap them downward. The sudden impact dislodges the weapons one at the time, sending them twirling away. One clatters across the cobblestones. The other embeds itself in the wall of a noodle shop.

Reinhart doesn't miss a beat, spinning and kicking twice in a row so fast that he nearly catches me. A simple leap back keeps me clear, but he turns that spin into momentum and charges, throwing a flurry of punches.

"You're skilled," I tell him, while deflecting his blows, doing my best to make it look like the job is effortless. "But you just—don't—have what it takes."

A quick deflection of his fist exposes his chest.

I thrust my palm into his solar plexus, knocking the wind out of his lungs, breaking a rib, and sprawling him back.

Could have broken all his ribs.

Killing him would have been easy.

But now he knows exactly what he's up against: a hardened soldier on another level. All the practice in the world can't make up for my years of experience, pain tolerance, or willingness to win by the most extreme measures, including sacrifice.

The moment he loses his patience—really loses it—I've won.

I'm lifted from the ground by an invisible force and am flung back. I bounce across the courtyard twice and then slam into the noodle shop's wall. Lying there stunned, I take a moment to scan the alley behind Reinhart. There are dozens of dead, but those still on their feet have managed to flee.

The sword handle protruding from the wall supports my weight. I pull myself up and yank the blade from the wall. Then I step back into the courtyard and stand my ground.

Reinhart doesn't bother picking up his staff or sword. He's done fighting. Has moved on to dominating.

And he's not alone.

Biologics arrive first. Gobi, Tyrne, Platamots, and Skitterlings. Even a Straub Hunt Squad. The rumbling of approaching Helions is impossible to mistake. Escape is impossible. Enemies fill the streets.

And the skies.

The Draun arrive one by one, coming in from all directions. Word has spread. A Kynolari has been cornered.

They'll fight over the honor of capturing me if the battle goes on much longer. But I have no intention of letting that happen.

I throw the sword underhand, the blade zinging through the air until it's caught, just inches from Reinhart's face.

He wasn't shielded. I very nearly killed him. And the Draun watching know it. I can hear them whispering to each other, debating how things will turn out, discussing which one of them will be the first to join the fray.

But they're not going to get the chance.

When Reinhart recovers from his shock, he focuses on the sword for just a moment. Then it spins around and launches toward me.

I see it coming.

Have time to move.

But…I don't.

The sword punches through my armor, slides through my body and out the back. I spin and fall to the ground.

Defeated.

"Pitiful," he says. "I have no idea why Lumen Sok is so afraid of you."

A telekinetic force drags me across the rough stones behind him, trailing blood. He walks to my shed gauntlet and picks up his prize. He slaps it onto his right arm and snaps it closed. Nothing happens. He's never seen a gauntlet before. Has no idea how it operates. But he's not interested if he can't use it to kill. Drops it on the ground and picks up the railgun. Points it at a nearby Skitterling and pulls the trigger. The shard shatters inside the small biologic and all but erases it. He chuckles and says, "That's more like it." Stuffs the weapon into his black pants.

Then he turns to me with a smile and says, "Night, night," before a sudden pressure compresses my mind and turns the world to darkness.

# 44

## CHIRK

"Halfway there," Denji says via the comms.

"You sure about that?" I grumble. "Because it feels like you're taking us on the scenic route through stank town."

"I do not know what stank town is," Denji says, "but your route is circuitous on purpose."

I roll my eyes. "And why is that?"

"You talk a lot. All of you. Complaining. Joking. Plotting. I am avoiding known Draun gathering places to ensure you're not—"

"Okay, okay. I get it." I shake my head. He's right. The underground gives us a false sense of security. All the concrete around us feels like a protective bubble, and who in their right mind would come down here to find us? Biologics, that's who. They don't care about smells, piss, or shit. "Probably not a bad idea."

"I know," he says.

If he wasn't in a wheelchair, he'd get a swift kick to the wrinkle berries the next time I saw him. I'm about to tell him as much when a chirp sounds from my regulator. It repeats two more times in rapid succession, once from Jess's regulator and once from Harth's.

The sound sends a twist of nausea through my body. It means that someone on the team has removed a gauntlet, someone's arm has been severed, or someone is dead.

"Harth," I say, looking back at the big guy, who is already tapping his gauntlet with a worried look on his face.

"Looking," he says.

Before he can finish the job of tracking the device's location—and owner—my comms comes to life again. This time it's Gruunlokar. "Chirk."

"I'm here," I say. "It's not us."

"Not us," he says, his voice low.

Harth confirms it at the same time Gruunlokar and I deduce the answer, all three of us speaking the name in unison. "Praxion."

"I've got a location," Harth says. "It's not far."

"What wrong with Praxion?" Grover asks, ears and tail down. He can smell my concern, even in this shithole.

"Not sure yet," I tell him. "Denji, we're going to be making a detour."

"What—why? *Where?*"

"Let you know when we get there," I say, "all we know right now is that we need to head—" I look to Harth.

"North," he says.

"North," I tell Denji. "Now."

"Next right," Denji says, adapting quickly.

As we double time it through the sewers, Jess falls back, joining me and Sean. "What's going on? Don't be vague."

"Yeah, dude," Sean says, looking down at me strapped to his chest. "Spill it."

"Praxion's gauntlet is offline. Means he's taken it off, had his arm removed…or is dead. When this happens, a signal is sent to our regulators—"

"I heard it," Jess says.

"—and a tracking beacon is activated." I look up at Sean. "Glad you know?"

"Not really," Sean says. "Geez. Do you think—"

"Don't guess," I say, and look up at Jess. "You humans have a bad habit of projecting possible futures and getting all worked up about them. Am I concerned? Yes. Am I making up gruesome stories of his potential demise and worrying about what it will mean for us? No. Fuck that. We deal in facts, okay?"

"Got it," Sean says.

Jess gives me a squinty-eyed side glance. She doesn't say it aloud, but she's calling bullshit on my declaration of Kynolari superiority. Because it *is* bullshit. I just don't want their worries to compound my own.

Denji leads us on an efficient, mostly straight course through the tunnels. While Harth provides Denji with compass directions, Denji responds with curt, "Left", "Right," and "Straight" instructions. The rest of us are silent, more aware of the enemy's proximity now, and that whatever we might find at the end of this journey was strong enough to take down Praxion.

After ten minutes, Harth says, "We're there. Need an exit."

"Straight ahead," Denji says. "Should be a manhole above you."

"What are we going to find up there?" I ask, "You know, structure-wise."

"Open courtyard, apartments, businesses, a yokocho…standard Tokyo."

"Harth," I say, "peek and sneak."

He nods, locates the manhole cover and holds out his hand. After unbuckling from Sean, I leap into Harth's hand. It's a little humiliating, but hey, I'm letting a human trot me around in a baby carrier. Harth climbs the ladder to the manhole, places his hand against its base and waits for my signal.

When I nod, he lifts the manhole.

It slides up smoothly and without a sound.

Just an inch, enough for me to do a quick sweep of the area. I'm looking for feet. The standing variety. Doesn't matter what they belong to.

But I don't see feet. I see… "Higher."

Harth lifts the manhole cover and me a few inches high. "Shit."

"What do you see?" he asks.

"Bodies," I tell him. "A lot."

"Praxion?"

"He's not here, but—" I spot his gauntlet lying on the ground. "Open fully. I'll be out and back in ten seconds, tops. Be ready to close it behind me."

Harth nods.

"Go!" I say, and I'm all but launched from the manhole as the cover rises. I dive and roll to my feet, taking a quick look at the carnage while sprinting toward the gauntlet.

The dead are fresh. Each one of them has a hole in their body, roughly the size of the cobble stones I'm running across. I know a Draun's work when I see it. Praxion must have been trying to save them.

The scene can't be more than fifteen minutes old. The smell of blood hangs thick in the air. I perk my ears, listening, but the city is quiet, like everyone has been invited to a party and decided to leave us out.

I slide to a stop, snag the gauntlet, and take one last look around. There're no major signs of a battle, which is unexpected. Praxion with his Sonizer, which can erase a Draun's consciousness, should have taken at least some baddies down. But I don't see a single Draun.

I spring back the way I came, and in two bounds reach the manhole. Sliding over the rough stones isn't a great idea, but I don't realize that until I've already done it. Sore-assed, I slip beneath the open manhole and drop down, right into Sean's waiting hands.

The manhole closes above us, and the others gather around to inspect the gauntlet with me.

"Sniffs like Praxion," Grover says. "Some blood."

"Not seeing any damage though," Jess says.

"So, he took it off?" Sean asks. "Why would he take it off?"

Sean's question hangs in the air for a good thirty seconds before Denji, still on open comms, chimes in. "Perhaps, it is because he wanted you to find it?"

"He would have known we'd hear the chime," Harth says. "That we would come for him."

"Yeah, but why?" I ask. "The only thing here is his gauntlet. What good is—"

"Oooh," Sean says with a little laugh. "My bros, he wants us to find the gauntlet so that we can use it. He knows the mission. That we can't complete our end without that resonant frequency shit. So, he left it for us, while he's doing his thing."

Harth and I share a look. It makes sense. But there is still a problem. "It needs an operator. Harth and Jess are out because using two different gauntlets can cause mental feedback issues. I'm too small. Grover…is Grover."

"I'm Grover!" Grover says, wagging his tail.

"And that leaves…" I twist myself around, still sitting in Sean's hands. I hold the gauntlet out to him.

His eyes widen. "No way."

"No way?" Harth asks, sounding offended.

"I mean that in a 'no way' kind of way, not in a 'no, I won't do it' kind of way."

"It's an expression of excited disbelief," Jess says.

Harth shakes his head. "I am beginning to detest your language. It makes no sense."

"So, what do you say?" I ask Sean.

"The legendary gauntlet of Commander Praxion, savior of the universe and maybe Earth and the universe again—"

"Hey, he had help," I say.

"—passed down to his gifted prodigy protégé, Lord Sean Huempfner."

"You must have regulators installed first," Harth says, "and the last we knew, your brainwaves weren't entirely in line with the Kynolari. It could be dangerous."

"Good thing I'm brave," he says.

"Or stupid," Jess says. "We *can* figure out something else."

Harth approaches with two halves of a regulator in his hands. I always made fun of him for carrying them. He's never had a reason to use them before, not even to replace a broken or malfunctioning set. But Sean will be the fourth recipient since our arrival on Earth. The only added risk this time is that this is a fresh regulator, built by Harth, to replace the ones given to Micah, Jess, and Grover. No one better than Harth for the job, but they're definitely not factory inspected units.

"Naw, dog, I'm good. Been livin' the Kyno life since that last test. No way I'm not one of you now. Hook me up. Strap me in. Benny Hinn me with that shit." He holds out his arm, waiting for the gauntlet.

"Regulators first," Harth says, placing them on the sides of Sean's head, just behind his ear. After a moment, Harth asks, "How do you feel?"

"Tickles," Sean says. "Feels a little fuzzy in my head. Just shy of being buzzed."

"He's fine," I declare and clamp the gauntlet onto his arm. He winces as it attaches itself to his bones. When the job is done, he lifts his arm, looks at the gauntlet, and says, "Huh, that wasn't bad at—"

Sean's eyes roll back, and his body topples straight back. I leap away just before he slaps into two feet of watery filth.

# 45

## MICAH

Here's a story. It's true. I once went to a science lecture with a girl I was trying to impress. The private event was held at a laboratory and attended by scientists from around the world. The subject was climate change—long before the news was actively covering the subject—and it was fascinating. But as I was sitting there next to the girl that I so desperately wanted to think I was a stud, and I was surrounded by fifty leading scientists...my stomach began to growl.

Not just growl. It felt like an irate wolverine had been let loose. Waves of nausea hit a minute later. I was going to pop. But I'd never been to this place before. Didn't know where the bathrooms were, and everyone who worked in the lab was attending the lecture. If I got up, it would make a scene. If I got up, I might puke instantly. If I got up...nothing good would happen, I was sure of it.

As my body roiled, desperate to free itself from whatever bad food I had eaten, I mentally prepped for war and by sheer force of will, stood my ground at the Hot Gates, fending off wave after wave of nausea. My body shook. I broke out into a sweat. But I held the pass, and the enemy didn't make it through. And just as quickly as it had hit me, the urge to throw-up ended. My body submitted. And not a single person noticed.

I mention all of this, because it's how I'm feeling right now, standing outside the Fukiage Palace, home to former Emperors and the most likely domicile for a world conquering megalomaniac. That's the theory anyway, after the imperial residence was a bust. There were guards, most of them silently dispatched from a distance by Gruunlokar and Jenna. Siloquin skewered the last of them, losing her patience with the lack of action. I think she wanted to prove her worth. She knows we're all holding silent grudges against her. How can we not? She's inhabiting the body of our friend, and we don't know if we're going to get her back or if we're stuck with doggy Joan of Arc.

Sliding out from the base of a tree, I inspect the Palace. The architecture blends traditional Japanese elements with modern features. The sprawling structures making up the Palace have sloping tiled roofs and broad eaves. The exterior walls look white in the moonlight. All of it feels like a natural extension of the meticulous gardens and trees surrounding the Palace.

The interior is as dark as the exterior, but that doesn't mean no one is home.

"Siloquin," I whisper into my comms.

"Here," she says.

"Eyes on?"

"Nothing," she says, "but I can smell them. Three targets. All inside. One of them is taking a shit. Would you like to know the details of his last meal?"

My stomach churns.

"No, thank you. Gruunlokar?"

"Nothing from here," he says. "They are avoiding windows on purpose. Or perhaps sleeping."

"Poppy?" I ask.

A chime is the only response. It's triggered with a thought on her end. A simple notification she can send without making a sound that means, 'Can't talk now. Bad guys are close.'

"Two chimes for yes, one for no," I say. "Did you go inside?"

Three chimes follow the questions.

"Three? Wait…is three chimes 'maybe.'"

Two chimes follow and I can't help but smile. "You're such a Pug."

"Okay team, we have one little sassy bitch on the inside, but since her gauntlet makes a lot of noise, and she's too small to strangle a caterpillar, I'm going to enter on the west. Siloquin, take the other side. Keep it *quiet*."

Knowing that I'm working with professionals helps ease my nerves some, but not enough. Because none of this feels right. We are Seal Team 6-ing our way through what should be the most protected compound under Draun control.

The Visionary has been skittish when it comes to the Kynolari. Since making an appearance—in orbit over Denver—he has remained in the background, an ethereal threat, preferring to send lackeys rather than face us himself.

Which means he's either terrified of the Kynolari, or a brilliant tactician who knows better than to risk his strongest asset—himself.

Either way, I'm starting to suspect the new emperor of Japan, and the world, isn't home at the moment. And if that's true, we need to know why.

"Do me a favor," I say. "Keep one of them alive."

I get a single chime from Poppy. *No.*

"That is a horrible idea," Gruunlokar says.

"If we get one of them outside, in the open, you can cover us. Shield or not, you and Jenna can put them down faster than they can make our eyeballs burst, yeah?"

"Yes," he says.

"Then that's the plan. Kill the strongest, extract the weakest. We need to know why this place is a ghost town."

Gruunlokar grunts. "Agreed."

After a begrudging silence, two chimes. Poppy is on board.

"One dead," Siloquin whispers. "I will do my best to spare one of the remaining two."

And right there is why I miss Torel. She's a team player. Siloquin is a one woman hit squad.

I slide up to the door beside me, take hold of the knob, and give it a turn. Opens right up. Too fucking easy. My nerves flare, but thanks to that laboratory experience, I know how to control my body's biologic responses when shit needs to get done. Puts me at a slight disadvantage, having to fight a war on two fronts, but my gauntlets more than make up the difference. They flare to life, lighting the way ahead.

"Hey," Haruto says, appearing by my side.

I flinch and nearly cut him in half. "How the hell did you—"

"I have the blood of Shoguns in my veins," he says with a double tap of his eyebrows.

"Just...stay here, okay? Things are about to get more dicey than a cabbage in the hands of a teppanyaki chef."

Haruto lets out a silent laugh, nodding and pointing at me.

"Stay," I say, and he nods vigorously. He's a man of his word, so I slip into the darkness and let the orange light of my gauntlets lead the way. The once opulent interior is in ruins. There's blood on the walls and a long smear of it across the floor where a body was dragged.

No one lives here. Not even a Draun would live in this mess. So why are they guarding it at all?

*They're not guards,* my subconscious screams from the depths.

*Doesn't matter,* I think. Still Draun. Still have answers. And we need them sooner than later.

"Two down," Siloquin says over the comms. "Never woke up."

"Do not, I repeat, do not kill the third."

A thump turns my eyes to the ceiling. Heavy footsteps follow, sprinting down a hallway toward an ornate staircase that descends into the foyer I'm currently standing in. So, I wait.

Much lighter and faster footsteps chase after the first. Poppy. She hasn't opened fire, which is great, but the Draun is running. It's not bad. It's just...weird.

"Kaiya!" Poppy shouts from above.

It's followed by an "Oof" and then the thunderous tumult of someone rolling down a really old staircase. The Draun, a young Japanese man, lands on the floor at my feet, upside down to me.

He groans and opens his eyes. Sees me, and the glowing gauntlets aimed at him, and panics.

"Inu ga suki desu!" he shouts, raising his hands. "Inu ga suki desu!"

The first two times he says it, my translation services miss it, probably because he's slobber-crying at the same time. I power down my weapons and put on my nice guy face. "Speak slowly. Tell me again."

This time when he speaks, I hear it in perfect English. "I like dogs."

My brow furrows, just for a moment, until I realize we've been completely duped, and killing the wrong people. "You're not Draun?"

He shakes his head. "No. NO. I…I am slave. They tell me to stay here."

"Why?" Poppy asks, crouching on the stairway banister.

He looks nervous about answering—until the point of Siloquin's spear slides across his shoulder and comes into view in front of his face. "Answer."

With his focus on me, he apologetically says, "Trap."

# 46

## CHIRK

"Yo," Sean says, groaning as he leans up onto his elbows. "Feel like I just had Snu Snu with She-Hulk."

Grover is the fastest to respond, descending on Sean with a barrage of licking. Sean laughs, "ahuh, ahuh," and it's good to hear. Thought we might have lobotomized him. "Love Sean," Grover says, smearing the side of his face, along with a strand of drool, along Sean's head.

"Oh good," I say, standing on his chest. "You're alive." I'm trying to act like I haven't been shaking in my little boots since he hit the water. I lean in close and whisper. "Love you, too, bud, but I got to look tough."

He nods, taps the side of his nose, and says, "I got you."

"Took you long enough," I say. "Twenty minutes. Harth had to drag your ass all the way here."

"With you riding him," Harth grumbles.

"I may have taken advantage of the situation." *So I could hear his heartbeat.* "But we're where we need to be, and he's awake."

"But is he okay?" Jess asks, crouching down beside Sean. Grover moves around her, wagging his tail, happily observing. Jess places a hand on Sean's forehead. "How are you feeling?"

Before he can answer, Jess's hand snaps up to her regulator. "Whoa."

We all feel it. Sean's regulators have just paired with the rest of ours and we quickly know exactly how he's feeling.

"Pretty damn good," he says. "Hey, I can kind of feel you guys, too! Whoa, this is badass. It's like we're all connected!"

"We *are* all connected," Harth says.

"Is this like some tantric shit? Like if one of us has an orgasm, we all—"

"No," Jess says, "not like that…and just in case it can be, don't even think about trying. The connection goes both ways."

"Right, right," he says. "Rad."

He looks up and around, noticing for the first time that he's not lying in a stream of ass sludge. "Where are we?"

"Beneath Mori JP Tower," Harth says.

"Oh snap," he says, whispering now. "We should be quiet, right?"

"You're four stories underground," Denji says in our comms. "There are four concrete subbasements above you. No one can hear you."

Sean twists back and forth, looking for where the voice came from. "What the—where is that sneaky little wheelchaired ninja?"

"In your head, dummy." I give him a smack upside the cranium. "You have comms now, too."

"Wait a second," Jess says, eyes widening with realization. "Hold on. He hasn't had comms. And no language services. How the hell can you understand what people are saying?"

"Uhh, well, it's not super hard to infer, you know. Everyone with regulators all sound like they're speaking English, even though it doesn't really look like it. BT-dubs, it's like a dubbed Kung-fu movie sometimes. But a lot of times I can tell what someone said based on how people respond. And you guys probably don't know it, but a lot of people just speak English to you. You might think it's translation services, but once peeps hear Jess, or Micah, or me speaking English, they just make the switch and you guys don't hear the difference. Like Denji. He's been speaking English the whole time. Haruto goes back and forth, but mostly just speaks English and shouts in Japanese."

Jess's mouth hangs open.

Sean shrugs. "What? It's not like I'm reading minds or some shit."

"Naw," Jess says. "It's just that...all the pot...and the way you talk... Just easy to forget you might actually be a genius."

"Ahuh, ahuh!" Sean laughs. Then he gives me a little smack. "You hear that? 'Genius!'"

"Maybe," I say. "For a human."

"Can we focus on the task at hand?" Harth asks, looking up to the grate through which we need to squeeze. Well, some of us might need to squeeze. Not me.

"Peek and sneak, part two," I say. Then to Sean, I ask, "Can you stand?"

He takes hold of me and all but bounds to his feet. Then his face crinkles up. He squirms around in his clothing. "Ugh. Still wet. Feels so...gooey. I think there might be a shit in my pant leg."

"We all agree?" Jess asks. "He's going up last?"

When we all nod, Sean raises his hands and says, "Makes sense, makes sense. But I am def shedding some of my garb."

"You shed," I say, as Harth takes me from Sean's hand. "We'll climb."

Harth lifts me up to the water grate. There's no ladder this time. People weren't meant to pass through here. Just water. But it's still our best bet.

Perched in Harth's meaty hand, I reach up and take hold of the grate. Then I push. It's tight, but *I'm a...mother...fucking...* The grate scrapes upward. *...Kynolari!*

The grate pops free. I keep it in my hands as Harth lifts me higher, up into a large, dark, echoey space. I place the grate on the floor and have a quick look around. Massive columns are scattered around, holding the extreme weight of the skyscraper above. At first glance, I don't see anything of significance.

But I smell it.

Death. And a lot of it.

As my eyes adjust to the pitch black, I find all the walls, but not a single body.

I stick my head back down and say, "Clear."

Jess is hoisted up next. She fits, but really has to squeeze what Micah calls her 'chunky bits' through the gap.

Grover goes next. No trouble there.

Then I hear Harth grumble.

"What is it?" I ask, lowering my head through the grate.

"I will not fit," he says.

"You haven't even tried."

"I have run the calculations. My dimensions and those of the opening are incompatible."

"Excuse me, good sir," Sean says from below. "Next floor please."

Harth grunts again, this time in disgust. Then Sean rises up toward me, head raised, hands on his hips like he's a Champion of Cliteous Prime. I stand back as he slides easily through the gap, maintaining his pose, now dressed in just a black 'Little Big' T-shirt and a pair of brown-stained tighty whities. And his gauntlet, which is glowing with a full charge. "Ahoy, me hearties. Let's board this bitch and get to plundering."

Jess averts her gaze, whispering curses to herself.

"Even Grover cannot look," Grover says, following Jess.

"Before you kill someone," I say to him. "Power down the gauntlet."

"Huh?" He looks at the space age tech connected to his arm. "Whoa. I didn't even mean to do that."

"That's the problem. You're going to have to learn on the go. But we both know how you are with accidental discharges."

"Ha!" He looks at the Sonizer. "So...I just think it, right? And then it should—"

The gauntlet powers down.

"Bazoom!" he says, pumping his fist.

"You're a natural," I say, far from impressed. "You forget something?"

Before he can answer, the object of my desire is flung up through the grate.

"Oh, right," he says, picking up the baby carrier. "Sorry, my dude."

While he gets my ride strapped to his chest, I poke my head down through the grate. "You got a plan?"

"Denji will assist me in finding another way inside, even if I must kick down the front doors. Then...then I'll probably just be cleaning up whatever mess you all leave behind."

I grin. "You're damn right."

"For Kyno," he says, holding his fist up.

"Kyno," I say, and bump his fist.

Then we part ways. I leap up into my waiting ride, snap myself in, and say, "Captain Beefcake! To the stairs!"

We arrive just a few seconds after Jess and Grover, who wait at the bottom.

"Here's the deal," I say. "We're down a heavy hitter, so we need to be stealthy as fuck, kill in silence, and have no mercy. You all get me?"

"Got it," Jess says, turning in my direction, seeing Sean, wincing, and then facing forward again.

"Affirmative," Grover says.

"Good, now fall in line behind—"

"Fuck that," Jess says. "I am not walking behind you."

Jess starts up the stairs, gauntlet charged. Grover hustles to stay by her side.

I can tell that Jess's time in the wild with Micah has changed her. She knows what she's doing now. Moving like an operator. Quiet, careful, sweeping before moving. She leads us up onto the second level and snaps a fist up in the air, stopping us.

She steps out first and a moment later whispers, "Oh my god..." Followed by, "Clear."

Sean carries me into the large open space, which looks a lot like the last subbasement with one stark difference. This one is full of bodies. They're months old and neatly stacked like wood, floor to ceiling. There's a four-foot-wide path leading between them.

"So many..." Sean says.

"They must have cleared them from the floors above," Jess says.

"I do not like," Grover says, tail between his legs. "Can...can feel their sadness."

"Same," Sean says, and then something catches his eye. "Little man," he says to me. "You cool with walking?"

I unclip myself and drop to the floor. "Needed to stretch my legs anyway. Also, you kind of stink." I point to the wall of corpses. "Worse than them."

"Yeah, yeah," he says, and he wanders away, behind a concrete post.

"If he comes back naked, I'm out."

"*I'm* out," Grover says.

Jess scruffs his head, which gets a quick, "Love Jess," in response.

Sean clears his throat, and we all turn to face him.

"What the hell?" Jess says.

Sean is dressed in a kind of chubby brown zip-up onesie. His feet are padded and shaped to look like some kind of clawed animal. His arms are stuffed into padded sleeves that end in a pair of mittens.

"I'm a mascot!" Sean says. He reaches back and yanks a bulbous head up from behind. It slips over his dome and completes the transformation. The creature has two pointy ears, a little nose, and whiskers, but it's the massive round eyes that hold my attention and make the whole thing strangely horrific. He does a little dance and in a muffled voice, adds, "I'm a kitty!"

He pulls the head off like a hood, pleased with himself. "Before anyone says anything, he says, "I know, I know, it's redonkulous. But check it out. I'm wearing clothes now, and I'm a cat. *A cat!* No one will think I'm actually a Kynolari. It's the perfect disguise."

Jess and I glance at each other. She shrugs. I roll my eyes.

"Fine," I say, "but…just tell me you didn't take that from a body."

"Eww, no," he says. "There's a stack of them over there. Might have been here before these guys." His excitement fades when he looks back to the dead.

"And try not to bump into anything," Jess says, before leading us into the catacombs.

The floor is stained dark brown so thoroughly that it looks painted. The bodies are mostly mummified now, but some are still oozing liquids, or twisted into a horrified pose. We double-time through the winding tunnel in silence, until we reach the stairwell, catch our breath, and head up to find the last basement packed with bodies. Jess wastes no time discussing what to do. She just moves into the tunnel and pushes through the nightmare.

The staircase is a welcome relief. Jess heads up the concrete stairs two at a time, stopping at the closed door at the top. She glances through the small window and then looks back. "It's the building's foyer."

"See anyone?" I ask.

She looks again, twisting her face around. "Nothing. But that doesn't mean they're not there."

I nod and say, "Weapons hot."

Then I take the lead and give Jess another nod. She opens the door slowly and silently. We slip out into the massive foyer and two things strike me at once. Bright lights and air conditioning. The building has power.

We move out into the white marble foyer that glistens under the lights. The place is opulent, as though made for a king. Before I have time to take in more details, Jess says, "There!" and points to what I think is a lift.

She hustles to the doors, reaching for the call button, when they open in front of her. She quickly charges her gauntlet and very nearly fires. But the lift is empty. I point above the door. "Motion sensor."

On our way to the top floor, Jess catches her breath.

When the elevator dings and the doors slide open, we rush out, ready for a fight. But all we find is an empty hallway. I take the lead now, pick a direction, and then take our ragtag strike team—which includes a dog and a mascot—to a T junction. Left will lead us deeper into the building, and that's where I suspect we need to go. So, I poke my little head around the corner, just for a second, before snapping back and bumping into Jess's leg.

There are two men facing each other in front of a set of double doors. But they're not just men. They're six foot tall, four-hundred-pound, god-damned sumo wrestlers, dressed only in mawashi—what most humans would call a 'loin cloth', because that's just about the only thing they cover. That's what the sumo documentary I watched with Sean said, anyway. On TV, they were fascinating. In person…I'm liable to get lost between their rolls.

For a moment, I'm not sure exactly what our play should be. We can get the drop on them, but it could be loud. We need to be a little more discreet. We need… I glance up at Sean—and grin. We need Captain Beefcake.

# 47

## MICAH

"Gruunlokar," I say, activating my comms. "Eyes sharp. We've been set up. Target is not here. I repeat, Lumen Sok is *not* here."

"Understood," he says. "Falling back or standing your ground?"

"They're here," I say. "But they don't know *we* know, yet. We could try to sneak back out, but they're most likely surveilling us from a distance. See if you can locate their spotters."

"On it."

"Should have known," Poppy says, shaking her head. "They don't call him the Visionary for nothing. There isn't much he's not able to predict."

"He's a precog?" Siloquin asks.

Poppy's head tilts to the side, and it's so adorable I nearly forget that we're about to be pounced on by god-knows-what. "A *what?*"

"Someone with precognitive abilities."

When Poppy still looks confused, I add. "They can see the future."

"What? No. He's just good at math or something. Calculating odds. Things like that. It wasn't really him who predicted we'd be here; it was a formula. The only real way to beat it is to be unpredictable and a bit reckless."

"*That's* why Praxion left," I realize. "Because it made no sense. It was unpredictable."

"Well," Poppy says. "I suggest we do the same. What would Lumen Sok expect us to do?"

While she ponders the question, Siloquin says to me, "Your knowledge of precognition is surprising for a human."

I shrug. "My knowledge of precogs doesn't go past *Minority Report.*"

"Interesting. So, your government has researched—"

"Not the government," I say. "Just Steven Spielberg."

"I would like to meet this man."

"Well, he'd love to meet you," I say with a smile. "And I hear he's a dog person, so it's not impossible."

I look down at the terrified man crouched on the floor, peering up at us with big teary anime eyes. There's not a lot I can do for him, and we can't risk the extra baggage.

"Find a place to hide. In a tub. Under a table. Things are about to get dicey. Stay there for a day."

"And—and then?"

"Come out. If you're captured or killed, we failed. If you're untouched, we succeeded."

He gives a quick nod, stands, and pauses. "Good luck." Then he scurries away, disappearing into the dark building's recesses.

"You know he probably doesn't stand a chance," Poppy says.

"Yeah, well, at least we didn't kill him," I say.

Poppy and Siloquin share an unamused glance and are about to tear me a new one when Gruunlokar's voice interrupts. "Contact. On the bridge. On every bridge."

"What are we looking at?" I ask.

"A Helion," he says. "On each bridge."

"That's it?" I ask.

"Each of them is followed by an army of biologics."

"Any Draun?" I ask.

"I have found three spotters," he says. "No way to know if they're human or Draun."

"Take them out," I say.

There's a pause.

Just a few seconds.

Then he's back.

"Done. You should be able to move freely for…sixty seconds."

"Any suggestions?" I ask.

"The logical choice would be to run while you can," he says.

"But that would also be the predictable choice," Poppy says.

"So, we stand and fight," Siloquin says, gripping her spear and smiling a little too much given the circumstances.

"That's not your body," I tell her. "Remember that when you throw yourself at the enemy."

Siloquin grunts.

"Okay," I say. "We fight. Lumen Sok doesn't know any of us. Not well, at least. So, they might not be prepared for what we can do."

"And what is our goal?" Siloquin asks. "Escape?"

I shake my head. "Nah. We're going to kill 'em all. Send a message."

Both of them look happy about my announcement.

"Either of you ever played a tower defense game?" I ask.

Poppy raises a small hand.

Siloquin says, "I have defended actual towers."

"That's the plan. We let them come to us. We back each other up. I'm going to take the roof, you two cover the ground from inside the building. Do not go outside. It won't be safe."

"I can handle—"

I cut Siloquin off, saying, "I'm not worried about the enemy hurting you. I'm worried about me."

"Mm," she says. "The Axiom. I have been curious about what you can do."

"So have I," I admit.

"We will cover from a distance," Gruunlokar says, "but I am conserving ammunition…for Lumen Sok."

"Understood," I say.

The ground shakes. "Here they come."

Poppy and Siloquin head for opposite sides of the building while I head for the second floor. After prying open a window, I extend the Hell Hound claws, lean out and latch onto the building's roof. Pulling myself up isn't what I'd call easy, mostly because I'm an obvious dingleberry, ready to be flicked off, but I manage to sling a leg up and roll onto the sloped tiles. I Super Mario my way up the other floors until I'm standing on the tallest spire at the building's core. I'm four stories up with a clear view of the surrounding Imperial park and…the enemy.

"Hey, Micah-San," Haruto calls from below. I flinch at the sound of his voice. In the chaos, I forgot he was with us. "Should…ahh, should I hide?"

I look over the side of the roof and find him looking up at me. "Blood of the Shoguns, huh?"

"Not all Shogun were fighters," he says, forcing a smile.

"Closet," I say.

He nods and dashes inside the building. I can hear him below, thumping around, looking for a hiding place. Motion pulls my attention back out to the Palace grounds.

Biologics are closing in from all sides. Looks like mostly big guys. Gobi in the front, their big bodies and powerful arms forming a wall in front of the next offensive line, the Tyrne. They stand twice the height of the Gobi, serrated limbs twitching with excitement, thumping on the ground. I can't see what's behind the towering Tyrne, but I'm guessing Platamots. Unlike their compatriots, they are not bound by the constraints created by bones. Like Earth octopi, their bodies can contort and bend unlike anything with a skeleton. And then…there's the real problem. Helions. While we've taken out several of them, they've learned from every attack. They'll be adapted against everything we've done before, so I'll need to attack in a new way. More than once.

*Or,* I think, *don't give them time to adapt.*

"Gruunlokar, how are we looking?"

"Would you like an honest assessment, or a hopeful one?"

"Got it," I say.

"What is your plan?" he asks.

"Simple," I tell him. "Lumen Sok knows we're here. No reason to conceal our firepower. So...I'm not going to hold back."

"Copy that," he says. "Happy hunting."

I rub my hands together, crack my knuckles, and then charge the gauntlets to full power, where I need them to stay until this fight is over, no matter how much it exhausts me.

We're surrounded on all sides, each army approaching in a calm, organized way. Are they waiting for something?

"Micah," Gruunlokar says over comms. "In the trees."

I shift my gaze from the armies to the trees surrounding the Fukiage Omiya Palace. The leaf cover is difficult to see through. Can't make out much more than movement and the tik tik tik of hundreds of little legs.

"Poppy, Siloquin, watch the treeline. Skitterlings incoming. I'll handle the big guys."

"Copy that," Poppy says. "'Bout time I get to let loose!"

"Okay," I say to myself, envisioning how I'm going to attack, where I'm going to hit first and how hard. "Fuck it," I say and lift my arms, pointing the gauntlets to the left and right of the closest biologic army. "Okay, Axiom...time to fulfill a prophecy."

I don't know any details about the Axiom prophecy other than he or she would one day exist. I'm still not convinced it's me. But it makes me feel better about our odds, so I lean into it.

Two beams of orange energy expand from my gauntlets, harmlessly enveloping my forearms and hands. They burst out and away at the speed of light. I twist my arms together at the elbows, creating what vaguely looks like a pair of laser scissors. Sparks fly from the stricken biologics, but I can't really see what's happening until the lasers clear my targets on the opposite end.

The orange light blooming from my still fully charged gauntlets dulls as I lower my arms and get a look at my targets. The line of Gobi stand motionless. Then one of them tips to the side at the waist, spilling its artificial guts. It bumps into the next beast and the same happens. Like gory dominos, the chain reaction spreads out across the hundred biologics. Severed waists, arms, legs, and torsos fall to pieces, unleashing waves of white, gooey entrails.

"Ohh...Ha!" I turn to the three remaining armies, laughing loudly. "You guys are so screwed!"

They stand still, just staring for a moment. Are they in shock or are they waiting for—

The crack of lightning sounds from below. It's followed by the screech of Skitterlings.

And that's when the three armies break up, moving in every direction, getting lost in the parks, gardens, groves, and buildings. I unleash on them as quickly as possible, swiping my arms back and forth, but they're onto me now, watching the beams' direction and getting out of the way. I'm still cutting down a number of them, but at this rate too many of them are going to reach the house.

And given the sound of constant thunder tearing through the air below, the Skitterlings might break through the line as well.

That's when it happens. It's that point in every tower defense game, when you think you just might survive and suddenly, everything goes wrong. Four remaining Helions hang back. Didn't even notice they were doing it. But now, all their rocket pods are open and facing this way. I sweep the lasers toward them, but only manage to detonate one pod before the other seven fire their six rockets each.

Back in eighth grade, there was nothing I hated more than 'math minutes.' Basically, just a sheet of paper with simple math problems on them. You had just a minute to complete it. While my friends would slap their pencils down after thirty seconds and declare, "Done!" I was busy counting numbers by making little dots beside each problem. Never did finish one of those in a minute.

But this calculation, with my life on the line, the number comes to me as though I'm hearing the voice of God. "Forty-two rockets."

I turn my gauntlets to the sky, just shaking my arms back and forth, hoping to hit all the rockets, but they're twisting and turning, impossible to hit. At the same time, I'm allowing the armies to close the distance.

With just seconds to impact and only ten of the rockets destroyed, my thoughts turn to Jess and Grover. I send my love to them, hoping they'll feel it, and with just a second until oblivion, I close my eyes.

# 48

## CHIRK

"Look into my eyes, they gleam and glow,
I'm the big cat with a heart that grows.
I meow and purr, oh so very sweet,
Calling kids from every street."

Sean does an impressive array of dance moves while completely concealed in the mascot suit. He works his way down the hall, toward the sumo wrestlers, who are now relaxed, smiling, and bopping their heads. When he first stepped around the corner, I thought he was a goner. Both men pivoted in his direction, stomped their legs down, leaned forward, and looked ready to charge. Then Sean began his one man show and chilled out.

"Watch my supple tail, it swings with grace,
Come and join me now, or face disgrace.
With tiny cat steps, I dance and twirl,
Bringing joy to every boy and girl."

Sean finishes the rap by crossing his arms in front of him, aiming the Sonizer beneath his suit at the two entertained behemoths.

"Meow Meow is in the hizouse!"

A high-pitched wail bursts from inside his suit, striking both unprotected men and bouncing off the walls around them, enhancing the effect.

None of us knows what setting Praxion left the Sonizer on. Honestly didn't think to check. Sloppy, but if he was fighting Draun, it can't be the setting that causes compulsive dancing—though that would be entertaining. Hopefully it's the frequency that erases Draun consciousness and—

When one of the two men leans forward, hands on his prodigious belly, which appears to be bulging...as though his insides were moving...straight toward his...

"Aww shit!" I shout. "Sean! Get baaa—" Time seems to stretch out as I leap away. Sean doesn't have time to react to my voice, or what's obviously about to happen.

*The Brown Note.*

Why the hell did Praxion leave—

"A tsunami roils in my stomach!" one of the men shouts.

"It cannot be stopped!" the other says.

"Quickly!" The first shouts. "To the bathroom or face disgrace!"

They each make it just a step before the effects of the Brown Note blossoms from their backsides. Liquified shit fills their loin clothes, bulging them out like balloons before spraying out along the edges. Both men are transformed into human shit sprinklers. They scream and wail, twisting about in revulsion and discomfort.

It's one of the worst things I've ever seen in my life.

When it ends, both men look a bit smaller. They fall to their knees, weeping in shame. I should feel bad for them. But they're Draun. Probably slaughtered hundreds of people each. That said, I *will* put them out of their misery.

Sean stood still throughout. Took the brunt of the brown hurricane and hasn't moved yet. So, I draw my mini-railguns, aim around him, and fire a single round from each. The men's crying and boundless shame comes to an end as they slump to the floor and slide through the sheet of nutty lubricant until both are face down in filth.

"Well," Sean says, voice muffled from the suit. "That worked. A little differently than I expected, but, ahhh...is that normal?"

"It happens," I say. Question is why did it happen this time? Why would Praxion change the Sonizer to the Brown Note? He'd have done it on purpose, because he could have easily erased whatever Draun he came into contact with.

Not only that, he left it behind on purpose.

Because...

Because why?

Because it wouldn't work for a Draun. Explains why he felt comfortable leaving it. Because he knew we would find it. Obviously. Because...he hoped we would use it? Because then we'd know it was set to unleash a wave of feces, rather than—

*He wants it kept secret.* The Draun don't know what it can do. If they did, the gauntlet would have been destroyed already. That would have been game over. I put myself in Praxion's much bigger shoes and try to see the chain of events from his perspective. A plan unfolds and I nod to myself.

*I see what you're up to...*

"So," Sean says bumbling around in his cat costume. "On a scale of one to ten, how bad is it?"

Jess, Grover, and I wince and reel back in unison. Grover even whines a little bit.

Sean is slathered from head to toe in diarrhea. Clumps of it slide down his bulbous body.

"Way over a ten," Jess says through her hands clasped over her mouth and nose.

"So, I should take it off, yeah?"

"Can you not smell inside there?" I ask.

"Naw, dude," he says. "Can't really see now, either."

I glance at the mascot's big eyes, coated chunky brown.

"Take off the suit," Jess says, "but let it fall dirty side down, clean side up so we can walk through without—"

"I get you," Sean says, and he does as asked. After a minute of carefully shedding the costume, it drops onto the floor like an animal rug. Then he hurries back to us, once more clothed only in a black T-shirt and tighty-whities. He's dried off some, so the smell isn't as bad…or the rank hallway is just masking it.

"Let's go," I say, "slow and stealthy. Recommend holding your breath if you can." I leap from the edge of the shit stew, onto the mascot's clear back. Sean follows me, then Grover and Jess. We're all perched atop the costume, trying to avoid the filth-covered bodies lying to either side.

"Poor Meow Meow," Sean says. "He didn't help us for long, and all we did was give him shit."

I turn around and find Sean grinning like a goof, thrilled with his double entendre.

I shake my head and lift my arms up. He picks me up.

"Door," I say, and he holds me out to the handle. I turn it and am surprised to find it unlocked. That said, Draun don't usually have to lock doors. The only one dumb enough to stroll right in would be another Draun, and locks have no meaning to someone who can unlock the bolt with a thought.

When we're all through and the door is closed behind us, I let out a sigh, take a deep breath of clean air, and say, "Huh…"

Ahead is a broad hallway with wall panels that curve up to form the ceiling. Looks nothing like the rest of the building. Light seeps out of the gaps between the arched panels.

"It's like a hospital from the future," Sean says.

We start down the hallway, pausing at the first door, which is nearly impossible to see. There's a razor thin seam, and a notch that Sean intuitively understands how to use. He grips the notch with two fingers and effortlessly slides the door open to reveal…a storage room.

*Fantastic.*

Then he gasps, leaps inside, and closes the door behind him.

"Rude," Grover says.

I put my hands on my hips and give him a nod. "Right?"

"Chirk?" he says.

"Yeah, Grove?"

"Love Chirk."

"I know you do, bud" I say, reaching up and patting his cheek.

"Also…" he says, and I'm expecting his adoration to swivel toward Jess. Instead, he says, "I sniff something. Something bad."

I take a long drag through my nose and am about to put his mind at ease when I catch it, too. It's faint. Distant. But unmistakable.

"What is it?" Jess asks, watching my forehead scrunch up.

"Blood," I say. "A lot of it."

"Not just blood," Grover says. "I sniff…" He takes in a few rapid breaths and then just about sneezes them out, trying to get rid of the scent he's caught. "Danger. Hunger. Predator?"

The hair on his back rises. Instinct telling him to fight…or run like hell.

Something on this floor, that I haven't picked up yet, has him freaked out.

The three of us stand in the hallway, looking down its length in silence, wondering what is waiting for us in Lumen Sok's custom made sanctuary.

"Taadaa!" Sean says, leaping from the storage room, dressed in doctor's scrubs. We all flinch back. I nearly shoot him. "Whoa! What's got all of you guys spooked?"

Before we can answer, the screaming starts. It's a woman. High pitched. In profound pain. Is she being tortured, or… "Did anyone actually look at the floor number before we stepped off the elevator?"

We exchange glances and shrugs.

"Shit," I say. "I don't think this is the penthouse."

"But we went to the top, dude," Sean says.

"Did we, though?" I ask.

"This is the sixty-*third* floor?" Jess asks. "The one filled with younglings that eat each other…"

"And anything else they come across," I say, taking a back step. "We do *not* want to be here."

"Hedo?" a cute little voice says from further down the hallway. A head pokes out from a doorway that slid open without us noticing. A little Japanese girl with braids pokes her head out. Her eyes widen when she sees us. "Oh, hedo." She giggles and then turns back toward the open door, whispering to whoever else is in the room.

"Be fwiends?" the girl asks.

"Oh, I don't think so," I say to myself, backing up another step.

Then she steps out into the hallway.

The top half is a three-year-old humanoid child. The bottom is almost insect-like, with human flesh stretched over the exo-skeleton. Its thin limbs are three feet long from body to knee, and another three to the ankle. She's only a few inches off the floor, though, her legs pulled in tight, knees above her head.

She leans forward, her eyes widening, her little chubby arms spreading wide to reveal hands with fingers tipped with foot-long, curved talons.

"Fwiends!" she says with a grin that reveals a shark-like mouth of teeth. Then she stretches her arms straight out and scrambles toward us, shrieking the whole way.

# 49

## MICAH

I've occasionally wondered what it feels like, being blown up. Do you feel pain? Heat? Does it happen so fast that you don't feel a thing at all? One second, you're a living person. The next, you're vapor. Seems like it would happen faster than the nervous system could transmit the pain, because it, too, ceases to exist.

The theory seems to be confirmed when I feel nothing at all.

No heat.

No body parts tearing away.

I don't even hear an impact.

I open my eyes and lower my raised arms. Several clouds of smoke roil up and away from me, the telltale sign of explosions. But I didn't even feel a shockwave.

*Because there is an invisible shield around me,* I realize. Not just me. The entire house. The shield fades and the smoke billows away. I turn to find Jenna floating down toward me.

"Thought you could use some help," she says.

"Kid," I say. "You just saved my life."

"You know," she says. "You could have done the same thing. Laser walls, remember?"

She's right.

"Yeah," I say.

"What happened?"

I smile at her. "Panicked. Happens to all of us, even now. The brain tells you you're going to die. The body believes it. Surviving is usually a matter of muscle memory. Training." I lift both gauntlets. "I'm still pretty new to these."

A bolt of electricity tears through the roof top. It's followed by Poppy shouting, "If you're done having a chit chat, can you clean up these little bitches?"

"Nonsense!" Siloquin shouts. She then crashes through a solid wall—not a window—dropping to the ground with three Skitterlings impaled on her spear. She lands amidst the horde. Follows the landing with a spin that flings the skewered biologics free. Then she spins the spear in a blur, facing off with the enemy surrounding her.

Electricity blooms from the Lancer gauntlet on her arm. It bends and twists, arcing down the spear, building in intensity. With a shout, she snaps the spear to a stop and unleashes a cascading wave of lightning that hops from one target to the next.

"Chain lightning," I whisper, remembering the epic power of the strike. Not from reality, but from my Amazon warrior in the Diablo 2 video game. Not even a horde of killer cows could withstand my wrath.

For a moment, I'm jealous. Then I remember—thanks to Jenna's reminder—that I've got her beat. I lift my gauntlets to the sky and fire a beam of orange energy that bursts out into the shape of a dome, coming down around us. Several Skitterlings are severed in two. Several more are inside the dome, but they won't last long against Siloquin, Poppy, and Jenna. And there are many more outside the dome.

Along with an army of biologics.

"Gruunlokar," I say.

"Copy," he says.

"You still in position?"

"Haven't moved," he says.

"Good." I smile. "Don't."

I don't need to move my arms to affect the shape, size, or direction of my laser light. My regulator connects my mind to the Hell Hounds and allows me to direct the path of destruction with a thought. In this case, it bursts out and away in every direction at once. A sun-hot tsunami of light rushes out, enveloping biologics, ancient buildings, and scores of trees. I feel bad about the destruction, but what's it matter if there won't be a humanity left to appreciate the history?

The deadly bubble expands throughout the Imperial Palace. When it strikes the western wall, I flip the mental switch and shut it down before it strikes the city, including the building where Gruunlokar is holed up.

"Impressive," the sniper says. "But a greater challenge is inbound from the east."

I turn east and find the incoming force in the last place I want them to be.

The sky.

"Draun," I say to myself. Looks like a dozen, give or take. Hard to tell. They're still a mile out.

Then, one of them spasms and falls. A dead weight.

It's followed by a second, and I smile. Gruunlokar is silently taking them out. After a third drops, Gruunlokar says, "They're shielded now. Can't do more without Jenna."

"I think we'd be better off with her here," I say.

"Agreed," he says.

When the building beneath me falls silent, I say, "Hey, guys?"

"What do you want, pretty boy? I've got sweat dripping from wrinkles you don't want to hear about. Need to catch my breath."

"No time," I say. "Draun incoming. Nine, I think. Airborne from the east. Shields up."

"If they're already shielded," Poppy says. "There's not a whole lot I can do. Not against nine of them."

"Nonsense!" Siloquin shouts. "I will gut them like—"

"Can't gut what you can't hit," Poppy says.

"Fall back to Gruunlokar's position," I say. "Jenna and I will handle this."

"No shame in retreat, but—" Poppy leaps up through a fresh hole in the ceiling and looks east, where the nine Draun are now incoming like missiles. If they don't find someone here, they'll catch us all running away.

"Ah," she says, understanding. "Never mind. Good luck. Toodles." With that, she leaps back down inside the building. "All right crazy ghost lady from the past. Time to go."

"Hey!" It's Haruto, voice muffled by the walls of whatever closet he's managed to hide himself in. "Don't go without me!"

Siloquin steps outside the house, looking up at us. "I do *not* run from—"

"Zip it, bitch!" Poppy shouts, sounding even more frightening than the ancient warrior reborn. "The man already told you that is *not* your body to risk."

Siloquin purses her lips, and stabs a nearby Skitterling corpse. "Rah!"

A moment later, Haruto stumbles from the building and Poppy leaps down from the roof. The trio heads west, moving among the scorched remains of trees, skeletal fingers poking up from the ground.

"You have a plan?" Jenna asks.

"Nope," I say.

"You trust me?" she asks.

"Sure do."

"Cool," she says, and we lift off the roof, carried by a telekinetic force. We start out slow but accelerate like a pair of missiles. Wind whips my hair and stings my eyes. Then the outside world and all its effects slip away. We're inside a telekinetic bubble.

Just like the Draun we're heading toward.

"So, do *you* have a plan?" I ask.

She smiles. "A couple of them. All untested, of course."

"Of course," I say. "What's the first one?"

"Talk to them," she says.

"*Talk* to them?" I ask. We're seconds away from reaching the group when she angles us upright and comes to a stop. To my surprise, they do the same.

"Turn back," she says with a dose of bravado. "Lumen Sok will meet his end today and I will lead—"

"Gemma," a young woman says. "You couldn't lead a dog to its own shit."

"Mm," Jenna says. "Good thing I'm not Gemma."

The group of Draun are all young adults. Five men, four women. They're all dressed similarly in mostly black with splashes of red. Closest thing to a Draun gang I've seen. Maybe Gemma was one of them once upon a time.

"She never was good at telling jokes," one of the men says.

They all have a good laugh, but it stops when Jenna says, "Gemma is dead."

"Uh-huh," The young woman says. "And who are you supposed to—"

"Jenna. With a J and two Ns. Jenna *Flood*. Maybe you've heard of me?"

They certainly have, but the fear in their eyes is just a flutter.

"Nice try, Gem," the man says. "We ain't got beef with you. Just give us the Kynolari symp and point us to your asshole sniper. You can either come back, or scurry along."

"My name is Jenna Flood," she says, hair billowing as power swirls around us. "And I do not scurry."

She spreads her arms out wide and I'm suddenly in the open air. My mind tells me I'm going to fall, and I nearly shout. But she's still got a hold on me. She's just turned the bubble around us into a wall.

The man taps on it with his fist. When he speaks, we can't hear his voice through the wall, but I can read his lips. "Cute."

Jenna grins. "Gruunlokar." She points at one of the other men in the group, and glances at me. "I call it sticky telekinesis."

A moment later, a small hole appears in the forehead of the man Jenna has pointed at. The back of his head is missing. He drops without a sound, following the remnants of his brain to the ground.

I nearly laugh.

The remaining eight Draun flinch back, oblivious as to how Jenna killed the shielded man. But it's clear to me. However Jenna wraps a shard in a telekinetic shield powerful enough to penetrate another, she doesn't need to be next to him, just in front of him. The bullet passed through her shield, became coated in it, and punched a hole in the man's head.

Jenna points at one of the women, who immediately turns away and launches in the other direction. She doesn't make it ten feet before going limp and dropping from the sky.

The group of Draun bursts apart and flees, headed in every direction, flying chaotically with the hope of not being gunned down next. They might be Draun, but they have no overwhelming loyalty to Lumen Sok. He leads them, but if death is guaranteed, not one of them will sacrifice their lives to the cause. It's one of our few advantages. And telekinesis-wrapped rail shards.

"I didn't even get to fire a laser," I say, feigning sadness.

"That was Plan B," she says, spinning us around and descending toward Gruunlokar's position. That's when I see the Mori JP Tower, remember who is likely there—Lumen Sok—and who is on a collision course to meet him: Grover and Jess.

"Jess," I say. "You copy?"

No response.

I look at Jenna and she shares my concern. Our speed doubles, but my twisting gut says we're already too late.

# 50

## CHIRK

"Shit," Grover says, spinning around on his back legs before springing away, back the way we came. "Shit. Shit. Shit."

The rest of us are right behind him, scrambling for the elevator.

"The hell is *that,* dude?" Sean shouts.

"Youngling!" I say. "Obviously!"

"That thing came out of a *woman?*" Jess asks.

"Probably not in the way you're imagining," I say, glancing back.

The youngling is faster than us, leaping forward on its long legs. The creature's making burbling sounds with its lips, enjoying the chase. It would almost be cute if I couldn't see the teeth behind its spit bubble lips, or its grotesque body…or its damn neck extending out and up.

"Ahh!" Sean shouts when he looks back and sees it, too. "It's got a telescoping tortoise neck!"

"I thought younglings would look human!" Jess shouts.

"Humanoid," I say, "but Lumen Sok has been known to genetically alter his children."

"*Why?*" she asks.

"Learning from his mistakes, I'd guess. Because I'm a Kyno Corps pilot who's seen the worst this universe has to offer and *I'm* damn near about to leave a streak of nervous diarrhea behind us!" The elevator is just ahead. Grover's nearly there, and the youngling is just a few lunges away.

Grover leaps up, paws smacking the call button. He scrabbles against the wall, claws clicking as he pushes the button over and over.

The doors don't open.

"I don't want to kill a baby," Jess says, understanding the situation the same way I do.

"That's what's he's counting on," I say. "Hesitation. Fear. Doubt. He's using our morality against us."

"Screw morality!" Sean says, powering up the Sonizer on his arm. The Sonizer that is still set to the Brown Note. No idea if the youngling is human enough to be affected by it, but there's no way in hell I'm going to let Sean find out.

I spring into the air. The top of my arc is level with Sean's face.

I haul back and give his nose a slap. "No!" I land on the floor, still running. "No more explosive bowel movements!"

*Ding!*

The elevator doors ahead finally open. But as they spread, a second monstrosity is revealed, this one larger. It's crammed into the elevator, its segmented body bent up toward the ceiling, ending in a pair of ass-end pincers. It doesn't have legs that I can see. What it does have is twenty arms, each ending in a human hand tipped with thick, yellow nails. The top half of its body is human. A teenage male youngling, with a human torso, two normal arms and long black hair that hangs like a curtain over his face. He's old enough for his telekinetic abilities to be fully active, though his control is likely still immature.

"Down!" Jess shouts.

I have no idea what she's got in mind, but I trust her. I don't need to duck. Can't get much lower than I already am. But I drop down to all fours anyway. Sean dives forward onto his belly. Grover, already leaping back from the elevator, flops down. Then Jess slides between Sean and me, aiming her charged Stinger gauntlet toward the baby behind us.

She fires.

The grappling hook cracks through the air.

Punches into the youngling's sternum and then crackles with electricity.

The youngling spasms, its talons tapping out a hyperactive rhythm on the floor. Before it can drop, the grappling hook retracts, yanking the youngling into the air.

Jess leans back to the floor as the partly human monster sails over us—and into the elevator, careening into the male. While he tries to free himself from the tangle of limbs, Jess's slide ends with her returning to her feet. She yanks her arm to the left and then back to the right, putting a wave into the grapple line that snaps toward the elevator.

By the time it reaches the teenage youngling, the line is glowing molten orange. It strikes with the liquifying heat of Harth's incinerator round, slicing through both younglings—and the elevator. Sparks and chunks of flesh burst out onto the floor around us, and then, all at once, the bottom half of the elevator car falls out of sight.

The bodies fall into two halves, the bottom falling first, then the top. All that remains is the top half of the elevator car.

We stand there for a moment, catching our breath, looking at the destruction.

"Not going to lie," I say to her. "That might have been the most titillating thing I've ever seen."

"Keep your pants on," Jess says to me with a grin.

Our relief is cut short by the sound of talons tapping on the floor behind us.

Sean rolls onto his back and sits up. "Ohh..."

Doors on either side of the hallway open.

Monstrosities step out.

"Guys," he says. "We're about to get spanked like Jean-Jacques Rousseau."

"What?" I say. "*Who?*"

"Doesn't matter," Jess says, and holds up her gauntlet. Her fancy moves drained her power by fifty percent. Which leaves me with two mini-railguns, Sean with a shitastic Sonizer and...what else? A dog with teeth.

"Do what you can," I tell Jess. "I'm going to adjust the Sonizer's setting."

"Do what I can..." Jess says, taking a step closer to the mass of freaks now scrambling in our direction. "Sure. Right... No problem..."

Teeth gnash. Talons clack. Mouths froth. It's like a single living organism composed of the worst parts of the nastiest demons in the universe. If they reach us, there will be no stopping them.

I snap my fingers at Sean and motion to the Sonizer. He crouches and holds the weapon system out. I don't use a gauntlet, but I'm trained on how to use them. How to change settings. How to remove and repair them. Just like every other member of the Kyno Corps.

A few taps on the control screen is all it takes. The Sonizer is now ready to detect a new resonant frequency, which it will store for future use, just as it did the Brown Note, and the Draun Consciousness Eraser. That needs a better name.

"With me," I say, hustling closer to the elevator. I locate a sizeable chunk of youngling flesh and pick it up.

Sean crouches down beside me. "What now?"

"Hand," I say.

When he turns his open palm up, I slap the jiggly globule of meat into his hand. "Hold it." He winces but grips the chunk. I turn his arm around and tap the controls. An orange progress bar appears, zipping down the length of his gauntlet.

While the gauntlet detects the ambient frequency of the flesh, I turn to see Jess, whipping her arm back and forth. Her extending grapple line fills the hallway like a slithering slime Flork from Erotomus Central in the throes of asexual passion.

As the grotesque mob closes in, Jess lets them walk over the line. It twists and tangles around their limbs. When they're nearly upon us, she unleashes the rest of her gauntlet's power as a massive burst of energy.

Bodies quiver and explode, chunks slapping against the walls like Micah's paint ball pellets on Sean's ass. The electricity snaps from one monster to the next, traveling along every body that's in contact with another.

Blue light rolls down the hall, eradicating everything it comes into contact with.

And then it stops.

When the last pieces of the dead fall to the floor, and the bloody mist fades from the air, I get a clear look at what's left.

The younglings at the back of the group have disengaged. And there are still more than enough of them to take care of us, unless… "Okay, Captain Beefcake. You're up. Remember how to use it?"

"Just got to focus," he says. "And let the juice flow. Not the juice. That sounds gross. You know what I mean."

"Let's just pretend that I do, my man." I give him a swat on the butt. "You got this."

When he stands all confident-like and steps in front of Jess, ready to face down the remaining younglings, I feel a sudden pride. He's come a long way. "Good boy," I whisper. "Get it done…"

"You think so?" Grover asks, sitting next to me, tongue hanging out, panting, and looking generally concerned. "Because I think maybe we go back to elevator."

"The elevator with no floor," I say.

He gives a doggy shrug. "Might be better."

I smile at him. "You might be right about that. Let's call it a solid Plan B."

"Plan G," he says, looking at me with one eyebrow raised and a slight smile on his face. I nearly burst out laughing, but then the younglings charge again, splashing through their dead brothers and sisters.

"Wait until they're close," I tell Sean. "You want to hit them all."

"Hit them all," he says, bracing himself like the Sonizer has a kick. "Hit them all…" Then he goes all rigid, like he's trying to lift the gauntlet, but can't. "Uhh, buddy… I can't move!"

One of the older younglings has a hold on him. Its technique isn't refined enough to crush him, but it locks him in place. When I try moving closer to help, I can't. I turn to Jess and find her fighting to move, but her legs are stuck to the floor.

"Chirk…" Sean says, his worry raising his voice's pitch.

*Fuck*, I think, and then realize that this might be the end for all of us. In that moment, I do something no one would expect from me at the moment of my death. "Love you guys."

"Love Chirk," Grover says.

"Love you so much, dude," Sean says, his frozen body now shaking in place.

Jess glances at me and gives a slight grin.

"Yeah, you're all right."

I'm about to close my eyes, but movement between us and the younglings catches my attention. The floor bumps up and glows orange. I realize what's happening a moment before the bulge explodes. "Look away!"

A shockwave slaps into us, but the telekinetic grip on our bodies holds us in place. When a second explosion tears through the floor, the grip disappears and we're flung to the floor. Ten more explosions tear through the hallway, shaking the floor beneath us.

When silence returns, it's complete. No child voices. No scratching claws. Just the sound of molten metal dripping down onto the floor beneath us. I get to my feet, which doesn't change my view much, but gives me just enough height to look down to the floor beneath us.

I find Harth looking up at me.

"You are on the sixty-third floor."

I throw up my hands. "I know that!"

His smile spreads wider. "Everyone okay?"

Jess, Sean, and Grover stand with me, looking down at him.

He nods, and says, "Good. I think this might be a wise time to call in Ridgeback."

Sean's eyes light up. He rubs his hands together. "Aww, yeah."

"You know what? Fuck it." I activate my tether with the battlesuit and send a signal that will bring it straight to me. "Done."

"Now," Harth says, "how do we get to the penthouse?"

I activate my comms. "Denji."

"Here," he says. "Are you okay?"

"Dandy," I say, "except the elevator doesn't go to the sixty-fourth floor, and even if it did—" I look back at the ruined car. "—it's currently out of service. So, I need a way to the next floor, and I need it now, before the rest of the nurseries on this floor wake up."

# 51

## PRAXION

"After all this time," he says. "The legendary Praxion, seated before me. Time has softened you. Or perhaps it is just this planet. Sad, what became of your people here. Reduced to animals, eating the scraps of this world's dominant species, who I must admit, I am surprised you care about."

Lumen Sok.

He sits inside his Visionary Sphere, the top half of it lowered behind him. A hovering throne for a King with no court. We're in the penthouse of the Mori JP Tower. I know because I was feigning unconsciousness when I arrived here, slung over Reinhart's shoulder and then dropped to the floor.

Reinhart remains, standing behind me. But the rest of the floor is empty, aside from concrete columns supporting the roof, and a control center at the room's core with stations for twenty, arranged in a circle around a central white shaft connecting floor to ceiling.

I can't see him. The Visionary. Only his silhouette. He is shrouded inside a circle of sheer fabric strips hanging from the ceiling.

But it's him.

I know his deep, rumbling, eternally calm voice.

And…I can't move. I am unbound but rooted to my chair. Even if I wasn't, there is nothing I could do. I have no weapons aside from the railgun Reinhart stole from me and now has tucked into his waist.

What I do have is hope.

And that will remain until the moment my enemy gets bored and kills me.

"Come now," he says. "You must have questions for me. Like, why?"

"I already know why," I say, breaking my silence. "There are no questions that need answering. Your mind and the desires of your heart are no secret."

He laughs as though an inside joke was told.

"Wrong already. I have no heart."

"Then why are you afraid?" I ask. "Why have you been hiding from us? Sending your lackeys instead of facing us yourself."

"Logic and strategy do not require a heart," he says.

"Nor does cowardice." I lean my head to the side, just about the only thing I can do aside from speaking and blinking. I try to see him between the thin strips as they wobble from the faint breeze of the electrified building's air conditioning. "Which is the only reason I can think of for you to be hiding from me, even now."

"Huh." The laugh is subtle, but deep. "The simple truth is that I find your kind wholly repulsive, but I will gaze upon you…out of respect. My adversary. I underestimated your resolve before. Not this time."

The sheets surrounding him twist upward like a cyclone, slapping against the ceiling and sticking there.

Lumen Sok is seated cross-legged atop a plush, ruby red cushion, padding the bottom half of his Sphere. It is a remarkably simple machine, capable of phenomenal feats of speed, agility, and even interplanetary travel. And we have no idea how it works.

The Visionary is clothed in loose white fabric, masquerading as a man of peace. A hood conceals his face.

"Still hiding," I say.

He doesn't move, but the hood peels away, sliding off the back of his head.

His face is revealed, and it is…unremarkable.

He is what this world calls Caucasian. The skin on his boxy face appears loose and puffy. His brown hair is short and awkward. He smiles at me and looks awkward doing it. "Satisfied?"

"But not impressed," I say.

"I could have taken any form I wanted. Replaced any human I chose. But this form suited me for its previous merits, and its simple and already graceless appearance. At first, I moved among them, and then I slowly conquered them, controlling them with money, shaping their culture. When the time came, they embraced my ten-thousand-strong satellite network. Of all the planets I have conquered and recruited, Earth was the easiest. They all but welcomed me as a savior."

Can't argue with him there. This planet had been seeded with Draun DNA so long ago that converting many of them to his cause was as simple as sending a signal out through his satellite network. I glance toward the control center in the middle of the vast, open room. What he doesn't know is that erasing all those Draun minds will be just as easy.

If everything goes to plan. The plan that no one knows.

As unlikely as it seems, a plan unknown to its participants is the only one he can't predict. But I trust my team. They'll get the job done.

Lumen Sok laughs, leaning forward, elbows on his knees. "You believe yourself the superior intellect. I can see it in your eyes."

"Just call me Khan," I say, and realize I've just made my first Earth movie reference. *Star Trek II: The Wrath of Khan* was a compelling story, and the ending, the self-sacrifice… It was inspired.

"Mm." He leans back now, relaxing, pleased with himself. "Have you ever wondered, how I do it? How I see you coming?"

"Not always," I say.

He grins. "The gaps in my knowledge base have been filled. There is nothing you can do now that I cannot forecast. Every choice you make. Every expression, follows a limb on a predictability tree, branching over and over until the limb ends. I have been following your progress. Watching how you fight. Your tactics and those of your human allies. Your strengths. Your weaknesses. You are all known to me, and as this is the end of our...relationship, I think it's only fitting that you see the truth and understand—you never stood a chance."

He waits for a response, but I don't give him one.

Despite his losses, he's not wrong. He is usually ten steps ahead. The fact that he is here, alive, with a new army, is a testament to his sinister genius.

"Not too sure of yourself now, are you?" He smiles, broad and toothy. "Would you like to see my face? My true face? That you might look into the eyes of your killer?"

"Honestly," I say, "if it's worse than this one, I'd rather not—"

Reinhart slaps the side of my head hard enough to daze me.

"Now, now, acolyte," Lumen Sok says, "this is a warrior of great renown, whose name is spoken throughout the universe. His death should be worthy of history, not steeped in the small-minded brutality of your people."

Reinhart grumbles but says nothing.

The Visionary reaches up, putting both of his hands inside his mouth. He takes hold of his upper and lower jaws and pulls. There's a pop and then the jaw unhinges. His skin stretches as he peels himself apart. His cheeks widen to a thin layer as he pulls his face up and over his head, like he was just wearing a hood. I expect to see a bloody skeletal figure beneath, like something out of Earthly demonic lore.

Instead, I see a robotic face.

His eyes are round and blue, flickering with streaks of what looks like lightning—living gems. His armor-plated head appears as though it was once black but has been aged by time and battle scars. It's flaked with something like rust, but colored almost a luminous turquoise, matching his eyes. No nose. No mouth.

The revelation answers a lot of questions about his intellect and the speed at which he's able to process information. But it creates a new dilemma.

"You're a *robot?*" Reinhart says, sounding irritated.

The Visionary holds up a hand while his eyes glow brighter. Reinhart clears his throat and doesn't speak again. Then the robotic eyes focus on me. "Questions within questions. Follow the branches, Praxion. Reach the conclusion."

I try to do as he requests, but I don't find a branch that makes sense.

"Simple-minded beast," he says, shaking his head. "Let me assist you. In the known universe, only living organisms possess the ability to access evolved states of mind. Europhids, the Draun, even a few Earthlings. But nothing robotic. No artificial intelligence, conscious or not. Telekinesis is a trait exclusive to living things. And yet..."

He motions to his metal face. "This shell changes nothing. It is simply a method for me to interact with the physical world."

His head...is not his head.

*That is why Gruunlokar's bullet failed to kill him.*

"Show me," I say.

"Ahh, *now* you're curious. I thought you might be." He rises from his Sphere, still in a seated position. He glides forward, unfolds his legs, and walks the last few steps. Then he sheds his loose clothing, standing before me in his accurate representation of a loosely fleshed human. He extends his arms out to either side, says, "It is finished," and then his flesh quivers. Bubbles form, bulge, and pop, releasing frothy steam.

His skin and the layers of actual fat beneath slip away in globules, slapping on the floor. Then, all at once, his outer body falls away as easily as his clothing had.

He is revealed.

And he is...surprising.

A machine from top to bottom.

"You said—"

I'm cut short when the armor plating over his chest slides apart at the center. For a moment, all I see is a sheet of glass. When the chest plates cease moving, a blue light fills the tank, illuminating Lumen Sok's true form.

To say I am shocked is an understatement. Lumen Sok is—

"Worms?" Reinhart says, once again aghast at what he's seeing. "Are you serious?! Fucking wor—"

There's a squelch behind me, followed by the sound of peeling flesh. The Visionary glances to the side and Reinhart's complete, intact, skeleton is flung across the floor. Behind me, his body drops.

Despite Reinhart's sudden, revolting demise, I remain focused on Lumen Sok, who is apparently a collection of long, aquatic worms. They writhe and twist, keeping themselves in something close to a sphere.

"Ordinary living things have bodies and minds. The Draun are one and the same. Every cell in me is capable of thought, making me a living brain with a brain-to-body ratio of 1 to 1. Telekinesis was a natural evolution for my kind and upon being mastered, we built an empire." He laughs and shakes his head. "Opposable thumbs. Humanoid species always believe themselves to be superior, but now... now at least you know the truth. You can take it to hell with you."

He returns to his Sphere, floats up and takes his seat. "All of you."

"All of us?" I ask without thinking.

"Mm," he says. "You. And your friends."

He glances to the right. A moment later, the wall he's looking at explodes inward, revealing Harth, Chirk, Sean, Jess, and Grover.

He turns the other way.

Glass shatters!

Micah, Jess, and Siloquin crash through, ready for a fight.

All of them are ready for a fight.

But they are not ready for Lumen Sok.

Neither am I. Unable to move, there is nothing I can do to stop or avoid the silver shard-like projectile rising from inside the sphere. "Praxion. It was a pleasure."

The silver shard launches toward me—

—and impales my chest.

# 52

## MICAH

I touch down inside the tower's top floor just in time to see a silver shard punch into Praxion's chest. He swivels toward me as he falls, making eye contact and giving me a subtle nod, as though everything was going according to plan. Then he hits the floor, eyes closed. Motionless.

I saw a dead dog once, when I was a kid. June. Beginning of summer break. It was laid out on a riverbank beneath a bridge in Rumney, New Hampshire. Looked a lot like Praxion does now. Lifeless. Face free of expression. Body limp. When I returned to that spot in September, the dog was still there, just bones and hair, partly swallowed by the sand. I buried it that time, and the memory has stuck with me my whole life. It disturbed me, then, but not nearly as much as seeing Praxion fall to the floor.

We stand there for a moment, the four of us, locked in place.

Then my training kicks in and I compartmentalize the trauma on an empty shelf in my mental warehouse of the shock and awe that comes from being a special operator in the U.S. military.

My eyes snap around the vast, empty space, taking in everything.

The broad columns—our only cover.

The command center at the tower's core. That's what we're here for.

The robot that has just slain Praxion, containing a floating mass of wriggling... *something*. Its chest has just finished closing, concealing and protecting the blue-lit blob inside. On the far side of the room, a wall has exploded inward, revealing Harth, Chirk, Sean, Jess, and Grover—alive and well. Relief at seeing them nearly drags a sob from my lungs.

Instead, I whisper, "Gruunlokar," activating the comms between us.

"I see it," he whispers. "But I'm not sure what I'm seeing."

"Poppy," I whisper, "circle right, slow and quiet. Jenna, you're *Gemma*. Do not show your hand until I say so." She gives a nod. "Siloquin," I say, glancing toward her. She doesn't acknowledge me. Her eyes are locked on Praxion, face frozen in confusion.

"*Siloquin*."

She blinks and turns toward me.

"Be ready to strike."

She grimaces. "I am *always* ready."

"Chirk," I say. "You know who this robotic ass clown is?"

"All I know is that he's about to be paste." On his side of the room, Sean, Jess, and Grover head in the same direction as Poppy—closer to the control center and away from the robot. Sean is wearing a gauntlet now, and I recognize it. I glance back to Praxion's body. His gauntlet is missing.

Chirk has his mini-railguns drawn. Harth has taken aim with his Incinerator, but I can see that its power is low from here. They're both stalking toward the robot.

I'm not sure how the switch from Praxion to Sean happened, but I understand the significance of that gauntlet. Sean heading closer to the control center now makes sense.

Between us, the robot, seated in a half sphere, spins around, calmly surveying the intruders. It's the sphere that holds my attention.

I never saw the Visionary Sphere, but I know someone who has.

"Jess," I say.

"Hey, babe," she whispers. "How's your day going?"

"The silver bowl this thing is sitting on. Look familiar to you?"

There's a pause and then, "Oh. Oh shit, yeah. I think it's him."

I'm not positive until I see the heap of human skin lying on the floor beneath the sphere.

*Holy T-800,* I think.

"Team," I say, connecting to everyone and charging both gauntlets, ready to unleash a tsunami of laser light into his body. "Target is Lumen Sok. I repeat, target is Lumen So—*hck*!"

An invisible hand grasps my throat. Lifts me off the ground.

I try to raise my gauntlets, but my arms are locked in place.

On the far side of the penthouse floor, Harth launches a volley of molten Incinerator rounds, using up the last of his gauntlet's power. The rounds arc toward the Visionary, but he ignores them, turning to me without a care in the world.

"The Axiom," he says. "It's not every day you get to meet a fulfilled prophecy. Probably even more rare to kill one." His turquoise eyes flare with bolts of energy. He raises his hand toward me.

"Hey, asshole!" Chirk shouts, firing both mini-railguns.

Harth's five Incinerator rounds strike an invisible telekinetic shield and lodge in place. A moment later, they're snuffed out, falling to the floor and rolling away. Chirk's shards strike the same shield, deflecting up into the ceiling, which is torn to shreds. Debris falls, slides around the protective, ten-foot-wide sphere, and flutters to the floor.

The robot, devoid of emotion, tilts its head and flicks a finger toward me.

Feels like I've been struck by a rhinoceros. My feet leave the floor just as quickly as the air coughs from my lungs. I flip over backward, land on my chest, and slide toward the window we destroyed while making our grand entrance, which in hindsight was a terrible idea.

Claws extending, I slap my hands down onto the tile floor. Eight troughs are left in my wake as the claws dig through the floor. But, there's not enough friction to stop me. My feet slide out over the edge. My waist next. Gravity is already pulling me down when my head clears the edge, and I get a look at the thousand-foot drop that awaits me.

The floor ends and my claws strike the window frame, digging deep into the metal.

It's not enough, because Lumen Sok is still pushing me.

The moment I fall out of sight, the pressure releases.

And then, I'm caught.

A second force brings me to a slow stop, out of sight. Jenna.

"Gruunlokar," I say. "You have eyes on?"

"That was…graceful," he says. "Are you injured?"

"I'm fine," I say, and I start to move along the building's side. Jenna is repositioning me without saying a word, which is smart. Better that everyone, including Lumen Sok, think I'm dead. "Can you see the target?"

"Negative," he says. "I need him closer to the window."

"Copy that," I say. "How's Haruto holding up?"

"He has made several comments about wishing he was a monkey."

I made the executive decision to leave Haruto with Gruunlokar. They are located near the top of Tokyo Tower—the Japanese answer to the Eiffel Tower, except painted red with three horizontal white stripes. It might not be as globally known, but it's been destroyed in a lot of Godzilla movies. It's also the tallest structure close to us. Gruunlokar's elevated position gives him a decent vantage point, but he's a little too high to see straight into the penthouse floor.

If we fail, the two of them will be left at the top of the tower with no way down.

"Tell him we've got this," I say, as I'm carried around the building's corner, out of sight from Tokyo Tower.

*How far is Jenna moving me?*

"I have," Gruunlokar says. "He is dubious."

"Overprepared is the dubious mind," I say. "We're all dubious."

A bending of light draws my eyes to the penthouse floor now ten feet above me. The glass is warping, distorting the reflection. What is… My eyes widen. The glass bows outward. It's going to—

The sound of a hundred windows shattering all at once makes me cringe. Glass falls from the building as every penthouse window bursts out and away. I raise my hands to shield my face. Not that it will help. Some of the shards are big enough to sever my head.

But I don't need to worry about protecting myself. Jenna thought of that, too. The broken glass bounces off the protective sphere surrounding me, fluttering to the ground far below, like glitter falling out of a greeting card gifted by some asshole.

My progress around the building stops.

I rise up toward the now open windows. Nothing I can do to change my position. I'm in Jenna's hands.

The moment my head clears the window I understand what she's up to. To the left, I can see Siloquin, Poppy, and Jenna. To my right, Chirk, Harth, Sean, Jess, and Grover. All of them are locked in place, grasped by Lumen Sok, who I can hear speaking on the far side of the control center. Jenna has brought me up in his blind spot and is moving me across the room, unseen by the Visionary.

As I float to my concealed destination, I manage to make eye contact with Jess and Grover. They can't make any facial expressions, but knowing they know I'm not dead puts my mind at ease. I give them two thumbs up and then touch down beside the control panel.

Sean isn't far, but there's no way I can reach him, or the gauntlet without exposing myself. Way I see it, I've only got one choice. Wait until the Visionary is turned toward Jenna, and then hit him with everything I've got from behind, and hope Jenna knows what I'm trying to accomplish.

I crouch low and move to the side of the control center, waiting for the sound of Lumen Sok's voice to project away from Chirk, instead of toward him.

# 53

## MICAH

I'm on my stomach when the volume of Lumen Sok's voice turns away from Harth and Chirk. I can't tell if they're in pain or not. Every part of their bodies is frozen in place like they're professional Red Light, Green Light players. No idea if they can see me. Just in case, I give them a thumbs up and slither along the floor, rounding the control center.

I peek around the edge of the nearest control console. Each of the twenty stations is separated from the others by a low cubical wall, which provides just enough cover to hide behind. Lumen Sok hovers thirty feet away, his back to me.

He's glided closer to the windows, but not quite close enough. His attention is on Jenna.

"When I sent you out, I believed you to be my most devious disciple. Your penchant for deceit was unmatched, and your ability to feign sympathy, even love..." He shakes his head. "It was art."

He glides a little closer.

"Almost," Gruunlokar says over the comms. "Five more feet."

Right. Five feet.

Just need to move him five feet.

"But now, here you are amidst my enemies. Taken in by them. It appears I am the one who has been deceived, hm? And yet, while you've fought your way back to my doorstep, you are not fighting my grasp, despite being quite powerful."

He swivels in a slow circle, taking in his surroundings as he says, "Perhaps you intend to beg for forgiveness?" He shakes his head. "You know I would never grant it. Then, what is your purpose?"

I slide back into one of the stations, curling around the rolling chair's base into a fetal position I hope will conceal me.

The Visionary's voice gets louder as he turns. "Unless... You are not who I believe you to be. You're no shape shifter. The Ferox were one of the first species to fall. And I've observed you—eyes everywhere, you know. You retain your abilities. You *are* Draun. I was either taken in by your consummate acting skills, or—"

His voice has turned away from me. I roll out from hiding and watch him glide a little closer to Gemma, still perched atop his half-sphere.

"You are somehow…not you." He glides a little closer, leaning his head closer to Jenna.

"I can see his legs," Gruunlokar says. "Nearly there."

"Who are you?" he asks, peering into Jenna's eyes. "Who is hiding inside my acolyte? Who dares desecrate my sanctuary?" He leans back. "Ahh, there you are, quivering behind eyes that do not belong to you. Tell me, before I draw your inverted intestines up through your esophagus… What is your name?"

He waits a moment. "Come now. I know you can speak. You can use your body. You might not be fighting, but you have retained control. This is your chance, after all, to ascend to the throne. To command an empire." His impatience gets the best of him. He shouts, "Give me your name!"

The air in the penthouse swirls with wind, but the moment he raises his voice, the air quivers. Feels like I'm lying on a subwoofer. I can feel the effect throughout my body, vibrating my organs. Pressure builds. My ears pop.

*Now or never,* I think, and climb to my feet. Moving with a silence that would make the Teenage Mutant Ninja Turtles envious, I walk out into the open penthouse, sliding around pillars until Lumen Sok is in position.

"Speak your name, now," he shouts, "or watch your friends burst, one by one, and when I am done, I will drown you in their blood!"

Jenna grimaces. "My name…" Her eyes flick to me. "…is Jenna Flood!"

She dives to the side, free to move despite Lumen Sok's effort to lock her in place. When she comes up, she thrusts her hands out toward the robot and tries pulling him. He moves a few inches, but they quickly reach a stalemate.

That's my cue.

Without making the kind of bold announcement like dumb heroes in movies do before striking an enemy, I just boost my power and give him both barrels. The round beam of brilliant orange light is ten feet across and strikes with the force of a tungsten train moving at the speed of light.

To my ever-loving delight, Lumen Sok shouts in surprise, sliding forward, inch by inch. The laser hasn't struck his body. It's hammering his personal shield, which he had no trouble maintaining while holding on to the team.

But now…now we have him distracted.

"Hit him with everything you've got!" I shout.

Chirk fires shards.

Harth's partially recharged Incinerator launches a handful of rounds.

Jess and Sean make for the control center while Grover… He heads for me, ears bouncing, tongue out. At first, I think he's having a ball, but then I notice his upturned eyebrows. A wave of concern washes over me as our connection peaks. He's not worried about himself.

He's worried about me, sensing something the rest of us have missed.

But I can't stop.

"Almost," Gruunlokar says. "Almost..."

The Visionary pulls his body in tight and rotates to face me. He hovers up away from his sphere, which closes and shoots straight down through the floor, leaving a perfectly round hole in its wake. Then he glides toward me, away from the window, resisting all our combined efforts.

His pushback draws more energy from me. I can feel myself tiring, while his robotic body is unaffected by the effort. I grit my teeth and put everything I've got into it, but I can already tell it's not going to be enough.

Siloquin and Poppy unleash waves of lightning from both sides, but they just crackle against his shield.

*How much more can he take?*

I have no idea. Neither do the Kynolari. No one has attempted something like this before. No one has been close enough.

No one has been *allowed* to get this close.

*He can beat us,* I realize, *and he knows it.* Has been watching us all this time, evaluating our strengths and weaknesses. Almost certainly knows that Gruunlokar is outside, waiting to take a shot. How could he not know about the sniper that nearly killed him once before?

Lumen Sok unfurls his arms and legs, unleashing a pulse of energy that would have taken out all the windows if Jenna hadn't already done it for him. Before it strikes me, Grover has my shirt in his mouth, yanking me behind a concrete pillar. "Back!" he shouts.

I don't see what happens next, but I can hear shouts of pain as the team is knocked outward—toward the windows.

My eyes snap to Jess. She and Sean slide side by side toward the thousand-foot drop. Jess rolls herself atop Sean, fires her Stinger grapple into the control center. The pair snap to a stop.

"Yo!" Sean shouts. "That was sick!"

His enthusiasm drops when Chirk slides past between us, limp and tumbling.

There's nothing I can do for him.

Nothing I can do for any of them.

Chirk bounces—and stops as though caught.

All of them stop.

*Jenna.*

I'm about to lean back out and put the pressure back on, but I'm stopped by Grover. "No! Not yet. Not until you see."

"See what?"

"Axiom," he says.

"I'm right here, Grove."

He shakes his doggy head. "See…with *my* eyes."

My vision shifts from my eyes to his. It used to be disorienting, but I quickly adjust to the gray, blue, and yellow view of the world from a much lower point-of-view. Grover turns his head up at me and I'm surprised to see a yellowish-blue haze flowing around me."

"Why didn't you say anything about this before?" I whisper.

"Thought you knew," he says. "But also…"

He turns his head to the floor. A river of the same spectral energy flows out from my foot…to his. "Do you understand?"

I smile. "I think I do, buddy. I think I do."

I step out from behind the column and find Jenna and the Visionary in a standoff, each trying to break through the other's defenses. It's a stalemate, for now.

A quick look around the penthouse fills in the knowledge gaps. Everyone is present, but mostly out for the count or struggling to stand back up. Only Sean and Jess are on the move, as she reels them in toward the control center. We still might have a chance, despite my belief that the Visionary is toying with us. He is Draun, after all, and hubris is their only weakness.

"Hey!" I shout.

The Visionary's head rotates one-eighty degrees, his blue eyes locking onto me, his body continuing the power struggle with Jenna, who appears to be weakening. "Ahh, the Axiom. Still alive. Perhaps you are everything these fools believe you to be, but it will not be enough. I have erased entire worlds. You…are nothing."

"On my own, yeah, I'm not much. But you've forgotten something."

His head tilts to the side, curious.

"I have a dog," I say.

Grover steps out from behind the column and slides himself between my legs. We face Lumen Sok together.

He laughs. Amused, but growing bored.

"You did get something wrong, though," I say. "*I* am not the Axiom."

"Oh?" he says.

Grover lifts his front paw and places it atop my foot.

"*We* are." I thrust both hands out, unleashing a blast of energy so vast and powerful that it eats the floor and ceiling in its path, letting in a streak of sunlight. The laser strikes Lumen Sok's shield, enveloping it in light so brilliant that I can't tell if he's still there or has just been erased.

A scream emerges from the light. It's Lumen Sok, but he sounds angry more than in pain. A bubble forms, expanding the laser blast out, eating the floor as it expands toward Poppy, Siloquin, and Praxion's body. I have no choice but to stop.

When the laser disappears, I find the Visionary on one knee, head lower, hand grasping the floor. His metal body smolders, smoke rising. Then he looks up—at me—eyes glowing white hot.

"Ahh, shit," I say.

"Now!" Jenna says, hands stretched out to the air just outside the window now framing Lumen Sok.

His head snaps toward her—and then shatters into a thousand pieces as Gruunlokar's sniper shard slips through Jenna's sticky telekinetic wall and then Lumen Sok's protective shield. His headless body topples forward and falls through the massive hole I've created.

"Holy shit," I say, leaning my hands on my knees. "Holy shit." I look down at Grover and give his head a scruff. "We did it. We actually did—"

"Yeeeaarrhahahaa!" The cackling laughing cuts me short, rising up from the hole into which the Visionary has just fallen.

Below me, Grover grumbles, "This is some bullshit."

# 54

## CHIRK

I wake up to the sound of laughter. Head is pounding. Body aches. A quick mental check-in with my body tells me the damage isn't bone deep, which is great. Already spent enough time with busted arms. I lean up into a sitting position and shake my head.

My blurred vision narrows for a moment, globules of light twirling around the periphery.

The laughter grows louder, drowning out the buzzing in my head.

"The hell is that sound?" I ask.

When no one responds, the memory of how I got here returns. Lumen Sok mentally flicked me across the top floor. I remember bouncing twice and the realization that I was going to roll out the window. Then nothing.

But I'm still on the top floor, and not even close to the far side of the building. Someone caught me. Mystery for another time. Right now...

I knock the side of my head, little knuckles clacking against my regulator. "C'mon, man, get my head straight. Advanced alien technology my—"

All at once, my head clears, and my vision focuses.

"More like it," I say and get a look at what the hell is going on.

My eyes dart around the vast space, collecting data. Sean and Jess have reached the control center. To my right, Micah and Grover stand beside a pillar. Everyone else is down for the count, but I don't smell even a hint of death. With a better understanding of the situation, I return my attention to Micah and the big ass hole in the floor—and ceiling—stretching forty feet out from where he and Grover are standing. Looks like he went full Axiom on the Visionary.

Based on the laughter, I don't think it got the job done.

At the far side of the hole, a headless Visionary rises into the air.

"Am I seeing this right?" Gruunlokar asks, broadcasting to the team.

"You mean the headless floating asshole?" I say. "Yeah, I see it."

Micah and Grover both turn around, looking relieved to see me awake. I give them a thumbs up. The touchscreen on my arm chimes. "By the way, help is incoming. ETA two minutes."

"Copy that," Gruunlokar says.

"Two minutes," Micah repeats. "Fucking hell."

"Fucking hell," Grover repeats.

When they move, it's together. At the same time. In sync.

"Fire when ready," Jenna whispers. I find her on the far side of Lumen Sok, lying on the ground, looking weak, but she has a hand raised.

Gruunlokar doesn't waste a moment.

The Visionary's arm bursts off as a shard—moving far too fast to register—slips through Jenna's telekinetic shield, Lumen Sok's shoulder, and who knows how many floors before reaching the ground. A moment later—the time it takes Gruunlokar to adjust his arm—Lumen Sok's other arm falls away.

If he feels pain, he doesn't express it. He just keeps on laughing.

That's when the severed arms float back up and reattach to the robotic body. A cloud of broken metal chunks swirls around him, reforming his head until it's whole once more, blue eyes glowing with power.

"Is that something space robots do?" Micah asks over comms.

"That ain't something anything does," I reply, "space or no space."

"It's not a robot," Micah says. "It's a Golem." Before anyone can ask, he adds, "The inanimate animated by an external force. God. Telekinesis. Whatever. Point is, we can't kill the body because it's not alive."

"Hey, my dudes," Sean chimes in. "You sound busy and all, but me and Jess are at the controls and this shit ain't Windows, if you know what I'm saying. How are we supposed to—"

A breeze kicks up, swirling dust and debris around the entire top floor. The speed at which it builds strength suggests its origin isn't natural. Lumen Sok hovers at the center of it, laughing, arms raised. Seems like he lost his mind when he lost his head, but I think he's just done screwing around.

"Any tips would be useful," Jess says, but she's already struggling to stay upright.

The ceiling peels away in sheets. Wires and cables snap, launching quickly extinguished sparks. It builds to a tornado force and then, all at once, the ceiling explodes upward. The entire roof comes apart and launches out and away from the building, leaving our column-covered floor exposed.

When the debris falls away, I spot Gruunlokar and Haruto, helpless in the Visionary's telekinetic grip. He's pulled them here all the way from Tokyo Tower. I hate to admit it, but after so long fighting Lumen Sok, we're still underestimating his power.

Then we're all caught up again, lifted into the air, helpless against him. Even Jenna, despite her struggling, is levitating. Micah manages to hold onto Grover, but they're floating now, too. Harth, Siloquin, and Poppy are still unconscious. Probably better for them that way.

"Shit," Jess says. "He has us!"

She and Sean are lifted up. Sean holds onto a desktop, but it's yanked away.

As we're moved around like toys in the tendrils of a Flavian Tentacle Larva, my hopelessness doubles. The sky around us is filled with the Draun.

Thousands of them.

They're here to witness his conquest and his display of power. They were made to fear us, and now he wants to cut us down in front of them. That's why we're here. Why he's here. Top floor of a tower, my ass. This place is a fucking stage. And the command center was the bait that turned us into unknowing characters in his spectacle. When we're dead, his control over the Draun, and this world, will be solidified.

"Jenna," I say.

"Here," she says with a grunt.

"I want you to stop fighting against Lumen Sok."

"Sounds like a bad idea, my dude," Sean says.

"She can't win," I say. "Not on her own. Not right now."

"Then what...do you want...me to do?" Jenna asks.

"Same thing you did to Gruunlokar's shards, but on something bigger. Well, two things, actually."

"She can do it," Gruunlokar says, not a trace of doubt in his growly voice.

"Hold up," Sean says. "Is it time?"

"Oh, it's fuckin' time, my man!" I look up to the sky and see a lone streak of light coming in faster than any Draun can. "Incoming! Clutch your nuggets and lick your puggets, here comes Ridgeback." My eyes flick to a second streak of light, following the first, "And Peregrine Two."

"What the what?" Sean says. "Peregrine *Two?*"

"What Harth was working on. Works just like the weapon systems except you're moving," I say. "Your regulators will connect you to all systems. It will respond to your thoughts. Got it?"

He doesn't have a chance to reply.

Peregrine and the Ridgeback armor swoop down, protected from the effects of Lumen Sok's shielding by Jenna. They are things of destructive beauty. Ridgeback is a powerhouse, built like a tank, as the humans would say. Heavily armored, covered in weapon systems, and in the rough form of a Kynolari. And when I'm inside of it, I'm a beast no one wants to mess with.

Peregrine is something else entirely. She is sleek, lightly armored, and built for speed. Both of them are stupid fast, like *Prowler* fast. They crossed the Pacific Ocean from Los Angeles—where they've been waiting for me to call them in—in twenty minutes, give or take. I haven't been keeping track of time. But Peregrine can move fast and maneuver unlike anything else on this planet. Nothing can catch her. She carries lasers, rockets, and shards, but not to the extent of Ridgeback. And it's not heavily armored, but it will shield Sean from the elements while he's pouring on the speed—if he doesn't immediately crash. The best part is that like the original *Peregrine*, Peregrine Two is iridescent purple, moving through the sky like a warbling blur.

The mechs scoop us both out of the air and curl upward as our bodies are automatically adjusted and slipped into place.

But then something odd happens.

It's just a blink of motion, but the moment Sean is picked up, his gauntlet drops away from his arm. He doesn't even notice—unless he did it on purpose. Maybe leaving it for Jess. Would be a smart move.

A HUD blinks to life in my vision and immediately starts locking on to targets.

"Oh, snap," Sean shouts, "this is wicked awesome, man! Whoo!"

"Fire at will, you sexy sunuvabitch!"

I unlock all my weapon systems and unleash hell. Lasers. Rockets. Shards. Sean does the same, spiraling straight up. A hundred of the slowest Draun are cut down and dropped from the sky.

"Watch your heads down there!" I say.

The only response I get is a pained gurgle. The Visionary isn't wasting any time striking back.

"Keep the pressure on, I'm going after the big guy!"

I swing around and rocket toward the tower's roof. I unleash a stream of shards and lasers, pummeling the Visionary's shield. Some of the shards sneak through, thanks to Jenna, although the damage they do is undone just as quickly. But the important thing is that I also get past his shield.

I crash down in front of him, and stand tall, looking down at him. "Can't touch this, Snausage Cock!" I wind up and throw a punch at him. His robotic hand snaps up and catches the fist. I try with the other and get the same result, except this time I'm clutching his fist in mine.

With a hysterical laugh meant to mock his, I unleash a point-blank barrage of shards and lasers. The space between us becomes a light display unlike anything ever seen as the orange lasers reflect off the shards—and their broken pieces.

Yeah, broken pieces.

Shards don't break. Unless, he's got some kind of unknown armor protecting his— I gasp inside my mech. "He's inside the chest! Inside the—ahh!"

My right arm is torn away, so I return the favor, wrenching his right arm off with a quick twist and a pull. He'll put it back together again, so I toss it as far as I can.

The floor beneath Jenna drops away, and she falls with it, letting out a shout. For a brief moment, she loses her concentration and the protection around me flickers. It's not long, but in that time, Ridgeback is torn in half and tossed to either side.

Intense pain snaps through my body and I think he's going to tear me in half next. Wouldn't be hard. But just as quickly as it begins, the pain ends. I'm spirited away in a protective bubble, courtesy of Jenna, who has floated back up. I extend both middle fingers as I glide away. Asshole doesn't even acknowledge me, in part because I'm insignificant to him, but also because he's on the defensive again. Sean divebombs, unleashing shards and lasers. Jenna is giving it everything she's got. Grover and Micah fire a massive energy pulse that would knock any ship in the Kyno Corps fleet out of orbit. And Siloquin, back on her feet, has snuck up behind him with Poppy. She thrusts her spear into Lumen Sok's back and unleashes a charge from her gauntlet. Poppy leaps up, grabs hold, and adds her gauntlet's power to the strike.

And at the center of it all, Lumen Sok screams.

He's felt pain, maybe for the first time in his life.

*This ain't gonna be good*, I think and then find myself distracted by a subtle motion. Reacting like an Earth dog, my head snaps toward it and I nearly bark. That's when I see what it is.

Sean's gauntlet.

It's sliding across the rooftop.

Headed toward Praxion's body…because it's his gauntlet. Because he's recalled it. Because…he's alive! I nearly shout it out but manage to hold my breath. All gauntlets have the ability to snap back on to a Kynolari's arm if it's outfitted with a recall system, which all of ours are. A combination of magnetic forces and a miniature repulse disc embedded within the device allow it to move and guide it home.

I almost piss myself when Praxion's hand lifts off the ground. Son-of-a-bitch has been playing dead this whole damn time, like a post-fornication Xelomant male, praying his mates don't consume him. He's waited for the right moment of maximum distraction, and only I see what's happening…or what needs to be done.

"Micah! Narrow that beam to the size of a fist! Jenna! Give him a hole to Lumen Sok's chest! Do it now!"

Micah's beam narrows, so bright now that it's impossible to look at. For a moment, it just reflects up into the sky. But then, it starts pushing its way through the field as Jenna puts her effort into carving a path to the Visionary's chest plate.

My invisible magic bubble pops and I drop to the roof. I'm exposed. An easy target. But I hold my ground, watching the chest plate as electricity arcs around his body and Micah's laser bursts through the telekinetic shield.

Lumen Sok shrieks now, and I suspect it's the first time he's felt fear, which I know from experience is far worse than pain.

The chest plate glows orange.

Cracks spread out from the laser.

And then I see it.

A hole.

About the size of a mini-Clufunk's dick, but sound waves don't care about size.

"Praxion!" I shout. "Now!"

The moving gauntlet shoots across the remaining distance, sliding back home onto Praxion's arm. He lifts the Sonizer up toward Lumen Sok and unleashes a burst of shrieking sound.

# 55

## MICAH

Following the shriek sound, it feels like the whole universe holds its breath.

The Draun in the sky around us, just watching.

I clutch onto Grover, both of us catching our breath, watching...

The Visionary, Lumen Sok, stands motionless over the body of Praxion, which has fallen still again. He held on, stayed quiet, and waited for the perfect moment to strike. And it might have cost him his life.

Around the rooftop, our people recover. Jess is back on her feet. Siloquin helps Poppy to her feet. Chirk dusts himself off, looking like a little badass. Jenna looks winded and tired but floats up and settles back down to her feet. Harth shakes his head, on his hands and knees. I think he missed most of what happened. Gruunlokar crouches by Harth's side, helping him find his feet. And Haruto... He is not only on his feet but is currently storming straight toward Lumen Sok.

He waggles a finger at the frozen robot. "Hey! You! Big metal man! You want to kill people. Want to kill Earth. But no! We say no! All of us. I do not care if you alien. If you robot. If you tele-kin-whatever! You are asshole! Now, get off my bus!"

Haruto winds up and slugs the robotic body—

—and immediately regrets it. "*Aita!*" he shouts, shaking his hand out. But then a piece of metal falls away and clatters on the floor.

We all watch in silence as the armor crumbles and falls to pieces.

Because it's no longer held together by Lumen Sok's telekinesis.

Because... I don't dare think it until I confirm it with my own eyes.

Before I get the chance, Sean shouts, "Incoming!" He swoops down from the sky and just a moment before impacting with the floor, twists around, slows, and lands on his feet. With augmented arms, he grasps hold of the Visionary's armored chest, catching it while the rest of the body falls to pieces. He carries it clear of the debris and sets it down.

As the team gathers around, he puts Peregrine Two to work, digging his fingers between the two plates and pulling them apart.

Inside is a leaking tank of water. A limp mass of black worms floats inside.

Sean points at it and says, "Now this...this is a dick-whore."

"May I?" I ask the group, holding up my fully charged gauntlets.

"By all means," Harth says. He picks up the tank, ready to throw.

"Pull!" I say, and he tosses the tank into the air above us.

With Grover's foot on mine, I take aim and unleash a bus-sized, orange laser pulse. It strikes the tank—vaporizing it, and its contents—and then disappears into the atmosphere.

Before any of us can celebrate the victory, Poppy shouts, "Clear!"

I'm immediately sobered by the sight of Poppy, Lancer hand pressed against Praxion's still chest. His body jolts from an electric shock. Poppy checks the readings on her gauntlets, adjusts the power, and shocks him again.

"C'mon old man," Poppy says.

In general, being connected to the other Kynolari via our regulators is an advantage. But now, faced with losing Praxion, I can feel all their worry, concern, and heartbreak mixing with my own. Loss is a communal experience for Kynolari. And it knocks the wind out of me, dropping me to one knee. Beside me, Grover whines. And we're not alone in our despair. Chirk, Harth, and Gruunlokar are driven to their knees.

Jenna…Jenna isn't paying attention.

Neither is Sean. Their backs are to us. Eyes on the sky. Shit.

We've killed Lumen Sok. But the Draun still populate the world, and several thousand of them are looking down at us, the Visionary's killers. Using Draun logic, it doesn't take much to deduce that we are all on their hit lists—not because we killed their leader, but because each and every one of them wants to take his place, and to do that, they need to take the lives of those who killed the Visionary.

"We need an exfil plan," I say.

Harth glances up and quickly understands the situation. He activates his radio and says, "Denji."

"You're alive!" Denji shouts. "Why you not contact sooner? I was—"

"Denji," Harth says. "We are on the roof. Need an exfil route. Fast, and underground."

"Copy," he says. "Working on it."

Harth nods like Denji can see it, and then fires up his Incinerator. One by one, our bedraggled team turns our back on our fallen leader, ready to fight for our lives.

"What about the control center?" Jess asks. "If we can get the gauntlet—"

"Negatory," Chirk says, pointing to the control center's top. It's a smoldering ruin. "He took it out, along with the roof."

Lumen Sok is dead…but the Earth is still lost. The best we can hope for now—if we survive the next ten minutes—is to eke out a life underground while a Draun with enough power becomes the next Visionary.

But we'll try. We'll fight. I look at my friends and see only resolve in their eyes.

All except one.

Siloquin.

Unlike the rest of us, she is still looking at Praxion.

She catches me looking and says, "He's still here. I can feel him."

I turn toward her, more curious than anything else.

"What did she say?" Chirk asks, turning his back to the Draun.

"He's still here," Siloquin says. "And I..." Her body convulses like she's about to puke.

Beside me, Grover starts barking at her, his hackles up.

And that gets everyone else's attention. Except for Jenna, who remains focused on the Draun. "Uh, guys?" she says.

"Buy us time," Gruunlokar says. "You are better than all of them."

"All of them individually, maybe, but all together?" When no one backs her up, she says, "Shit," and raises her hands. I can't see it, but I know there is a telekinetic shield around us now.

"What's happening?" Poppy asks Siloquin.

"I—I don't know." She winces, clutching her body as though trying to contain something inside. "I feel...sad. I feel love. Desperation."

My eyes widen and I whisper, "Torel."

Siloquin falls to her knees and lets out an anguished wail that breaks my heart. Grover's barking becomes a whimper. We're all feeling it with her. The profound sense of loss, like waking up to find all your limbs have been amputated.

There isn't a dry eye among us. Even though I can't see Sean's face behind the Peregrine armor, I can hear him hiccup-crying. Our collective loss is profound—but it is the worst for Siloquin. Because she is not feeling just our pain, she is feeling Torel's.

She screams.

Pounds her fists into the floor.

"Noooo!" she screams, and then... She begins glowing blue.

"Uhh," Chirk says. "That ain't normal." He takes a step back and the rest of us follow suit.

The glow becomes an ethereal flame, engulfing Siloquin and Praxion. And it's not hot. It's freezing. We step back farther.

"Might be time to worry more about the living," Jenna says, grunting, "and less about the dead." In the sky above, several of the Draun are pushing back against her shield. Won't be long until she can no longer hold them back. "Sorry if that's cold, but—" She looks over her shoulder and sees the blue glow for herself.

"Oh. Shit."

A shockwave of blue light explodes out from Siloquin's core, sliding through all of us. My stomach twists and I nearly drop to the floor. "What the—"

Siloquin's head snaps toward the sky, eyes wide, mouth open, blue light surging from both. She opens her arms and lets out an inhuman shriek. A second shockwave explodes from her mouth, unleashing a column of blue energy, straight up into the sky.

Then, and I shit you not, it's like something out of *Raiders of the Lost Ark*, souls of the god damned dead swirl up into the sky, each of them shrieking, each of their pained faces vaguely Kynolari.

"The Lost Tribe," Grover says, sounding reverent, which I suppose makes sense. They're his ancestors, too.

The spiritual tornado strikes Jenna's shield and bursts though, unleashing a shockwave of light. Jenna is knocked to the floor, but okay, turning her head up to watch with the rest of us. The unleashed souls explode out in every direction, as more continue to pour out of Torel's body.

It's at this very moment that the Draun—and the rest of us—realize they are well and truly fucked.

As the smartest Draun begin to flee, the souls impact them one at a time. Streaks of light seep out of their every pore as a cacophony of screams roll over the city of Tokyo. Each one screams as their former selves are scraped from every cell in their bodies and are replaced. You can hear it in the screams. Horror shifting into relief.

Even those who fled are swallowed up.

Not a single Draun escapes.

And yet, they remain. Alive. Floating.

When the light fades from Siloquin, she topples forward over Praxion, sobbing.

All around us, the floating mass of spectators float closer. But I sense no ill will from them now. A lone woman takes the lead, the others falling in line behind her. She lands in front of us, dressed in a cloak, which she sheds to reveal a young Japanese woman with dark black eyes. Siloquin's dropped spear lies at her feet. When she bends down, picks it up, and gives it a spin before shoving the base against the floor, we all know who we're looking at.

"Siloqun," Poppy says.

"If that's Siloquin," Chirk says. "Then..."

We all turn back to the woman sobbing over Praxion's body. Chirk steps closer and crouches by her face. "Torel?"

When she looks up, tears in her eyes, we all see that it's her.

Body no longer a vessel for the trapped Lost Tribe, she has returned to herself just in time to find her love dead.

Chirk leans against her head, embracing her.

"That is...very sweet. But I'd appreciate it...if you stopped touching my girl... and get your dick out of my face."

Chirk staggers back.

Torel gasps, leaning back.

Everyone sees him together, returned from the dead.

*Praxion is alive!*

But far from out of the woods. He's still impaled. It's a mortal wound, whether or not his soul has been dragged back into his body.

"Talon-One," a voice says. "*Prowler*-Actual. I am incoming with help."

Harth looks to the sky. "Baarfolir?"

A streak of light descends toward us. It's followed by thousands more. Then hundreds of thousands.

"That's my name," Baarfolir says. "Hope you glory-hogs don't mind sharing some of the action. I brought some help."

Gruunlokar watches the descending lights with a smile on his face. "The fleet. They're here."

The streak leading the others arcs toward the tower, slowing as it approaches and touches down. When the dust clears, we find Baarfolir, now dressed in battle armor. There's a smile on his face, until he sees Praxion. "Gallent-Actual, *Prowler*-Actual, med-evac on me. One severe injury incoming."

In a blink, three more Kynolari dressed in white combat gear arrive. They spot Praxion and without a word, hurry over to him. In seconds, they have him hovering off the floor and gliding toward their leap node.

"Keep him steady!" Torel barks, following them. As she passes Baarfolir, she touches his shoulder and says, "Thank you."

He nods and says, "I'm sorry we did not return soon enough to avoid all... of...umm." He points at the thousands of human beings floating around us. "None of you seem concerned."

"They're not Draun," I tell him.

"Who...are they, then?"

"You ain't going to believe this, bud," Chirk says. "This...this is the Lost Tribe."

"And we are glad to finally be free."

Baarfolir looks up at the woman who spoke, clutching her spear, chin raised. She places a fist against her chest. "We meet again, little man. I am Siloquin, Prefect of the Kynolari Guard."

His eyes widen. He smiles. "Oh my."

"Before you start twenty questions," Chirk says. "How'd you do it? We all saw you—"

"Oh dear," he says. "I'm sorry if you all believed I was— That must have been horrible."

"Some of us were happy about it," Chirk says, and slugs Baarfolir.

Baarfolir laughs and it's looser and more relaxed than I remember. "I ejected a spare fusion core into their line of fire. Honestly, I wasn't sure the explosion would be as big as it was…but it would appear it was convincing."

"Sneaky little bastard," Chirk says. "Nice work."

All around us, streaks of light descend into the city. Some land on rooftops, some on the ground. It's not long before the sounds of battle ring out through the city. There might not be any Draun left here, but there are plenty of biologics.

I walk to the edge of the tower with Grover and Jess, hand on the G-man's head, arm around my lady. Streaks of light descend as far as I can see. The others stand with us. Jenna, Gruunlokar, Harth, Baarfolir, Haruto, Poppy, Chirk, and Sean…still wearing his Peregrine armor. Not sure he'll ever take it off.

"So," I say, "we're going to win this, right?"

Harth nods. "It will be like this all over Earth."

"And they know to confirm a Draun mind before striking," Baarfolir says. "Humanity will be spared."

"Uh," Haruto says, raising his hand. "Maybe we tell Denji to stay in hole for now, just in case dog-aliens get trigger happy."

"Denji," Harth says into his radio.

"Sorry! Sorry!" Denji says. "Almost done with escape route!"

"No longer required," Harth says. "The battle is over. But…you should stay where you are until we retrieve you."

"Copy—wait. We *won?*"

"Affirmative," Harth says. "The Battle for Earth is nearly over."

"Hell to the yes!" Sean shouts. "Fuckin' awesome!" With that, he leaps off the side of the building. A moment later, he launches skyward, cruising past us, up into the sky.

I lean my head against Jess's. "So. Second date?"

"Fuck, no," she says, smiling. She takes hold of my cheeks, pulls me down, and kisses me. "Still love you, though."

Beneath us, Grover gasps. "I love, too! Love Micah. Love Jess. Love everyone." He turns around, looking at the Lost Tribe turned human. Siloquin stands before them, all watching the Kynolari descend from the sky, smiles on their faces.

Grover trots over to her.

She looks down at him. Then, she crouches.

He reaches up to give her his paw, and to my surprise, she takes it.

"Love everyone," Grover says. "Love Siloquin."

She smiles. "Brother. Welcome to the Guard."

# Epilogue

**PRAXION**

I'm alive.

For a time, I wasn't.

Outside my body, I watched my friends. Watched Torel. They mourned my death, and it broke my motionless heart. As I observed them, I drifted away, pulled toward a light from which there was no escape. I was on the event horizon of another plane when I heard her.

Torel's scream. The anguish. The pain.

My reaction was instinctual and more powerful than the light was prepared for. I shot back to my body, weaving between an explosion of souls headed in the opposite direction. When I opened my eyes again, she was with me. And she was herself.

I'm told I blacked out soon after that. The next thing I remember, apparently three days later, was waking up in the flagship's med-bay, attended to by the very best doctors in the fleet, including Torel and Poppy, who technically shouldn't have been there—being field medics. But no one was about to argue with two Kyno Corps operators that had just slain Lumen Sok and prevented a second Draun invasion.

Despite that, I can't help but feel partly responsible for the devastation wrought on this world. Had we put a stop to this in Denver, the world's population would have never become Draun. Would have never done Lumen Sok's bidding. And their corrupted DNA would have remained silent.

Now, much of this planet's human population has been slain in one way or another. Some died at the hands of the Draun. Others became acolytes of the Visionary and have now been hunted and cut down by the Kyno Corps residing in orbit. And they will not leave until there is no doubt that every single Draun has been killed, once and for all.

Most of my guilt stems from the fact that I reported Lumen Sok deceased once before. If not for that, he would have been tracked down long ago, and Earth's people wouldn't have even known the universe was at risk.

Gruunlokar shares my weight, though, as the soldier who reported a successful headshot. But how was he supposed to know Lumen Sok wasn't humanoid? If I'm kind to myself, how was I to know?

We have yet to identify the species Lumen Sok belonged to. The collection of wriggling worms was unfamiliar to me, and when we described it to Baarfolir, he couldn't recall anything else like it in the historical records. Doesn't help that Sok's remains were vaporized, but given the threat level, everyone has agreed that it was the right thing to do. We can't risk another threat like the Visionary. Which is why I've been put in command of a battlegroup tasked with locating his species and assessing their threat level. If Lumen Sok was an outlier, we will leave them be. If not... Well, that's something I don't want to consider until the time comes.

Torel, Harth, and Gruunlokar are joining me, along with a special guest who begged to be included, and bowed all the way to his toes when approval was granted. Haruto is Earth's first official emissary, but mostly he just wants to see the universe, surrounded by 'dog-aliens.' And he deserves it. We could not have prevailed without him.

Chirk...is staying behind. He and Sean are a duo now, neither wanting to leave the other. But...they're also not staying on Earth. Sean wants to see the universe. Wants to meet other species. His mind, less clouded by marijuana, has opened to the vast possibilities the endless void has to offer. Chirk had no trouble getting a ship of his own, complete with a fully repaired Ridgeback, and an improved Peregrine Two.

Jenna is also staying behind. She and Baarfolir are leading a Lost Tribe relations team along with Siloquin. They have a two-fold mission: to help catch the Lost Tribe up on thirty-seven thousand years of history, including changes in Kynolari customs. They will also be teaching them how to be humans—with the telekinetic abilities of the Draun. Siloquin has already announced plans to reform the Kynolari Guard as protectors of the Earth. They are doing well and have been instrumental with reconstruction efforts.

Humanity has dwindled down to roughly 500 million people. They've been relocated to several colonies surrounding the world. Two on every continent, aside from Antarctica. There are no countries any longer. Just one Earth. In part because those who remain feel a kinship through their Kynolari brain waves courtesy of their love for Earth dogs, but also because they're now part of a larger universe, filled with opportunities and dangers. To join the Union of Species, which is led by the Kynolari, Earth must become a centralized government, free of secrets, internal corruption, and infighting. If humanity fights another war, it will not be with themselves. And it will not sneak up on them.

Elections will be held only after every human on Earth—and their dogs, which they will be allowed to keep—is housed, fed, and safe. Likely within the year. That said, it's almost a certainty that the person leading this world into the future will be Micah.

Not only because of his close association with the Kynolari, or the fact that he and Grover are the prophesied Axiom, but because it is no secret that his actions led to the Draun's defeat and Lumen Sok's eradication. He would deny it. Would credit me for the act, but the Sonizer would have never worked without him first putting a hole in the Visionary's armor.

The happiest news is that he and Jess decided to forgo what humans call 'dating' and skip straight to marriage, which is a concept Kynolari, as a mostly monogamous species—excluding Chirk—understand. Grover is the happiest of all and is demanding that all of us leaving, return for the ceremony.

Right now, we are gathered for a different kind of ceremony.

I believe humans call it a housewarming.

Micah's home in New Hampshire was partially destroyed, and much of its contents unrecoverable. But enough remained for Kynolari builders to replace the home with an improved version. Same layout, but the plumbing and electrical systems are…advanced. And the doors no longer squeak. It doesn't smell the same, but that will change after a few years of burning wood fires, cooking bacon, and having three muddy dogs running around.

And that starts today. It's late afternoon, but the kitchen is alive with action as the team that saved the world is arguing about how to make pancakes and who gets the most bacon. I'm no cook, so I retreated to the living room along with Torel, Micah, Jess, Grover, Crip, and Blood.

"Excited to be leaving?" Micah asks.

"Space…can be a lonely place, and our friends will be missed, but—" I squeeze Torel against me. "I will not be nearly as alone on this voyage."

"Right," he says. "Because you have Haruto now."

"Hey!" Haruto shouts from the kitchen. "I hear my name! You no talk about me when I'm—hey! No, no, no. Three egg! *Three!* Yare yare."

We share a laugh, and then Jess says, "What about you two? Any chance of getting hitched?"

Torel and I look at each other, confused by the expression.

"Married!" Grover says, wagging his tail.

"Geez, you two," Micah says. "Don't pry." He turns to me. "So, when's the date? Do we get to go to Kyno?"

Torel smiles. "It is Kynolari tradition to not be conjoined for life until children are conceived."

"On Earth," Micah says. "That's called a 'shotgun wedding.'"

"What…does a shotgun have to do with a wedding?"

"It's usually held by the father of the bride," Micah says.

I laugh and she says, "I see."

"Seriously, though," I say. "Do it when it feels right. If that's tomorrow or in five years."

"But don't wait five years," Jess says. "Women hate that." She gives Torel a wink and they share a laugh that makes me wonder if that was genuine advice I should abide by.

"Can *I* get married?" Grover asks.

"You need to find a bitch first," I say, and quickly follow it up with, "Apologies. Translation services is still using a word that is offensive to human females."

"Meh," Jess says. "Only if you're talking about human women. Although some of them can really be bitches. But all female dogs are bitches. And I'm not sure why that would be an insult because female dogs are generally adorable and kind."

"The English language is confounding," I say, shaking my head. "Perhaps you will choose something new after you've been civilized."

My joke falls flat until my discomfort shows on my face. Then everyone laughs at me. I can navigate a battlefield, but not a conversation with witty and sarcastic humans. But it doesn't bother me as it once might have. I laugh with them, my psyche forever expanded thanks to my time on Earth.

"Time to eat!" Poppy shouts.

Grover and his two larger adopted siblings are up and running before I have time to fully register what has been said.

We gather in the kitchen, crammed into the space that is still small despite my insistence that we could expand everything. It's a tight fit, and the smell of cooked pigs, eggs, and pancakes has my stomach growling. I pick up a glass of cow's milk, which I might miss most of all, and hold it up. "To our friends turned family. May your days be filled with happiness, peace, love, and—"

"And lots of sexy time!" Chirk adds, and I notice the way he's looking at Poppy when he says it…and the way she's looking back.

Everyone has a laugh, and I surprise them all by lifting my glass as is customary in the human tradition of 'giving a toast'—another confounding phrase as it has nothing to do with warmed bread. It was taught to me by Micah, as I will be what is called his 'best man,' and a toast is part of my duties. "I'll drink to that!" I say, and drink. To friends. To family. All the other nice things I said. And yes, sexy time.

# Epilogue Two

**GROVER**

"Micah," I whisper. "Hey, Micah."

He rolls over to see me, because I lie in bed, between him and Jess, except for when they do *thumping* time. Then I downstairs with Crip and Blood. But now sleeping time.

"Yeah, bud?" he says.

"I sad."

"I miss our friends, too. But they'll be back, or we'll go see them out in space."

"Not because friends," I say. "I miss...Mom and Dad."

He's quiet.

"I miss them, too," he says. "But I think...I *know*...we will see them again."

"Because of Lost Tribe?"

"Yeah, Grove. We don't need to start going to church or anything, but we know there is a life after this one. We don't know what it looks like, but it's not nothing. It's kind of an adventure. Going somewhere new. Making discoveries. Reuniting with friends. Mom and Dad, too."

"That nice," I say. "That...make me happy. But, I still miss."

"Always will," Micah says, and wraps his arm around me.

I wait to say next part. "Also... I miss leg humping."

He laughs. "*What?*"

"I no leg hump anymore," I say, "because I know it not funny for other people. Because I smarter now. Because of regulators."

"Wait," he says. "You were trying to be *funny?*"

"*I* thought it was funny."

"Holy shit," he says with laugh. "You know what, it *was* funny. How about this, from now on, you can leg hump people, but only when I tell you to."

"So, people think it funny."

"Meh," he says, shrugging. "Might just be us who find it funny."

"Okay," I say. "That work for me. We can sleep now."

"Thank god," Jess groans. She behind me now. Puts her arm over me and Micah's arm.

I cozy and warm and safe.

Close my eyes.

"Micah."

"Yeah, bud?"

"Love Micah."

"Love you, too, Grover McRover.

"Love Jess."

"Love Grover," she says.

I sigh, close my eyes, and dream of chasing tennis balls.

# AUTHOR'S NOTE

If you're reading this, you've just finished *Good Boys – The Visionary*, book three of the next great American trilogy. Forget *Star Wars*...wait, there's like ten of those movies now. Forget *The Matrix*. No...they made a fourth. Indiana Jones! That's the one—huh? *Five* of them? Are we just recycling movies now?!

You know what, just forget any story that was a trilogy once upon a time and move *Good Boys* to the top of your list. Then tell everyone you know about the absolutely bonkers trilogy that's now your favorite and maybe, just maybe, we can pressure Hollywood into making something stupidly original. There've got to be some dog-people there who will share the vision. Even posting a review on Amazon or Audible will help.

I really enjoyed writing these novels. When I started the first book, I thought it was going to be a stand-alone, but saying goodbye to these characters so quickly felt wrong. I wanted to spend more time with them. Halfway through with Book 1, I decided it would be a trilogy and enjoyed every second writing them, Grover by my side, under foot, sometimes on my lap, looking at me with wide eyes, asking to wrestle. He might have slowed me down a bit but inspired me far more. Not only did I write three books, I wrote them back to back, something I've never done with a series before. I just couldn't resist the characters, and I hope you feel the same.

The actual Grover says "heff, heff, woof, lick," which translates to "Me hope you enjoy books." I told him you did, so hopefully I wasn't lying. These books aren't a lifelong dream come true, but they were inspired by and guided by a life of dog ownership and love. I like to think that if dog aliens appeared in my backyard, that Grover and I would help them just as Micah and Grover did. If the many worlds theory of the universe is real, then I suppose there is a world out there where we did. And where you did. How cool is that?!

To those who found the...gratuitous/gross scenes in these books offensive...you might not own a dog. They have no shame, and before they are neutered, are humping machines that don't mind the sight or smell of vomit, feces, or every other dog's butts. I wasn't trying to be crude, just realistically portraying things I've observed over 50 years of dogs. You thought I was going to apologize, didn't you? Hogwash. I have no dog-shame.

If you want to stay in the loop on upcoming releases, and all the exciting news about future comic books, movies, TV series, and more, head over to bewareofmonsters.com and sign up for the newsletter. You can also join the Tribe at facebook.com/groups/JRTribe—a fantastic group of fans where all the cool announcements drop first. Plus, we give away free stuff every week!

Thanks for joining me on another wild ride. You have amazing taste, and don't let anyone giving you strange looks for laughing or crying while reading convince you otherwise. I can't wait to share what's coming next!

*—Jeremy Robinson*

# ACKNOWLEDGEMENTS

Upon threat of life and limb, I must, for the third time, thank Alex Maddern for putting the concept of talking dogs from another planet looking for their lost tribe in my mind. It is a conversation that will live in my mind forever, because he will never let me forget it.

Massive gratitude goes out to Kane Gilmour, the maestro who helps transform rough drafts into polished, entertaining reads. And a big shoutout to our dedicated team of proofreaders (Julie Carter, Elizabeth Cooper, Gavin Gregory, Matt Ingram, Marcy Jaqua, Andre Jenkin, Scott Kehoe, Rebecca Laurent, Janis Levonitis, Stefanie Maubach, Kyle Mohr, Jessica Otterstål, and Courtney Westendorf), who work tirelessly to hide the fact that my typing skills rival my spelling prowess.

When I started this series, I was nervous for a few reasons. First, talking dogs. Second, what kind of insane narrator has the character range to pull off so many different BIG personalities. When I heard Tom Taylorson's audition, I knew he was the man for the job. His voices and clear narration brought this trilogy to life in the way I had hoped it would, but I wasn't sure was even possible. So, thanks to Tom, for exceeding my expectations and making this insanity sound great.

A huge thanks to you, the readers. Because of you, I get to write stories about intergalactic talking dogs saving the planet. Swearing dogs! Horny dogs! Pot smoking dogs! YOU made all this possible. Feel proud—I know I do.

—JR

# ABOUT THE AUTHOR

**Jeremy Robinson** is the *New York Times* and #1 Audible bestselling author of over eighty novels and novellas, including *Infinite, The Others,* and *The Dark,* as well as the Jack Sigler thriller series, and *Project Nemesis,* the highest selling, original kaiju novel of all time (which is in development for TV with Chad Stahelski, director of John Wick). Robinson is known for mixing elements of science, history, and mythology, which has earned him the #1 spot in Science Fiction and Action-Adventure, and secured him as the top creature feature author. Many of his novels have been adapted into comic books, optioned for film and TV, and translated into fourteen languages. He lives in New Hampshire with his wife and three children.

Visit him at www.bewareofmonsters.com.